Sword
Cross
and
Crown

Michael O'Gara

Michael O'Gara

ISBN 9780615801124

1st Printing 2017

Heartland Indie Publishing LLC

Chapter 1 - Narrow Escape

It was his one defense; the quickness. He saw his half-brother's fist coming and Wolf ducked and twisted off his chair. His half-brother Ragnar half fell from his chair as the vicious swing pulled him off balance. The large amounts of strong drink had affected Ragnar's balance as well as his judgment. He cursed in anger as he rose from his seat.

In his father's absence, Wolf knew his life was in the balance as he vaulted over the table, scattering cups, plates, and food. The men in the hall were hooting and shouting now as their attention had been drawn away from their tales and arguments to the entertainment developing at their lord's table. Some sat speechless realizing the danger.

Wolf ran full out for the great hall's main door. Ragnar tried to follow, but in his drunken rage he miscalculated. A grown man, staggering drunk, could not do what the boy Wolf had done so effortlessly. When Ragnar attempted to vault over the table, his large mass tipped the table and he went face first onto the floor. Food and drink followed, and covered in it, Ragnar struggled to rise. The laughter of the men in the hall fed his anger to a killing rage.

Wolf slowed at the door and looked back to see his half-brother bellow as he drew his sword and the chase was on. It would be murder if Ragnar, a drunken warrior, a giant of a man and proven killer, killed his unarmed thirteen year old half-brother Wolf. Some in the hall realized the danger should Ragnar catch and kill his half-brother. Ragnar's reputation and how quickly events transpired, led to inaction by others who might have otherwise intervened. Ubbe, charged with Wolf's wellbeing in Wolf's father's absence, was outside the hall relieving his bladder. That was just as well, for Ubbe would surely have died if he had tried to stop Ragnar, which he undoubtedly would. Ubbe would have only slowed Ragnar, not stopped him.

Wolf ran into the night and for the gate to the castle. He realized that Ragnar followed. He knew his brother would not catch him on foot. He heard Ragnar call for a horse. Wolf headed for the wood. He knew his life would probably be forfeit should he not reach the woods before Ragnar rode from the gate. He had almost reached it by the time his pursuer rode through the gate. He was into the wood by the time Ragnar had ridden half way across the field.

It was a moonless night and pitch-dark in the wood, so Wolf slowed for a moment, assessed his best route and took off running. He had chosen a way in which his being on foot was an advantage. He could slip between the densely packed trees, ducking the large overhanging branches, at almost a full run. Wolf thought his brother would have to dismount in order to follow him and be at a disadvantage. Thus, Wolf might live to see another day.

Ragnar's rage was in full control of him. Killing was all he could think of. He heard the usurper running to the right and he spurred his horse, brandishing his sword. His rage and drunken state, combined with his disdain and hatred for his half-brother, led him to make a near fatal mistake. Ragnar's head was almost taken off as he hit the overhead branch he did not see in the pitch black. His horse tripped simultaneously, letting out a scream as it collapsed, its forelegs broken by the log over which it tripped. Ragnar was thrown almost clear of the horse but was close enough that one of its thrashing rear legs caught him on the right leg, shattering it to pulp. Ragnar was semiconscious as he pulled himself out of range of the thrashing hooves. His skull was fractured and his leg broken. His prized sword was gone. He drew his short blade with great effort. He realized his horse had stopped screaming.

Ragnar saw him then. The boy Wolf, the threat to his ambitions, was standing close. He screamed at the boy, "I will gut you, skin you, and leave you for the carrion eaters."

Wolf knew that if Ragnar lived, he might not be able to fulfill that threat himself, but he could get others to do his bidding. Yet, to kill Ragnar now would be cold blooded murder and not an act of self-defense. Wolf stood for a moment assessing the situation. From the injuries it was clear that if Ragnar lived he would be a cripple. Indeed, he might still die of his injuries. Wolf could easily kill his brother now and end the threat from him even if it was small. If he did so, it would still be an unlawful murder and there was no way of knowing how his father would respond, but he knew how his God would. It was calculation and conscience, not fear nor bravery, which caused him to act.

Ragnar had just a moment to realize tonight he might die at the hands of an untrained boy. Had he not slayed brave warriors; Danes and Saxons, bandits, and worthy opponents? He deserved to die in glorious battle. He felt humiliated as he saw the boy had his sword which dripped the horse's blood. Oh how the gods had had toyed with him. Ragnar realized the boy was out of range of the short blade.

Wolf darted into the thick brush and Ragnar slipped into unconsciousness, his last conscious thoughts of the boy's cowardice in running away when he should have killed.

Wolf heard the shouts. Men were coming and he recognized the voices. Ragnar's men for certain came, perhaps others. His life was still in danger. This was not a time to take chances here in the dark. He ran deeper into the woods. He ran and ran until he could run no more. He was lost deep in the woods. There was a small clearing in front of him, but he did not have the energy to sprint across it or to go on, so he sat leaning against a tree. He knew he had run for hours, for the soft light of the predawn was growing in the sky.

As he sat, Wolf's weariness overcame his restless spirit. He laid the sword by his side and pulled his knees to his chest and wrapped his arms around his legs. The tears started. He would not cry. He would not let himself sob. He was a, it was then he realized he did not know what he was. He was caught between two worlds and born into conflict.

His father was a Dane bred of warriors; his mother a Saxon noble woman and a Christian. His father proclaimed to be a Christian for political reasons, but in private he worshipped the old gods. Their marriage was a political one. His father resented him, but his mother loved him. What am I, he wondered? His half-brother lay dead or near dead. His oldest half-brother, the bastard Ulrich, would eventually seek revenge for his brother Ragnar's crippling. Ragnar was now certainly a permanent enemy. Wolf thought about it. He lost nothing for Ulrich and Ragnar would always have been his enemy until he or they died. At least now, Ragnar's threat was limited. His mind was unsettled, but his body was exhausted and sleep came.

He awoke shortly to the sound of movement. He stayed very still.

A man was practicing sword movements in the clearing. His fighting style was like nothing Wolf had ever seen. The man was not a brute like his half-brothers Ragnar and Ulrich. He was more like Wolf thought he would be when he was grown, if he lived that long. The man was lean and muscular, well proportioned, and quick as lighting. Wolf watched the man for what seemed like an eternity. It was a style that would suit a quicker man like Wolf would be. He would never have the brute strength of his father's line. He knew his mother's father was a feared warrior, and perhaps this was more how he fought? He quieted his mind and concentrated on his observation.

The man seemed to have stamina as Wolf had never seen, although Wolf had seen much single combat. Was this the way he would live beyond his boyhood? When he became a man and outgrew his father's protection, he could be challenged by his brothers. He had often thought that his life would be short unless he became a priest as his mother has suggested. This would mean forsaking his rightful inheritance in both his father's and mother's lines. It was a path he knew he could not take.

It happened suddenly. He saw the flash coming for his head, and Wolf moved just enough to the left so that the knife's blade plunged into the tree by his head. He watched the man coming toward him. Wolf considered his options and remained motionless.

The stranger stopped a few feet from wolf, sword in hand. "Are you spying on me boy?"

Wolf considered his answer. "No, just admiring your style of fighting and wondering if you would teach me."

The stranger tilted his head as he regarded wolf. "Why did you not run?"

To Wolf the reply was simple and he gave it without thought. "If you had wanted me dead, I would be. At worst, the thrown knife would have taken part of my ear. What use to run? I have run all night and can run no more."

Wolf regarded the blade imbedded in the tree next to his head. It was like none he had seen before. He reached back and pulled it from the tree and examined it then offered it to its owner as he asked, "Will you teach me?"

The man sheathed his sword reached forward and took the weapon which seemed to disappear into his garments. The man laughed.

"Why should I teach you?"

Wolf had watched the horse traders and knew what was expected, "I can pay you."

The man laughed. "And what could a boy like you offer me as pay?"

Wolf knew the risk in what he was about to divulge. He could be held for ransom. If it was not paid he would die. He had quickly weighed it in his mind; his mother's priest had often said he had a quick mind. If he did not learn to fight, he would either die or be sent to a monastery, and he thought he would prefer death.

"Silver", was all Wolf said.

The man again tilted his head as he watched the boy, "And where will this silver come from?"

"My family who rule this land," Wolf replied and then added, "but there will be a condition of secrecy."

The man squatted. Wolf could tell he was thinking.

"Are you stupid boy? Telling a stranger this, could lead to your ransoming or death."

Wolf smiled and said, "I am already a walking corpse. My oldest bastard brother Ulrich is a brute and savage killer. When I am of age and no longer under my father's protection, he will kill me if I cannot fight and live. My other alternative is to become a priest and renounce my inheritance. I think for me death would be the better choice."

The man considered then said, "You have lost your bargaining power by telling me this."

Wolf paused. "If you are greedy you will try to ransom me and it does not matter. If you are a warrior, you will turn me down or your oath to train me will be worth a goodly price, but it cannot be beyond what I can secretly raise."

The man considered. "How old are you boy?"

"Thirteen," Wolf answered.

The man looked troubled. "You do not talk like a boy of thirteen nor do you act and reason like one."

Wolf sat quietly and waited while the man squatted there. Wolf was tempted to break the silence, but he did not. Minutes passed and the man finally spoke as he nodded toward the bloodied sword lying beside Wolf, "Tell me about the sword."

"My father and mother are away. In a drunken rage, my bastard half-brother tried to ride me down and kill me. I tricked him. He is near death or dead. It is his sword and I put his mount out of its suffering with it. My half-brother had a twisted and shattered leg and broken head, was swooning, had but a short blade, and could not have attacked me then. He may not live and if he does, he will surely be crippled."

"How old is your brother?" the man asked.

Wolf looked up and his eyes locked with the man's. "He is nineteen."

The man nodded. "Not exactly a fair fight. You did well to trick him. Still, if he lives he has many years to plan revenge, even if through others."

Wolf confessed, "It was part cunning, but mostly providence and my brother's drunkenness that led to his defeat. I feared I would die."

The man smiled, "Yes, it is always like that in battle. Are you followed?

Wolf shrugged for in truth he did not know.

The man accepted that and said, "Come to my camp, sleep, and then we will eat and talk."

When Wolf woke, it was with a start. He looked up and realized it was late afternoon. He felt for the purse he always carried. It was still there and the sword was still by his side. He smelled food cooking. Wolf's host had roasted a pair of rabbits over an open flame. The man motioned to Wolf to come and eat. The man watched as Wolf crossed himself then bowed his head for a moment before eating. They ate in silence.

Wolf spoke first, "Thank you for the rabbit."

The man smiled. "What do they call you boy?"

"Though it is not my given name, everyone calls me Wolf. I am called that because my mother's family banner bears the wolf. To my father I am just a tool to further his ambitions. My father and

6

brothers call me runt. I think my father wants others to think of me as my mother's son, not his."

The man sat silently considering this. "Think Wolf. Are your brothers and father taller than the others who are warriors?"

Wolf was dumbfounded as he considered this. "Why, yes."

"Then could it be that you are seeing things through eyes tainted by what your father and brothers see? It has been my experience that large men can be killed in the same way as other men. Could it be that you are just a normal size boy who will become a regular size man?"

Wolf instinctively knew the answer. How could he have not seen this? He nodded in agreement.

The stranger smiled, "They call me Shadow. That is what you should call me. I may be willing to train you if the price is right. What do you offer?"

Though only a boy, Wolf had seen enough bargaining, watching secretly to know how it was done. "I will give you a silver coin each month, but you must train me in secret."

For most, the silver coin would be a small fortune.

Shadow smiled. "Consider Wolf, is that all my service is worth? What is my loyalty worth?"

Wolf considered. "Service is one thing, loyalty another. My mother says loyalty is a priceless thing."

Shadow was taken aback by the boy's wisdom. How could so young a lad be so measured in his thinking? If he lived, he might become a leader worth following, and Shadow knew there were few enough of those. "What then young Wolf is the best you can do? I do not even know if you are who you say you are."

Shadow already believed the boy for he was too well reasoned not to be of noble birth and exceptionally bright. Shadow thought he knew who this boy was.

Wolf gave a measured response as he had learned to do from watching the traders. It gave him time to think.

"It is true you do not know me but neither do I know you. Why do you have no Lord? Are you an oath breaker?"

Shadow looked at him, "I have broken no oath because I have not given one, and my Lord died in battle."

Wolf nodded. "It is not then a matter of worth, but what I can give you. I have not yet any inheritance so I cannot promise what I do not have. I will pay you 3 pieces of silver each month for your oath to train me in secret for at least two years and to protect me for I am still a boy. This may be extended if we both agree, and if I do not pay you are released. You should know I am a Christian like my mother and the Danes do not like that. If I am who I say I am and with your training if I can learn to fight well enough to perhaps succeed in holding an inheritance, I will reward you further. I may then give you the option to become my man and serve me."

Shadow wondered if he was being tested by this boy and decided he was. "I will make no oath, but my yes is yes and my no is no, as the scriptures demand."

Wolf asked him, "What talisman do you wear?"

Shadow pulled the chain from his tunic and showed Wolf the cross hanging from it and said. "No talisman."

Wolf smiled, for truly God had answered his prayers. "It is good you are a Christian, if you were not, or had not become one, I would be limited in my dealings with you. I will reward you in accordance with your service when I come of age and if I gain an inheritance. However, you must prove your ability to fight in battle, as I must to you, before we are bound. Are you agreeable?"

It was then Shadow knew Wolf was who he said he was. No other boy would dare to offer such conditions, for if his birthright was proven to be falsely stated, it would justify Shadow killing him.

"Young Wolf, you ask much for so little. To teach you is one thing, but by being your protector, your enemies become mine, and yours are formidable."

"That is true. I can tell you why, with your help, my future, thus yours, is more likely to be a successful one"

Wolf revealed more of himself than he had ever before. He knew this was one of those turning points when one risked all.

"When my father returns, he will be furious that my life was sought. My half-brother Ragnar's life will be forfeit, but he will flee. My mother's family has no male heirs for all but I have died in battles. My father seeks to acquire my grandfather's lands. My abdication is his only way to obtain my inheritance on my mother's side and thus be Lord of both lands. The Saxons will not accept him if I am dead. If I become a priest and take a vow of poverty, they will be more likely to accept his claim for it will be stronger, as will his warriors, then any who stand in his way. I think it is for this reason he does not train me to be a warrior. I do not think he has the love for his bastard sons that he leads others to believe he has. They are the leverage to force me into the priesthood. Only they, as my father's sons, can be seen to challenge me without my father intervening."

Shadow was stunned by the boy's insights.

"How do you know these things?

"I have my ways."

Indeed Wolf did. He had learned well from both his mother and father who did not realize that Wolf's spies were more numerous and less visible then theirs. A child was often ignored when even a servant was suspected. The cost of orphan children's eyes and ears was so small and their loyalty was easily earned. His kindness, freely given, was the only goodness many of them experienced. There were many such children working in the castle. Between these and what his mother's priest Father Bryan taught him about political intrigue in his family, and what he secretly overheard, had given him a unique understanding of how others saw him. He also had paid other adult spies who he knew were in one of his parents' service, though he used them clumsily so they did not regard him seriously. They had their uses in misleading others.

Wolf had feigned physical inability because that was expected. He also had until now let no one know just how much he really understood or learned. Father Bryan saw him as a hard working but ungifted scholar struggling through his letters, but the truth was that Wolf had mastered them long ago and learned languages with ease. He understood the Danes when they spoke in front of him, though they did not know it. The problem was he had little chance to practice speaking it.

Wolf looked at Shadow seriously, "The real danger comes the closer I come to manhood. I must train in secret while leading others to believe I will skulk off to a monastery. If I am found out, I do not know what will happen. I think I can do it, God willing, for two and a half years until I reach sixteen. Then I will either have to defend myself against my oldest brother Ulrich, flee to my maternal grandfather, or die. I hope Ragnar, crippled permanently, will no longer be a direct threat. He was my worst nightmare to face sober, but strong drink was his weakness. Ulrich is slower of both mind and body, but he also is a natural killer and though he drinks, never too much. I also know if I chose to go to a monastery I would soon thereafter have some fatal accident or illness. My mother would probably die soon after my father assumes control of my grandfather's lands. If I am forced into fighting him and Ulrich thinks I will be a lamb to the slaughter, I may have some advantage if I have learned to fight well."

Shadow considered what Wolf had told him. The two of them sat in silence for some time before Shadow responded.

"You reason well. In one instance you die with no gain, in the other you may live or die, but if you live you may gain much. What happens if you defeat Ulrich? What will your father do? What will you do?"

Wolf replied without hesitation, "I have a plan to avoid fighting him, but I may not be able to avoid it. You will have to decide whether to help upon what you now know."

Shadow answered, "Before answering I need to know why you want to rule lands."

Wolf's answer was immediate "The people have lived in fear and despair, subject to hardship and attack. It is time for them to live in peace and prosperity. As they prosper, so will their Lord. I seek a land ruled righteously based upon the law and where God's church will prosper as its people do. My desire is for peace for my people, at least for a time during which my children and grandchildren can take root in the land."

Shadow knew then what his answer would be.

"You fight not only flesh and blood, but on the spiritual plain. The old gods will not be given up easily or without conflict. The devil will be your adversary. Yet still, it is a just dream worth fighting and dying for, so I agree to train you."

Wolf responded, "Greater is Christ who is in me, than he who is in the world."

Wolf reached beneath his cloak and came out with his fist tight over coins. He dropped nine silver coins into Shadow's hand, "For the first three months."

The teaching started. Wolf's parents would be gone for some time and Wolf wanted to make the most of the time he had available.

In the days that followed, Shadow was surprised to find the boy was in fine physical condition. He was strong for his age, fast, had exceptional reflexes and had phenomenal stamina. Wolf had exercised in secret and ran every day. His drive for self-preservation had resulted in his dedication to becoming as fit as possible. Away from the castle he had moved about stones of increasing size. His loose clothes hid a wiry body.

Wolf was also a very quick learner. They started with the basics. It seemed Wolf had a talent for integrating things he had seen his father's warriors do with the training he was receiving. As a result, his teacher found new ways of thinking about fighting technique. Wolf knew he was progressing very quickly. He also realized that his past practice of privately mimicking the moves he had observed in the training yard of his father's castle had been both a blessing and a curse. They had given him some flexibility and strength he would not otherwise have. Some things blended nicely with how Shadow was training him, but some bad habits had to be unlearned as Shadow showed Wolf their inherent weaknesses that could lead to death.

Several days after starting their training, they heard a voice far off calling Wolf's name. They stopped their practice.

Wolf looked at Shadow, "Sounds like Ubbe. I had better see him and send him back. It might be better if you keep out of sight for now".

Ubbe was wandering the woods calling Wolf's name. He was worried for his life. If Wolf was not at the castle when his father returned, Ubbe feared he would be executed. He was charged to protect the boy, not that he could have overcome Ragnar, but it was his duty to try. He had failed. When the boy stepped out from behind a tree, Ubbe exclaimed, "Thank the gods you are safe."

Wolf played the frightened boy screaming, "Go away, I will not come back until my parents return. They will kill me! They will kill me!"

Ubbe tried to placate Wolf. "It is alright now. No one is going to harm you. Ragnar has gone daft, and they had to cut off his leg. He will not harm you. Everyone else knows what will happen if harm comes to you. "

Wolf looked around, pretending he was deciding whether to bolt.

Ubbe made the judgment Wolf expected and warned, "Don't make me chase you boy."

"The others could not catch me, so what makes you think you, with your limp can? I could just run away and never come back."

Ubbe was now near panic. He was so close to saving his own life, yet he knew he could not catch the boy if he ran. "Now, now, let's not be hasty."

Wolf stammered, "Leave now and I will return to the castle when my parents return. I will hide in these woods where I am safe until then. I will tell my father I was kept safe in these woods. Go. Go, or I run and you will not find me."

Ubbe hesitated. "Promise you will come back when your parents return?"

"Yes", and then Wolf slipped into the woods and disappeared before Ubbe could say anymore.

Ubbe was lost and short on food, but he would find his way back. It seemed the boy was faring better than he had. At least now there was a chance his life might be saved. He started walking.

Shadow had been watching from the woods and was impressed by the way his pupil had played out the scene. Shadow could hardly believe the boy talking to Ubbe was Wolf. They just might succeed with God's help.

Some days later word had come to the castle that their Lord was returning and was just a day away. Ragnar's friends prepared for his escape. In the end there were only three that were prepared to go with him. Ragnar was a doer, not a thinker, and he had accumulated only these three oath men. They prepared a cart to transport Ragnar for his stump had not fully healed and much of the time he was unconscious. There was no way he could sit a horse even tied to the saddle. When he was awake, in spite of the rumor he was daft, he was fully aware. Everyone knew he was surely facing a death sentence if he stayed. Ragnar and his small band left in a panic.

Ulrich knew it was necessary his brother leave. His attitude toward Ragnar had changed with the crippling injury. Ragnar's status had changed from a threat to Ulrich's ambitions which would be eliminated by murder, to that of a brother who had been wronged. What had happened to his brother Ragnar was because of that sniveling whelp Wolf. Ulrich knew his time for revenge would come in the not too distant future. In the meantime, he would wait.

Chapter 2 – Homecoming

Lord Vilhelm's party was just a day's journey from the castle but nightfall was coming, so they made camp in a place that was very defensible. It was unlikely any would be foolish enough to attack the party of Lord Vilhelm that consisted of so many warriors armed to the teeth and battle hardened. Yet old habits die hard and Vilhelm knew those who were careless died even harder and often unexpectedly. Even in his own lands, he was careful.

His wife's tent was erected, but Vilhelm would not share it. He was afraid of siring another legitimate heir and that would complicate matters. He must control his father-in-laws land before he bred more legitimate heirs. He would sleep with his men and they would see their Lord sharing their warrior's life. He knew his power over these men was part respect and part fear. He needed both from them to keep them in line. Some day one of Vilhelm's future sons would rule, but not his bastard sons.   Ulrich, like Wolf, would have to eventually be eliminated, for they were threats to his power. Through his spies, Vilhelm knew of Ulrich's ambition and threat. For the time being, he was content to keep Ulrich constrained for use as a weapon against the runt.

The guards had been posted and so his mother almost shouted the alarm when she saw the movement in the shadows, but Wolf stepped forward and she embraced him. She whispered, "My dear, dear son, what are you doing here?" As she hugged him, she noticed that his body had become even harder since she had left, though his clothes hid the fact. She never really took note of it and later would realize her error.

Wolf led her to a bench, knelt down beside her and told her all of what had happened with Ragnar while she was gone. He also told her about Shadow, though he left out his plans and the training, mentioning only that Shadow was his bodyguard. She listened intently to what she heard. She whispered, "Do you judge this Shadow a man to trust with your life?"

Wolf nodded. His mothered smiled, for it was obvious her son did not know Shadow's former employment with her deceased brother.

Wolf spoke softly, "I will need your help mother. When you see him with me at the castle, call him by name and others will think you heard about the incident and sent him to protect me. Father already knows you have spies and will be troubled by what happened. Do you think he will challenge Shadow's presence?"

"No son. It is in his interest to be seen as wanting to do everything he can to protect you. He knows Shadow will not be able to intervene in a legal challenge when you come of age. Until then, he does not want any harm to come to you. He knows you will have to go to the priesthood to survive. He still has Ulrich to use against you. I wish it were otherwise, but my father is no longer strong enough to ward off my husband if I were to send you. You would never be allowed to leave anyway." She brought a small chest which she gave to Wolf. "It is a gift from your grandfather. You will need it. Hide it well."

Wolf knew his mother's spirit was being beat down bit by bit and it broke his heart. "I must leave now mother. I will see you at the castle." He slipped away.

Wolf had no sooner left than the messenger came from the castle. He was taken directly to Vilhelm who listened to the messenger saying nothing. As the telling continued, his seasoned men who knew him well enough, saw the controlled anger on their Lord's face. At the end of the telling the messenger was thanked and sent to be fed and find a place to sleep.

Vilhelm sat silently going over his plans. He decided that only minor changes to his strategy had to be made. It could have been worse. If Ragnar had succeeded in killing the runt Saxon, the only way he would have gotten his wife's family lands would have been by force. He would eventually win, but the cost would be so great in warriors and treasure that all his holdings would be subject to threat. His ambitions would have been thwarted. The gods were with him, for by luck, the runt had survived and so the goal was still attainable.

Ragnar's stupidity rankled Vilhelm. He must be seen to be sought after to be put to death if still within these lands. He would, if not found, have to be exiled upon penalty of death.

As Vilhelm set out for the castle, his messenger went in search of Ragnar. Vilhelm's searchers would go out in two days and by then

Ragnar must be away from the lands his father ruled.

Two hours before his father returned, Wolf and Shadow came from the woods, crossing the open field to the castle's gate. Shadow led his war horse, and a second horse which carried his baggage. The guard at the castle recognized the boy and called into the courtyard. Several men came to the gate. Among them were Ubbe and Ulrich.

Ubbe was the only one to greet the lad, "Welcome back Wolf. Your father and mother will be here soon."

Wolf nodded, "I know."

Ulrich stepped into the path of Wolf. "Who is this with you?"

Wolf responded, "Ask my mother." He knew Ulrich would not.

Ulrich changed his tactic. He moved in front of Shadow. "Who are you?" he challenged.

Shadow looked him up and down, almost as though with contempt. "I am Osmund, the Shadow Killer, slayer of too many to number, and now protector of Wolf. Do you mean the boy or me harm?"

Wolf had never seen Ulrich taken aback. He knew then that Shadow was indeed a man of reputation.

Ulrich stood aside. "I was only seeing to my brother's wellbeing. He is young and I was concerned he did not have good sense in his choosing of companions."

Shadow replied, "His mother certainly has good sense."

The implication floated on the air like a fog of malice. Shadow had dealt with too many bullies, not to recognize one when he saw one. Some were very dangerous and this man surely was. Nevertheless, not to assert one's self was to give power to the enemy.

Shadow turned to Wolf, "Lead on, Wolf."

As Shadow's general belongings were taken to Wolf's lodgings and his horses handed over for stabling, Shadow and Wolf carried the belongings that they did not trust others to handle; weapons mainly. Ragnar's sword and the small chest filled with treasure were safely hidden in the woods.

They had barely gotten settled when the announcement was made of the return of Wolf's father and mother. Wolf looked at Shadow, "I think we need to meet them."

Wolf's father and mother rode into the castle and dismounted as the warriors followed. Wolf went toward his parents and his mother came forward to embrace him. Wolf smiled, "Welcome home, mother."

Shadow came forward. He knelt on one knee to the lady. "Greetings, Ethelind, my lady."

She smiled and said, "Rise, Shadow. I thank you for looking after my son." She, always concerned with the political, added, "Between you and Ubbe my son was in good hands."

Shadow got up, "Thank you, my lady."

She motioned to him and led him to Vilhelm. "Husband, let me introduce Osmund, the Shadow Killer. He protects our son. He was my brother's War Chief."

Vilhelm nodded. "Your reputation precedes you Osmund. You are a warrior of accomplishment. Welcome. Thank you for your service in protecting my son."

Shadow nodded but did not bow, "Thank you, Lord Vilhelm."

Vilhelm turned and left.

The exchange had not been lost on Wolf. His mother knew Shadow all too well. His father also knew of Shadow. He was not the only one playing the wily fox. He and Shadow would have to talk. When they were alone, Wolf asked Shadow why he did not mention his service to Wolf's uncle.

"Your uncle is dead. At first, I did not know who you were. Once I realized who you are, I sensed why God had arranged for me to be here. I had come at your uncle's dying request to see if your mother and you were safe. Once I gave my word to serve you, what difference did it make? You had not asked who I served before."

Wolf realized that it was a lapse in judgment not to have asked that question. He would learn from that omission.

The following months were uneventful. Wolf spent time each morning supposedly learning his letters. When Father Bryan left, he read the ancient texts. He memorized key portions. The more he read the more intrigued he was. Father Bryan was willing to let Wolf increasingly study by himself because his progress seemed to be a little improved when left to his own ways. Little did the good Father realize just how much his young student was digesting. Each morning after ensuring Wolf was started on his studies, Father Bryan was content to spend more time on his other duties.

Wolf not only studied the church papers and the scriptures, but in the priest's absence studied the grants, deeds and laws. It was there he came to realize the importance of the written word. Words on a page could change a meaning or a future. They could grant or take away, condemn or pardon, motivate or destroy. He was determined to learn ever more.

Afternoons were spent in the woods. There, secretly, the art of arms were practiced with Shadow. Wolf had always been seen to take his books into the woods each afternoon, weather permitting. Everyone thought he went to study. So generally, no one paid attention to his absence nor questioned Shadow's accompanying him.

A few times they had been followed. Wolf had sat and read while Shadow went to intimidate the spy. After a while, no one tried to follow them. There in the woods, they practiced unhindered with wooden sword and shields. Wolf's skills increased quickly and dramatically. In the beginning Wolf had suffered many bruises, but over the months they became fewer and fewer.

One afternoon they spared for almost two hours without stopping. Shadow signaled a stop and motioned for Wolf to follow him. They both sat, their bodies soaked with sweat.

Wolf spoke first, "That was a good workout; I am exhausted. You pushed me and pushed me, but perhaps it is time you do not hold back?"

Shadow laughed so hard he was bending over trying to catch his breath. Finally he stopped laughing. "Wolf, I have not been holding back for two weeks. You match me on equal basis. If we were to fight in mortal combat, I would probably still triumph because I am fully grown and still have a few tricks up my sleeve. In a few months, who knows? You are now keeping me sharp. Few men in the castle would overcome you in single combat and you are still a boy. You are as fast as I am, and strong enough. I am called Shadow Killer because they say I am so swift with the sword that my blade kills a man before its shadow is seen. I have not seen anyone who could match my speed until now." Shadow went silent for a moment before continuing, "The only real challengers would be your brother and father. I have seen them in battle and they are formidable. The trick with the big ones is to avoid fighting, if you can, or if you have to, to kill them quickly."

Wolf became serious. "Then you had better teach me how to kill the big ones quickly."

Shadow chuckled, "I think you already know how to do that. The thing you need to learn is how to avoid killing them. That would be more pleasing to God."

Wolf considered. "Good point, but how?" It was a question that Wolf did not expect an answer to.

Shadow answered anyway, "A man of experience can overcome sometimes by reputation or by commanding superior numbers, thus creating in the enemy fear or a reluctance to pay a high cost. This may persuade the other not to attack in the first place."

Wolf rose and started walking back to the castle forgetting to gather his belongings. Shadow lagged behind as he collected wolf's books and hid their other belongings. Wolf walked back to the castle lost in his thoughts.

"Well who is this?" Wolf looked up and saw four youths standing before him and it was the biggest who had spoken. The big lad spoke again, "Hand it over!"

Wolf was for just a brief moment angry at himself for not being alert enough. Then he determined to let that emotion go.

Wolf asked seemingly with an innocent voice, "Give what over." The big boy swung at Wolf and lost his balance as his arm arced through empty space. Wolf was standing there just out of his reach and the boy lunged forward to tackle him and felt blinding pain in his gut as he dropped to the ground. His smaller opponent was standing back watching him. Wolf was keeping the larger boy between himself and the other three. It was then Wolf's attacker made the mortal mistake, he drew a blade and attacked. It wasn't a fancy blade, but it was a lethal weapon. Wolf waited until the last moment.

His attacker was sure of the kill, but his blade swept thin air and then he felt the pain for only an instant. Then he fell to the ground and died from the single cut. The other boys stood not knowing what to do.

Wolf looked at them and demanded, "Who was he to you?

The lad standing closest replied, "He was our cousin. Those two are brothers," he said nodding in the direction of the other lads, "and I am their cousin." He moved a little toward Wolf.

Wolf warned, "Be careful what you do and say. If you attack me, or declare a blood feud, first you, then all your relatives will surely die. I am Wolf, son of the Lord of this castle and my brother is Ulrich, called Axe Slayer." Wolf knew the boys would probably know nothing of castle politics. He could tell they were all terrified now. "You three, pick him up. We go to the water." They did as ordered. The body was thrown in and was carried away by the current.

Wolf looked at the boys. "Who are your family?

The boys looked at each other, and the new leader, the oldest cousin responded, "We are. We have no others. All died at the hands of raiders."

Wolf regarded them carefully. They probably were orphans doing whatever they could to stay alive. He locked eyes with the elder cousin.

"Consider carefully. If you mention this, you will be guilty of my attempted murder and will surely die. You will always have to guard yourself to keep your foul secret. I give you an alternative. You may kneel to me and take an oath to be my sworn men. You will be paid for your service. Decide."

One of the brothers was about to leave, but the other brother stopped him and whispered to him. They called their cousin over. After some minutes, all three approached Wolf stopping at a respectful distance. The cousin spoke for them. "What would you pay us?" The moon had come out from the clouds and it was obvious that their clothes were in tatters. They were the poorest of the poor and they did not look like they ate regularly.

Wolf tossed a small copper coin to the spokesman. "One at the end of each month. That, food, and a roof. Later, if you serve me well, there may be more. If you do not perform your duties, you will be treated like any other oath man who fails in his duties. Talk about it quickly, I have other business."

The lads huddled together. They were not sure what 'being treated like other oath men who failed' meant. They all thought the punishment would be harsh. They worried about their safety. If they refused they would have to go far away and quickly. Slavers might get them. That was worse than the meager meals they earned working the docks. Being a sworn man would be a better life than they faced now. They would eat regularly and they were desperate as well as very hungry. They were not afraid of hard work so they agreed. They would live or die together in the service of this young noble.

Wolf took their oath right then. He led them through it and explained the consequences of being an oath breaker in vague terms, but the lads understood the seriousness of the matter. He warned them to tell no one of what had taken place. They had bent their knees to him and he told them to meet him at sunrise and where.

When they left, he said, "You may come out now."

Shadow had been observing the encounter. He appeared from the dark, "I see you have a plan on how to raise future men," just a little sarcastically.

Shadow had discussed with Wolf the difficulty of finding reliable trained and experienced men at arms to help him claim his inheritance. Most were already aligned and Shadow and some of his old company, due to unusual circumstances might be the only reliable and available men at arms who were not aligned with a Lord, but there were not enough of them.

Wolf replied seriously, "Yes, but not like this. I just took mercy on these boys as Christ would have me do. They did, however, give me an idea - the orphans of the monasteries. Some young men may be candidates for service and become proficient. There are many who would seek a better life and if we could only recruit some of them we could provide it. I need to find out where to obtain youth to train. We need to find some place and a master at arms to train them. We will also need some seasoned warriors to anchor the trainees."

Shadow was again struck by Wolf's intelligence. It might just work.

Shadow asked, "Can you afford the arms, the bribes, and the pay?"

Wolf nodded, "Yes, thanks to my grandfather and mother."

"Then Wolf, I know where I can find a master of arms to train the lads, some seasoned warriors that are trustworthy, and an abbot who will provide orphan youth to train if the gift to the church is adequate."

Wolf smiled. "There are priests and then there are priests."

"Indeed!"

And with that Shadow chuckled. Wolf was no fool. Even at his young age he recognized the difference between the called priesthood and the purchased office. Wolf knew that some who professed publicly to be Christians still worshipped the old gods like his father Vilhelm did. There were also clergymen who were not truly Christians.

The next morning Wolf and Shadow met the boys and arranged work for them as well as new clothes. Shadow left Wolf with Father Bryan and met with a reliable man known to Lady Ethelind. He was hired to bring a common message to men he had led. He knew Lady Ethelind would learn of the messages, but he also knew she had no love for her cruel and pagan husband. Vilhelm would learn nothing of the messages.

It turned out a number of the men sent messages were still unaligned and accepted the payment to stay that way until Shadow called for them. They had served under Shadow's command before and trusted him.

Chapter 3 - The pilgrimage

As late summer came the year he turned fifteen, Wolf approached Father Bryan about going on a pilgrimage. Father Bryan was elated with the suggestion and discussed it with Wolf's mother. After some discussion between Wolf's parents, it was decided that Wolf, Father Bryan and Shadow would make the pilgrimage along with a guard sufficient to ward off bandits. Vilhelm was happy that Wolf was taking an interest in things religious. He saw it as a movement forward in his plan and was quite willing to support the trip. Ulrich would not be part of the party. Vilhelm did not want to take any more chances that would undermine his ambition.

Of course, no one but Shadow and Wolf knew of the side trips that Shadow would make while Wolf visited at the Cathedral, nor the plan Wolf had formulated. So it was that the group, including four of Vilhelm's seasoned warriors and three boys driving an oxen pulled cart filled with camp gear set out on the journey. The journey was only a few days in length and during that time Wolf missed the opportunity to practice at arms. He did take the opportunity to listen to the campfire talk of the warriors, which was very revealing given that they did not know he understood every word they said.

He and Shadow slept with the three boys near. The Warriors ignored the boys. They were employed setting up Wolf's camp, cooking, and packing. He still played the role of the scholar concerned with his creature comforts and the warriors kept their distance. Each morning at sunrise, Father Bryan prayed briefly with Wolf and Shadow as the boys stood by listening.

The leader of the assigned warriors communicated seldom and then only with Shadow. He would not talk to Wolf. He was careful to make sure nothing could be reported to Vilhelm that would call his loyalty into question.

Initially, Father Bryan talked for hours as they rode. He talked continuously about the books, the relics, and the grandeur of the Cathedral they would visit. He told of the bishop and his priests, about each one's specialty and of the large nunnery. After a day's riding, the priest's enthusiasm for conversation dissolved as his pain increased. He was a poor horseman at best.

It was easy for Shadow to slip away once they reached the Cathedral.

Wolf did not have to pretend interest in the work of the bishop and his staff. He had reason to want to understand better the workings of the church. He charmed everyone and gave the appearance of a pleasant and humble student who was solid and devoted, but not outstanding. He was just the kind of nobleman's son who would render valuable service to the bishop; not the least of which was the lad would bring a good donation from his father. Nominally it was for his son's education and support. The gift of course would end up in the bishop's purse because the young man would take a vow of poverty.

Wolf had no trouble quickly sorting out the pious from the ambitious. He learned things that the bishop would not want him to know. Once the bishop had decided Wolf was no threat, he was placed in the care of an elderly and jolly priest. The priest was happy to show him the library and let him read at his leisure, though Wolf was careful to hide his true interest.

Wolf was allowed to interact with the younger priests. He identified a young and pious priest, Aert, who was obviously unhappy with the bishop's sinful life style but was smart enough not to criticize it. Brother Aert was disaffected but cooperative. He always had a positive attitude and did the most unlikely thing; he often actually quoted scripture to make a theological point.

Wolf liked the young priest and it was he who Wolf approached to be his personal priest until he came of age. Wolf expected, God willing, the relationship would continue for many years for Wolf had no intention of entering a monastery. After a small gift was made to the church, the bishop was pleased to grant Wolf's request that the priest be assigned to him immediately. The bishop expected the additional benefit of having a spy in the midst of Wolf's family, but in that he would be disappointed.

The Cathedral building was not that impressive. Wolf had expected something more and was disappointed with the structure. It was a dark and dank place.

Two warriors followed Wolf everywhere. They were always bored, but working in shifts they had time to spend in the local ale houses in the town. Wolf had heard two of the warriors joking about seeing the bishop and two of the priests drunk at the whorehouse they frequented during their visit. It neither shocked nor surprised Wolf.

The days passed quickly as Wolf learned about the inner workings of the diocese. In the evenings in his room, when the priests were at study, Wolf exercised in silence until the sweat poured off his young body. He would not allow his stay at the Cathedral to soften him.

While Wolf was at the Cathedral, Shadow searched out an old colleague, Aewel, who l had fought many battles with Shadow. Aewel was a deadly fighter and also a gifted trainer. He had taught many warriors how to use all sorts of weapons to efficiently kill. He was skilled at determining which weapon would be the best for each fighter based on their physicality and personality. He was also skilled at choosing men who would become good fighters.

Shadow found him sitting on a bench leaning against the wall of his small house. Aewel sat seemingly half asleep and unconcerned. Wolf saw the spear and shield nearby and knew his friend's appearance was deceptive. Once Aewel recognized Shadow, he jumped up and came forward to greet Shadow as he dismounted.

They embraced and exchanged friendly insults. Shadow remarked that Aewel had gained a few pounds, although he had in fact been of the same build since his youth, but his rotund appearance was deceiving. Aewel remarked that Shadow was not getting any younger and seemed to move with all the speed of a fast turtle. The aging part was true, but at twenty four Shadow was certainly not old, and if anything, his work with Wolf had made him faster.

Shadow inquired as to what his friend was doing now. Aewel admitted to being at loose ends and drinking too much to relieve the boredom. He was desperate because he was broke and the tavern owner had his armor as collateral against the debt for food and ale. After his armor was pledged, Aewel had survived on the coins Shadow had sent to keep him unaligned. The message had been a God send for Aewel who awaited his new employment.

Shadow explained his proposal and gave him some background, but not all. He trusted Aewel with his life, but it was not his life he would be risking to divulge too much. Aewel was told only that which was necessary for him to understand the urgency and necessity. Aewel trusted Shadow, so he accepted the task and committed his service to Wolf. The price of services was agreed and it was in keeping with Aewel's ability. Coins changed hands. They both went to the local alehouse to celebrate their new adventure and to reclaim Aewel's armor.

Neither of the men were drunkards, but they shared ale and a meal for which Shadow paid. The food was basic but good, and the ale mediocre. To the friends it was a feast because they shared it.

They went to Aewel's lodgings early. The next morning after prayer, Aewel gathered his belongings saddled his battle horse and led his burdened spare horse as he and Shadow set out for their next stop. When they arrived it was indeed as they suspected; abandoned. Part of the structure, the eastern wing was unusable having been totally destroyed by raiders years before. The front and west roof was still intact but the shutters were gone from the windows. The enclosed court yard could not be seen from the road.

They camped there and took inventory of what would be required to make it serviceable to start the training. They decided it would serve as a training place. The great hall still had a good roof and two hearths so it would be the barracks. If the windows were properly packed, and heavy cloth draped over the doors, the room could be kept warm on winter nights and their meals could be prepared there.

Aewel went recruiting from the list Shadow provided and Shadow returned to the Cathedral to report to Wolf on the progress. Shadow remained two days and then he left again, this time with Wolf's priest Aert.

Shadow and Aert camped near the monastery in late afternoon to wait for the others to arrive. Shadow heard riders in the woods. He told Aert to stay with the horses and went to investigate. Shadow recognized the seven men who led packhorses. He stepped from behind a tree and proclaimed, "You are so noisy you will wake the dead."

The riders laughed, stopped, dismounted, and greeted Shadow with embraces. He knew them all well for they had served under him. He took them to his camp where they paid courtesies to the priest for they were all Christians. There were three less than Shadow had hoped, but it was a sufficient start. He was told the three others would come later. They spent time getting reacquainted. They were given a brief explanation as to what they would be doing, and what they could expect. They all recognized the risk and opportunity presented to them and agreed to the terms of employment.

In the morning, they dressed in full battle gear, mounted and headed for their destination. The battle gear was for intimidation and it was probably not going to be required.

At the monastery, they entered the courtyard, dismounted and Shadow went to the door. An acolyte came to answer the pounding. Shadow's voice was commanding, "Tell Abbot Adamnan that Osmund, the Shadow Killer, is here and demands an audience."

The acolyte responded officiously, "I will see if the abbot will receive you."

Shadow's voice rose into a threatening tone, "He will see me or this place will come down around his ears. Now go boy and tell your master I am here."

Shadow had dealt with the Abbot before on other business and knew the right amount of coercion and bribery to apply. He would not act the way he planned to if the abbot was a true man of God, but in truth he was an evil ambitious little man who hid behind a veneer of pious service.

A monk returned scurrying and opened the door.

"The Abbot will of course see the renowned warrior Osmund, his old friend and servant of Christendom."

Shadow entered with Aewel and brother Aert, leaving the rest of the warriors in the courtyard. Aert had been cautioned to remain silent and observe.

They were led into the abbot's room, a poor imitation of a bishop's throne room. The abbot rose from his chair to greet Shadow.

"My dear friend, how good to see you again."

He put out his hand so Shadow could kiss his ring which gesture Shadow ignored for Adamnan was no bishop. The abbot held it out to Aert who followed Shadow's lead. Shadow appreciated the young priest's quick take on what was happening. He had passed the test by remaining silent.

The abbot returned to his chair. Shadow walked to the elevated chair and stepped up onto the platform while Aewel wore a menacing glare and kept his hand on his sword as though expecting to have to kill someone any moment. The priests in the room began small restless movements afraid of what was happening.

The abbot recognized his attempt to gain the upper hand on this warrior had failed. With the threat that Shadow represented standing beside him while he sat, the abbot began to sweat. This was not going well.

Shadow changed strategy. "My dear friend Adamnan, I come to pay you honor and make a gift to your charitable works. God has blessed the Lord I serve, who wishes to donate anonymously."

The last negated any chance for the abbot to ask questions. Shadow would not in any event answer the Abbot's questions. Better to have the abbot make wild assumptions as he was prone to do. He would surely think a renowned warrior like Shadow would be in service to some powerful lord. This would make negotiations simpler. Shadow leaned over and spoke softly so no other could hear.

"In return my Lord would appreciate some young men for service in the advancement of Christendom."

The abbot rose and called out to the monk who had led them in, "Tell brother Petrus that we have guests who need refreshments. We will partake in the garden."

The garden was the one place where no one could be close enough to overhear what they would be discussing. Shadow and the Abbot sat at a small table while Aewel and Aert stood close by and heard all that was said. The negotiations went quickly for the abbot was always uncomfortable with armed warriors in the courtyard. Less than a half an hour after arriving, Shadow and his two companions left the main building and headed to the fields to make their choices, the bribe having been agreed to. The amount paid would depend on the number chosen. The amount for the letter and secrecy surrounding it was already paid. Shadow had gotten it for a bargain, treating it like a side issue. Yet it was very important to their plans.

It was clear that Aewel was disgusted as he approached the fields.

The young men working there wore tattered clothes. "Orphans they are not. Slaves more like it. They were sold by their parents for a few small coins to stave off the starvation of the rest of their family. If this abbot is a Christian, then so is the god Thor."

Aewel spat. The monks supervising the field work were in earshot. Shadow told Aewel to concentrate on the task at hand. Aewel realized it was a warning.

The first one Aewel chose was a stout lad who was alert to what was happening and seemed to be measuring his chances to survive a sprint for the woods close by. Aewel picked up a shovel and holding it upright tossed it at the lad, who dropped his hoe and caught the handle of the shovel before it hit him.

Aewel went through the fields for the rest of the day. There were almost a hundred young men working in the field. Aewel found seventeen who might have the right stuff. They needed at least twelve fully trained, and some might not make it.

That night the seventeen ate in the camp of the warriors. They were given new clothes and bedding before the evening meal. Some of the young men were given the chore of cooking the meal. Others cut wood. None tried to sneak off. Just as well for they would not have made it far.

After supper, around the campfire, Shadow addressed them. "You are being given an extraordinary opportunity. The offer is to be ransomed from the monastery to serve a Christian noble as warriors. You have been chosen to be trained for service beyond your station. You may become a sworn man with opportunity you have not dreamed of. You will keep the peace in Christian ruled lands. You will protect the inhabitants from bandits, marauders, and invaders. You will prosper as your Lord does. You will have the right to marry. I do not, however, wish to pay the ransom for a man who is not going willingly. You each have an hour to decide. If you come with us, my Lord will pay your ransom and there will be no turning back. You will be required to become sworn men to the Christian Lord who pays your ransom. One hour to decide, that is all. Think it over; I will come back in one hour to see who goes and who stays."

Shadow returned in an hour. Two had decided to stay. They

were stripped of their new clothes and given their tattered clothes and returned to the monastery. To let them keep the clothes would have not benefited the two young men, for the clothes would have been confiscated. The bribe had been paid for seventeen. The lives of the two who had returned to the monastery would be a living trial, for the abbot would have to refund their ransom price, and thus be deprived of a profit.

Unexpectedly as the men were preparing for sleep, the young priest Aert approached Shadow. He spoke quietly to Shadow, "I expect my Lord Wolf has arranged all this. If he agrees, may I train with the others? I would like to be a soldier for Christ in the physical sense as well as the spiritual."

Shadow considered and replied, "Unless Wolf disapproves, most certainly. You will of course have to first agree to fealty to our young leader."

Aert responded affirmatively, "Of course, as long as what he requires of me is in accordance with God's laws."

Shadow smiled, "But not necessarily the church's directives?"

Aert laughed, "You read me too well, Shadow. I know the difference."

Shadow expected Wolf would be agreeable to the proposal. He would certainly advise Wolf to agree. The young priest could be helpful in so many ways.

After morning prayer and a light meal, fifteen youth from the monastery left with the mounted warriors and the priest. They left on foot in their new clothes and boots. Their old rags had been burned as a symbol of the life left behind. What they wore was all they had. Shadow and Aewel observed that the youngsters were in good shape and did not complain about the marching. They also noticed that the young priest was an accomplished horseman.

It took all day to reach the training site. As they rode, Shadow talked with the young priest. He came from a noble line which was blessed with too many sons; an unusual event in these times.

He had been sent to train for the priesthood at an early age. Aert found the life not disagreeable, but he was careful not to cross his betters, a lesson he had learned well as a youngest son in a large family where intrigue and the struggle for power was a daily game.

Shadow found him refreshing. He was a young man not afraid of work, not overtly ambitious but also not afraid of responsibility, and, most importatantly, a truly God fearing Christian.

When they arrived at their destination, three warriors were waiting; their horses nearby. They were men Aewel had recruited and who had family arrangements to make before they came. Shadow and Aewel greeted them with embraces and much laughter. Shadow introduced them to Aert.

Shadow arranged the watches and saw that each man had a place assigned. The new recruits fell asleep after being fed a cold meal of cheese, bread, and water. They slept heads to the walls in the barracks room wrapped in warm blankets. There would be trusted warriors sleeping by the three doorways and on sentry duty all night.

Some of the seasoned warriors who were not standing sentry, sat for a time around a fire in the courtyard bringing their comrades up to date on what had happened while they had been apart. They soon retired. The last few days had been hectic for them all.

Shadow was pleased, for there were ten seasoned warriors here, eleven counting him, all of whom were mounted. If the young men worked out well they had the potential for over twice that number either on foot or horse. He hoped they would all be mounted for mobility would be their ally.

The next day Shadow was inventorying, and inspecting the state of the warrior's armament and clothing. To the untrained eye they looked intimidating in their battle array, but the truth was that much of their weaponry and armor needed replacement. It was worn, outdated, or of inferior quality. Only two mounts besides Shadows were really fit for battle.

Shadow called the experienced men together to discuss mounts. He told them of his plans and they all agreed. The horses after all were each man's private property. Wolf had given Shadow enough treasure to outfit twenty five men with the finest armor and purchase the needed horses and that is how the money would be spent, on the finest.

Aewel recommended Herewood to be his assistant. Herewood was a steady and battle hardened warrior and very smart. He had helped Aewel to train before. His recommendation was accepted by

Shadow.

The recruits were rousted at sunrise. The warriors were already about. Aewel announced that each morning brother Aert would hold prayer at sunrise and say a mass on Sunday. On Sunday there would be no training, and the only duty would be sentry duty. Brother Aert would teach about Christ for an hour at midafternoon. All, except those standing sentry, would be in attendance. The group was happy at the announcement for it was seldom than anyone had rest on the Lord's Day, even in Christian lands. A small morning meal would be served each day. There would be a mid-day and evening meal. Each evening the day would end in group prayer.

Accordingly, the training schedule was implemented that first morning. The new recruits were told there would be riding lessons each day. They would learn to fight mounted and on foot. That was a surprise to everyone. Horses were very expensive and men did not customarily fight from horseback. The group was told that until Shadow acquired more horses, the existing mounts would be shared and riding classes would be staggered. Two of the warriors would teach the recruits to ride while Aewel and Herewood would teach them to use weaponry.

Shadow made several procurement trips and half of the warriors would stay at the training site with the recruits. The rest went with Shadow to procure the armor, equipment, and clothing they needed. It took longer than expected even though Shadow had arranged for measuring of the men before he had left. Aert had taken measurements of the men according to Shadow's instructions. Shadow had done this before. Shadow knew exactly what he wanted and negotiated very good prices on the very best quality. The men knew that Shadow was ordering armament to be made, but they were not privy to the specifics.

God was blessing them. There were few major conflicts at this time and many of the Lords were either unwilling or too broke to equip well, and so at present it was a buyer's market on high quality armor and arms. Most nobles would be no better equipped than any of Wolf's warriors when all was done.

Shadow had made two trips back to the camp with the boys driving the oxen pulling their cart laden with goods. It would take time for the armor to be made.

Shadow had been able to purchase or commission enough equipment to arm thirty warriors, though not all in the same place. At present they expected to need twenty six sets so there would be extra. He arranged enough equipment for a half dozen archers, and a great number of arrows, for more archers would come later.

Many thought that to be an archer was dishonorable. Their position was that only in hand to hand combat was there any honor. Shadow knew from experience that a dead enemy was preferable to your own demise, no matter how that enemy was killed. He had no qualms about using archers. He doubted many would criticize his honor to his face.

The need for good well trained battle mounts presented problems. Shadow had purchased only six from those available in the region, although at a reasonable price. The rest he had seen were of poor quality. He would have to range further afield and he did with great profit.

One issue caused Shadow some concern. He had three warriors approach him when they were in towns. They had heard about his purchases and sought employment. He knew only one of them, and that one was not trustworthy. The other two he did not know. They were the dregs of soldiering and he told them his master did not need them. This was the truth, for these men would be a hindrance at best and a threat at worst. Shadow was only bringing in those he knew and trusted with his life. He had been careful not to be followed back to the training site.

Life at the training site had fallen into a military routine and the training progressed. The new goods were stored and the three boys were charged with keeping the items clean, oiled, and rust free, and were diligent to do so. Life here was good to them. They were well fed and more comfortable then they could ever remember being. They prepared food, cleaned, and tended the fires. They had full bellies, good clothes, warm fires, and warm blankets. They did not even mind that they were required to attend the Christian services. The boys approached brother Aert about learning about Christ and he started spending more time with the boys. Eventually, they proclaimed they would follow Christ as well as Wolf and asked to be baptized. Father Aert was ecstatic.

Shadow left Aewel in charge when he left for the cathedral.

Wolf received the letter Shadow had arranged about three weeks after arriving at the Cathedral. Father Bryan was elated that Wolf had received the invitation and would be spending an extended visit to the monastery of Abbot Adamnan. His father was sent a message and he agreed to the arrangement. Wolf would be safe at the monastery with Shadow, and Vilhelm could bring the warriors guarding his son home and save a considerable sum in their maintenance. Father Bryan was called back to the castle by Wolf's mother and was dispatched with two warriors. Wolf sent a message to his mother, that he would like to meet her at the Cathedral on his sixteenth birthday when he publicly made his decision. Wolf knew his father would learn of the message and hoped he would not come.

Shadow was suddenly again Wolf's companion at the cathedral. So it was Wolf, accompanied by his father's men, was escorted to the monastery. He and Shadow waited for a few hours making sure Vilhelm's men at arms were well on their way before they left.

In the many months his parents thought him at the monastery guarded by Shadow, he would be training his men and practicing at arms.

Chapter 4 - The Warriors

When Shadow appeared with Wolf, everyone wondered who the youth was to whom Shadow gave so much deference. The pair immediately went to the training yard where they watched the young men training.

Wolf turned to Shadow, "Now is as good a time as ever".

Shadow nodded and Wolf followed Shadow's lead as they both removed their capes. Both were muscular and lithe, though Shadow was slightly taller than the lad. The two took training swords and shields.

Aewel cleared the courtyard and sat the student's around the edge. He had seen Shadow humble an uppity student before and it was a thing to behold. Shadow and Wolf stood on opposing side then proceeded to circle. They engaged quickly. Aewel's worry grew as time went on. For almost a full hour Wolf and Shadow put on a demonstration that had their audience enthralled. Both suffered minor cuts and bruises, in spite of using only practice weapons. Sometimes the movements were so swift the onlookers could hardly follow them. At last both, sweating and breathing hard, backed away from each other. They bowed to each other smiling.

Shadow turned to Aewel, "Finally an opponent with whom I can really test myself." He looked around. "Don't just stand there, someone get salve and bandages for our cuts." Two of the trainees scurried off for bandages.

Wolf started laughing, "Shadow either I am getting faster or you are slowing down."

Shadow responded, "I think we are both getting faster."

The two embraced, and then sat in silence as their minor wounds were bandaged. They were both bruised and would be sore in the morning. It was a necessary exercise to establish Wolf.

Aewel was looking at the shields and swords. The sword blades were so nicked he did not know if they could be repaired. The shields were ruined. He had known Shadow could kill him in a heartbeat in single combat, but know he knew this youth, not yet a man could also. The others were thinking the same thing. The seasoned warriors came to inspect after Aewel. They all knew this had been a combat in which either opponent could have been seriously injured. The blades had moved too quickly for too long a time for this to be a practiced show.

When the bandaging was complete, Shadow announced at the top of his voice, "Tonight we feast for our young master is here to meet his sworn men. I present to you Aelle, also known as Wolf, heir to two holdings, who with your aid will ensure his inheritance and defend Christendom."

The men had been awed by the display of arms and cheered. The sentries were set by lot and, after a blessing, the meal began.

During the months of training, the new recruits became journeymen with their weapons and the warriors honed their skills. The men became deadly with both spear and sword. The only surprise was all the men learned to ride well. They all worked hard joking that they would not be the one to walk. Some were naturals, and some struggled, but all did what they needed to do to become good riders.

Only one man was found to be unsuitable for training as a man at arms; a young man named Palne. It did turn out that he was an archer of uncanny skill. So his training was altered so that he would be a bowman able defend himself close in with a short blade if all else failed. This worked well. It also solved the problem of integrating archers when the time came.

In time the three boys approached Shadow and asked him to train them enough to protect themselves and the baggage cart. They promised to keep up their other duties. They were given to Palne to train in archery and close in fighting for several hours each day. The boys were strong and soon could draw a bow and became bowman. Though not outstanding archers, they were passable. Palne was put in charge of the three.

The months passed and the band became closer to being a combat ready company. They could maneuver on foot or on horseback to commands. The training had been arduous.

The winter came and was harsh. It seemed the company was forever chopping wood for the fires. Everyone took a turn, even Wolf and Shadow when they were in camp. The company continued to train. It had become close knit and in spite of the hardship the men were happy. They were paid regularly; something to which even the warriors were not used. With no way to spend the money, many of the men for the first time in their lives had purses with coins in them. Two men were sent to deliver coins to the families of the three warriors who had dependents.

In late winter, Shadow travelled again, this time with Wolf along to observe and learn. All those they visited assumed Wolf was Shadow's man, not the reverse. They visited several of the mail and weapons makers Shadow had contracted with. Twice Shadow refused armor that was not of the quality negotiated. Shadow could be fierce when provoked. He had paid a deposit and threatened the armorers with bodily harm if they should not have what he ordered when he came in the spring.

When spring came, Wolf and Shadow ranged far with some of the warriors to find good trained mounts. They were able to procure what they needed as well as spare mounts. They also purchased a second cart and quality draft horses for both carts. When they returned with the last of the mounts, a message came to Wolf that the uniforms he had commissioned, along with his banners were ready.

Shadow went with Herewood and half the warriors to fetch their armament. Although acquiring, training, equipping, and maintaining his men had cost him slightly over half of the sizeable fortune he had been gifted, Wolf was pleased with his investment. He thought his grandfather must have sent the money to aid in his escape from his father. That was not how it would be used. It would soon be time to make his move. Scouts were sent out and returned with the needed reports.

It was a warm spring morning when Wolf called for a break in the regular training. His men, except those standing guard, were instructed to assemble and those who had them were to carry their armor, shields and weapons to the courtyard. The empty ox cart was already in middle of the yard.

When the men were assembled Wolf spoke. "Aewel put all your armor and equipment into that cart." The men were looking at each other. Aewel rose and carried his equipment to the cart, lifted it up and dropped it over the side rail into the cart. His was a partial set of mail and his weapons were serviceable.

Wolf spoke again, "Bring Aewel's."

Two of the young archers brought two large bound packages while another carried a six foot table upright to a place in front Wolf, set it down on edge, then rolled it upright in front of Wolf. The packages were laid on the table. The archers moved away. Wolf motioned Aewel forward as he cut the binding on the first package.

"Aewel, this is the finest equipment for a fine warrior." Wolf drew out the gambeson, the padding that goes under mail armor. "You will find this material sandwiched between the fine cotton liners will absorb impact as well as any available." He handed it to Aewel who slipped the garment over his head. It seemed too long and there appeared to be a defect for it was split front and back but he said nothing.

Wolf next took the mail from the package and offered it to Aewel, "You will note that this armor is split front and back for it is longer than the normal mail and offers more protection. The split allows freedom of movement and allows its user to sit a horse. It has full sleeves. I have tested this new design and it provides good freedom of movement."

Aewel put the mail on. He tested how it moved and smiled. In spite of being longer, it weighed no more than his old mail. Aewel had been around and knew it was better armor than most nobles wore.

Wolf opened the second package, "Here are your mail leggings. This is also of the finest mail."

Aewel strapped the mail on his legs.

The men standing around were watching intently. The seasoned warriors knew if the equipment they received was half as good, they would indeed be well armored. They whispered to the new men about the quality and effectiveness of what was being shown. The men knew that the armor cost a small fortune and the Wolf must expect them to be very successful to invest so much.

Wolf signaled and the two archers brought out a helmet of superb craftsmanship which had mail hanging from it that protected the neck. Everyone saw that the inside of the helmet was padded. This was something that they had never seen before. Wolf placed the helmet on Aewel's head. It fit firmly, and now the men remembered Aert taking their measurements, some of which seemed strange at the time. They hoped their armor would fit as well. The other archer removed a cloth from over a shield which Wolf handed to Aewel. Aewel slipped it over his arm. It was also of the finest quality and obviously strong.

Wolf motioned, and a long and short sword in fine belted scabbards on a wide belt was brought forward and strapped around Aewel's waist. Wolf spoke again, "You may draw the sword Aewel." This was a great honor, for only the most trusted warriors would be allowed to draw a sword in striking distance of their Lord. Aewel drew the sword. It was a marvelous weapon. He turned away from Wolf and tested it.

Aewel did not realize he was speaking, "Such balance, and such workmanship!" A tear came to Aewel's eyes. He raised his arms as if in triumph and the men cheered. When the cheering ceased, Wolf motioned again and Aewel's steed was led in armored. It was an awesome display and the men cheered. Aewel sheathed his sword turned toward Wolf and went down on one knee to his liege Lord. It was so quiet that one could hear a pin drop.

Wolf spoke, "Arise Aewel, my good and faithful master at arms." Aewel rose. Wolf continued, "I will have a task for you to perform shortly, distributing the very same armor for each of the company." There was silence for a moment for the company could not believe what they had heard. Surely not every man would be so outfitted with mail?

Aewel broke the silence, "All of them, Lord?"

"Except the four archers Aewel, their mail is shorter to allow for drawing their bows, and their helmets are different to allow them better line of sight, and they will have no mail leggings to slow them down in redeployment. They also only have a short sword. However, of course, they have a sizeable supply of arrows." The men realized then that their Lord was serious and a cheer went up.

Wolf addressed the men. "You have all done well. I am proud that you are my warriors. You will serve God and me with honor and success. Everyone here today is now accepted as a man at arms in the service of our God and me."

Another cheer went up.

"I am Wolf and you are my Wolf Pack."

The men stood and cheered again.

Wolf motioned again, and two of the archers brought out two spears while Palne brought a new saddle out and placed it on the table. "You will note the metal stirrups are a new design which protects the feet from attack. These leather cups at the end of the strap to the right of the saddle are to hold the spears from which banners are to flown. See how they are attached. Two of you will have the honor to carry the banners as we ride. Palne, show them."

Palne to the laughter of the company climbed on the table and mounted the saddle resting on his knees. A spear was brought by another archer and it had a fabric wrapped around it. The archer leaned the long spear over and unfurled it to show a red cross on a white background. The company cheered. He handed it to Palne and he slipped into the cup which hung down from the saddle sitting on the table. After demonstrating, he handed the spear off, and got down from the table and bowed to the company's continued laughter. He walked away to store the spear.

Wolf waited for the cheering to die down. Next, a black folded cloth was fetched.

Wolf addressed the company again, "Each man will have a cape which is reversible, black on one side and on the other", he held the cape up over his head by its ties and again it was a cross, this time a red cross outlined in white against the dark blue cloth of the cape.

"Aewel now is the time for you to complete your task."

Aewel responded with enthusiasm, "Certainly, my Lord."

Wolf moved off to join Shadow, and they sat in the shade sipping some fine wine. The men were formed into two lines and sat until Aewel and Herewood distributed the armor. It took all day. The fitting had been so well done that only minor adjustments would be needed and that would soon be resolved. The evening meal was late but everyone was in a jubilant mood and the fare seemed like a king's feast.

The next morning, the company turned out in their new armor for inspection. Wolf and Shadow had discussed the assignments. Wolf addressed the company, "My War Chief Shadow will now proceed with the inspection. After the inspection Aewel the senior sergeant will divide you into groups. Sergeant Herewood will be in charge of one group. Our priest warrior Aert will be my aid. He will now lead us in morning prayer."

The entire company as one went down on one knee as the priest led them in a responsive prayer. Aewel and Herewood had difficulty focusing for they knew the impact of their new appointments on their incomes and the added responsibilities that would be required of them past the training period.

The inspection proceeded with deliberateness. The experienced warriors had helped the new recruits prepare without being asked, which spoke well of the unit cohesion. As a result, the inspection went well. The men were proud of their armor and weapons. They learned from the seasoned warriors how blessed they were. Father Aert followed Shadow as he inspected and made note of any adjustments that would be needed to be made by a skilled armorer.

After the inspection, the men were led in a series of practice movements to become used to moving in their new armor. The men increasingly appreciated the quality and workmanship of their weapons. Their superb balance made their use less tiring over long periods. The armor was well fitted and there were only a few blisters and irritations. Adjustments would solve those problems. Aert made notes of additional adjustments that would be needed.

At noon the company, and those not standing sentry, stored their armor and took a meal break which was longer than normal. After the meal, the company was assembled without armor.

Wolf conducted a ceremony that none of the men had witnessed before. That was because it was new.

Wolf spoke, "Father Aert has prepared a document of commission for each of you attesting to your appointment as sworn men at arms of the elite Wolf Pack. It also shows you are entitled to a share in any spoils the company acquires. No other Lord can legally require your services according to the law of this land, as long as I or my heirs live. Further, you are receiving two changes of clothes. You will note the large cross on back of the tunics. The two crests on the front are my family crests. Unless otherwise ordered, you will wear your uniforms proudly at all times. I trust you will honor your commitment to Jesus and through me to my family."

The men cheered.

After a moment, Shadow stepped forward and held up his hand for silence. He then called each man forward starting with the sergeants. Father Aert prayed over each of them as they came forward and called them individually to repeat an oath of fidelity to Jesus and to their earthly Lord. Each man was then given his commission parchment, and his new uniforms. The men took the ceremony seriously, for it was indeed a serious time. The ceremony was meant to tie them all together.

The men were dismissed at the end of the ceremony. Aewel and Herewood found a spot to talk. Aewel spoke first.

"At first I thought I was a fool helping out an old friend and comrade because I had no other hope. When Shadow came to me last night to offer a permanent position I thought beyond my wildest dreams, I could not believe my good fortune."

Herewood nodded," I too was as surprised as a man who finds an honest innkeeper."

They both laughed and then discussed their good fortune. Approaching thirty, many would have thought them too old for advancement in a fighting company.

Herewood summed it up. "If we die in the service of God and our good Wolf and his man Shadow, then so be it. I am grateful for the opportunity. Perhaps I will die old, with a full belly, a good woman beside me, and many little ones." Little did Herewood know that this was God's plan for his life.

Chapter 5 - Call to Action

Preparations and planning for their departure completed, the company started out for its destination on a warm spring morning. The company travelled for a day to a place where a man was camped and had set up a portable armorer's worksite. The company set up camp and sentries were posted and a patrol sent out to scout the immediate area.

The company was informed that this man was going to be their armorer. Those who needed adjustments came to have them made. During the day the men stayed in their armor to become used to it. During the night half the company, one squad, along with their sergeant, was in armor during their watch. After two nights and one day, the company broke camp and started travelling to their destination. Only Wolf and Shadow knew where they were going.

They had not travelled far along the river road before they met a group of villagers heading in the opposite direction. The Company stopped while Shadow went to question them. They were fleeing raiders, Danes, who had come up river. Shadow got what information he could.

He came to Wolf. "We will need to move quickly. Danish raiders and from where their boat landed I would say they are headed toward the abbey. There is a shrine there and loot from the pilgrims' donations. Just one boat beached below the village. They seldom come this far inland and usually not at this time of year."

Wolf motioned to Father Aert. "Take two of Palne's archers, the brothers, and hide the wagons in the woods. Put on your armor and wait until we return. Tell Palne and the archer Pehr to come mounted with as many arrows as they can manage. And pray."

Father Aert nodded and started to ride for the back of the column. He had heard the report and understood why the company must act. There would be a massacre at the abbey. Shadow called the sergeants forward.

Wolf spoke, "Danish raiders headed for the abbey. Their boat is at the shore below the village. How many will likely be guarding it, Shadow?"

"Two, probably. The archers and two experienced men should go to the boat, kill the guards and do it quietly, remove any valuables, and hole the boat. If God blesses us, the archers may be able to kill the guards from hiding. The men could then hide near the boat and kill any stragglers who retreat that far. If they come in force, our men should just hide until we arrive."

Wolf ordered, "Let it be so."

Aewel assigned two men at arms, and the four men left for the boat. The rest of the company headed for the abbey. They could hear screams as they neared. The column halted. Shadow and Aewel dismounted and ran forward to the crest of the hill to assess the situation. When they returned Shadow gave the report.

"There are bodies everywhere. It seems the raiding crew consists of thirty or forty. Most of them are drunk. About a dozen have started on foot toward the boat with loot. The monks are probably all dead and the nuns are being raped. I suggest you take half the men on horse through the woods and take those with the loot by surprise once you hear the battle start at the abbey. Kill them from horse then come to the abbey. The other half should go with me on foot and we will sneak in and take those in the monastery by surprise. There is enough cover that we can circle from the west and be in the buildings before they know we are there. Agreed?

Wolf answered, "Agreed. We will wait for the sound of your attack before we ride on the others. You will take Herewood and I will take Aewel."

Shadow knew the last was open to discussion, but it made sense. Wolf was new to this and sending him with the more experienced sergeant made sense. Shadow nodded. The company split.

Wolf's group made their way at a quick gallop along their side of the ridge. After riding about a mile, they stopped, Aewel dismounted and walked to the top of the ridge. He returned shortly. "We are about a half a mile ahead of them. We should enter the woods on the top of the ridge over there and form battle line."

Wolf leaned toward Aewel as he mounted. "I will take the end of the line nearest the enemy and you anchor the other."

Aewel nodded agreement though he was worried. The lad was a good fighter, but in battle he was untested. Aewel was nervous, hoping the lad would not unleash the dogs of war too soon.

Wolf gave orders in a low voice. "We will form a battle line at the tree line. Stay quiet where you are until I give the signal and then we charge the enemy. Kill them quickly as we will be needed at the abbey. Pray as you ride."

Wolf displayed a confidence he did not really have. It was now or never.

Wolf's group was in line just inside the trees out of sight waiting patiently for the sound of battle for what seemed a long time. It was a blessing that the enemy, laden with loot, was moving so slowly on foot. They were talking loudly and laughing at their good fortune. They were close enough that Wolf could understand what they were saying. Several cursed when they dropped items they were carrying and had to stop to pick them up.

The enemy was almost abreast of them, and only a few dozen yards away when the first sounds of commotion came from the monastery. The enemy was close to the tree line and they turned facing back to the monastery at the first sounds.

Wolf, instinctively shouted, "For justice and God!" and his warriors burst in line from the woods. By the time the raiders realized they were in danger the horsemen were upon them. Wolf's warriors swept the enemy away before them.

Wolf's first adversary was quick to drop his loot and the shield on which he was carrying it. He drew sword and quickly tried to move to the shield side of Wolf's horse. The horse was well trained and it responded instantly to the pressure of Wolf's knees turning sideways blocking the move and knocking the raider off balance. Wolf swung his sword as fast as lightening and the man was down.

Wolf straightened his horse and charged on. The next two were quicker kills. Many of the raiders were cut down before they dropped their loot, and those who did draw weapons were too late. It seemed only a moment and all the Danish raiders were down.

"Leave them, form line, to the monastery!" Wolf shouted. The horsemen formed a line and galloped forward.

Shadow's group had been in the monastery and had killed several drunken raiders before the alarm was raised. Several raiders tried to form a shield line in the church hall. Wolf led two men in a wedge through the middle of a dozen raiders to keep the group from forming the line. Several raiders were struck down before the line could be successfully assembled. As the rest of Shadow's men rushed into the room, the raiders realized the danger. The raiders fled from the abbey toward their boat. They did not know the size of the force attacking them. In the dark they ran directly into Wolf's horsemen who cut several of them down before they could organize. The survivors were caught in the open and in a panic. Wolf's men slew another half dozen raiders as about fifteen others retreated to form a defense only to realize too late that Shadow's men were attacking from the rear. The raiders were not cowards, but the surprise had been almost total. Some, who had been raping nuns, were not even fully clothed. Engaged by better armed and trained men the fight was fierce but short. The last three raiders were overwhelmed and taken alive.

Wolf turned to Aewel. "Any wounded leave here to be treated. Take the rest to the boat to make sure it has been captured and our men are not threatened. If all is well, return quickly." Aewel's warriors rode toward the boat.

Shadow ordered Herewood, "Check to see if we have any wounded."

Herewood returned quickly and reported, "One of the lads has a broken leg. Clean break. The mail leggings saved his leg from being severed. Brother Aert says it will heal. The lad will be out of service for a while. There will be lots of bruises and such, and there are some minor cuts. One of the mounts is lame, although I do not yet know how serious the injury is. It is a miracle our injuries were so light. God was with us this day."

The three captured raiders sat disarmed, tied, and sullen, guarded by two warriors who stood over them with swords drawn. Shadow ordered his men to check the raiders lying about. All but two were dead. Wolf and Shadow's men stripped the raiders of their arms, armor and purses. Two badly wounded raiders were found alive but probably would not live. Shadow ordered that the prisoners carry their wounded to the monastery. One died as he was picked up and the other survived the carry to the building.

The men who were sent to the boat had found six men guarding it. The boat was too close to the woods for there was not much of a beach where it was grounded. Four of the men were asleep on the boat and the two standing on the beach were not wearing full armor and their helmets were resting on the boat. The range was so close the archers could not miss their mark. Their arrows penetrated deeply and the two men fell without raising an alarm.

The two men at arms slipped onto the boat as the archers came forward to cover them. The men on the boat wore no armor though their swords and shields were beside them. The first man died quickly and easily. The other man knocked over his shield resting against the bench on which he was sleeping flinging his arm as his throat was cut. The two other warriors jumped up to take up arms but before they could, they fell to arrows. The engagement was over as quickly as it started.

Palne searched the boat, and the men discussed what they should do and retreated to the woods with what they could carry in addition to their weapons. As they were entering the woods, they heard the sounds of battle as Wolf and Shadow's forces engaged the enemy.

Aewel later arrived at the boat and approached with a cautious eye on the woods and the boat. All seemed well but he had learned to take nothing for granted. "Form line", he ordered and his men did it automatically as they drew their swords.

Palne came from the woods.

Aewel asked, "Is all well? Your orders fulfilled?"

Palne answered. "Yes we are well, but we were not able to remove the plunder on the boat."

"Why not?" Aewel asked.

Palne shrugged. "There is just too much, and we just removed what we could carry into the woods. A large wagon will be needed, maybe two."

Aewel went to see for himself. He came back smiling, "A good night's work and surely God smiles on those who enforce justice and keep the peace."

He left half his men and Palne's group to guard the boat and returned to the monastery. He found Shadow and Wolf. He approached and spoke quietly so others could not hear. "A large wagon or two will be needed; there is too much loot on the boat to move otherwise. This lot has been raiding far and wide for a long time."

Wolf looked at Shadow then said. "See to it Aewel, but keep the loot from here separate and bring it here. Tell the men not to mention the loot from the boat in front of the priests who live or they may claim it is all from here. The loot from here is still in the field. Send some men to collect it and send for our own baggage wagons. See if you can find extra wagons and purchase them outright with good draft animals." Aewel went to see it was all done as ordered.

Only two priests were still alive; their torture had just started when Shadow and his men arrived. Five of the nuns survived. All had been raped, and three might not live. They were put into two rooms, the priests in one and the nuns in another. Beds had been arranged. One of the nuns had thankfully kept her wits, and was doctoring the others as she wept. She was apparently a skilled healer.

Before sunrise, everything had been arranged. Sentries had been set. The treasure had been packed in two wagons and the monastery's loot had been taken to the main hall. One of the priest's was able to hobble aided by a crutch into the main hall where Shadow and Wolf waited. He bowed to them. "My thanks for our rescue, sirs. Will you now take our goods in payment?"

Wolf answered. "Good priest, we came without thought of payment, for it is our duty to protect my family lands and the church. Are these all your goods?"

It was then the priest saw the cross worn by one of the men at arms. The priest broke into tears. "My good Lord, what is your name that I may announce this good deed far and wide."

Wolf answered, "I am Aelle, heir to these lands. They also call me Wolf. This man is my War Chief, Osmund, also renowned as Shadow Killer. You will be returned to holy mother church with your goods we have recovered here."

"Thank you, my Lord", the priest replied, tears flowing with relief and happiness. He prostrated himself before Wolf.

It was then that Wolf realized he must appear to others differently than he regarded himself. "Rise, my good priest. Aert has drawn up an attestation which I will ask you to sign, along with the other survivors, so that I may legally return the goods to you. It attests that you claim ownership in the name of the church, lists all the goods to be returned, and I ask you make certain it is a complete accounting of all that was taken from here. All the survivors will sign it. Agreed?"

The priest replied, "Most certainly my Lord. I will fetch the parchment with our inventory list to compare."

Wolf continued, "As is my right under law according to my birthright, I will assemble a trial tomorrow for the men who committed murder, rape and pillage here. One of my men will accompany you to fetch the inventory list, and men will stand guard over you this night so you may sleep soundly. You may go." The priest left filled with joy at his good fortune to be rescued by such a Christian noble.

At sunrise, the company was assembled for prayer in the meadow. Afterwards, there, away from the abbey so they could not be overheard Wolf addressed his men. "God has blessed us because we came to protect and enforce justice without thought of cost or profit. There will be a share that will make each of you rich. It will be divided fairly. We will not divide it here lest the word get out as to what we have.

We are going to my grandfather's castle, where we can safeguard our riches and establish ourselves. We are presently near the border of his lands. Keep quiet and keep your riches. Just one loose tongue can bring all sorts of trouble upon us. One item will be used to make a gift which will pave our way home. It will come from my share. Shadow will now give you instructions." Wolf strode toward the abbey.

Shadow wanted the company gone from here so he spoke quickly. "Aewel see that the weapons of the slain are displayed rising from the sides of our baggage carts and upon them are placed the helmets of the raiders. If they are bloodied, so much the better; do not clean them. We want to make an impression and serve notice. Now everyone to their duties and sergeants are to take the sentries aside and instruct them as to the need for secrecy. Palne go to the village and hire grave diggers, take two men at arms. Ready yourselves to leave after we perform funeral rights."

Shadow took Aewel aside, "Make sure the wagon's contents are well crated and bagged and tied down. Our wounded warrior can sit atop one to the wagons. Cover the wagons with the captured armor and other goods. Make sure men are sleeping very close. Very close."

One of the men came and asked about the bodies of the raiders. Shadow's response was cold. "Pile them in the field away from the abbey and leave them for the carrion eaters."

Preparations were started for the journey. There had been forty two raiders but more than fifty six swords and helmets adorned the company's carts, for as usual Aewel took his task seriously and that's how many pairs of helmets and weapons were on the raiders and the boat.

There was a cart and oxen belonging to the abbey that would be used to transport its goods. Only one item was missing from the abbey inventory, the ring of the Prior. Aert instructed the prisoners be searched, and sure enough the ring of office was found. Aert put the ring with the other abbey treasure and ensured the papers of attestation were signed and he had obtained the signed copy of the original Abbey inventory.

While the company was working, Wolf and Shadow convened court. The priests and nuns were first brought in and they sat on benches. Then the three Danes hobbled in, a very short rope tied to their ankles and their hands closely bound. The wounded Dane was brought in on a stretcher. Aert was there to make a written record of the trial. Shadow stood beside Wolf as an official of the court.

Wolf addressed the prisoners in Danish, much to their surprise, "What are your names." They responded with pride and Aert entered it into the record of the trial.

Wolf continued, "Will the witnesses please identify themselves." Each of the clergy stated their name and Aert dutifully entered in the record.

One of the prisoners, the most senior, interrupted, "What horse piss is this? We came to plunder and rape and you have taken us prisoner. Our families will pay the ransom. Why do you not treat us as valuable hostages?"

Wolf interpreted for Aert and asked, "Did you get all that?" The priest nodded and wolf turned to the witnesses, "Are these men some of those who attacked you, murdered priests, and raped the nuns, and stole the abbey goods, including relics?" All but one nun, who still had not spoken, replied yes. The last nun nodded and started whimpering softly.

Wolf turned to the men and spoke in Danish, interpreting for Aert as he went, "As a rightful noble of this land I duly assembled this court to hear the charges against you. They include murder of five priests, six nuns, as well as the rape of nuns, torture of priests, and the thievery of church property including relics. You have admitted your guilt and your guilt has been established by these witnesses to your foul deeds. Sentence is hereby declared that your right hands are to be cut off for your thievery and then immediately thereafter for the murder and rape you are to be hung by the neck until dead and left hanging as warning of the swift justice that will be upon the heads of those who raid my family's lands." Wolf repeated his verdict in Danish and then added, "Court is ended. Take the prisoners away."

The Danes started cursing. The one shouted, "We will be ransomed! Ransom!"

Wolf turned to the witnesses, "You may watch the execution of sentence to report that justice has been done."

The raiders were taken outside and all the surviving clergy watched them as sentence was executed.

After the executions were over, Wolf looked at Shadow and said, "A very nasty business that, but it had to be done."

Wolf then went into the bushes and threw up.

Shadow was waiting when Wolf returned.

Shadow continued as though there had been no pause in their talk, "And well done. One would think that was an everyday thing for you. I know you did not notice, but the men now hold you in even higher regard, not just as a warrior, but now as their noble and just Lord as well."

Wolf sighed and then said "Good."

Shadow saw the sadness in the young Lord. "What troubles you wolf."

Wolf looked at Shadow, "Today I turned sixteen and look how it was spent. Added to this, I killed several men yesterday. I hope it will not always be like this. Please say nothing to the men about my coming of age for we cannot afford to stop for celebration."

Shadow nodded in agreement. They must make it on time to the Cathedral and they were still inside Wolf's father's lands.

Chapter 6 – Unexpected Events

The company made an impressive display as it travelled. The men all rode in armor with banners flying and the crosses on their capes displayed. The news of the victory had travelled faster than they travelled. The number of raiders killed in battle grew with retelling. The display of swords and helmets had been magnified as Shadow knew it would. The reality had been triumph enough, but the reputation for the company had grown as had Wolf and Shadow's.

Wolf was concerned as what he would find when he reached the Cathedral. When his company arrived there was much fanfare. They were heroes and received a heroes' welcome as they rode through the town to the cathedral. The people threw flower pedals and cheered. Once through the bishop's gate, the company was out of sight of the crowds.

His mother had heard of his approach and was there to meet him. He embraced her and whispered in her ear, "is father here?"

She whispered back, "No, but word should be reaching him now and he will come."

Wolf released his mother and said softly, "Slip away and be ready to leave for grandfather's castle. We will leave directly. Two of my men have been told to go with you and will follow when you go."

His mother did not reply but stepped aside as the bishop approached.

"Welcome young Lord Wolf. You serve mother church well. Come let us celebrate."

Wolf motioned for one of the men who brought a chest guarded by four of Wolf's men at arms. "Dear Bishop, we have urgent business and we need to conduct it out of sight of prying eyes."

Wolf noticed his mother had left and he had planned this, playing on the bishop's greed. Wolf had no intention of being delayed. His men stayed in place as they had been ordered.

The bishop, anticipating gain, led the way, with Wolf, Shadow, and the other five men with the chest following. Aert was carrying the chest. The company stayed together in ranks. The bishop entered his personal library and Wolf nodded to Shadow who ordered the chest be put on the only table in the room and that the four guards go into the hall and guard the door.

The bishop was anticipating gain and his eyes were almost glowing with greed.

Wolf opened the chest as he spoke, "My dear bishop, here is the inventory of what was at the abbey and the attestation that it is all in the abbey's wagon and that we returned it to your servants." He reached into the box and removed the parchments. "Here also is a copy of the court record of the trial. The men responsible for the atrocity against the church have been punished."

The bishop had been disappointed when only parchments had been taken from the chest. He already knew the abbey goods were being returned. He curiously took up the parchments and read.

The bishop lost his temper upon reading the trial transcript. "You forfeited the ransom? What gave you the right? The ransoms would have funded many good works. The damage was already done!"

Wolf had expected the bishop would be officious, but this was just too much. Wolf paused to consider for a moment before acting. He walked around the table and got face to face with the bishop.

Wolf spoke evenly and threateningly "You pus ball! You Pharisee! You ungrateful greedy fool, count yourself blessed I am a Christian for a pagan lord would kill you here and now for the insult. Is this how you reward those who do you good service? I will stay in your presence no longer."

Wolf reached into the chest and withdrew an item wrapped in cloth. He un-wrapped a most intricately carved one foot high solid silver Celtic cross and slammed it down on the table. "This was to be my gift to you on my coming of age. Not now. We leave with it. Consider yourself fortunate we do not take a share of the treasures we recovered as rightful reward for rescue. Aert bring the cross."

Wolf stomped from the room and the building his men following. Wolf was relieved his mother was mounted on her horse surrounded by his men. The company mounted and rode away. There were friendly faces waving and shouting praises as they again rode through the town.

On the road Wolf rode with his mother between him and Shadow. He turned to her, "Where are your servants, mother?"

"Back there. They were truly your father's and more my prison guards than my servants. If you had not sent your men, I would either not be leaving or leaving on foot without any of my possessions. My faithful servants and my spies started disappearing some months ago. Father Bryan also disappeared. I am happy you rescued me son, but your father will come you know."

Wolf nodded, "But we will be ready."

Wolf's mother looked worried. Shadow saw the worry. He spoke, "Lady Ethelind, if your husband came this moment we would be at worst evenly matched. Once we reach your father's lands, he would be a fool to come. Combined with your father's men, our company would be too large for him to overcome. He would not be able to raise a large enough force to overcome even this company until at least spring and by then that will not be enough."

His mother looked about. "You have done well my son, but the fortune I gave you was all we had. We cannot raise the funds to prepare for war with your father."

Wolf laughed, "Mother, that is least of our worries, for we are much richer now than in the beginning."

His mother turned to Shadow in disbelief. He just smiled and nodded.

The company did not stop riding until they were well within the lands of Wolf's grandfather. They camped late, rose early, and rode steadily until they reached the innermost parts of the holding.

The "Death's Neck Wall" had been built by the Romans. The gates were gone but the stone walls and tower were as sturdy as the day they were built. The company stopped for a meal and Wolf and Shadow examined the fortifications. They went through the tower to the top of the fortification.

Shadow was pleased, "The scouts were right. If proper gates were installed, a few men could defend this pass against hundreds. The passage between the cliffs is narrow and only a small number could approach at once. See those spouts on top of the wall, they are angled downward so hot oil can be poured onto attackers trying to put up ladders against the walls or batter the gates. Even if the gates were breached the losses to take the tower would be grave. The one winding stairway is easily defended and the defenders could retreat floor by floor. Large iron balls could be stored on each floor and rolled down the walled in stairs to break legs and bodies. It would be a murderous ascent for any attacking force. Meanwhile archers could pour down arrows on those below outside.

The cliffs are steep, difficult to scale, and any attacker attempting to do so would be an easy target for archers. Climbing in armor would be almost impossible. If attempted, most of the force would die from falls before they could attack.

The tower is high enough with a line of sight such that a signal fire could be seen throughout the valley. Overwhelming reinforcements would arrive in a very short time. Why this is not manned I cannot understand."

The last remark worried Wolf.

Shadow continued, "According to the scouts, this passage and the river flowing through the valley are the only ways to invade with any sizeable force. If we can find a way to defend the river we could hold this valley indefinitely against any force your father could possibly raise."

Wolf nodded, "We must find a way in order to dissuade my father from attacking. He will not risk everything on a long chance. He is ambitious, but not stupid. He is as brave as he is devious, but he is not reckless."

The company mounted and rode toward the castle. They saw no people along the way, and that made them wonder. They stopped at one farm and found a family in hiding. Wolf and Shadow questioned them while Wolf's mother listened. Raiders had overrun the valley several weeks ago and left. The family was given food and Wolf told the man to come to the castle some days hence. It was less than an hour's ride from the Neck to the castle that stood beside the river.

As the company approached the castle, Wolf was alarmed to see no guards. When they rode to the gate they found a guard asleep against the gate post. He did not wake until Shadow's blade brought a trickle of blood from a nick in his throat. The man came awake with a start to see the disgust on Shadow's face and feel the sword at his throat.

Shadow demanded, "How many men here?"

The reply came and it shocked Shadow, "Seven."

The man's eyes grew even more as he saw the heavily armored mounted warriors riding through the gate into the courtyard.

Shadow turned and shouted to Wolf, "Seven."

Wolf gave orders, "Aewel, four men to secure the gate, search the castle. Bring me the men you find. Mother, please stay here. Shadow, bring your prisoner."

The man was brought to him. "Take me to Lord Cuthbert." Wolf demanded. The man started off, Shadow holding him by the collar and with a blade at the man's throat. In a hall he pointed at a door guarded by a man who looked surprised to see them. Wolf strode toward him. When he was a few feet away the guard started to draw his sword, but only had it half way out of the scabbard when Wolf had his blade at the man's throat.

"Step aside or die." The man did as he was ordered and two of Wolf's men took him into custody. Shadow turned over the man he held prisoner as well. Wolf motioned Aert and Shadow forward. Wolf entered first with Shadow and Aert following.

The smell was of a sick room. Wolf went to his grandfather. He was unconscious. Aert came forward. He examined Cuthbert. He looked last at his fingernails. His diagnosis was quick.

"Poison. Get him into the fresh air. I will prepare some medicine. It may not be too late. Someone is using a slow poison either so he will suffer or to make it look like a natural illness."

A thought occurred to Wolf. "Could it be used to be certain of the time of death, to prolong life and terminate it about a certain time?"

Aert considered the question and then gave his answer, "It could be done if someone was practiced with such things."

Men were called and carried Cuthbert on a stretcher into the spring sunshine. They brought a table into the yard and laid Cuthbert on it. Wolf's mother came to see her father.

She gasped and started trembling. She said, "He looks so weak and has lost so much weight. What is his illness?"

Wolf spat the answer, "Poison. Aert thinks he can be saved.'

Shadow called for food to be brought. The cook brought it.

Shadow motioned to the food and said to the cook, "You eat it."

It was obvious from the cook's response that she knew the food was poisoned.

Shadow drew his knife, "Consider carefully now for your life hangs in the balance."

The woman fell to her knees and started sobbing. "Please sir, I had no choice. Staffan made me do it"

Shadow called for Aert. When he came Shadow demanded of the woman, "Tell this priest healer what you used and give him the poison."

She did as she was told then was taken away.

Wolf called for Palne and nodded to Aert, "Your instructions."

Aert told Palne that the brothers were to be the only ones to cook for Cuthbert. He would sleep on the table by the warm hearth at night and be brought into the sun during the day if the weather was good. Wolf repeated one of the brothers and a guard was to be with his grandfather at all times. Each night there would be prayers for Cuthbert.

It was ordered that no one in the company would eat anything from the castle until Aart determined it was safe.

The seven men that had been captured were questioned. It turned out they were in the employ of a man called Staffan. They were mercenaries and Shadow determined they knew little beyond where Staffan was lodged and how many men he had with him. The seven were locked up within the castle.

Wolf, his mother, and Shadow got together to discuss the situation over a meal. Wolf learned Staffan had been a lower official in the castle. How he had come to have so much power was a mystery. Wolf pronounced that he saw his father's hand in this. It was decided that in the morning Staffan would be found and captured if possible.

For the first time in weeks, the gates to the castle were locked and alert sentries posted. The castle was lit and those lights could be seen for miles. Within in the walls, the treasure the company had was distributed according to each man's rightful portion. Divided such, it was taken away to be hidden and safeguarded.

Before the company bedded down for the night, Aewel came to Wolf with Shadow.

Aewel spoke, "Some of the men had asked if they could purchase the arms, armor, and mounts you so generously supplied. They would then truly be free sworn men. There is also a request from the men with families to bring their family's here."

Wolf agreed with the provision the families would have to arrange to come on their own or wait. No men could be spared to fetch the families until the valley was fully under control. It was thus that Shadow's treasure was added to by repayment for the outfitting of his men. In the end, all of the company purchased their arms and armor for they could well afford to even though each set cost a small fortune.

At sunrise, the company had held its morning prayer then set about preparing for the day's duties or action. A dozen men at arms and the two brothers under Aewel would hold the castle while the rest of the company sought Staffan. Aert would stay and continue to minister to Cuthbert. Wolf's mother would help the men staying behind inspect the castle to see if anything was unusual.

Before the company could leave, the gate sentry called that men were approaching. They appeared to be unarmed. Wolf had the men who would be going on patrol form line inside the gate and had it opened. The men approaching stopped when the gates opened and they saw Wolf's warriors. Wolf, his helmet held in the crook of his left arm, stepped into the gateway and Shadow was at his side his helmet held similarly.

The lead man screamed, "Osmund!", and ran forward arms out, and Shadow went to him where they embraced. Shadow looked at the other men, and started calling them by name. Wolf counted, there were fifteen men.

After Shadow greeted the men, he led them forward.

Wolf smiled, "My Lord Wolf, let me introduce some of Lord Cuthbert's sworn men led by my old friend Ragnvald. My fellow warriors let me present Lord Cuthbert's grandson and heir, Aelle, also known as Wolf."

The men in unison went to one knee. Wolf motioned and told the new arrivals to rise. He signaled Herewood with a slight gesture and Herewood ordered the men to move to the side. The men moved to Wolf's left and to the untrained eye seemed to be at ease. Ragnvald recognized they were positioned to quickly form line if they needed to.

He let it be known he had seen, "Your men are well trained Lord Wolf; a credit to you."

Wolf laughed, "More credit to my War Chief Shadow and Sergeant Aewel."

It was Shadow's turn to chuckle, "Ragnvald was always too smart for his own good. He is a good friend in spite of his name. He has a Danish name because his mother was Danish, though his father was a good Christian Saxon. His father never could deny his wife anything, even burdening her son with such a name."

Wolf laughed again. "He is not the only one with a mixed heritage, so I can certainly not hold that against him. However, being your friend calls his character into question." All three men laughed.

They sought a spot where they could talk. Shadow was the one who asked what had happened. The answer was betrayal. All the men had been taken at their homes in their sleep by mercenaries whose entrance to the valley was arranged cunningly and secretly by Staffan. False orders had been given to them. They did not realize that all the key men had been furloughed at the same time. Ragnvald and the others had been taken prisoner. When Wolf's company had come to the valley, their guards had simply fled. Ragnvald's men had heard the mercenaries discussing the reputation and danger, having heard of the company's deeds. Ragnvald speculated that they had worked themselves into fear like a bunch of old women. When unguarded, Ragnvald's men had broken out of their makeshift prison. Wolf listened intently.

He finally spoke after Ragnvald had finished, "Go to the others and give Wolf and I time to consider a course of action."

Ragnvald left.

Shadow answered the question he knew was in Wolf's mind, "I believe him. I have known him all his life. There is not an ounce of treachery in him. He is still loyal. I would stake my life on it."

Wolf added, "And perhaps my family's. What about the others?"

"The same. I have fought with them all."

Wolf got up, "Let's go talk to them." Shadow rose and followed Wolf.

He went to the new arrivals. "You are my grandfather's sworn men, and so in his incapacity, as his heir, you are my men. We will arm you so that you may guard my grandfather and my mother, and this castle, and aid me in putting my grandfather's lands in order and defending it. I want to hear your agreement."

They all stood and bowed answering with a yes. Wolf called for Palne. He was ordered to bring the Danish weapons and armor for the men to select from. Once they were armed, Wolf gathered the men all together again.

He introduced his grandfather's men to his company, "This is Ragnvald and his men. They are sworn men of my grandfather. While my grandfather is incapacitated, they are also my men, your comrades at arms. Aewel, Ragnvald, and Herewood see the men are introduced to each other. We will leave in an hour. Sergeant Aewel will remain here and Sergeant Ragnvald will accompany us." That was how Ragnvald's position was made official. "Seven of our company and seven of my grandfather's soldiers will guard the castle. The rest will go to find Staffan. Prepare."

Shadow intercepted Wolf. "I hope we find horses on our patrol. Lord Cuthbert's horses are missing along with all his goods and much of the food. We will be stretched thin for mounts. Hopefully this expedition will be short. We have one battle injured mount still healing and some of the mounts need to be rested and tended to."

Wolf nodded. He called Herewood and Ragnvald. "Shadow has pointed out that we do not have enough healthy and rested mounts for all the men who are to go on patrol, even using our spares. Ten of my company will remain here with my grandfather's seven."

The Company got organized and the patrol rode out in column two abreast, the new men riding in the left line of the column. It gave the two groups who were now forming one an opportunity to talk with their new comrades. Ragnvald rode beside Herewood behind Wolf and Shadow. The company was only a little nervous for they knew where they were going they would be the overwhelming force. When they got close, they sent Ragnvald and one of the local men to scout the site. They returned and reported the men were in the manner house and that no guard was seen.

The company simply rode up to the manner house and surrounded it; Herewood leading men to the front and Ragnvald his men to the rear as a dozen men dismounted entered and unopposed pulled men out of bed and into the yard. Two men bolted from the back door only to be ridden down. One had a sword and resisted. He was cut down. The other man was Staffan and he was rounded up with the others.

Wolf ordered, "Herewood, have the men search the barns for mounts and saddles. Search the house for my grandfather's goods and any other loot. See if there is a wagon or wagons."

Ragnvald was herding the captives together. In various stages of undress, the prisoners were bound with their hands behind their back and ropes strung from one neck to another in line.

The house was searched and a significant amount of loot was discovered and confiscated. Arms and armor were found, some of it formerly belonging to Ragnvald's men. Two wagons were found and draft horses. There was so much to be transported a third wagon had to be hired from a nearby farm. The farmer was surprised when he was told he would be paid for his services and use of his wagon and team. The wagons were well packed as only soldiers and merchants can, then secured well.

Some furniture was left at the manner. Wolf ordered the locals that no one was to enter the building until it was decided who would occupy it.

The company rode smartly back to the castle. The captives were paraded through the countryside and hung their heads. People were appearing from hiding. They pelted the prisoners with various things, some of which were very unpleasant, but Wolf supposed they deserved it. Good words of encouragement and welcome were shouted to the company, the news of Aelle's appearance with his men having spread quickly.

They arrived back at the castle in midafternoon. The prisoners were locked away. Wolf asked Shadow to assemble all the men except the sentries. The sentries chose proxy men to choose for them. The loot from the manor that did not belong to Lord Cuthbert was shared amongst all the men according to their station, with the exception that all agreed the men from the valley would have the choice to reclaim their old armor or keep the Danish. When it was finished a sentry duty roster was established.

Late that afternoon, Lord Cuthbert came to consciousness for a very short time. His daughter and grandson spoke to him briefly before he fell to sleep. Aert was smiling. He was of the opinion Lord Cuthbert would recover.

In the early morning hours, Ragnvald was summoned to Lord Cuthbert's room. Wolf, his mother, Shadow and Aert were already there. Cuthbert was sitting up spooning soup in continuous labored movements. Tears came to Ragnvald's eyes as he came to his Lord Cuthbert and knelt beside the bed. With sincerity, he asked for forgiveness for failing to see the treachery that put his Lord at risk.

Cuthbert's motioned to have the empty bowl taken. His speech was labored, but he managed to say, "The fault is mine. It seems we all needed my grandson to rescue us." He smiled, and then fell off to sleep.

Wolf had Staffan brought out of the dungeon into the courtyard where he was forced to his knees in front of Wolf who was sipping a drink of cool water as Shadow stood leaning against the wall. Wolf spoke calmly, "Listen closely Staffan for your life hangs in the balance. Tell me what you know about the treachery here and you will be allowed to live to be expelled from these lands."

Staffan raised his head, "You give your word I will live."

Wolf answered, "Yes."

Staffan proceeded to tell him about how a mercenary captain had approached him with the plan and promises of great riches. He revealed who in the valley had aided him in his plan and how they had profited. He told of how once the plan was being executed, many of Cuthbert's loyal men had been murdered in their bed and some taken prisoner. He admitted to being behind his grandfather's poisoning. He knew where the mercenaries were now and how many there were. He did not know who had hired them. Given where they had taken up residence, it was clear to Wolf that they served his father.

It was also clear Staffan was a greedy fool and had betrayed his lord for little gain. He also acknowledged to himself that his grandfather had grown careless with age. It was a warning as to what could happen to him unless he had a strong family, a strong army, strong allies, and relied on God.

Wolf had Staffan sent to be cleaned up and put in a separate cell from where in a few days he would be sent out of these lands. Staffan was relieved his life was being spared. He did not consider that his being expelled alive might still allow for other punishment. Wolf realized his father did not know that Staffan had been taken and his plans exposed, but as time passed that knowledge would become common.

Two riders were dispatched to spy up the valley to confirm Staffan's telling. It would be easy to confirm if what Wolf had been told was true.

That evening Aert held a prayer service and Ragnvald's men attended. Praise and thanks to God was given for Cuthbert's recovery and the successes.

During the night a rider came and Wolf was awakened. He went to meet the messenger who was in the kitchen where he was being given food and drink. He started to rise as Wolf entered but Wolf motioned him down.

"What news?" Wolf asked.

"If I am first Lord, then treachery is afoot and I am the only one to have escaped with my life. I am your mother's man and the message is for her."

Wolf nodded agreement, "I will honor your service to my mother." He turned to the man who had fetched him, "Summon my mother and Shadow." Wolf sat back and said to the man, "Eat, drink, you have come a long way."

Wolf's mother arrived shortly. The man rose when she entered the room and went to her and bent on one knee to his sworn lady, "My lady, I have urgent news."

"Rise, dear Vagn. What is the news?" Ethelind asked.

"Your husband rides with armed men to rescue you; to take you by force. He is furious his plans have not worked. He thinks to strike while your son is weak. Others went to the bishop to find you, and should have been here by now. I came directly overland. Your husband should be here in no more than two days if he comes quickly behind and directly as I did."

Wolf thought for a moment. "How many warriors with him?"

Vagn had the answer, "Twenty one on horse. He had to leave a few to guard the castle."

Wolf turned to Shadow, "He will not come directly. For some reason we do not understand, my father must be desperate."

Shadow nodded, "He will collect the mercenaries. Also his men are not riding light as Vagn was, but will becoming armed so they will be slower. We have time to prepare a defense and he will be coming through the Neck hoping to attack us by surprise. He probably still thinks everything is in chaos."

"We will assume he has only the twenty mercenaries that Staffan reported." Wolf added, "If they are like the ones we captured they will not have much stomach for a real fight." Wolf turned to Vagn, "You are welcome here as long as my family controls this land."

Wolf's mother smiled at Vagn, "If my son fights your future is more assured that Vilhelm's. I may yet be a happy widow."

Vilhelm had been furious to find out his runt son had not joined the church and taken a vow of poverty, but had somehow kidnapped his wife. Wolf would find when he fled to his grandfather that there was no safety there. Vilhelm had already weakened Cuthbert's rule in anticipation of taking control of the land when Wolf forsook his inheritance. He had kept the old man alive to facilitate a timely death. Vilhelm was determined to crush Wolf and seize his father-in-laws lands. He thought it was what he should have done in the beginning.

Vilhelm had heard rumors that Shadow had gathered some men. There could not have been many for Vilhelm knew the time and resources it took to organize a worthy fighting force. There had not been much time. In any event, it was always preferable to intimidate an enemy into submission or overwhelm them if necessary with superior numbers. The mercenaries were not dependable, but they would serve a purpose.

When Vilhelm's men arrived at the village where the mercenaries were staying, he went directly to the ale house and dismounted. He knew that is where he would find Waldemar, the mercenary leader. He threw open the door and saw the man at a table drinking ale with some of his fellows. When Waldemar saw him, he said something and his comrades left.

Vilhelm sat opposite Waldemar. "We have more business."

"Do we?" Waldemar asked.

Vilhelm smiled, "I go to destroy my son and his hired man Shadow. I will now take the land of Cuthbert and rescue my wife."

Waldemar sighed, "That will be a dangerous business, and I have heard rumors that your son has gathered a company that has defeated many Danes. I do not wish to risk losing all my men for small pay in a battle that cannot be won."

Vilhelm sniggered, "Rumors. My son is a weakling coward who could hardly lift a sword let alone use it. Shadow can have no more than a dozen men, and those being old warriors from his past, nothing to match your stout men. We will have over forty fighting men." Vilhelm took a heavy purse and slammed it on the table. "It is yours when we win. You may look."

Waldemar did and exclaimed, "Gold!"

Vilhelm knew he had Waldemar and said, "A fourth now, the rest when we win."

Waldemar smiled, "We leave with you in the morning."

Vilhelm counted out the coins.

It was on the third day when Vilhelm's men entered the gorge and approached the Neck. There still was still no gate and the walls seemed unmanned. They were within a few dozen yards of the fortifications when suddenly there were men at arms on the walls and on the tower, and there was Shadow astride a horse in the middle of the gate.

Vilhelm looked at the men. There were over forty on the walls. They could ride directly through as a last resort. Then he saw the smoke rising and knew there were fires for oil burning on top of those walls. Vilhelm, called out to Shadow, "Stand aside, I come for my wife and son over whom I have rightful rule"

It was then that he heard Wolf's voice. It came from behind the wall. So like him, the little coward, Vilhelm thought.

"This is my grandfather's land, you have no claim here."

Ulrich moved up beside his father, "I challenge you Wolf for inheritance."

Wolf called back, "You have no inheritance here, bastard. These are my grandfather's lands. My father surely does not want to kill me himself."

Vilhelm gave one of few emotional responses he had ever made, "I challenge you to individual combat!"

It was then that over forty mounted men at arms fell in beside Shadow and Wolf fully armored rode out beside him and shouted, "In front of these witnesses I accept, father. If I win your lands are rightfully mine." Wolf turned to Shadow and proclaimed loudly so all could hear, "If he wins kill them all for he has no claim to my grandfather's lands while my grandfather still lives."

The mercenaries were now feeling fear as they realized just how dangerous this situation was. There were men at arms facing them in fortified positions and waiting. There was twice their number of armored men, half of them on horse. It was worse than Waldemar's worst nightmare. The rumors had been true, he knew it then. He would be forced to flee to avoid death.

Waldemar decided to wait to see the result as Vilhelm charged forward. Usually it was the son who challenged but nothing about this had been usual.

Much to Vilhelm's surprise, Wolf did not flee but also charged forward. Vilhelm raised his shield and swung his sword but it swept through thin air as he passed the head of the other horse, but as he went by he felt excruciating pain as he was knocked from his horse. The fall partially knocked his breath from him. He staggered to his feet.

Wolf was dismounting! The young fool would pay for that insult and Vilhelm mustered his strength and charged. His blade met shield but his shield met no resistance but rather one of his legs gave way as he felt the back of his knee kicked viciously. The pain was excruciating. He staggered forward and turned breathing hard. The knee would hardly support him. Had the stories been true? His son, the one he despised, had he become the warrior son he had always hoped for?

Wolf spoke, "Yield father, I have no wish to kill you."

Vilhelm's pride was too great and he hobbled as he circled. He noticed that Wolf glided effortlessly. Vilhelm hoped to take time to gather his breath, but the attack came swiftly and vigorously. It was all he could do to ward off the blows of blade and shield, they were too fast. He knew he was now being cut and losing strength and blood. The attacks kept coming and his breathing was becoming labored.

Wolf ceased the attack, "Yield, father. You need not die."

With a battle cry Vilhelm made one desperate lunge and felt his blade deflected to the side, his shield thrown with all his might swung through the air encountering nothing. It was then in an instant of realization that he looked down. The blade had come from underneath his shield and penetrated under his ribcage into his heart. He looked down to see Wolf, a victorious warrior on one knee, his arm an extension of the blade that had just killed. In that moment, Vilhelm was proud and died.

The mercenaries fled, as did Ulrich and some of Vilhelm's men, all fearing slaughter. Some of his father's men hesitated.

Wolf ordered, "I am your Lord now, sheath your weapons and come to me with oath or leave my lands by your own free will. Decide!" Some came and some rode off unhindered. As those few who stayed bent knees, a cheer went up from Wolf's men-at-arms and those wearing captured armor who imitated warriors standing ready. In truth the two forces had been evenly matched and though the outcome would have been no different, the cost would have been much higher if Wolf had not entered single combat. The men knew this and loved Wolf all the more for his risk.

After taking the oaths and turning the five new men over to Ragnvald's care, Wolf went to his father's body. He took his father's seal ring, the pouch of gold, and removed his armor. He ordered the body prepared for transport to the castle to be buried.

Wolf went off with Aert and they both prayed to God and gave thanks. All around the Neck small groups of men were kneeling and giving thanks to God. None of Vilhelm's former five men were among those groups.

Shadow saw Wolf rise and come towards him, "You did nothing wrong in killing Vilhelm, Wolf."

Wolf looked Shadow in the eyes, "Yes I did; I enjoyed it. For that, I had to ask God for forgiveness."

Shadow could think of no response but just followed Wolf and sat beside him against the wall. After a brief rest, Shadow and Wolf consulted, and then called the sergeants.

Wolf gave orders, "Ragnvald, you will have to defend the castle and my relatives in our absence. I must leave to go to my father's land to assert my claim before his goods are plundered. I will take Shadow, Aewel and Herewood and those men who came with me here and the five from my castle. Hold my grandfather's castle for that is primary. Arrange sentries to light alarm fires. Here we are most likely under no immediate threat. Recruit additional men if you can, and if you trust them, as you think wise. We will return as soon as possible. Here is a letter with my seal. Give it to my mother and she will provide you the money."

Wolf and Shadow set out with their men riding the freshest and strongest mounts as the rest of the men returned to the castle.

Ulrich was determined to get to his home and take as much loot as possible for his future. He had been able to find six men who had bolted from the Neck. They joined him for the promise of gain. They did not make good time for their mounts were tiring. The group had to stay overnight in a tavern sleeping on the floor.

In the night, Ulrich heard riders passing in the distance. It did not occur to him who it might be. He rose early and the men ate before they set out. They alternately rode and walked their horses to conserve their mounts and make all the distance they could. That night they kept going until late and made camp in the dark. They started out at daylight.

Wolf's company was far ahead of Ulrich. Their fresh and better mounts made excellent distance quickly and the first night the company did not set up camp to sleep but took only four hours dismounted rest. They ate cold rations in the saddle. The roads were good, at nights the moon was bright, and so the company made good time. They arrived at Wolf's new castle almost a day ahead of Ulrich.

It was mid-morning when the company arrived, banners flowing, to the astonishment of the people who witnessed them pass. Wolf was coming with more men than Vilhelm had left with. Everyone they passed knew the meaning of their coming. Shadow saw a rider dashing across the field toward the castle and pointed. The company did not speed up. As they approached the gate they saw the indecision of the guards. Wolf signaled a stop.

He dismounted and walked forward leading his horse the

company following. "Open the gates for I am your Lord Aelle, known as Wolf, and I am here to claim my rightful inheritance gained by successful challenge. My father is dead. "

A voice came from behind the wall, "How do I know what you say is true?"

Wolf's recognized the voice. His reply was commanding, "Come and see me Skjold, see my seal ring, then yield or die!"

After a moment's hesitation the gate opened and Skjold came out, looked at Wolf, saw some of the men who had went with Vilhelm, and went to one knee, "My Lord Wolf."

"Rise, I wish to take charge of my possessions."

Wolf entered the castle followed by his troops. He ordered the men of the castle to assemble. There were nine and clearly three of these were men who were not expected to fight until their wounds healed.

Wolf ordered the men of the castle to wait in the barracks to meet with their new Lord. Shadow had the company search the castle. Wolf went to his dead father's quarters which were locked. He had the door broken in. He was left alone, and searched the rooms. It took two hours, but by systematic searching he found the hide. It had been well done. He decided to leave it where it was for the night and re-hid it.

The castle also yielded up a goodly supply of weapons, some silverware, and a few good mounts. A wagon and draft animals were in the barns. They would be used to transport the inheritance. Half of the armor would be left here for outfitting future recruits or replacement.

Wolf and shadow locked the castle for the night, set the guard, and sat down to talk. The castle and the lands they had passed through were actually quite good, but there were no crops planted. The land was good but not being managed. Deciding how the holds would be combined would be a challenge, but there was a good living to be made from them.

That evening Wolf visited the children working in the castle that he had used as sources of information. He was shocked at the tatters they wore and the conditions of the castle generally. He had not realized how filthy it was. When he lived here the castle had been much better kept and he realized that probably had a lot to do with his mother's efforts.

In the morning, Wolf met with the men from the barracks and the five he brought from here that had returned with him. They had already told the story of Vilhelm's defeat and Wolf's strength. Wolf spoke to the men truthfully.

"The reason my father wanted my grandfather's lands is that his lands could no longer support him when his neighbors became too strong or poor to raid at will. My father was only a warrior. My father had not seen the wealth that could be wrought from these lands by hard work. The lands here are not managed well. The people were overtaxed and abused so many died or left.

My other lands are fertile and profitable. These will be also. Combining the two will provide a good income so all can prosper. This castle will anchor this end of my lands, so there is no reason you and your families cannot prosper. If you give me your oath, you will be paid to keep the peace in this area, collect reasonable rents or taxes, and serve me through the man I decide to put in command. For those of you who have not given me oath, if you decide to leave, you are free to go now and I will release you, but if you decide to stay, you must be my oath men and honor all that entails. You will be bound. I will pay you according to the custom. You may bring your families to the castle. If the commander decides to employ your family members, there will be additional pay. Skjold, I know you will keep oath, so if you stay you will be sergeant to the commander. What will it be?"

The men were enthusiastic in their response. They all gave their oaths. Wolf's reputation was useful in more ways than one. The offer and the fact he was the rightful heir, an obvious warrior, and a strong lord, sealed the deal. They would serve a stronger lord and one who was fair as well.

When asked, Herewood agreed to take command and hold this castle. He was to be assigned four of the company. Herewood would command the fourteen inherited men and four from the company. Wolf gave him a sufficient purse with which to run the castle for a time. Herewood protested that he did not know how to keep accounts, but one of the men said he had some training from the monastery and was assigned as one of the four.

Wolf instructed Herewood to see the children were cleaned up and got new clothes, and that they set about cleaning the castle thoroughly. He instructed the children were to be well fed and he would see they received a small monthly stipend that Herewood was to use for their clothing and upkeep. Permanent quarters were to be allocated for sleeping. He did not want them sleeping in the halls propped against a wall.

Wolf went and removed the contents of his father's hidden treasure, packing it for travel. It was a goodly fortune, but not as much as the family already possessed. It would have been enough to put these lands into production several times over. Wolf realized his father had been a warrior lord but also ignorant and greedy. He had not known how to govern.

Ulrich and his band came within sight of the castle to find Wolf's banner flying. One of his hired men went into the village and found out how many men were here. He reported to Ulrich who cursed his luck. He would find a way to even the score eventually. The men with him were angry, but the gold Ulrich carried would pacify them. Perhaps he could find his brother. He set off.

The Wolf Pack departed leaving the castle under the guard of men Wolf had fought with and other men in whom he had seen hope for a new future.

In Wolf's absence, his father was buried. There was no funeral mass for Wolf's father because he was a pagan. There was a short memorial service and burial in unhallowed ground on top of a hill overlooking the river. A marker was set.

Lord Cuthbert was much revived by news of the victory and Aert's medicine. Though there was no festival to celebrate the victory, Cuthbert did attend the mass of thanksgiving after the memorial. The Lady Ethelind did not wear black as widows customarily did, for she openly proclaimed to be a happy widow and no hypocrite. She did not hold her bad arranged marriage against her father, for she was blessed from it by Wolf.

At the time of the marriage, Ethelind knew it had been a necessity of survival for her family who had been harried on all sides. In the beginning, it had not been so bad, then Vilhelm had taken up again with the mother of his bastard sons behind Ethelind's back. The woman had darkened Vilhelm's soul. Ethelind prayed to God for forgiveness of her hard heart toward the woman who had caused the alienation with her husband.

Chapter 7 – Rebuilding

There was much gladness when the company returned. Wolf went immediately to see his mother and grandfather. His grandfather was recovering and alert, but still thin and weak.

Shadow came after the men had been dismissed. He was the one who recounted the story of their journey. Shadow told of the inheritance that Wolf had claimed. This was not spoil and so not sharable. Wolf decided, however, that the men would nevertheless receive a small gift as would the church. Shadow was charged with seeing all the men received theirs, including the men at the other castle.

After storing the treasure, Shadow and Wolf excused themselves to get rest. Before retiring, Wolf went to see how the warrior whose leg had been broken was faring. He asked where the man could be found. Grimbold was in the foundry sitting on a hay bale, with his leg still stinted and bound, sticking straight out. He was sharpening blades with a whetstone. He did not see Wolf coming.

"I see you are keeping busy, Grimbold."

"Yes, my Lord. Since you insist on continuing to pay me, I felt I should make myself useful."

He turned to the armorer, "Greetings, Aldwyn."

"My Lord", Aldwyn acknowledged. Not one to stand on ceremony when he was working hot metal, he kept working on the sword he was making.

"What does Aert say?"

Grimbold explained that Aert was sure of a full recovery, God willing, if Grimbold took care to follow instructions. He showed the crutches he had started using. He said his comrades had started calling him three legs and he hoped the name did not stick. Wolf excused himself and retired.

The men of the company were exhausted and all slept until the next morning, rising only to relieve themselves in a night pot or go to the kitchen to eat some bread and cheese. Aert held morning prayer service as usual, but he made it known that the returned company should be allowed to continue to rest this one morning. A few showed up anyway before returning to sleep some more.

Wolf rose late the next morning, washed, shaved, put on a clean uniform and went into the courtyard to where his grandfather usually could be found. Shadow, Ethelind, and Aert were already with Cuthbert in the courtyard where he sat on a large chair in the warm sun. Cuthbert was eating more soup. He smiled and nodded between each spoonful.

Wolf smiled at Shadow, "It seems my grandfather loves soup."

They all laughed.

Lord Cuthbert appeared in good spirits. He talked without difficulty, "Praise God for He has seen fit to rescue me through my grandson. Father Aert has given me a full account of what has transpired in the last months. I am joyful that my daughter is now a happy widow, though I wish the circumstances had been different for your sake. It seems my grandson is wise, brave, and capable beyond his years and is surrounded by wise advisors and loyal warriors. You are all my witnesses that he has my full authority to rule here."

The old man sighed. "I need to rest now and can for I now have my grandson to do all the work." He chuckled, then simply laid his head back and went to sleep sitting in the comfortable chair.

Aert just shrugged. The visitors left Lord Cuthbert in the care of Aert and one of the archer brothers who were always with Cuthbert. A guard stood nearby.

It was at the time Wolf was leaving his grandfather that a grizzled old man appeared at the gate and asked to see Lord Cuthbert. He was told that Lord Cuthbert was recuperating and that his grandson Lord Aelle, known as Lord Wolf, had authority here. The man asked for an audience in the name of the risen Christ.

When the request came it intrigued Wolf. He was told the old man was hungry and thirsty so Wolf ordered he be taken to the kitchen and fed. Wolf waited until it was reported the man had eaten his fill before appearing.

The man got up when Wolf entered. Wolf motioned him to sit down. Wolf observed the grey haired and bearded smiling man. He was a little rotund, but reminded Wolf of Aewel who was anything but soft.

The man addressed Wolf, "I have heard good things about you, Lord Aelle. The last time I saw you, you were a small child. I am called Wilfred. I was your grandfather's house master until I was sent away by force of arms. I managed the household of the castle, though you would not know it to look at me now."

Wolf called for his mother to be fetched.

Wolf smiled, "We could use a good household staff. Probably right now we could use any household staff." Wolf chuckled at his own humor.

Wolf's mother glided into the room and held out her hands, "Wilfred, I wondered when you would magically appear."

Wilfred took her hands as he bowed, "My Lady."

She turned to her son. "He will be a great help son."

Wolf nodded, and simply said, "You are hired Wilfred for I can hardly deny my dear mother." Wolf then became serious, "You must have had quarters and you may return to them, and operate as you did before."

"What is my budget, my Lord?" Wilfred asked.

Wolf looked at his mother, "I suppose we can afford what it used to be?"

His mother nodded and Wilfred looked surprised.

"May I visit Lord Cuthbert?" Wilfred asked.

Wolf answered enthusiastically, "Of course, as soon as he is awake and whenever your duties allow. I am sure he will be delighted to see you. I will leave you to start your duties for you are sorely needed."

Wilfred seemed much relieved by the answer. It occurred to Wolf that Wilfred may have been concerned Cuthbert was under duress from Wolf. It spoke highly of the man's loyalty.

There was still much to be done to secure the lands now that the immediate threat was gone. Later in the afternoon, Lord Cuthbert, Wolf, Shadow, Ragnvald and Aewel gathered together to discuss what would come next. Lord Cuthbert deferred to Wolf to lead the informal council. Lady Ethelind was also present.

It was decided that they would continue with the plan to make sure crops were planted, the lands combined, and the defenses strengthened. Wolf and Shadow prepared to execute the immediate plans.

Wolf met with Ragnvald after the meeting, "You and your men know all too well that much work has to be done to restore this castle, my grandfather's lands, and our collective futures. I want you and nine men from here and one of Aewel's to travel the valley. Ask Aewel for capes, so your men will display the cross as they march. Tell the leaders to make a list of what is needed to plant the spring harvest and what will be needed for survival. Let everyone know that my grandfather is well, we are strong, and law and order will be enforced.

Call the Sheriffs together from each area for they are the ones the people trust and turn to for everyday affairs. I wish to meet them. Tell them to prepare a list of what our people need to start working their farms again. Warn them not to be greedy, only ask for what is necessary to maintain life and bring the fields and orchards to productivity. I will decide who will be helped and how much based to a large extent on your knowledge, so be observant. I have two men I want you to tell to come in addition to the Sheriffs. Tell no one that the two are called by me.

One last thing, we still have four suits of the new armor and you may take one if you wish. My men have been successful and have now purchased their armor. You may do so in the future as you prosper in my service, if you choose to take my offer."

Wolf then had Ragnvald call his troop together. He motioned them to sit.

"We have a lot of work to do if we are to make sure of the protection and prosperity of our people. We need to hire men to train at arms. I also need carpenters and tradesmen to repair our defenses starting with the Neck's gate. You know the men here so make your recommendations to Ragnvald who will speak for me. Only the appointment of men at arms will be subject to Aewel's approval for he is a good judge of whether and how a man is trainable to arms. They will be paid the established rate. Tell the tradesmen to come as soon as possible.

I will give you coin to purchase food. Ragnvald, you may take mounts and you will fly my banner. I want a show of force so it sinks in that this valley will no longer be lawless and we are able to move about swiftly.

If you encounter raiders or lawlessness, deal with it as you see fit. If you happen to catch any law breakers, have them held until you are on the return journey and bring them to me as we brought the last group. I want the people to see them in their shame and that justice prevails. Before you leave, if you need repairs or service to your arms or armor, see our armorer who has set up in the castle's forge. Questions?"

Ragnvald's answer was direct, "No questions. We will carry out your orders, Lord Wolf."

"Very well, we have much to do." He stretched out his arm and the two men clasped each other's. "God be with you and your men, Ragnvald." Wolf turned and headed for the main hall.

Ragnvald took charge, "Alright you lot, let's get organized and prepared for the march." The men scurried off to prepare. Ragnvald watched Wolf walking away. He thought to himself that it was hard to believe this lad of sixteen was already a seasoned warrior, a natural leader, and a pious noble. God had indeed blessed the people of this realm. He would do his part to see Lord Cuthbert's lands restored. Ragnvald was determined Wolf would inherit a prosperous land. Ragnvald looked to the future and wanted his children and grandchildren to know life under a worthy lord.

After Ragnvald's unit departed, Wolf and Shadow assembled twelve men to travel the river side to determine how to best defend the valley. The mountain streams coming into the valley from the north came together to create the river and the rugged terrain there provided no easy access to the valley. The waters downriver from the castle were another matter. From that direction it was possible for attackers to come by boat. That is where they headed first. Wolf, Shadow and company travelled for some time. The progress was slow, not because of the distance or the terrain, but because of the people who came out to greet them. Wolf stopped to greet and interact with them for they needed to know who he was.

At one place near the end of the valley, several men and women came running to tell about a group of bandits that had taken over a small village and were terrorizing the residents. Only a handful had managed to escape. One of the locals agreed to take the patrol there. He was helped up behind one of the riders and they set out to rescue the villagers.

The company stopped on a hill overlooking the village. It was not a rich village but neither was it the poorest. The bandits appeared ill armed and merely evil men looking for opportunity to steal and rape where there was little resistance.

Wolf muttered out loud, "There are quite a number of the rogues, but we should make quick work of the rabble."

The guide was lowered, and the company formed battle line and galloped down the hill toward the village. The bandits sounded the alarm and because of their superior numbers thought to defend themselves. The company went to full charge at Wolf's command and the bandits, as they were cut down, realized they were facing a foe that would decimate them and some attempted unsuccessfully to flee. For Wolf's men it was a skirmish that lasted but for the briefest few minutes. The account would be retold of the successful charge and battle against greater numbers of armed raiders and how those raiders were massacred by the outnumbered forces of Lord Wolf and his War Chief Shadow.

Two bandits were captured and trussed up. The village had suffered. The men of the company found murdered men, many of whom had been taken from behind as they ran. Some had tried to fight with hoes and been struck down. They found women in the homes who had been repeatedly raped and beaten. The guide had walked down into the village by the time the company was gathering the survivors together. Wolf sent two men with him to fetch healers and a priest. Some villagers came from the woods where they had been hiding. They started to seek their family members to look after them or mourn.

Wolf's men gathered the weapons of the bandits. They were of poor quality but had been very effective against the farm implements of the villagers. Everything else was left for the villagers who had suffered so much. The villagers were reluctant to pick the corpses until given permission to do so.

The company went to the top of the hill, which was both defensible and close to the village, to establish camp. Wolf's company needed to be out of the way of the families. Wolf decided they would stay the night.

Two of the villagers, old men, came to the camp to ask for the leader and to inquire who it was who had come to their rescue.

When they were told, they asked to see Wolf who came to meet them. They fell to their knees before him. He bid them rise which they did, their heads still bowed. Wolf asked for blankets and at his beckoning they moved into the shade and sat on the blankets laid out on the grass.

One of the men spoke. "Good Lord Aelle, grandson of our famous and clever Lord, we thank you for our rescue. We come to plead for food so we will not go hungry. Our crops have been stolen and our homes plundered. We have no means to pay for more."

Wolf regarded the men. "Do you have a cart and oxen?"

One of the men replied, "We have a cart, but no oxen, they were taken."

Wolf asked, "Is there a place close by where food may be purchased if you had money?"

One of the men nodded, and pointed, saying, "Down the river a day's journey, within your grandfather's rule outside the valley, but we have no boat. Many people at this end of the valley are without food."

Wolf looked at Shadow. The problem was greater than they had supposed. Wolf told the men to wait there. He and Shadow retired a distance to discuss the matter. Shadow suggested they split up. He would take six men to find a boat and travel downriver to buy food and bring it to the castle to be distributed. They had enough coin with them to pay for a large boat to travel and to purchase food to bring back.

Wolf was concerned one boatload would probably not be enough to see them through until harvest. Wolf suggested Shadow come to the castle with a hired boat so more men could be sent downriver. Perhaps more boats could be hired downriver to bring more food back on the return trip. The cargo ships would need protection and a show of force would discourage bandits. Shadow agreed that it was a good plan.

Wolf arranged for the villagers to send a cart to the castle to be given enough provisions to sustain them until supplies arrived. They went and advised the village men of what was decided and that one of them would go with Shadow to help him find his way. The company had brought three days rations, and they shared two thirds of their food with the villagers. It was a meager amount but appreciated. There was much mourning in the village but relief that the immediate threat was over. The villagers got busy putting things in order as best they could. The company stayed out of the way on the hilltop.

The next morning the local priest assisted the company as it held its regular morning prayers. Wolf held court and the two captive bandits were tried and executed. They were hung by the neck and left hanging in sight of the road some distance from the village. All thirty three of the raiders were now dead. Those killed in battle were heaped in a mass funeral pyre and burned to ash and bone fragments.

There would be funerals and burials this day, but the company would be gone. They were on a mission to save the villagers at this end of the valley from starvation. Wolf headed back to the castle and Shadow went to hire a boat.

Wolf's party arrived at the castle in the late afternoon. Grain from the castle's stores was loaded on a cart and sent back to the village with a guard.

Wolf went to see his grandfather who was much better. Wolf found him sitting in the courtyard talking to his mother and the priest Aert.

Wolf took a seat near his grandfather who spoke first, "It seems grandson that God has truly blessed me and your mother. You are a son for my daughter to be proud of and an heir any man would be proud to leave. I have already been informed by Father Aert that you fought and won a battle against raiders down the valley."

"How can this be grandfather? How does Brother Aert know of this? I have just returned?"

His grandfather just smiled, "You know these priests have their noses into everything."

Wolf recounted factually what had happened and the action that had been taken. He revealed the plans made. He told his grandfather that when the men from the valley arrived the prisoners now held in the dungeon would be tried and executed for their crimes or their treason. Staffan's life would be spared for he had revealed all those who had conspired with him. Throughout Wolf's recounting his grandfather kept nodding agreement.

81

When Wolf had finished, his grandfather spoke, "Well done! When the valley men come I will announce that I am turning rule over to you and Aert will draw up the documents." Wolf started to object, but his grandfather stilled him.

"It is best; I will recover and I may live some years yet, but I will never fight in the field again or will I likely have the energy to govern. I am old. I was advanced in years when your mother was born. I was forty one years old. As long as our God allows, I will be here to advise you and aid you. You should probably know, even though you are apparently wealthy in your own right and were prepared to ransom our people from poverty with your own wealth, that I have treasure your mother did not know about hidden away. The documents that will be drawn will be witnessed by all present at the upcoming meeting and copies sent to the bishops and lords in the surrounding lands."

Wolf looked at his mother who nodded agreement. "It is best for the family son."

His grandfather was not finished. "Once the defenses have been strengthened we must find you a suitable Christian wife who will provide heirs. The right marriage will also establish alliances that will help ensure the security of our lands and people."

Wolf nodded. He had expected that this would be part of his responsibility. He looked at his grandfather smiling, "We need to pray that God gives me a good Christian wife who will be a good help mate in the years to come. Even though Godly character, family and intelligence are more important than appearances, I hope she will not be too homely."

His grandfather returned his smile, put his head back, and went to sleep.

The village near the castle had started to be repopulated. In years past, Cuthbert had ordered the village be kept away from the castle so it could not provide cover for an attack on the castle. Yet it was close enough for the people to reach the walls if the alarm was raised at the Neck. Now people were returning from hiding. Some had been with other family and some had camped in the woods. Now that the castle was manned with a strong company, the village here was the safest place to be.

A few men had turned up with their families claiming to be Ragnvald's men. They were given some provisions and told to wait in the village until Ragnvald returned. They went to find places to stay. These men were sent away when Ragnvald came back for they had been the ones who fled when their leaders had been captured or killed. Their arms had not been taken, but they had attempted no rescue. They would become field hands for soldiers who would not fight were of no use.

As night approached, a boat came upriver. The alarm was sounded and the troops went to their stations. Wolf sent Ragnvald and twelve warriors to the docks. It turned out that Shadow was on the boat. A few hours later Shadow's men arrived leading his mount. The boat would soon enough be dispatched downriver. In the meantime the boatmen were paid to wait.

It was then that Wolf had the next idea. It would require considerable expenditure, but it would no doubt be profitable and provide a sound defense. He would discuss it with his grandfather, his mother, Shadow, Aewel and Ragnvald.

Ragnvald returned in the morning with five prisoners. He and his men had marched only half the planned circle of the upper valley before the leaders had come to him. The valley was reported to be quiet at the moment. Most of the food and seed had been stolen as well as anything of value. The Sheriffs would come as ordered. They would spread the word.

In the afternoon, Wolf sat down with his grandfather, Shadow, Ragnvald, Aewel, and his mother to discuss his idea regarding river trade and defense. It was agreed it was a marvelous plan. Wolf then committed that it would be implemented.

Ragnvald gave his report on his investigation regarding what had happened in the valley. Wolf shared what he had learned from Staffan whose accounts meshed with what Ragnvald had said. They now had a clearer picture of the treachery which had been executed. When the spies returned that night, they confirmed it.

In operation it had been simple. Vilhelm had hired the mercenaries to create lawlessness so the people would want a strong leader to protect them; one who could put a stop to the raiding. The mercenaries, most likely at Vilhelm's order, had bribed Staffan.

Cuthbert's loyal men had been removed by treachery. Staffan had used the cook to ensure Cuthbert's illness and the timing of his death. Staffan had left a nominal guard provided by the mercenaries, to make sure no one interfered with Cuthbert's illness.

All that had been needed was for Wolf to take the vow of poverty and enter the church. The strike had been at the heart of Cuthbert's lands, with those outside being relatively unaffected and able to provide income. Vilhelm with a rightful claim and with his wife at his side would have ridden in, saved the day, and taken power.

The next day leaders started to arrive in the morning and were all there by noon. Several priests had also arrived as they had also been summoned by Aert at Wolf's request. A modest noon meal was served in the great hall following which the meeting was to be held. The priests took the attendance and checked it against the list. No one was missing.

The men were finishing the meal when Lord Cuthbert, Wolf, and Shadow entered. The hall went silent. Lord Cuthbert was leaning slightly on Aert for he was still weak. They walked the Lord's place of honor where there was a pair of throne chairs at the top of three steps. For years since Cuthbert's wife's death, there had only been one. The party went to the steps and Cuthbert and Wolf took the seats. Shadow stood beside Wolf. Men at arms entered and stood to either side. The priest Aert went down the stairs and sat at the middle chair at a table in front of the dais, facing the audience. Four other priests came and sat at the table.

Lord Cuthbert started making his announcement, "My dear subjects and honored guests, my grandson and I greet you. We will now have a prayer to start our meeting and ask for God's guidance."

Aert stood and led the assembly in prayers. It was short and when he finished he sat.

Lord Cuthbert continued, "We are grateful that my grandson came in our hour of need to rescue us from danger. He came with his own men and spent his own treasure to do so. A man was never so blessed to have such a brave, pious, and just heir as my grandson is." Cuthbert paused to let that sink in. "I will now turn the meeting over to my grandson."

Wolf stood and paused for effect before starting his speech, "Here in this hall are the men who are the natural leaders of our people. You are the leaders whom the people respect and trust to give them advice in day to day affairs and arbitrate disputes. They have priests to give them spiritual advice and their sheriffs to help them in their daily lives. We ask you to advise us of the needs of your area necessary for the planting of crops, feeding the people, and putting our farms back into production. This growing season will be difficult for all of us. For this reason, my family will provide you with the necessary supplies at our expense."

There was a gasp in the assembly and then a spontaneous cheering.

Wolf waited for the cheering to subside and held his hand up for quiet, then continued, "There are two men in this hall who deserve special recognition. Come forward now."

Aert announced their names. It seemed the men were about to receive some honor but Wolf simply said, "Guards, seize these traitors."

The assembly started buzzing.

Wolf continued, "In the morning, these men will be tried for high treason, and you may all attend their trial so you may assure our subjects that there is justice in this land."

Lord Cuthbert raised his hand for attention and the hall fell silent. "In the interest of my people, I have decided that it is time my heir, my grandson Aelle, known as the great warrior Wolf, take charge of my lands for the good of his family and his people. I therefore proclaim him heir and ruler. He will rule our family land. The good priests have made copies of my signed formal declaration which will be posted for all to see."

Cheers started. A chant went up for God to bless Lord Aelle. Cuthbert smiled and waved encouraging the response.

Those assembled were brought forward in line to bend their knee to Wolf and swear allegiance. They then returned to their seats and conversations started in the hall. When everyone had completed their part, Aert called for silence.

It was Wolf's turn to speak again, "God has blessed us and we thank Him. He has blessed to provide riches to rebuild our land and its defenses. I pledge to devote my life and treasure to, God willing, make our land a safe and prosperous land. It is larger now that my father's and mother's lands have been joined. Together we will rebuild and make these lands secure and productive. I will require help in doing this. I will meet with each of you individually to discuss the needs of the people in your area with you. Once you have met with me you may return home, unless you want to stay to see the trial." The last was met with laughter. Everyone would want to see the trial.

"As you know, my personal War Chief is Osmund, also known as the great warrior Shadow Killer. I now appoint him War Chief over all of our forces and a judge who speaks with my authority. If you need a place to rest this night, see Wilfred.

"And lastly, my other lands are fertile but much has no one to work it. If any family has land that is insufficient for its size and there are those sons of the family who would move to farm other larger fields, please list those and send them to me. Those farmers will be reestablished within my lands on fertile ground and given what is needed to start."

Wolf motioned to Aert.

Aert rose, "All stand."

Everyone in the room stood up as Wolf and his grandfather left the great hall.

The rest of the day was a flurry of activity. Wolf spent time with each of the Sheriffs starting with those who were from the farthest distance. Aert and Cuthbert sat as advisors to Wolf, and they worked through the requests. The greatest need was for seed and food. Wolf was impressed by the concern about the lack of churches that were within reasonable travelling distances. Apparently the only church in the valley was the chapel in the castle and it was in disrepair. An accomplished trader from the shire was recommended by several of the leaders to go down river to acquire what was needed.

The trader Beorn was summoned to meet and came directly and was waiting when the last Sherriff left.

Wolf greeted Beorn as he entered the room, "You must be Beorn the trader."

Beorn knelt on one knee and bowed saying, "Lord."

Wolf smiled, "Rise my good fellow. I have heard good things about you. How can you be of help?"

Beorn bowed, "Lord, may I be so bold as to ask for a prayer before we start?"

Wolf became serious, "Yes, good Beorn. It was my failing and may God forgive me for not thinking to do so."

They prayed for God's guidance. Wolf had been told Beorn's story by elder men. He had fled when the mercenaries came. Placing greater value on his family than his possessions, at the last minute Beorn had escaped with them on foot with only the food they could carry and a few meager possessions. His storehouse had been emptied by the thieves who plundered his home as well. After prayer, Wolf again asked Beorn how he could be of help.

Beorn spoke, "To answer your question, sir, I come seeking employment for I have lost everything and my family will go hungry if I do not find work. I have knowledge of the river trade, boats and such so perhaps in some way I could be of use to you."

Wolf noted that there was no whining, no excuse, and no request for a loan or handout. He was impressed by the man.

Wolf replied, "I will not offer you employment," and at that moment he saw disappointment on Beorn's face, a face Wolf expected was usually unreadable. "I do, however, have a business proposition." Beorn's disappointment disappeared.

Wolf stated plainly, the he needed to establish river trade and defense and that Beorn could play a key role in the matter of trade doing the kind of business he had in the past. Wolf would purchase river craft and provide the initial capital to purchase goods for resale. Beorn could also advise him on how to defend against a river invasion.

Wolf completed the offer, "Beorn you supply the knowledge of the trade and run the business. The business will pay only the customary taxes, and we will split the profits."

Beorn perceived that this Lord was a man trying to do good. He answered, "I of course accept your generous offer, Lord, but I have a condition."

Wolf had not expected this response, but he was curious, "What is the condition?"

"If we are to share profits equally, then you must let me repay half the cost of the original investment out of my share of the profits."

Wolf was elated, for this served to confirm Wolf's trust in the man. "Done", he said and stood to clasp the man's arm and so seal the bargain. Wolf continued, "There is a hired boat waiting to take you down river and Brother Aert has a list of critical items and quantities needed. Shadow will assign you men-at-arms to guard you and your cargo."

Beorn asked, "Lord, could the soldiers not be in uniform so they look like hired guards. I will be more likely to get better prices if those who I do business with think I am on my own business."

Wolf nodded, "Very well, I will be a secret partner".

Beorn nodded and smiled. "Is there some place my family could be housed, they are waiting in the yard."

Wolf asked, "Why not your own home?"

Beorn said simply, "Squatters and I have no provisions."

Wolf became stern, "My men will evict the trespassers and see your family is safely installed. Is there someone you can hire to guard your house until you return?"

Beorn nodded. Wolf gave him two large purses, one as the initial investment and one to purchase the goods for the valley then bid him hire a guard and hurry on his journey. Beorn worked quickly and two days later the first boatload of goods arrived. Beorn was not present for the shipment delivery so the manifest and accounting was brought to Wolf who called on Aert to administer the shipment.

It was then that Wolf realized he would need someone to keep his family's accounts and spoke to Wilfred who made the arrangements for a man named Modig who was talented at such things to come to meet Wolf. Modig was accustomed to keeping secrets upon penalty of having one's tongue cut out and being thrown in a dungeon to rot, though those threats were unnecessary. Wolf was told the man was honest and feared God's wrath in the next life more than any threat mere man could make.

Before hiring him, Wolf conferred with his grandfather and mother. They knew of the man and thought he would be a good appointment. Only a small portion of the family's fortune was included in the accounting and that had come from Wolf's father's wealth. Aert recommended one of the local clerks to help Modig. He would be keeping a second eye on the accounts.

Wolf asked Aert to take a beverage with him. Alone in the kitchen, Wolf expressed his concern that the Castle's chapel was in disrepair. He told Aert to have the carpenters come up with a plan for repair and a cost. If the price was reasonable, the work would start as soon as the Neck gate was repaired. They also discussed the need for churches throughout the valley. It was decided that five more would be built at strategically located places. Priests would be needed, to minister in the churches to be built eventually throughout the family lands. The present bishop would be an impediment to that.

Aelle stated the obvious, "We must have a new bishop."

The cost of such appointment and how it could be achieved was discussed. Aert asked if Wolf knew how they could find someone to fill the post. Wolf said he had someone in mind. Aert asked who that would be.

Wolf simply said, "You" and got up and went to visit his grandfather.

Wolf went to bed late after visiting with his grandfather. Shadow made a round of the sentries before retiring.

The next morning, Wolf ate breakfast with Shadow after prayer service. It was agreed that Shadow would ensure the army was expanded and trained while Wolf spent most of his time in governance. They agreed when they were both in the castle they would spend an hour in private each morning sparring with each other to keep their skills sharp for war.

The matter of archers was discussed. Ragnvald was called to provide his perspective. There were a fairly good number of archers who hunted and were reasonably proficient with the long bow. There was a discussion of the role archers could play in the defense of the valley. It was decided the use of archers and fire arrows on boats bringing raiders upriver would be effective. They would also be able to keep climbers off the cliffs at the Neck. Wolf's next discussion met with some concern.

Aewel and Palne were called in. Wolf pointed out that archers would be particularly effective against horseman if the targets were the horses. Horses in full charge that were taken down were likely to injure their riders when they went down. It might be distasteful, but might be very effective. A hunter, who could bring down a deer at the run, could bring down a horse. The question was range and tactics.

Ragnar and Palne volunteered to find the answer to the question of range and develop possible tactics. Aewel would develop counter tactics, and methods for the archers' losses to be minimized. The plan was to be kept secret.

It was decided that in any event the archers could be used and should be organized. They could be organized as a part-time force. A few would be hired full time. The others could be trained, as Palne was, to defend themselves close in and practice intermittently between working the farms or other jobs.

It was delegated to Ragnar to determine and recommend the best place to establish a river watch and defensive position for Shadow's approval. The defensive tactics would be included and Beorn was to be consulted because of his knowledge of the river.

It was reported that gates for the Neck were under construction. The group finished their planning at mid-day.

The trials started after the noon meal with Shadow presiding. Wolf and Cuthbert purposely stayed away so Shadow's authority to judge would not be questioned in the future. Shadow had been more nervous about the trial than he had ever been about facing battle. He had slept fitfully and prayed each of the numerous times he woke.

There were so many people wanting to see the trials that they had to be held in the field between the village and the castle. This only served to add to Shadow's queasy stomach. It was almost a festival atmosphere. When it came time for the trial to start, Shadow had to have a horn blown to get the crowd silenced.

Shadow, summoning up the same brave front that he often used in battle, forged ahead following the procedure established by Wolf. Two priests kept a written record of the proceedings. The trials started with the matter of treason.

The two men who had been involved with Staffan were brought out. Shadow told them the charges against them. They proclaimed their innocence. The first witness was Staffan, then men and women who worked for the two men. It was clearly established that the men had plotted the overthrow of Cuthbert in order to line their pockets. They had purchased all the food and goods plundered by Staffan for next to nothing. The two men's servants testified they had stored the goods delivered in the middle of the night by Staffan and his band. Some of these goods were still on the men's lands.

The men were asked if they had anything to say for themselves. They quickly in panic pleaded for mercy. The verdict by Shadow, who later was sure the words came from God in answer to his prayers, was later to be recounted throughout the lands.

"You have by your deeds betrayed not only your rightful lord but the good subjects of this valley who you would have condemned to poverty and starvation but for the intervention of Lord Aelle and his brave men-at-arms. This court finds you guilty of the charges against you, thievery and treason."

A cheer rose up. It was a fine thing in the people's eyes to see justice dispensed on behalf of their lord and his people. After a few moments, Shadow raised his hand for silence and the crowd hushed. Everyone waited for the sentence.

"On the charge of thievery, it is the sentence of this court that you shall be taken immediately and that your right hand shall be chopped off at the wrist and that your right to lands and all your goods are forfeit to Lord Aelle. On the charge of treason, it is the sentence of this court that you be taken from this place and hung by the neck until you are dead, such sentence to be carried out after execution of the sentence on the charge of thievery."

Another cheer went up.

"This court will sit again in the morning to hear the remaining cases."

The crowds stayed to watch the carrying out of the sentences. Priests were present for any of the convicted who wanted their ministrations. None did.

Wolf, Cuthbert, and Lady Ethelind came to witness the executions from horseback. The crowds waved and cheered as they rode into the field.

That evening, Wolf, his grandfather, mother, and Shadow met to discuss more general matters. The elders were starting to submit the names of young families desiring to relocate to the other lands. The method and cost of the relocation was discussed. They had no doubt the taxes and rents would justify the investment. The valley would be the hub of the family lands as it was the most defensible position. It decided to start patrols outside the valley immediately.

In the morning, after their weapons practice, Shadow told Wolf he did not like being a judge. Wolf told him he understood and Wolf said there were times he did not like being lord, but he still had to do it. Wolf explained that he thought it was necessary for Shadow to do this in order to be seen as a man with great authority outside the military realm. The work they had to do was far reaching and Wolf did not want anybody to even think about questioning Shadow's authority. They discussed the things they were going to have to do that would be outside their roles as warriors. They even discussed that perhaps this was a natural progression, more peace less battle, more prosperity yielding more strength, more strength less challenge. They decided human nature would not change, so the force of arms would always be necessary.

That afternoon the trials for the other prisoners were held. The crowds were large but somewhat diminished from the day before. The orderly distribution of goods was taking longer than anticipated. People were leaving as they received their apportionment of the goods that had come up river. In addition, the seized goods were now being used to fill the needs in the valley and there were now two distribution sites that Modig organized and administered.

Staffan's trial was the least anticipated. People knew he would be exiled for his treason. They had not expected he would still be tried for thievery and have his hand removed before being sentenced to exile. There was a mass hanging of prisoners. The mercenaries were employed by Stephan in treason and not as combatants so were treated accordingly and hung.

The people of the valley were very satisfied with the outcomes. Hope prevailed as people went back to their homes and work. Shadow was a little depressed. Governing was not as easy as he thought. It had been easy in the past to criticize how others had ruled, but when you were the one in the seat of power it was different. It took a different kind of courage.

Shadow now realized why Wolf had wanted him to judge and be involved in governing. Like battle, you could only know the experience in the doing of it. Shadow was more impressed with young Lord Wolf. The lad was tutoring him and the roles were now reversed.

It was just a few days until the families that were to relocate were coming to the village. A temporary camp was set up for them as it would take a few days to arrange the additional resources needed to start the new farms. Ragnar and Modig worked to ensure the group was properly outfitted. It turned out that Modig had a talent for organization as well as keeping accounts, so as a result Modig became Wolf's logistics expert.

It was still early spring when the group set out for their new assigned farmlands. There were thirty seven young couples or young families setting out in carts and wagons. They followed Shadow and ten mounted men-at-arms and two archers. The archers were placed directly behind the banner bearers. The archers wore their mail and helmets with their bows proudly carried across their backs. Wolf and Shadow wanted the status of an archer to be seen as an important part of the company.

Chapter 8 - A New Beginning

Herewood found he liked garrison command. He enjoyed the structure of military routine and the autonomy. He took his job seriously, set high standards, and treated his men with respect and a strong hand. The men responded positively to their new set of circumstances. They seemed happy in their new role. They also liked being paid regularly. Some of the men had family and they moved them into the castle and the castle became a busy and happy place.

The first week he was in command, Herewood had called the tenants that were still in the area together. He advised them of the rent and taxes the new lord would expect. They were shocked. They could not only make a decent living but perhaps prosper under their new lord. The problem was that there was a shortage of some critical goods. They had been bled near death by their previous ruler. Herewood told them their Lord Aelle was sending supplies, took a list of what was needed, and hired a rider to take the message to Aelle.

Herewood's men patrolled regularly with instructions they were to protect and be friendly to the people of the land. The folk in the surrounding area came to trust the garrison. The castle became an integral part of the social fabric of the region. A market again started up in the village and garrison troops patrolled the market on foot and kept the peace on market day. Several thieves were caught and punished. Thieves seemed unwilling to risk the loss of a hand and they soon stopped coming to the market. The merchants did not grumble about the small market tax as their businesses began to prosper in the secure environment. In the past much of their goods had been simply confiscated by Vilhelm. It had been just possible then to eke out a living.

Herewood made sure the area between the castle and the village remained clear and unoccupied so as not to impair defense of the castle. People starting coming to Herewood to arbitrate disputes and his common sense approach and fairness gained respect.

The remaining tenants had started working the land. They trusted help was coming. Repairs to barns and homes were started. Things were turning around.

The news of Shadow's pending arrival spread quickly. There was much celebration when the column reached the castle. The new residents stopped and camped at the outskirts of the village.

Herewood was waiting in the courtyard when Shadow rode in. The men embraced.

Herewood spoke first. "It is so good to see you, my Lord. Your arrival is timely, for some farmers are waiting for the goods you brought."

Shadow laughed, "That is all I have become, a bearer of goods."

Shadow ordered the men to dismount and dismissed them. He accepted Herewood's invitation for a tour of the castle and to be shown to his quarters. Shadow was impressed with the way Herewood had ordered the castle. After putting his gear in his quarters, Shadow accompanied Herewood to the village. They were greeted warmly by the residents. Many of the people expressed their happiness with the changes and since Shadow had arrived on market day, he had the opportunity to walk amongst the vendors. He could not get over the changes since the last time he had been here.

Herewood had recruited four new trainees and two seasoned men since Shadow had been there. Shadow met the men and watched some of the training that was taking place. Sergeant Skjold was putting them through spear practice. All of his troops trained five times a week as part of their regular routine. As a soldier first, the garrison commander wanted to make sure his troops were battle ready at all times. There had been dozens of sets of armor at the castle, some of which Wolf had left, and by sorting through it Herewood had fitted all the new men. The only things he ordered new were the distinctive capes and uniforms. He gave the accounting to Shadow who was impressed with Herewood's management. The castle had even started to receive income from the market tax and the small court fees Herewood charged to arbitrate disputes. There were also fines that were levied on troublemakers.

Shadow took the opportunity of his visit to distribute the gifts of coin to the men who had been a part of Wolf's claiming of his inheritance. The men were surprised and happy at the windfall.

The new settlers were allocated land, the goods brought by Shadow distributed as would be most beneficial, and a late spring planting went ahead smoothly. Life was settling into a pattern of hard work and peace.

Bishop Gimm had been dismayed when he heard of the defeat of Vilhelm and the assumption of the rule of the land by Aelle. As the days passed he received reports of Aelle's consolidation of power. He could ill afford a powerful enemy like Lord Aelle who was, to make matters worse, apparently a true Christian. He considered the matter and how to shore up his own office.

He found it strange that the young man who he had thought to have under his thumb turned out to be a threat. Well, Gimm thought, life was like that and one had to make do as best one could with what one was handed. His thoughts turned to how he could buy his way out of the present dilemma and ensure his own comfort. He weighed the risk and gain over and over. He started to make his wealth portable just in case.

It had been a grievous error to allow Lady Ethelind's servants to basically keep her under house arrest, that much was now clear. He had received a letter demanding they be released to the custody of Lady Ethelind. Bishop Gimm did not want to face Aelle's men-at-arms, so he immediately sent a letter saying as now the land was safe for travel he would send the servants to her forthwith. He expressed regret for the delay but proclaimed deep concern for their safety. The day after the letter was dispatched the servants were released but they did not go to Ethelind. They headed out of Aelle's lands.

He heard that the upstart priest Brother Aert had started to build a church in Vilhelm's lands. He sent a scathing letter demanding to know what right Aert had to undertake such work without the bishop's permission. The use of money given to the church was properly administered by the bishop's office. He ordered that the work cease and that Aert report to him and bring any money donated for the building of churches.

There was no response from Aert, but within a week Bishop Gimm received a letter by rider summoning him. Somehow his superiors had apparently learned of his propensity for sins of the flesh, greed, and that he was impeding missionary work. He was being called to come to account for his alleged sins.

In the past he had balanced the power of his church superiors and

Lord Vilhelm against each other. His church superiors had been well aware of Vilhelm's true beliefs, and saw the survival of the church in the lands ruled by and near Vilhelm's as a delicate balance. It was a balance Gimm had controlled, so his superiors had tolerated him. Gimm had been useful to Vilhelm's ambitions and Vilhelm's bribes had been generous. Gimm's services were no longer needed for balance with the Christian Lord Aelle ruling. Gimm had some time before he had to appear before the council reviewing his conduct.

After much thought, Gimm decided that the wisest course of action was to leave. He had lost the gamble, but he was rich and could live out his life in comfort elsewhere. He gathered his riches and simply left one night with his body guards.

Gimm had not been aware that the charges against him were more about his impeding the true work of spreading the gospel and thus growing the churches than his propensity for sin. In spite of Gimm's efforts to the contrary, the matter of the lack of churches in the valley and outside of it had been solved in a most practical manner. Wooden structures, basically large barns, were erected at barn raisings with the cost of materials borne by the ruling family; Wolf's family. Wolf just considered it his family's tithing of the wealth that had been added to their fortune. The people did the manual work on Sundays. The carpenters and masons were hired to work full time to finish the insides and to construct hearths for keeping the churches warm in winter. The carpenters constructed rough benches.

The resulting structures were functional and affordable. Each church was of exactly of the same construction although the interior finishes differed depending on the carpenter doing the work and the materials available. Two small rooms were attached to each church behind the hearth to house priests. The warmth from the hearth would keep the rooms warm in winter and serve for cooking of the priest's meals.

Once five churches were built in the valley and one in Wolf's paternal lands, the next step would be to staff them. The castle chapel had been repaired and the four priests at the castle were more than were needed to do the clerical work required at the castle. There were many priests at the Cathedral, some of whom were actually true men of God. They would make very good parish priests, but Bishop Gimm was an impediment to their reassignment, so Grimm had to be removed.

Reports started to filter to the highest ecclesiastical circles of the churches being built in Aelle's lands. The stories of the Christian influence of Aert on the people of the valley and his ministry to the ruling family started to circulate. The building of the first church in Aelle's paternal lands was circulated as a story of a great missionary accomplishment, which it was. It was the first church in a formerly pagan holding and the church had been needed to serve the people that had newly settled. Aert had sent the best of the priest's from the castle to temporarily be pastor there.

At the same time, reports of the letter Bishop Gimm sent to Aert became well known. Reports of the bishop's malfeasance also started to be sent by various priests and lay people. All of the reports were true, but Gimm's reputation and influence had previously suppressed them. Once it was apparent his power was waning, the flood gates were opened.

This had resulted in the letter calling Gimm to come before the ecclesiastical court, but instead he had fled.

Wolf received the report of Gimm's flight which was brought by a rider who had come on his own imitative and on a plow horse. The man was well rewarded and taken care of. Wolf called for the assembling of a dozen mounted men-at-arms provisioned for two days. Within a half hour of the rider's arrival the patrol left.

Bishop Gimm was feeling smug for his party was only a short distance from leaving the lands of Aelle. His party had made reasonably good time given the speed with which the wagons moved. Liking his creature comforts, the party had camped early each evening and departed late each morning. The patrol in pursuit had cut across country and ridden long, ate in the saddle, slept only briefly, and departed before sunrise. It was not the first time they had done so.

Bishop Gimm's carriage came to a sudden halt and he yelled at the driver, "What is the delay?"

The driver replied, "Armed men, Your Grace."

Bishop Gimm alighted from his carriage and walked toward the front of his body guard, Gimm was demanding, "Who is holding up my progress? Who dares?" He became silent as he came to the front and saw who was blocking his way. In front of him were thirty mounted men-at-arms and then the realization hit him. It was Wolf.

Gimm took a commanding posture, "Stand aside. You have no right to detain me or my party."

Wolf removed his helmet and smiled, "You are indeed correct, Excellency." The tone was sarcastic. "But neither do you have the right to steal the property of the church in my realm."

Gimm was angered, "This property is mine not the church's!"

Wolf kept smiling, "And how does an honest clergyman, with no inheritance, from a poor farm family, come to have such a treasure if he did not steal it from mother church or others?"

Gimm turned to the head of his body guard, "You have more men than he, attack!"

The leader of the guard hesitated for just a moment, taken aback by the order, and then Wolf started laughing. It was not a chuckle but a full out belly laugh, through which he forced the words, "This man is no fool. He and his men would be like lambs to the slaughter and in the chaos I could not even assure your safety, Bishop."

It was then Gimm understood the threat to his life was real.

Wolf now commanded the bodyguard's leader, "Tell your men to ride away now and leave my lands."

The leader of the guard motioned his men and they rode off. Bishop Gimm was left standing alone in the road. Wolf continued, "You are free to leave Bishop with your driver and your carriage, but the goods of the church remain." He motioned at the wagons, "You drivers turn your wagons around and return to the Cathedral."

Gimm made one last attempt, "My personal baggage, surely ...", but he could not finish for Wolf interrupted him.

"Leave now with what is in your carriage before I lose my temper." He motioned his men and they rode forward forming in column of two.

The bishop stood in the middle of the road tears of frustration flowing from his face as the men-at-arms rode to either side of him. He scarcely had enough gold coin on his person to keep him modestly in food and drink for two or three years. It was certainly not enough to buy another office. He mounted his carriage and left.

He had no other choice. His career was in ruins and his fortune gone. What was he to do?

Wolf ensured the cargo was guarded day and night on the trip to the Cathedral. The bishop's wagon train had been well provisioned so the company camped that night and ate a hot meal at dark. At sunrise they were readying to eat and move out. It took two full days and part of a third, to travel to the Cathedral; the draft horses were tired. As Wolf and his troop rode into town the people came out to greet their lord and his men.

The troop entered the gate to the Bishop's residence and Wolf called out the priests into the courtyard and shut the gates to hide the unloading from prying eyes. Wolf had the goods removed from the wagons and everything inventoried. The expensive furniture was returned to the Bishop's residence from where it had been taken. The silver chalices and plates were taken and locked away. Some of the items bore the crest of Wolf's paternal family. The priests made notes of this on the inventories and turned the items over to Wolf who signed a receipt in acknowledgement. The items were obviously stolen for no one in the church would want to speculate they had been part of bribes.

Wolf's men rested overnight in the Bishop's residence. The next morning Wolf called the priests together and they shared morning service and then ate a hearty breakfast together. Wolf had met most of the priests and knew which ones truly sought to be pious and could be trusted. Those he asked to stay and the rest he sent away to wait elsewhere.

"Who is senior here?"

The jolly older priest stepped forward, "I am."

Wolf tilted his head.

The priest only bowed slightly and said, "Things are not always as they appear, Lord. You should know that better than most."

Wolf laughed, because he knew then that both he and the priest had played their roles as necessary when he had been a visitor here.

"Brother Kenric, when I was in your care, I did not realize your authority here. May I suggest that the brothers not present be bundled up and sent away to a place as you see fit so they do not hamper the true work of the church which is the saving of souls?"

Kenric roared with laughter then said, "Well put, Sire, but what about the good Bishop?"

Wolf shrugged, "It appears his misdeeds have been found out and he is fleeing justice. I do not think you need make allowance for him for I understand he was called to appear before an ecclesiastical court but chose to flee instead. I imagine he is outside my jurisdiction now. I fully expect a new bishop to be appointed soon and it is my hope he will be a true saintly man. Perhaps in the meantime, you can manage without a bishop if I leave some men to guard the Cathedral?"

Kenric smiled, "Certainly, sir. Would you care to rest up another day and be our guest for supper? I think perhaps we have much to discuss."

Wolf nodded, "Indeed we do my brother, indeed we do."

*****

The harvest was bountiful, the river trade lucrative, and the land peaceful. After just two growing seasons, Wolf's holdings could support seventy full time men-at-arms and twenty full time archers with another thirty in the part-time reserve force. It was a strong standing company.

In addition, there were helmets, shields, leather breastplates, and spears for the young men of his lands should all-out war break out. Some training for war was also being given to the men of the land by Wolf's troops during the winter months.

After some time it came to pass that a bishop was appointed for the lands of Lord Aelle. The bishop was pleasing to Aelle. The church leaders felt certain that the new Bishop would be a good influence on the young ruler Aelle and that the church in those lands would flourish as a result.

So it came about that the Bishop Aert was to be invested at the Cathedral with great pomp and ceremony. Nobles came from the surrounding lands and for the first time, Aelle was to meet his peers.

Wolf's grandfather and mother tried with all their persuasion to have Wolf dress in the latest fashion. He knew they were hip deep in potential matchmaking, but Wolf insisted on wearing his uniform. Finally as a compromise, he agreed to have a uniform made of the finest cloth and embroidered with his coats of arms and the cross. He also agreed to wear a ceremonial sword with a silver scabbard as a sign of his rank. His family thought it a ceremonial sword, but Wolf ever the soldier, made sure it was fully functional and it was just the guard and scabbard that appeared ceremonial. The hilt, though of twisted silver braid provided a solid grip and the blade was of finest steel. The hilt guard appeared decorative but underlying the silver braided cord lay hard steel. The scabbard that carried the deadly blade was pure show and would be quickly damaged on a battlefield, but then it was not intended for the battlefield. On the surface the sword appeared to be a rich decoration and symbol of rank, but appearances can be deceiving.

The investiture ceremony was a great deal of pomp and circumstance; really an opportunity for the church leaders to have a regal display of religious authority. After the ceremony there would be a feast at the bishop's residence. The following day there would be games at which the young men would compete for prizes. Wolf was host and he had arranged a feast to impress. There would be noble rulers from a dozen other families visiting with their entourages.

Wolf and his family travelled to the Cathedral while Shadow stayed at the valley castle. Three dozen men at arms and ten archers travelled with Wolf and his family. It was an impressive display for few families could afford such a show of strength.

Wolf and his family would be staying at the Bishop's residence. As Wolf's family approached the town they saw large colorful tents forming camps encircling the town. Wolf turned to his mother and grandfather, "What say you we put on a show and gallop into town with banners flying?"

His mother and grandfather looked at each other and smiled. The company started at the gallop and sped down the road. It made for a striking image as the armored men rode into and through town to the cheers of the town folk. Those nobles who were encamped or visiting the town were left with no doubt who had just arrived.

The company rode into the bishop's residence and Aert came out with Kenric to greet them. Wolf dismissed the company and after greeting and embraces, his mother and grandfather went inside. Aert noticed Wolf hanging back examining the front shoe of his horse.

"Is something the matter, my friend?"

Wolf nodded, "I need to take my mount to have this looked at. I will be back directly." Wolf added playfully, "Please excuse me, Excellency."

Aert gave an equally playful wave of dismissal, "Of course, Lord."

They both laughed and Wolf set off for the ferrier. There were many new faces among the many visitors in the Town. He was in his mail and uniform and dusty from the journey so no one paid him any attention.

Wolf was strolling along when he bumped into a young woman who stepped into his path.

Wolf bowed and said, "Excuse me."

The young woman gave him a look of disgust. "Certainly not. You need to be taught some manners. Men-at-arms should be on watch for their betters. If your master was here I would tell him of the manners of his men."

Wolf smiled, "I am sure he knows, my lady." The young woman huffed, stuck her head in the air, and marched off.

Another woman, slightly older had been trailing the young woman. She said, "You will have to excuse my little sister; she is full of herself, a fault I hope she will overcome with time. That was rude of her for the fault was clearly hers. If she causes you trouble with your lord, please tell him Lady Cenedred will attest the fault is not yours."

Wolf smiled, "That is kind of you, my Lady."

Cenedred smiled and walked on. Wolf thought about the encounter. The younger woman was a true physical beauty to behold, but with a character as ugly as a horn toad. Now Cenedred was not the beauty her younger sister was, but nonetheless attractive. Cenedred's character was altogether pleasing and kind. Wolf put the thought out of his mind and took his horse to be cared for.

On the walk back to the bishop's residence someone from the town recognized him and bowed saying, "Lord." Wolf engaged the man in conversation for a few moments and then went on his way. It was then he noticed Cenedred had witnessed the exchange. He smiled and nodded to her. To his amazement, she blushed.

His mother and grandfather, to Wolf's chagrin, had arranged an evening meal with the nobles who had marriageable daughters thus a third of the families came. Wolf knew there was a time to yield and a time to fight and this was one of those times it was not worth the battle. He cleaned himself up and put on his 'dandy uniform' as he called it, and with his mother between him and his grandfather, went to the hall.

Aert had given Wolf a crash course on how a noble gentlemen should interact with "princes of the church" in order to give them respect without subservience. Wolf charmed them and his mother and grandfather seemed pleased with his performance. Introductions were made.

Wolf had met several families before being introduced to Lord Eadgard, his wife Hilde and his two daughters, Ava and Cenedred. Ava pretended she did not recognize Wolf when he was introduced as His Lord Aelle, also known as the great warrior Lord Wolf.

Cenedred on the other hand smiled and said she had met Aelle that afternoon in Town, to which her sister told her she must be mistaken.

The dinner was pleasant and the conversation boring. Wolf found himself the center of inane questions from any number of young women who obviously did not either have a brain or know how to use the one God had given them. When an opportunity presented itself, Wolf slipped outside and leaned against the stone railing.

He saw movement in the shadows. "Do you always lurk in the shadows?"

Cenedred walked into the light and stood beside him. "Sometimes one just needs to have room to breathe, Lord."

Wolf nodded.

Cenedred spoke candidly, "I watched you in there. You are very accomplished. I would have thought you much older than your eighteen years. If half the stories about you are true, you are quite talented."

Wolf inquired, "What do the stories say?"

"That you are an accomplished warrior and conqueror of many women."

Wolf laughed. "I am but a virgin warrior."

Cenedred seemed surprised, "Really?"

"Yes and I will go to my marriage bed that way as I expect my bride to?"

Cenedred asked simply, "Why?"

Wolf's answer was without hesitation. "The epistle to the Galatians tells us that those who practice fornication and adultery will not inherit the kingdom of God. What would it profit me to gain the entire world but lose my eternal soul? Besides, since a man and his wife become one flesh, a husband should not want another woman to be part of that union."

Cenedred said nothing for a few moments. "It is true then that you are a good Christian."

Wolf shook his head, "No one is good but God. Scripture tells us that. I am but a sinner turned saint by grace and that not of my own doing, but it is a gift from God, so I cannot boast."

Cenedred smiled, "So serious for such a young man."

"God is a serious business."

"Yes, but we are to have joy in Christ our Lord," and with that she turned on her heel and went back into the dining hall. She left Wolf in wonderment; a woman who knew scripture? Is it possible she could read and was learned?

The next morning the pageantry of the investiture was something to see and many came to watch. Aert was held in high esteem by the people of the land and when the ceremony was finished there was much cheering.

At the noon meal, Wolf's mother imposed on him to advise she had invited guests to the castle. They were the nobles who ruled the lands to the north and Lord Eadgard was bringing his wife and daughters. His mother hoped Wolf would find some time at the feast this evening to talk to the family. Wolf agreed to talk with them, but what he really wanted was to find out more about Cenedred.

The banquet hall was filled with the noises of celebration and congratulations. Aelle had only a moment with the new bishop in which he took the opportunity to congratulate him. The church officials came to Aelle to discuss church work. Aelle expressed his pleasure with the new bishop, and his hope that the bishop would not be too busy to continue to be his spiritual advisor as well as his partner and mentor in spreading churches and winning souls for Christ. In this Aelle was sincere and the churchmen assured him it would be so.

Aelle initiated the deal when he said he supposed he would now have to station men here to protect the Cathedral. The problem was, he noted, that there was no castle. The closest thing was the walled in Bishop's residence, the stone one the Romans had built that sat atop the hill.

The churchmen suggested that a residence could be built near the Cathedral and the existing residence turned into a fortress. Aelle supposed another residence could be built closer to the Cathedral and he supposed he could grant more land to the church to do so. In truth, Aelle needed to post men here because it was midway between the two castles and was a natural defensive lynch pin.

Bishop Aert was called to participate in the discussion, and he advised Wolf that the suggestion made sense both for the expansion of the Church and the protection of the citizens. The churchmen inquired if the property on which the new churches had been built could be transferred to the church. Wolf had prayed to be eventually shed of the cost of continued maintenance of the churches, but this was sooner than he could have hoped.

Aert talked to Aelle in support of the idea of the fortress, the new residence and the church taking ownership of the churches. Aert and Aelle had already discussed the mutual needs. The church officials saw it as a sign of the great influence of Aert when Aelle agreed to provide land to build a residence suitable for the Bishop, grant the land the five churches were on to the church and accept in return the existing Bishop's residence to fortify at his own expense. It had taken less than ten minutes for the dealing to be done. The documents would be drawn and executed before the parties left.

Aelle started circulating and made for Eadgard to introduce himself. He walked up to the man and did so, and before he knew it his youngest daughter Ava had attached herself to his arm. Ava just stood there like some decoration while Eadgard and Aelle talked.

"I hear you have had good crops in your lands, Aelle?" Eadgard inquired.

"Yes we have been blessed. God has seen fit to bless us with abundance and good fortune."

Eadgard smiled, "God blesses those who work hard, rule well, and give Him glory."

"That is true Eadgard. And you have been blessed also with fine daughters. Your lands are prosperous so you too have worked hard, ruled well, and given God the glory." The plural was not lost on Eadgard who smiled and nodded.

Eadgard spoke to his daughter, "Ava dear, would you be so kind as to leave us to discuss man things."

"Yes, daddy," was all she said and was off like a butterfly in a garden full of beautiful flowers to investigate.

Eadgard asked, "You are not upset with your mother inviting us without your approval, for she admitted she had done so."

"I am not upset. My mother is a wise woman and she knows that I will not be forced into a marriage I am not agreeable to. She also knows she has not raised a fool. Eadgard you have ruled your land longer than I have lived. You are smart and you have prospered by your wits. You have inquired after my deeds and my character. I know this as surely as you know me by the reports of your spies and I have done the same." Wolf paused before continuing.

"There is gain for both our families in a good marriage. But for me, marriage is a sacred bond and I will not be made one flesh with a woman without substance. I wish you to come and visit with us. I tell you directly I am not interested in Ava, but Cenedred is another matter. I will consider her if she will consent to consider me. Only by mutual agreement between us will there be marriage."

Eadgard nodded. "I will ask Cenedred. You do realize that she is twenty and you are but eighteen?"

Wolf smiled, "Now two years may seem substantial, but in time surrounded by children and grandchildren it would seem as nothing, assuming we marry and live that long."

Eadgard smiled, "Good enough. Let us go to the banquet table, they are getting ready to serve the meal."

Eadgard was a good judge of character and this young ruler was everything the reports had stated. He was more impressive in person. It was hard to accept he was only eighteen.

Eadgard and Aelle sat next to each other, and Cenedred sat to Aelle's right and Eadgard's wife Hilde to his left. It messed up the seating arrangement, but no one challenged the two lords. The two men, in spite of the difference in their ages, got along well. Hilde spoke mainly to the lady to her left and Cenedred spoke little.

When the meal was finished, Cenedred leaned across toward her father and asked, "Father would it be permitted to step outside for a breath of fresh air."

Eadgard asked Aelle, "Would you accompany her?"

"My pleasure."

The two young people stepped outside and stood again at the stone rail. "What is afoot? Why am I sitting next to you instead of Ava? It was my father's intent to arrange marriage with her."

"You are sitting beside me because I told your father I was not in the least interested in Ava." Wolf turned at looked at Cenedred, "But you, now that is a different matter. I told your father I was definitely interested. Do not worry, we may find we are not suited, though I doubt that is likely. There will be no arranged marriage unless you and I arrange it."

Cenedred was blushing. Aelle could see it even in the semi-darkness. She put her arm through his. They started to walk without thinking as he spoke. "There would be advantage to our families in our marriage. But I am not going to become one flesh if it is unlikely we are suited to spend our lives together. Your visit to my family castle will allow us and our families' time to get to know each other."

Wolf froze. Cenedred let out a scream as Wolf pushed her to the ground hard. She saw the flash of steel.

Two men came rushing out of the dark swords drawn. One hardly had time to realize he had been gutted before he fell and the other almost lost his balance pivoting to face the attack that he expected to come from where his partner fell, but it was now Wolf, not Aelle that the man faced. Wolf had reversed back to where he started and his blade almost decapitated the second attacker. The two men lay bloodied and dead on the ground. Cenedred was getting to her feet as men with torches came running. Wolf wiped his blade clean on one of the men's cloak and sheathed his sword.

Cenedred took Wolf's arm, "You are an entirely dangerous man."

Wolf smiled, "Not to you my dear Cenedred, not to you."

Eadgard arrived with the torch men, his sword drawn. Wolf simply said, "Assassins. It appears someone has not taken kindly to the prospect of our families being united."

Cenedred looked at her father, "They were not just stories father; they did not have a chance. They were dead as soon as they attacked. He is that good!" There was just a hint of pride in her voice.

The bodies were taken away. Wolf did not recognize them, nor did anyone else. Wolf expected that Bishop Aert would do some investigating.

Wolf walked Cenedred back to the hall. Security was tightened that evening. There were extra guards and extra vigilance.

The next morning Wolf and Aert had an early breakfast together with the visiting clergy and documents were signed. After breakfast, the visitors left for they had a long journey.

The new bishop advised Wolf he had decided Kenric was to replace a certain abbot who was to be retired. On a related matter, a part of the treasure recovered from Gimm was to be used to repair the Abbey and the shrine from which a portion came. The pair speculated who was the culprit that hired the assassins. The list included: one of Eadgard's enemy's Lord Sievert; Gimm; Staffan; and the brothers Ulrich and Ragnar. The problem was the last four probably did not have the money to hire assassins. Wolf would talk with Eadgard.

Acrt had a proposal for which he asked Wolf's approval and help. The bishop wanted his lord's permission to train warrior priests, soldiers of Jesus like himself to protect church lands. Wolf agreed on condition that they would be subject to Aert's commitment to Wolf's family also; they would be required to make an oath.

By mid-morning Eadgard's group had broken camp and was ready to join Wolf's company. Wolf's company was coming down the road just as Eadgard's group had finished departure preparations. As always when travelling with his men, Wolf was in mail, though he was not wearing his helmet which was on his saddle horn.

Wolf halted the company on the road and came to meet Eadgard.

Eadgard greeted Wolf, "Good morning Aelle, or should I call you Wolf?"

"Wolf. That is what my friends call me and I hope we will be friends."

Eadgard looked at his group, "How do you want to do this?"

"I suggest you and I ride in front, then my mother and your wife, then my grandfather and Cenedred, then Ava and my sergeant. We could ride in column of twos, your men on the right and mine on the left, with the balance of mine following, then the baggage wagons."

Eadgard nodded, "Let's do it."

The combined column started out. Wolf and Eadgard discussed who might have hired the assassins. Eadgard thought it might be his neighbor, Lord Sievert, who though not strong enough to challenge him directly, knew he had no heirs, and would like to keep it that way. Sievert would like to destabilize Eadgard's rule if he could do it indirectly. The prospect of an alliance between Eadgard and Wolf would be a direct threat to his ambitions. Eadgard felt this was the most likely source of the threat.

Eadgard said his neighbors held themselves out to be Christians, but their actions betrayed their proclamations. Eadgard, like Wolf, looked at what people did rather than what they said. People who practiced thievery, all sorts of immorality, and were involved in occult practices were definitely not Christians.

Wolf was thoughtful. He told Eadgard that he had no ambitions to expand his rule. The lands he had were sufficient to provide a good living for his people and his family. It was also relatively easy to defend.

Eadgard considered this, "Yes, but sometimes God calls us to do that which we would rather not."

Wolf had studied enough scripture to know the truth of the statement. "If it is God's will that will be revealed in time. In the meantime, let us enjoy becoming friends and perhaps allies."

Eadgard smiled, "Or even family."

Wolf laughed.

During the ride Eadgard suggested that riding partners be changed so everyone could have a chance to become acquainted. Wolf suddenly found himself riding beside Cenedred. He smiled looking back at his mother and Eadgard and turned to Cenedred. "Do you get the idea our parents are matchmaking?"

Cenedred laughed, "It is rather obvious isn't it? My poor sister Ava is pouting. She is not used to not being the center of attention."

Wolf smiled, "Perhaps we can do some matchmaking of our own. Surely it should not be too hard to find men interested in a fourteen year old beauty."

"As opposed to an old woman like me?" Cenedred quipped.

Wolf looked at her with interest, "Are you trying to bait me or fishing for a complement. If it is the latter you have no need to go fishing for you would make any man of substance take note."

"Well thank you, kind sir," Cenedred said with a slight blush, "but I was teasing you, but alas you are entirely too evasive for me."

"Oh forbid. You I do not want to elude."

Cenedred smiled, "Good."

Wolf asked Cenedred about her home and her family. It seemed that her family's lands were productive farmlands and there was good timber in the hills. The people were mainly Christians though in the north some of the people held to the old pagan gods. The priests were trying to bring Christianity to them but were meeting with resistance and some missionaries had disappeared.

The lands to the north were ruled by the family of Lord Sievert who did not follow the Christ. They had tried to buy Eadgard's daughters in marriage and professed to be Christian so their family could marry into the inheritance of her father's lands. Her father had spied on them and knew they followed pagan gods and rejected them. He would not have his daughters unequally yoked.

Cenedred spoke freely about the strengths of her land and confessed their family's biggest weakness was the lack of a male heir. Her only brother and his two bodyguards had allegedly been killed by bandits when in the north. Eadgard almost went to war over the matter, but at the time his land had been weakened by a war he had won, but at a substantial cost.

Eadgard thought Sievert was behind his son's death. The people in the north had hung three men who they claimed were responsible. Eadgard felt sure those men were innocent scapegoats. The men he had sent with his son were formidable and it was unlikely three men could have even begun to overcome them, even with surprise. Her family was certain that if the natural barrier between her father's lands and those of Lord Sievert did not exist, the people in the far north of her father's lands would join their pagan neighbors in rising up against her father.

Cenedred asked, "What would you do about the people in the north if the land was under your rule."

Wolf considered. "It's a hard question with a hard answer. From what you say, they are a sore on your lands and a knife at your throats. I would tell them their leases were not being renewed and give them until after the crops are harvested to leave the hold."

"What if they did not want to leave?" Cenedred inquired.

Wolf replied seriously, "It would not be a request."

"What if they burned the homes and barns before they left?"

"It would be difficult for them to do with men-at-arms in the area, especially if they wanted to leave with any of their shares of the crops and any possessions."

"What if they had the support of outsiders?" Cenedred asked.

Wolf understood what she was really asking, "It is my experience that ambitious lords do not start wars they know they will lose. They just need to be faced with a force that is formidable; better still if it is overwhelming. The ambitious usually count the cost and risk against the potential gain."

Cenedred said, "You really are wise beyond your years, sort of a modern Solomon."

Wolf asked, "You know scripture?"

Cenedred smiled, "I really struggle. It was difficult for me to persuade a priest to teach me, a woman, to read, but money talks. Once I learned, I tried to get him to teach me Latin. For a price, he agreed. No one knows I acquired a copy of some of the Old Testament writings and all of the gospels. I do not have any of the epistles. I really struggle to read and understand what I do have. It is very slow going, a snail's pace, but what else does an unmarried woman have to do? Do you read Latin?"

Wolf nodded, "At one time I was studying with priests. I was fortunate enough to have a good teacher in my mother's priest. He disappeared; probably a victim of my father's treachery."

Wolf heard a horse coming up beside them. He heard his mother's voice.

"My dear son, do you mind if I borrow Cenedred for a while? We have not really had time to talk."

Wolf said, "Yes I mind, but I suppose she will go off with you anyway."

Lady Ethelind laughed, "So perceptive, my dear son. You will make some lucky woman a good husband."

Wolf found himself riding beside his grandfather who asked, "I suppose, Wolf, they have been testing you? Have you learned anything?"

"The answers grandfather are yes and yes. Cenedred seems very bright and seems to have as much knowledge of her father's lands and affairs as a son would."

Cuthbert agreed, "Indeed. She is a very unusual young woman. She could be either a blessing or a curse, depending on the character of the man she became wife to."

Wolf asked, "Which to you think she would be to me?"

"A blessing."

That was all Cuthbert said and they rode along for some time lost in their own thoughts. The two of them were comfortable with each other and often did not feel the need to make small talk; being together was enough.

They rode past well-kept fields and were greeted warmly by their subjects. Women would come to the road with fresh water and the younger women brought flowers for the men-at-arms for it was known that most of them were still single.

That evening they set up camp early. Wolf chose a spot that was defensible. He not only placed sentries but sent out roving patrols. The attack by the two assassins had left a bad taste in his mouth. He felt uneasy.

The families had an enjoyable meal and pleasant conversation. Wolf excused himself and left the fire circle to visit the sentries. He had an uneasy feeling and had learned to trust his instincts. He doubled the guard and brought in the patrols. He stationed half of the archers and men-at-arms under cover, ready to put up an immediate defense. He told his men to appear to take off their mail but in the dark to put it back on and sleep in it. He would do the same.

After a while, Wolf's mother came to his tent with Cuthbert. She made inquiries as to what Wolf had learned about Eadgard's lands and family. Wolf told his mother and grandfather what he had learned. What they had been told matched the reports they had received. They agreed they felt comfortable going forward.

Wolf saw his mother back to her tent. He was unusually tense. His instincts told him something was not right. The attack came in the early morning. The first riders went down as their horses collapsed under a flurry of arrows. Those following were met by fully armored men-at-arms and the attack faltered.

Instantly, Wolf and four of his men rushed into the attackers. The first man was pulled from his mount by Wolf and was slain before he could raise his shield. The battle mind was now upon Wolf and more of his men were engaging the attackers. Wolf fought with a natural instinct that only great warrior leaders possess. He had killed three opponents before the enemy retreated in full flight. He recognized one of the fleeing attackers – Ulrich!

Eadgard and his men had armed and come to the fight as it was close to ending. Wolf called for his company to reestablish line which they did swiftly and smoothly. The circle around the camp had held. It had not been penetrated. The engagement had lasted only two or three minutes, but dead or wounded attackers and mounts lay everywhere. He took roll, and only one of his men had been significantly wounded. Eadgard's healer was tending to him. One of Eadgard's men had been killed.

Wolf sent two men to check that everyone in the camp was alright. The reports were positive. Eadgard came to him.

"How did you know?" he asked.

Wolf his sword still drawn, covered in blood, shrugged, "Instinct and a suspicious mind. If we were to be attacked again it should be tonight, for tomorrow we will be where attack would be more difficult, perhaps suicidal."

Eadgard added, "It appears the attack tonight was almost suicidal for the attackers."

Wolf shook his head, "It would have been a close thing if we had not been ready. There must have been over forty of them. One of the attackers was my half-brother Ulrich who fled when I slew my father. How he could gather such a force is beyond me."

Eadgard became serious, "He didn't. I recognized one of Sievert's sons amongst the attackers. It seems our enemies have thrown their lots together."

Wolf said ominously, "In that they have made a grave error." Wolf went and wiped his sword clean on a dead horse's saddle blanket.

Some of Wolf's men went among the attackers, stripping bodies and gathering the wounded. Lame and badly wounded horses were put out of their misery. When the count was completed, it was found that seventeen attackers had died in the battle. In addition, five of the attackers lived and mainly had broken bones, mostly legs, from the falling of their mounts. One had to be removed from under his horse.

The men were questioned by Wolf and Eadgard. They were mercenaries. It came out the man who had been taken out from under his mount was their captain. In return for promise of his life, he revealed he had been hired by Sievert. He said that a half dozen of Sievert's men had accompanied the attackers. Wolf found out by questioning, that Ulrich had been one of those six. It was also discovered that the assassins had been the initial threat and only if they failed were the mercenaries to attack.

Eadgard asked, "What do we do with the wounded."

Wolf pointed at them. It was an order to his men, "Hang them all but the captain, for him I have given my word he would not die at my hand. Leave him here with a horse. They came to conduct banditry and murder in my lands so their lives are forfeit. Leave their bodies for the carrion."

One of the men called out, "We are not bandits; we are soldiers!"

Wolf replied, "No Lord has declared war on my family. Has such been declared on you Lord Eadgard?"

Eadgard replied simply, "No."

"Then bandits you are,." Wolf declared and marched off.

It was nearing dawn, so the camp met. A short funeral mass was said for Eadgard's young man who had died in the battle. He was buried and a marker erected. The bandits were hung and the mercenary captain put on a nag that had been captured.

After the hangings, the group started breakfast. Cenedred ate with her father. When they finished eating she declared, "Wolf is hard when he needs to be but has a tender heart for the good. I will go to see him."

She rose and without any objection from her father went looking for him. She found him kneeling at the edge of the camp praying. She stopped some distance behind him, knelt and started praying. She was startled by his voice for she had not heard him coming.

"Ruling is hard, but God is my rock and my shield. What were you praying for?"

Cenedred looked up at him then stretched out her hand for assistance in rising. Wolf helped her up.

"I was praying for you, for all of us. Evil is about, and the prince of the air seems determined that Christian rulers should be brought down." In that statement, Cenedred had summed up their struggle.

Wolf responded, "Yes indeed, my good Cenedred." He took her arm and they walked back to the tents.

Eadgard had been watching from a short distance. He marveled at these young people. How had his daughter and this young man become wise beyond their years? His daughter Ava was a beauty that had most men stop to look at her, but she was spoiled and would need a strong man to straighten her out.

Wolf asked Eadgard to meet and inquired if Eadgard was concerned that his land might now be attacked. Eadgard said he doubted there would be any immediate danger. Sievert had committed too many men to this attack and the attackers were mainly mercenaries which would have cost Sievert dearly. Sievert's forces were not that large. Eadgard was certain his war chief could fend off any attack in the unlikely event there was one. As a precaution, a fast rider would be sent with a message to warn his castle.

The rest of the journey to the Neck was uneventful. At the Neck the party stopped while the gate was opened and then they dismounted to rest. Wolf greeted his men on guard and introductions were made. Eadgard was given a tour of the defenses and was impressed by the state of preparation. He was of the opinion that just a few men could successfully hold the pass against a large force.

Eadgard noted that Wolf interacted with his men without aloofness, yet they had a respectful deference. He assumed this meant that they liked, respected, and were somewhat in awe of theirlord. This man would be a match for his eldest daughter and an answer to his prayers and a hope for the future of his people. Now if God just arranged for the two young people to be enamored with each other.

The party continued on at a leisurely pace toward the castle, enjoying the sunny day, riding past fruitful orchards and fertile fields. People came to the lane to greet them waving and shouting greetings. The people were friendly and Wolf was happy because his people were content.

Shadow was waiting in the yard of the castle to greet the arriving company. When everyone had dismounted, the servants took over and the company was dismissed. Introductions were made all around. It seemed Ava was taken by Shadow and took a place on his arm. Shadow seemed more than a little uncomfortable with the attention and Wolf was amused at his discomfort.

The guests were shown to their quarters. Wolf then showed Eadgard around the castle and they walked to the village and drank a mug of ale. Eadgard noted the deference of the people and that Wolf was comfortable being with his subjects. They bowed slightly in acknowledgement or greeted him briefly, but they did not intrude when the two lords were talking.

That evening the families had dinner and there was merriment. It was decided that the next day the guests would be taken on a short ride in the valley if the weather was good. It rained all day and the families spent all day in the castle. After breakfast, Wolf spent a half hour in the library with Cenedred, while a priest worked in a corner copying a text. They discussed the Gospel of John and Wolf explained about the meaning of some verses Cenedred was struggling to understand. They then went to sit beside the hearth in the kitchen and talked. Throughout the day various groupings of the families informally met and talked, getting to know each other.

In the afternoon, Wolf had business to conduct and excused himself. He met individually with Beorn, Modig, and then Shadow. Trade was profitable and the family income from rents and taxes were at a record high because productivity was high and sources of income were expanding. Shadow reported the defenses were completed for the valley and the construction of the Bishop's new residence had been started. The renovations to fortify the old residence would be started when the Bishop's residence was completed and tradesmen became available. They discussed the possibility of expanding the standing military force, for as their riches and income grew so would the temptation for raiders. A strong military would deter attack.

It was agreed to recruit new men. Wolf told Shadow that as their military grew he thought Herewood and Aewel should be promoted to Captain with increase in pay so that sergeants could be promoted under them. Herewood could command the other castle and a garrison at the Cathedral. He would need a sergeant at the castle and another at the Cathedral. Shadow added that Aewel could command the main castle, the Neck, and the river defenses. He would need sergeants to assist him. It was agreed that the captains would be appointed and they would choose their own sergeants. They also agreed that Palne should be appointed sergeant of the archers.

Shadow and Wolf called the men at the castle together and announced the promotions of the captains. They also announced that the captains would be appointing sergeants and that Palne would be sergeant of archers. Congratulations were offered to the newly promoted.

At dinner Eadgard invited Wolf and Shadow to accompany him on his return and visit. Wolf suggested Shadow accompany him and said he would love to visit also, but he had much business that needed attention. Eadgard agreed. Lady Ethelind invited the daughters to stay for a time if their father permitted and assured Eadgard she and Cuthbert would take good care of them. Wolf understood it was agreed that way for Wolf's mother and grandfather were taking responsibility to see the girls were properly chaperoned. It was all agreed.

The next day was pleasant and the families accompanied by a select group of men-at-arms travelled up the valley. Wolf continued to be amused at the way Ava made Shadow uncomfortable by attaching herself to his arm every chance she got. On one such occasion Wolf glanced at Eadgard who smiled and leaned over to discreetly say to Wolf, "It seems Ava has gotten over you and found a new focus for her attention."

Wolf, not to be outdone, told Eadgard that he found it humorous to see Shadow made so uncomfortable by the young woman when towering warriors quaked at his presence.

The party ate a cold lunch outdoors by the river and visited two of the smaller villages and two churches. The visitors were introduced to the parish priests and shown the churches. It was all in all a pleasant outing.

At the evening dinner it was decided that Eadgard would return to his castle the next day accompanied by his wife and Shadow, while his daughters stayed with Ethelind and Cuthbert. After dinner, Shadow and Wolf strolled in the garden with the daughters, chaperoned by Lady Ethelind and the girls' mother Hilde. It was a thoroughly enjoyable evening. Wolf did notice that his mother was taking great delight in Shadow's discomfort with Ava. He wondered about it.

Later that evening Wolf went to the kitchen alone to get a beverage and Shadow was there. He appeared to be deep in thought. Wolf sat across from Shadow. He said nothing, waiting for Shadow to start the conversation. When Shadow finally did, what he said took Wolf by surprise.

"I am quite taken with her.," Shadow paused before continuing, "The problem is that I do not know what her father would say, but more importantly, how it would affect us."

"How so?" Wolf asked.

"Well, assuming her father was agreeable, and she was, if we married how would it affect the relationship between you and I? We could end up in a relationship that might be awkward. What would be her father's expectation if he did agree?"

Wolf chuckled and Shadow gave him a glare.

"Shadow, I would have no problem at all you being my relative, assuming it all happened the way you think. Any father should be happy to have a man of character like you as a son-in-law. You have done well and have riches. I could certainly provide you titled land. If Eadgard is reluctant because of your birth, so much the poorer a man he would be."

Shadow looked up, "Eadgard? You think I am talking about that child Ava. No, I mean your mother."

Wolf's mouth was hanging open. "My mother?"

Shadow simply replied, "Of course. Your mother and I are as close in age as you and Cenedred. Your mother is an attractive and intelligent widow, and still young enough to marry and have children."

Wolf thought for a moment, "As strange as it seems at first, it would be a good match. I would argue for you with my grandfather. I do not know if he would hold a common birth against you."

Shadow chuckled, "Penniless I might have been, but my lineage has never been common; to that your mother and grandfather can both attest.

Wolf just shrugged, "I did not know, neither did I care."

Shadow nodded, "I know; the more to your credit. It is one of the reasons the men love you. You demand nothing, earn everything, and are respected as a result." He smiled, 'I would be honored to be family and still serve you as I committed. "

Wolf smiled, "I guess we will both have to see how things progress." Wolf laughed and shook his head, "One just never knows what is going to happen next around here. God must certainly find us entertaining."

It was still early morning when Eadgard's party headed home accompanied by Shadow and a dozen of Wolf's men-at-arms and four archers. Combined with Eadgard's men, the group was an impressive size military force. The journey during that first day was uneventful and Shadow got to spend some time talking to Lady Hilde, who was altogether a pleasant and intelligent woman. Eadgard and Shadow also had the opportunity to get to know each other better.

Eadgard knew of Shadow's family, even though they were far off. Shadow had been the youngest son of a large family of brothers and a natural soldier. He had come to the aid of Lord Cuthbert's brother who had later been killed in battle.

Eadgard asked Shadow about his relationship with Wolf. Shadow told him that Wolf had been his student in many things and had now had become the teacher. He respected the young man and they had bonded together in battle and hardships. In response to Eadgard's further inquiry, Shadow told Eadgard that Wolf was wealthy. He had also saved his own family from Vilhelm and made his estates healthy again. Eadgard asked about Wolf's character. Shadow told him that Wolf was a devout Christian, loyal and honest, generous with those who served him, and loved by his people. Wolf demanded nothing, earned everything, worked as hard as those who served him, guarded his subjects' welfare, sought their prosperity, and was respected and loved as a result.

By answering the questions, Shadow had revealed much about his own character and what he valued. Eadgard had learned that because of his service with Wolf, Shadow was wealthy in his own right and Wolf had let him know that morning that Shadow held his own titled land. Shadow had worked none of this into their conversation.

Eadgard had made it his business to learn about Shadow when his youngest daughter starting showing an interest in him. He thought she might be getting serious and more than one man had succumbed to a woman's physical beauty. He had embraced the opportunity to spend time with Shadow. He knew about Wolf from first hand reports, but Shadow only from stories and rumors.

They camped well within the bounds of Wolf's lands that evening. Shadow knew this area and had no trouble identifying a good defensible campsite. The next morning the party departed and in late afternoon they had not quite left Wolf's family lands and they camped early.

Given their recent experience, Shadow had chosen another very defensible site and conferred with Eadgard who agreed they would probably not find a better site before sunset. Shadow had an uneasy feeling for he had spied a rider in the woods earlier in the day. On the chance he might have been a scout, he ordered his men to sleep in their mail and half the men stood watch at any time, though he tried to ensure that would not be apparent to watchers. There were many empty sleeping rolls around the camp plumped up with various things. Shadow did not expect a repeat attack but to not prepare would be reckless. That kind of mistake had been the downfall of many a warrior. Shadow shared his concerns with Eadgard who followed the example.

In the early morning a very quiet notice was circulated around the camp to be ready for an attack. A sentry had spotted men in the woods. Those still in their sleeping rolls remained there by the fires so as not to alert the attackers. Lord Eadgard roused his wife and moved her from the tent, moving in the shadows to where several of his men were hidden.

It was a sudden and ferocious attack. Arrows struck empty bed rolls and harmlessly struck mailed men who lay in others. The attackers were only half way across the open ground to the campsite when their horses began to collapse. The leader ordered his men-at-arms to dismount and attack on foot. Some still fell under horses as they tried to comply.

When the attackers reached the camp they found the defenders had collapsed into a shield line and the charge was broken against it as attacking warriors started falling. The men they had attacked were very skilled and experienced warriors.

In one area the attackers formed a wedge and struck for Eadgard's tent. The line did not hold there, but neither did the experienced warriors fold. They fell back and reformed. The attackers had been intent on slaying those in the tent and this had allowed the line precious moments to reform. The attackers charged again and their charge was broken.

Elsewhere Shadow and his men were holding. The man next to Shadow was plunging his spear overhand. It struck over an attackers shield and the point struck home. As the attacker fell, Shadow punched forward with his shield and thrust his sword under another's shield and twisted the sword so he could withdraw it easily. Another attacker tried to attack Shadow but tripped forward over his fallen comrade and in an instant fell to Shadow's swift blade, his guts spilling out onto the ground. The ground in front of the defenders was now slippery and the attack slowed and then the sound of retreat was called and the attackers retreated. Shadow called the men to hold. None followed after the attackers.

Shadow ordered recently appointed Sergeant Grimbold to have the men form a defense in preparation to repel another attack. Shadow turned and crossed the camp to find Lord Eadgard standing next to his wife who was receiving treatment for an arrow wound to her left arm.

Lord Eadgard was furious, "The target was the tent. They were after my family. They killed all my wife's servants. They were after my wife and daughters. They slaughtered everyone in there; treacherous dogs."

Grimbold was efficient so the report came quickly. There were twenty seven attackers dead or wounded in the field. The defenders had lost six men, two of Shadows and four of Eadgard's and two more had been wounded, and they were Shadow's men. Sergeant Ody, Eadgard's man, had estimated the attacking force had been made up of at least seventy. Shadow thanked the soldier who then turned and ran back to his position.

Shadow looked at Eadgard, "I think we had better get out of here in case they decide to attack again. It is almost daylight."

Eadgard nodded agreement, "Going back makes more sense than pushing on. I will send a fast rider to warn the castle and to pull in my people. We do not know which way they will go."

Shadow agreed, "Good. I will send a fast rider to Wolf. They may think they have killed your family and that may buy us time. We will make it seem we are travelling with your family's bodies. We will put your wife in mail so she can ride with the other wounded in the middle of the company. We usually have a wounded man ride beside a healthy one. I suggest you put one of your best men next to your wife and two behind her. She cannot be seen to receive favorable treatment.

We can wrap the female bodies in blankets and tie them over the horses so the attackers will think they killed your daughters and wife. We will put our dead over horses the same way."

Eadgard considered, "Good plan. It may buy us time." Eadgard turned to Ody and said, "Make it happen before the sun rises. We leave as soon as we can. Burn the baggage carts. Horses only for we will travel hard overland."

When the preparations were completed the party stood beside their horses for a moment and prayed in thanksgiving for their deliverance and victory. They also prayed for their safe return and the safety of their people. They then mounted up and set out.

In the attacker's camp Ulrich was strutting around like a fighting cock. "We did it. We got the whole family."

Sievert's captain Uno was not happy. "At what price? We lost more than a third of our force whose bodies still are lying out there in a field. I have a dozen more wounded men being doctored. It was an expensive victory."

"Yes, but Eadgard's family is dead, and as our allies strike unexpectedly allowing us to move south to plunder. Soon this land will be yours and I will reclaim my rightful inheritance."

Uno shook his head, "We cannot afford any more victories like the last one. In the morning we move to strike at the cathedral. That may divert Wolf's attention from the main attack."

The fast rider came to Cuthbert's castle. His horse was lathered and its wind almost broken. One horse had already been discarded at a farm along the way. Wolf knew it was trouble when he was told there was a signal fire from the neck and a fast rider coming.

He was shocked by the message. His orders were given quickly. He called his captain. "Aewel call out all the reserves. Our land has been attacked. I want the river defenses alerted and fully manned and guarded. I want a full garrison at the Neck. Garrison the castle with one of the sergeants and half dozen regulars and some reserves. I want the balance of the men, regular and reserves, summoned and ready to march by mid-day. Tell the priests to start prayer vigils. Send scouts up the valley just in case some few attackers attempt to climb down along the streams and cause havoc in our rear. We need to know if a blocking force should be sent."

Wolf called for one of the priests and told him, "Send an urgent message to Bishop Aert. Tell him to evacuate the town and take all his people and valuables to Herewood. The cathedral town fortification is not done so the few men we have there will escort the bishop. Ask the bishop to send a return message as soon as he has left the town.

Send a message to Herewood; tell him to prepare for an attack. It may come from the opposite direction but we are not certain. Tell him I will come to reinforce him soon. In the meantime, tell him to hold. Tell him to send me a message if enemy movements are scouted."

Wolf called the family together and explained what had happened. He assured the girls that although their mother was wounded, she was returning to the castle alive and well. He told them what to expect. Cuthbert agreed to oversee the defense of the castle if it should come to that. Wolf would leave one of the capable sergeants to help.

Wilfred was called by Cuthbert, he had prepared for this before. He received his marching orders and immediately went to start preparing in case of a siege.

Wolf called for Beorn and told him to commandeer every craft at the docks, off load any cargo, and prepare to embark troops, provisions and weapons.

By the time Shadow was approaching the Neck he met reserves straggling along with the people flowing through the Neck to sanctuary in the valley. Shadow knew that the people would retreat to one of the castles for protection, whichever was closer. At present, the people were orderly and calm.

Shadow suggested Eadgard go on with the wounded and take the party through the field path and told him which of the men knew the way. He told Eadgard he would be along directly. Shadow had seen the road below as he came to the Neck. The reserves had up to then been rushing forward to the assembly point and clogging the road in their rush, even though the civilians had been calm and orderly.

Shadow called for the Neck's sergeant and ordered him to organize the reserves as they arrived and send them into the valley in groups of ten using the field footpaths so the roads could be used for the civilians. The sergeant was to assign men who knew the valley to direct the arriving reserves. The orderly movement sped up.

When Shadow arrived at the castle just shortly after Eadgard and the company, a makeshift hospital was already treating the wounded. Lady Hilde had been taken to her rooms and her daughters were seeing she was tended to. One of the men at arms came with a message that Shadow's presence was needed in the library. When Shadow arrived, the family was there as well as Eadgard and Captain Aewel, sitting around a table.

Wolf rose and came over and embraced Shadow. Neither man said anything as they took seats at the table.

Wolf wore a troubled look as he started, "I am glad you are all here. I want to share my thoughts with you and get your reactions. Please let me finish before making any comments. Eadgard, I ask your indulgence in this."

Eadgard motioned wolf to continue saying, "Of course, my friend."

Wolf resumed, "The attack against Lord Eadgard on our lands was clearly an act of war. The first thing I asked myself is what would Sievert hope to gain by killing Eadgard's family? Certainly, it would ensure no future heirs were sired but that would not explain his provocation to my family. It does not explain why Sievert did not wait until Eadgard was in his own lands.

If he had waited there would have been no act of war against my family. Obviously there must be another motivation for Sievert is no fool and not entirely reckless. How could the odds be in his favor? How could this vicious attack profit him? I thought there must be more to it. Wolf paused before continuing.

"Sievert was apparently not with the attackers, and yet he had committed a large portion of his military strength to the attack. Alone his forces are inadequate to do anything but penetrate our lands, be forced out, and eventually conquered in his own lands. It is inconceivable that Sievert would do such a thing unless he has lost his wits, which I think unlikely. It occurred to me that the attack might be an attempt to draw me and my forces from the valley. If that was so, another attack from a different source must be pending, perhaps more than one. What if our heathen enemies on three sides allied together to attack us and after conquering us planned to divide our lands?"

Wolf pointed to the map on the table moving his finger as he talked, "One would strike here trying with one blow to decimate Eadgard's family and draw me out and leave the valley weakened. Sievert would simply lead me further and further from the valley, probably into an ambush where the rest of his forces lay in wait. Another enemy from the south would attack upriver and take the valley, while my father's lands would simultaneously be attacked from the south. If they conquer our lands, Eadgard's then would be subjected to the enemies combined strength. Since Eadgard's castle has not been attacked, I think my suppositions are reasonable."

At the last Eadgard raised his eyebrows and demanded, "How do you know my castle has not been attacked?"

"I ask your forgiveness Eadgard, but I have spies in your lands and please do not ask me how I received a message so quickly, just be assured it is so."

Eadgard half smiled not knowing whether he should be offended or pleased, "When this is all over, we will need to talk man to man."

Wolf nodded. "I think there will be two main attacks, one against Herewood, and one upriver. It is my intention to concentrate my forces on the river defense, destroy the attackers, move my troops downriver by boat to here," Wolf said pointing to a place on the map, "March overland and relieve Herewood and defeat the remaining forces. Shadow would then ride north with whatever force we could send mounted to pursue Sievert's forces, although I doubt if we are successful in relieving Herewood that he will stand and fight. The rest of the force sails back to the castle and then we march on Sievert's lands and take them by force. In the meantime, I expect our other neighbors will be suing for peace and willing to pay large reparations."

There was silence for a few moments while the group thought about the plan.

Eadgard asked the first question, "What is Herewood's latest report?"

Wolf told him, "He is bringing the people and his patrols in and preparing for siege. Bishop Aert is on his way to Herewood. The cathedral town was already abandoned by the time our scouts reported Sievert's men were half a day away. His captain is leading and he commands about forty men-at-arms. He has two scouts watching the Neck and I have ordered them left alone. I have a use for them."

Eadgard was amazed and told Wolf, "I am glad I am not at war against you."

Wolf smiled, "So am I. It would make things, er, awkward."

They all laughed.

Eadgard asked, "How can I and my men help?"

Wolf smiled, "I would be most grateful if you would help my

grandfather in defense of the valley. If we need to send men here or there to deflect marauders," Wolf turned to his grandfather, "with all due respect grandfather, that is work for a younger man."

Eadgard banged the table enthusiastically with his fist, "Certainly, my pleasure."

It was Cuthbert's turn to smile and affect the manner of a feeble man, "Yes I will be most pleased to stay here in the castle and watch the valley from my chair on top of the highest tower."

There was more laughter for Cuthbert was healthy enough now and experienced enough to direct the defense of the castle. If it came to that, he would have a sword in his hand even if he was not the warrior he once was. He would be marching around atop the castle walls giving appropriate orders.

Later, Sievert's man Uno received word that fifty men-at-arms had left the valley. Somehow they had killed one scout and the other had lost them in the woods and returned. Uno knew the game was afoot. He would lead them a merry chase. The plan was falling in place.

Uno arrived at the cathedral town to find it empty. There was no food, no beverage, nothing useful, except a little hay for the horses. When the doors to the cathedral were broken down they found it empty of anything of value. In frustration, they burned the cathedral down. They spent the night in the town.

Uno's men spotted a scout briefly and Uno moved his men out. They marched away from the valley. Occasionally a scout was spotted and Uno would lead his men away from the scout. Uno was sure he was being followed by the troop that left the valley. He did not recognize that five men were playing hide and seek with him, making him think they were scouts for a larger pursuing force. In fact, the fifty men who had left the valley had returned there. Once, Uno sent out a scout to find the larger force. He had not returned, which Uno took to mean they were still being chased. All day, the game went on.

At dark Uno's men camped. In the far distance they saw campfires, which were quickly extinguished. Uno had his men do the same thinking a scout had reported their position. They moved out, thinking they were being chased in the dark.

The primary attack came up river as Wolf had anticipated. It was a windy day. There were nine large boats loaded with men sailing upriver. They were running before the wind, sails full, making good time with no need to row. Two more bends and it would be straight up the valley to the castle and plunder.

It was better than Wolf could have hoped. When the first boat hit the first chain, it did so with such force that its bow beam broke and men were thrown forward, two being thrown into the river where they promptly drowned weighed down by their armor. The boat immediately started to take on water and there was panic. The second boat tried to avoid the first. They had been too close together and the boat leaned dangerously, loaded to overflowing with men. It started to take on water. Then the arrows came.

It was a boatman's worst nightmare; fire! Flaming arrows, coated with pitch struck the sails and stuck in the wood. Two boats were already sinking and two more were dangerously aflame as their helmsmen tried to beach their boats. One boat tried to turn and go downriver only to see a chain come up to the water's surface as large gear wheels lifted it from the bottom as half a dozen men cranked the large wheel hidden on the only solid spot along the banks. The boat struck it and its occupants were tossed about. The captain ordered the oars to be shipped. Under a hail of fire arrows the crew made for shore.

Two boats had sunk with their crews, two more were a mass of flames and much of their crew was burning alive before the boats could be beached. Most of those men jumped in the river and drowned weighed down by their armor. The boats peeled to opposite shores. All were afire now to varying degrees.

The warriors, furious at the turn of events jumped from their boats as they were beached only to find themselves knee deep in muck. They slogged forward. By the time they reached the more solid part of the river bank their legs were coated with thick mud and their legs burned from exertion. It was then they were attacked by an overwhelming force.

Mercenary Captain Waldemar cursed that he had been foolish enough to challenge this Wolf. The man's name said it all. He knew all the attackers were doomed. He did not try to slog through the mud but stripped all his possessions off and in loincloth swam to the middle of the river. He found a piece of wood and started kicking downstream as he saw the hell on the banks take place. He swam under the chain and just kept going down river.

Wolf commanded from the hilltop overlooking one side of the river and Shadow from the other. They had not had to engage their reserves and enter battle themselves. Aldwyn was not at the battle, but his work had made it a massacre.

The defenders were using long spears which had long spear tips and iron wraps around the first two feet of shaft. Swords would not chop the ends off. The majority of the attackers died in the muck before they could reach solid footing. What the spears didn't get the archers did. They were so close that any opening in an attacker's armor was exploited. The few, who did reach solid footing, were overwhelmed by defenders. The river ran red with blood.

It was all over within two hours of the first boat hitting the chain. Shadow was brought three prisoners. He was told one claimed to be Lord Yingvar. Yingvar claimed he would be ransomed.

Shadow looked at him with disdain, "You may not have a family or a land to ransom you when we finish what you started."

Shadow ordered the prisoners be bound and held. There were hardly any prisoners as all but two of the attacking boats had sunk or burned to the water line.

It took another half hour to regroup the men and then another hour to march upriver to where the banks were solid enough to ground and load the boats. In the meantime, the fire barges that had been deployed upriver from the battle as a second line of defense were drawn to one bank.

Only half the men were able to load onto the available boats. The rest of the men marched back toward the castle. The men on the boats were the most experienced men-at-arms and the best archers.

The boats passed Waldemar floating downstream and the troops jeered at him as they passed but no arrows were shot at him. Waldemar knew what he would find by the time he went downstream. Waldemar knew he was going to have to go far away. He watched as the boats, sails furled, rowed out of sight. The boats were making good time with the current even though the wind was against them.

The expedition was way ahead of schedule. They grounded that evening before dark and were on the road marching as the sun set. They marched all night and just before sunrise they closed on the castle. Scouts were deployed ahead and brought back a report that the enemy was camped within striking distance. They were in the fields surrounding the castle between the woods and the castle. The enemy was pinned between Wolf's force and the castle next to the other river. The camp was not fully roused and just started to wake.

Knowing they vastly outnumbered the men in the castle the enemy was lax. It was obvious the enemy did not know Wolf's force was here. There was no great strategy, they prayed silently, then simply slipped into battle line in the woods, moved to the edge of the woods and at Wolf's signal the line charged from the woods under an umbrella of arrows. The panic in the camp started with the first flight of arrows as the un-mailed men in the camp started falling. Wolf's men came screaming war cries and slashed into the camp as the grey light started to rise in the east.

The first man came to engage Wolf and his sword thrust glanced off Wolf's shield. Wolf spun a hundred and eighty degrees his sword cutting the man nearly in half from the side. He thrust his shield into the next man so swiftly that man was unbalanced as Wolf thrust his sword under the man's shield and twisted and drew it out. He started cutting a path through the camp and men followed him.

Shadow was near the other end of the line and he was cutting men down like a scythe through wheat and his men were following him through the field. Some of the enemy warriors were still scrambling for weapons and armor. The gates to the castle opened and Herewood and his men came charging out on horseback and rolled up the enemy line from the rear. Some of the enemy tried to stand against the attack, but it was too far advanced. Men were breaking and running, some had started to swim the river on the other side of the castle, while others were mounting horses to escape. Herewood's men were running down the fleeing enemy. The battle turned into a full rout.

It ended as suddenly as it started. There just were no more enemy warriors standing. Wolf looked around. It was another blood bath. It had been a vicious and decisive battle and suddenly Wolf was concerned about casualties.

Herewood rode up and greeted Wolf, "Lord, when you said you would reinforce us I did not expect you before we were even attacked."

Wolf quipped without thinking, "If I had known you would be disappointed, we could have waited."

Everyone standing nearby laughed. It must have been nerves. It had all happened so quickly; two battles within thirty six hours and both so short. This was a major battle and it had lasted less than two hours. Wolf found a place to sit.

"Someone get me a report of casualties!"

Shadow came and sat down beside Wolf. "I cannot believe it. In all my life I have never seen battles go so quickly. Truly God was with us."

A sergeant came to Wolf and reported, "Lord, three dead, seventeen wounded. Enemy dead are fifty seven and we are still rounding up the wounded."

Wolf, head hung, waved the sergeant off, "Thank you, Sergeant, carry on." Wolf was experiencing adrenalin let down after the battle fever.

Shadow was hanging his head and turned toward Wolf, "Amazing; a bloody miracle."

The two men just sat there as Herewood took charge of the after battle command. They let him. They were exhausted emotionally. People started leaving the castle and were warned away from the battlefield. The troops were stripping the dead and wounded.

A wounded man was brought to Wolf by the sergeant. "My Lord, this man claims to be Lord Asbjorn."

Wolf looked up, "Keep him bound and guarded in the castle, I'll deal with him later."

Wolf rose and Shadow followed. They both realized about the same time that they were still holding their swords, so they wiped them clean on whatever was handy and sheathed them. They went to the castle to find a bed.

Ten hours later Wolf was roused out of bed by Shadow. His mail was lying on the floor, he was half dressed, and his sword was on the bed beside him. Still groggy, he sat up.

"Come on lazy Lord, we have a funeral to attend. You need to get cleaned up."

Shadow was motioning two servants who had brought in basins to get out of the room. Shadow said, "Lord, here is hot water to shave and another to wash. Herewood got us some clean uniforms. Yours is there on the table. I'll be back in fifteen minutes."

Everyone who was not on duty attended the funeral and Bishop Aert officiated. After the funeral and internment, the company was dismissed to have a meal. Wolf, Shadow, Aert and Herewood were on their way to the hall when Wolf saw Skjold and asked him to come to breakfast and the men had a pleasant meal.

Wolf told his men he would travel back upriver by boat. Shadow would mount part of the force and pursue Sievert's men. The goal was to find and destroy them if they were caught in Wolf's lands. After Wolf got to the valley castle, he would see how Eadgard wanted to proceed with a northern campaign. By noon one column under Wolf was marching toward the river and another mounted column under Shadow headed north.

Chapter 9 - Taking It to the Enemy

Wolf took captive Lord Asbjorn with him upriver. Asbjorn was bound and well-guarded. Two of the three Lords who had mounted the attack were now captive. The wind was still blowing upriver and the boats went under sail. It was an easy journey, much easier than Shadow was faced with.

The boats returned to a hero's welcome. Before being dismissed, the men were told to report for duty in twenty four hours. They had done very well and deserved a break while they could get it. There was much work to be done before an expedition could be mounted. Wolf put Modig and Captain Aewel to organizing the mounts, wagons and supplies for an expedition even before he got to the castle.

The walk from dock to the castle took some time because of the press of the crowds, even though people made way for him. There was much celebration. Wolf knew three families would not be celebrating and as he walked he told Ragnvald to call the mothers, fathers and wives of the deceased men to meet with him later in the day at the castle.

Wolf's family had stayed in the castle anticipating the press of crowds. When he entered the courtyard, his mother and Cenedred were the first to come to greet him. Wolf noticed his mother slow down to let Cenedred get to him first. He embraced her.

Cenedred simply said, "I prayed. I prayed a lot."

Then she moved to the side to allow his mother to hug him and the other's to greet him. His grandfather and Eadgard clasped his arm in greeting and gave him congratulations on the great victory. Lady Hilde's arm was still in a sling so she had remained back. Wolf went to her, smiled, and greeted her. She put out her hand and he took it in both of his.

The party moved inside and the men went to the library. There were chairs around the table they had last used for planning. Wolf sat and summarized the situation.

"We, thanks be to God, have defeated two prongs of the attack of the enemies allied against us and captured their leaders. Their forces have been destroyed and their lands are open to us. Only Sievert remains and his force has been diminished substantially. Shadow is now pursuing that force. I expect Sievert's forces to flee our lands and pass into Eadgard's and then home. The question as to what to do next is to a large degree in Eadgard's hands. Eadgard what is your wish? We cannot pursue Sievert without crossing your lands."

Eadgard paused before starting, "I have given the matter much thought. Chasing Sievert out of my lands will only postpone the problem. The people in the north of my lands support him. I would pray to destroy his forces and remove the threat of those who ferment internal rebellion. The truth is that I am not strong enough to do this alone and would need your help."

Wolf leaned forward and spoke, "I understand, Eadgard. Would you give my family time alone to discuss the matter please? Perhaps we can meet again after lunch.'

Eadgard rose, "Of course. I understand this is an important decision."

Lady Ethelind was called and the family seriously discussed the situation at length. At lunch, they left the library. Wolf asked one of the servants to seek out Cenedred and asked her to have lunch with him on the balcony. She was led to a small table set out and apart.

Wolf was arriving and a smile brightened his face as he saw Cenedred also approaching the table and Wolf said, "Cenedred, you could not have timed that better."

She said, "Lord," leaned over and kissed him on the cheek, increasing the size of his smile. A servant drew her chair and she sat down as Wolf took his chair.

Wolf started, "Thank you for coming to break bread with me. Let us give thanks to God."

They bowed their heads and said a short prayer of thanksgiving for their meal and God's many recent blessings, including the victories.

They said amen and then Cenedred spoke after a short pause, "I prayed ever so fervently for your safe return and that of your friend. We have known each other for such a short time yet I missed you terribly while you were gone and worried for your safety."

Wolf smile, "I am happy to hear that, which brings me to what I want to ask you."

Cenedred tilted her head inquisitively.

"Please hear all I have to say before you answer. I ask your consent to marry me if I can persuade your father? Your father wants us to ally with him, and quite frankly that will happen whatever your answer, so do not let that affect your decision. You must want to marry me or I am not interested. I must warn you however, my heart will be broken if you should turn me down."

For a moment Wolf was concerned as Cenedred shook her head back and forth, "Oh Wolf, you are really naïve. You had my heart the first time we met. Of course I will marry you. You must not make it known to my father that we desire it. Make him squirm a little, and get a good dowry from him for I would like to see how much he really wants to be shed of me," and with that they laughed.

The lunch was marvelous and the two of them plotted together. When Wolf went to his family to discuss their plans, Cenedred went to her father. She found him pacing in the garden. "What is the matter father?"

"I have asked our friends to ally with us. They have been discussing it for some time. I have not yet received an answer"

Cenedred made a tsk sound several times and her father stopped pacing and looked at her.

"Father, please look at it from their point of view; they have nothing to gain and much cost to bear to just help us out of the goodness of their hearts. Being people of conscience they are struggling over the decision. Do they ask their people to risk their lives for their neighbors out of Christian charity? How do they justify the danger? There seems only one thing to do."

"What is that Cenedred?" her father asked.

"Wolf seems a little interested in me and I do not find him all that unappealing. I suppose I could do worse," she smiled a little impishly. "Offer me in marriage to him. If they accept, then they have a stake in our wellbeing. Offer them estates as a dowry for my wedding. If they accept my offspring will inherit anyway. The new land will be stronger and more prosperous for all the people."

Eadgard took only a moment to consider, "I will do as you suggest." Eadgard half suspected his daughter might not be at all opposed to the marriage but in any event it made sense. He sent a servant to ask for a meeting with his hosts.

Eadgard and Lady Hilde were warmly welcomed into the library and offered seats.

Cuthbert was the one who asked, "What would you have of us Eadgard?"

"I have come to make you a proposition. I have come to offer my daughter Cenedred in marriage to His Lord. I will provide a dowry of estates in my land. In this way our families would be allied, and their marriage would be benefit to both our people. Our lands allied now and becoming one under a new heir of Wolf and Cenedred. It would ensure greater security and prosperity for all our subjects."

Lady Ethelind smiled, "I must admit I do not find the prospect displeasing but my son rules here now and he will be the one to marry."

Wolf tried to keep a serious expression, "Which estates do you propose to offer as dowry?" Eadgard stood and bent over the map showing the areas. Wolf paused a moment before responding, "I consent to the marriage."

There was much joy in the room as Wolf shook Eadgard's hand solemnly. There was much embracing and congratulations. Cenedred was summoned and came. When she entered the room she stood beside her father, who simply said, "Daughter, meet your betrothed, Lord Aelle."

Immediately, Wolf took a ring from his pocket and placed it on Cenedred's finger. She leaned over and kissed him on the cheek, moved beside him and took his hand.

Eadgard slammed the table, "Hoodwinked by my own daughter. Who would have thought!" and he burst into laughter and all followed him.

Wolf offered Cenedred a chair beside his, "This affects our future dear Cenedred and I want you to be part of these deliberations. We have set the unusual precedent of having women involved in affairs of government," Wolf smiled at his mother, "so we might as well continue to use that to our advantage. Eadgard, we have received word from Shadow that Sievert's troops are fleeing north. Shadow will pursue them to the borders of your lands with your consent."

Eadgard nodded, "Of course."

"I will send a rider to him. We can maintain our lands and still comfortably field a hundred men, including Shadow's present company, plus the men you bring, so the question is how you would have us proceed."

"When I came here, I never imagined you would be able to raise such an army. I suspect neither did our enemies."

Eadgard looked around the table and to everyone's surprise Cenedred joined in, "Father, I think Wolf was correct in stating that the northerners are a knife at our throat. Since they aided Sievert's men by our reports, let us not leave them at our back but expel them now. Then march on Sievert."

Eadgard shook his head, "Daughter you have been around soldiers too long. You are beginning to think like one."

Lady Ethelind added, "She is right."

Eadgard nodded, "Of course." He turned to Wolf, "How long before we could mount an expedition?"

"We can leave day after tomorrow. We can still strike while the element of surprise is on our side. Sievert's people will be stunned by our victories and by our sudden appearance. They are likely to offer minimal resistance to being driven off the land by an overwhelming force. We give them a head start to let them spread rumor and panic of the approach of our army then follow them. Drive Sievert's people further north and threaten them if they return south of the castle. Sievert will retreat to his castle. We need not capture it but just take everything that is not nailed down and burn the rest. Impoverish him. That will deprive Sievert of the income from those lands and weaken him."

Eadgard looked at everyone around the table. "It is a good plan. Any thoughts?"

Wolf laughed, "It just occurred to me that in this plan you recover control over enough lands to replace those of Cenedred's dowry."

Eadgard just shrugged, "God protects fathers from scheming daughters and future son-in-laws."

There was more laughter. The planning for the expedition was discussed in detail. Bringing back goods might create a logistical problem that would have to be solved in the field. The women left to conduct business over which the men had no interest.

Ava came to meet with her mother, sister and Ethelind. There were wedding plans to discuss. Ava was just a little pouty that she was not the one to be married, but it took only a short time for her to get caught up in the enthusiasm. No time was lost in making the announcement of the betrothal public, if not quite official. The excitement over the victories and the upcoming marriage created optimism among the citizens. Within hours other families around the valley were announcing engagements.

While the women were planning his wedding, Wolf met with the families of the slain soldiers. Two sets of parents had lost single sons. Wolf expressed his condolences and how his family and the people of the land appreciated the heroism of their sons. Expressing that no amount of money could make up for the loss of their son, Wolf asked the families to accept a gift of money. They were very thankful.

The young widow of the other soldier was quite young, had no child, and was pleasant in appearance. Wolf knew she would marry soon enough. He expressed to her his sympathy and told her she would receive a pension for a year unless she married before then in which case her remaining pension would be paid as a lump sum. Wolf hoped the arrangement would encourage her to get on with her life.

Wolf should not have been happy preparing for war, but he was.

Meanwhile, Shadow's troop rode hard until they arrived at the Cathedral to find it burned to the ground. One of the scouts came to them there. The company rested in the town that night with a strong guard posted. They spent an uneventful night and departed early the next morning not to the area were the scout had last seen the enemy, but on an intersecting line to the direction they would generally have to take to retreat to Lord Sievert's lands.

That morning two more of the scouts joined the company. Shadow conferred with them and they concluded that the enemy was indeed retreating toward Eadgard's lands, but not in a straight line and where they would cross over was still hard to determine. Two scouts had not yet come to them and even then Shadow did not have enough men to scout the entire border. They would just head north and continue sending out scouts.

That afternoon the rider Wolf had dispatched intercepted the company. It was Vagn, Lady Ethelind's trusted man. His horse appeared worn out, but the one he was leading was fresh. He delivered the message advising Shadow he had authority to enter Eadgard's lands to intercept Sievert's men. If he could not intercept them, he was to meet Wolf at Eadgard's castle. Vagn also brought a letter from Lady Ethelind. Shadow wrote a quick note of acknowledgment of his orders and a note for Ethelind, and gave them to Vagn. Vagn changed horses and headed back.

The company picked up the fourth scout late in the afternoon. He advised that the enemy was a half day ahead. Shadow did not know what shape the enemy's horses were in so he would conserve his own mounts and hope that the enemy's would give out in time to allow him to catch them. His company camped at dusk and rode at dawn. The next morning they met the last scout who walked out from a wooded area and waved to the column from a distance. One of the men was dispatched with one of the extra mounts to fetch him.

The scout's horse had gone lame and had to be destroyed and left. The Scout had spent the night in the woods. Based on his information, the company was not yet gaining on the enemy. They entered Eadgard's lands that day and it was late afternoon when they stopped at a village for water. When the villager's realized they were friends pursuing Sievert's men, they came out of hiding.

The villager's related that over a dozen men had come to meet the retreating column. Shadow asked if they were men-at-arms. The villagers told Shadow the men had been lightly armed and had been leading a large number of horses. Shadow knew then that he had lost the race for the border. He had been out maneuvered. The villagers told Shadow the enemy had left about four hours before they arrived. In a desperate hope, Shadow sent out four scouts on spare mounts and rested the company.

One scout came back in half an hour. The enemy had just abandoned their old mounts to pasture in a nearby field so they would not slow the retreat. Those horses were just about done in. Shadow ordered the horses rounded up and brought in. They would be of use in the future. The scout set out with two additional riders for that was all the spare fresh mounts available. Shadow arranged for the villagers to provide his troops hot food and beverage. He paid fairly, perhaps just a little high, for the work. The village was much impressed when they heard the news of the victories from Shadow's troops. They heard that Lord Eadgard would soon be returning with his new ally.

Uno was riding hard with the remainder of his troops. He had been ordered to salvage as many men as possible for the defense of Sievert's castle. None of them would have made it back if it had not been for the fresh horses. His Lord could ill afford to lose the horses left behind, but it was either that or the troops. Ulrich had complained about the loss of his horses. If Uno had his way, he would gut the useless heap of dung. Uno had noticed that during the attacks Ulrich had always been at the fringe not exactly in the midst of battle. When Uno finally entered his Lord's lands, he slowed the retreat but kept a respectable pace as they travelled towards Lord Sievert's castle.

Shadow's men made camp on the edge of the village and rested their mounts. They stayed overnight. They left a couple hours after sunrise for Eadgard's castle. There was no longer any urgency so they travelled at a leisurely pace for Shadow could estimate when Wolf could arrive at the earliest.

The company arrived late in the afternoon and Aldin, Eadgard's castle captain, rode out to meet them. Shadow noticed that when he came out the gate closed behind him. Shadow noticed that he also only rode out far enough that he was still within bowshot of the walls. If he had to retreat any horseman following him would probably experience a severe case of flying. That would be an experience resulting from multiple arrows taking the horse out from under him.

Shadow spoke first, "Well done, just as a matter of curiosity, how many archers are covering your back?"

The man smiled, "You must be Shadow."

"And you are Aldin." Shadow leaned over and offered his arm. The two men clasped arms.

Aldin turned his horse, "Welcome to our castle. We were told to expect you, but I had to make sure it wasn't Uno and his men in your uniforms. I am the only one here who knows him by sight."

They rode to the castle and dismounted in the yard. Aldin called one of the sergeants to help Shadow's men get squared away. Aldin took Shadow to his temporary quarters to drop off his gear then to the kitchen where they sat and a cook was called to prepare something for Shadow to eat.

Aldin told Shadow that food was being prepared for his men. He expected Eadgard in the next day or so and Aelle would be with him. Aldin asked Shadow about the battles they had won. Shadow told him between bites.

After Shadow ate, Aldin gave him a tour of the castle. Shadow was introduced to the men. There were some similarities with Wolf's castles. The builders had built them to a similar design. The castles were very functional and could be defended with a small force. Aldin did not take Shadow to the village, for they were on a war footing and the village had been evacuated.

Shadow could see that Aldin knew his business and was good. His men were well disciplined. The castle was well kept and the defenses were prepared for war. Extra bundles of arrows and spears were placed at strategic positions on the walls. There were pots full of oil with wood ready to fire under them. The guard was well positioned and alert. Shadow would be able to sleep well. Aldin and Shadow shared a mug of ale before retiring.

It was an impressive force that left the Neck. Wolf and Eadgard led the column. The mounted troops rode first, followed by the marching men-at-arms, archers and spearmen. Numerous wagons full of provisions and weapons were in the column. The people they passed stopped their work, waved, and watched the column pass. No one had ever seen such an army. The word went out before them.

When the column entered Eadgard's lands the people came out to greet their Lord and his new ally. The column stopped to rest and eat twice each day. Eadgard introduced his future son-in-law to those who came to greet them. The news of Cenedred's pending marriage spread quickly as did the fact that she was to marry the famous Warrior Lord Aelle. The news about the size of the army also went before the column. It seemed that news and rumor always travelled faster than troops.

The column arrived at the castle with much fanfare. People had seemingly appeared out of nowhere. The citizens had become adept at disappearing from the dangers of war.

Shadow and Aldin came out to meet the column. With the return of Lord Eadgard and the arrival of the army, people started repopulating the village and opening their homes and businesses again. The army camped in the open fields beyond the village. Eadgard and Wolf went to the castle with Aldin and Shadow.

Some of the people of the north began to worry. The implications of the news of Cenedred's betrothal were not lost of some of Sievert's followers. Some packed up and left their crops growing in the fields and headed for Sievert's realm anticipating the army would march north. Others stayed thinking that ignoring the army would save them from any repercussions because of the participation of their friends, family, and neighbors in the rebellion against Eadgard. It had always worked in the past. They would find out they were wrong.

On the day of their arrival Eadgard and Wolf called a council of war. Shadow and Aldin brought their senior men. The meeting started with a prayer. Eadgard then told those assembled that the basics of the plan were Wolf's and he would present it. The strategic plan was laid out. The men were told it would be up to them to determine the best tactics to implement the strategic plan.

In the first phase, large patrols would immediately be sent to guard the three major river fords and the one bridge. Riders would be sent immediately to priests in the areas north of the river and they would be told to immediately bring any loyalists to the nearest river crossing and safety on the south side of the river. Once the army had cleared the area they had left, they will be allowed to return. There were not many loyalists in the area to be swept and it was expected the group would be small.

In the second phase, the day after tomorrow the rest of the army would sweep in a large arc north from the castle travelling west to east along this side of the escarpment and north of the river. The army would cross the most western ford and split into two columns. Each column would consist of half the force available.

The columns would travel in as close to parallel movement as possible and work to stay in close proximity, no more than two or three miles apart. As they swept past each of the fords, the patrol from that ford would join the main force. The people of the area between the river and the escarpment would be made to pack up their goods and leave the land ahead of the army. Resistance to the immediate move would be met with overwhelming force. The army would live off the land as all crops and goods that were not already removed by those loyal to Sievert were forfeited.

Those who had supported Sievert would be given only an hour to leave with their possessions so it is unlikely they would be able to take any but their most immediate possessions. They would be told if the army caught up to them south of Sievert's castle, their lives and goods would be forfeit. The goal was to cause mass flight.

In phase three, the army herding the refugees before them, would invade Sievert's lands and destroy every building, burn every field, or take anything of value that was not nailed down south of Sievert's castle. Once Sievert's borders were crossed people would not be given the time to pack. They would be expected to flee ahead of the army.

Wolf gave one caution; it was to be made clear that this army would not inflict unnecessary cruelty. There would be no rape or beatings. Confiscated goods would be collected in an orderly manner. They would be placed in the common spoils wagons to be distributed later according to shares. Wagons would be commandeered to move the goods.

After laying out the plan, Wolf asked if there were any questions or suggestions. The first one was who would be leading the columns.

Eadgard volunteered the answer. I suggest Shadow lead the most northern and Aldin the southern. Eadgard added, "Once the army has reached the eastern passage to Sievert's lands Wolf and I will gather the remaining forces not needed for defense of the castle and join the army for the invasion of Sievert's lands.'

The second major question was how large would the invasion force be. The men were stunned when they were told almost three hundred trained warriors would be participating in the invasion. None of the men had ever been a part of such a large force.

Wolf added that initially about eighty trained men would be

dispatched to the crossings with sixty or so armed citizens. The citizens would not be participating in the invasion. The two columns would each consist of a little over one hundred trained men. The force sweeping from east to west would number about two hundred and twenty five men, and about one hundred and fifty would be mounted. The last statement left all the men looking at each other. That was truly an army like none other they had known.

The men asked if they were going to lay siege to Sievert's castle.

Wolf simply said, "We plan to impoverish Sievert so he can do us no more harm, we do not intend to occupy his lands. We will simply let it be known that anyone settling south of Sievert's castle is subject to attack at any time. Lord Eadgard have you anything else to add?"

Eadgard smiled, "I suppose you have all heard that Lord Aelle will soon be my son-in-law. Let's make quick work of this so he can get to work on an heir for me."

There was laughter all around.

That afternoon, patrols and riders departed northward from the castle. The stationing of guards at the crossings and the southward flight of the loyalists families had a frightening effect on those left north of the river. The next day saw most northern families start packing as much of their belongings as possible on their wagons and leaving of their own accord as rumors spread of the pending scourge of the area. Word had been circulated that anyone who left of their own accord and did not burn their land and buildings before leaving were to be let go. They were not to settle south of Sievert's castle because anyone there was to be killed and their crops and buildings burned.

The army left the castle as a large column and went north crossing the western ford at mid-day. It split into two columns and roving patrols went ahead of them. One such patrol was led by Sergeant Skjold who had come north with Shadow.

Coming to one hillcrest, he saw smoke and immediately responded riding in that direction. He came upon six armed men torching a homestead and his patrol of eight charged into the men. Four of them were slain and two fled on foot. Two of Skjold's men were wounded, one seriously. A rider went for a healer and the fire was contained. Skjold left two men with the wounded and took three men, one of them leading the two horses of his wounded men left behind. Skjold and his three men tracked and rode down the two who had fled. The two enemy warriors were wounded in the capture but Skjold bound them up and tied them to the two horses. He and his three men rode quite far east deep among the fleeing enemy. On the main road they hung the two men with signs on them indicating this was the punishment for those who set fires in Eadgard's lands. There were no more fires set.

The army travelled at a steady pace, both columns finding that they had no one to chase off the land. A rider came telling of the encounter of Skjold's patrol and Shadow sent a half dozen men and a healer. The column caught up to the patrol's wounded an hour after the healer had arrived. Shadow was informed Skjold had gone in pursuit of the two who had fled. Shadow wondered why Skjold had done that.

The column kept travelling east until dusk when they found a place to establish camp. A scout came in to confirm that Aldin's men were also establishing camp. Just before dark, Skjold and his three men arrived at the camp. Their horses were tired and it was apparent they had been ridden far. Shadow went to him as he was dismounting.

Shadow greeted him, "I was starting to wonder if you had invaded Sievert's land already."

Skjold chuckled, "Almost, my Lord. We caught the two and took them as far east as we could and still make it back by nightfall to where we thought you might be camped. We hung the two we caught by the main road and left them hanging with signs on them that simply said 'set a fire, get hung'."

Shadow laughed, "Well it worked for we have found no fires and your riding all over the country has frightened them into Sievert's lands."

Skjold replied, "Good, then it was worth the long ride. With your permission I would now like something to eat and drink. We haven't had anything to eat all day."

The following day the army proceeded with the sweep unopposed. It was clear that people had fled before them and even the village merchants had left in a panic. Many useful items had been left behind, including livestock. The two columns had arrived at the border with Sievert's lands much earlier than anyone had expected and within minutes of each other. The Lords had not arrived so the army camped and waited overnight.

The Lord's Aelle and Eadgard arrived at mid-morning. They had camped just a few miles back not expecting the army to arrive until at least this day. There was much cheering as the Lord's rode into camp. The army started preparation to move out when sentries came to report three riders were coming under a truce signal. Eadgard and Wolf flipped a coin to see whose man would go with them. Wolf won and so Shadow went with them.

Wolf's party came forward at a leisurely pace. When the two parties were just feet apart they stopped. The man opposite them spoke first, "Good morning, Eadgard."

"Good morning, Sievert. Let me introduce Lord Aelle, my future son-in-law and his War Chief Osmund known as Shadow Killer."

Sievert bowed slightly, "I cannot truly say on a personal level I am pleased to meet you, but as I come to seek terms I will, because not to be pleased is to be fighting a war we all know I cannot win. Let me introduce Uno my captain and my War Chief Siegfried."

All the men nodded to each other.

Eadgard knew but asked anyway as formality dictated, "What would you have, Sievert?"

"Terms."

Eadgard looked at Wolf, "Is that agreeable, Aelle?"

"As you wish, Eadgard."

Eadgard looked up, "It is going to be a hot day. I will have a tent erected here with a table and chairs and perhaps we can come together again to negotiate when it is up. I also propose both sides bring one priest to record the terms. Is that agreeable?"

Sievert simply said, "Agreed."

About twenty minutes later everything was in place and the parties rode out to the tent. The men dismounted and went to the table. Sievert was the first to speak.

"Lord Aelle, if I knew you could field such an army or fight so well, I would never have agreed to join forces against you. I let my greed overcome me. I will admit to being an opportunist for which I will now pay a price. I just ask that you not make the price so high that honor calls for me to fight to the death."

Wolf regarded the man before speaking, "If it was death we wanted Lord Sievert, then I am quite certain that under the circumstances that is what we would have. However, we are more interested in the future than what has happened yesterday."

Sievert raised his eyebrows. "Good. I had hoped this was not some kind of holy war you waged against me and my people."

Eadgard said without rancor, "Lord Sievert, we were not the ones who instigated this conflict, but we are determined to have it finished."

Sievert raised his hands, "Very well. I offer for peace to pay tribute annually and a lump sum for reparations now."

Wolf nodded, "I see a financial arrangement as part of any agreement and do not think it should be so onerous as to preclude the prosperity of the subjects in this land. We want more than that, to let you remain ruling here."

Sievert's face reddened, "To let me remain ruling? And what is that Aelle?"

The lapse in putting Lord in front of the name under the circumstances bordered on insult, but Wolf let it pass.

Wolf held up the five fingers of his right hand. "We require five things and they are all things you can do: first you are to pay to us a tenth of all the taxes and rents that you collect and a lump sum of two thousand silver coins;" Wolf bent one finger down;

"Second, the refugees are to be given a place in this land and to be told that we negotiated that for them" and a second finger came down;

"Third, your personal guard and standing military force combined will never be greater than thirty soldiers of any kind and for the time being they will be from our force with your present men being reassigned elsewhere" and the third finger came down;

"Fourth, you will turn my half-brother Ulrich over to us" and the fourth finger came down.

"And finally, I want you to swear oath and bind your descendants to that oath, that you will give to me and my descendants, allegiance in time of war and peace, ruling here as our vassal." Wolf's last finger came down and now his hand was a fist and he lowered it.

Sievert was now beet red and he jumped up. "I will never agree to the last. Do you know what the cost to you will be to lay siege to my castle?"

Wolf looked at him and said in a calm even tone, "Please sit and listen carefully, Lord Sievert."

Sievert looked for a moment like he might storm out, but he was a horse trader and knew the negotiations were not over. He intended for the negotiations to continue. He sat down.

Wolf continued, "We have no intention or any need to lay siege to your castle. We will just march on your land and take what we want and burn everything else. We will impoverish you. If you come out of your castle to protect your land we will utterly destroy you and your men. Even with the forces we have in the field all our castles are still manned against attack. We have the two Lords with whom you allied captive. You have no leverage.

Leaving a noble to rule here makes sense for us, and as long as you are willing to accept your role, that can be you. You plotted to kill our families. Do you have any inkling how hard it is for us to put that aside and not just seek revenge. Our combined lands will be prosperous beyond anything your people have dreamed of. You will be richer by this arrangement than you ever have been because we will increase trade. We have proven we know how to make that happen. You will be richer than ever and semi-autonomous and you will be given that by men whose family you tried to murder. You tell me, what will it be?"

Sievert now sat silently, "May I have time to think it over."

Wolf looked at Eadgard who nodded.

"Very well, sleep on it and give us your answer in the morning."

The men walked off leading their horses back to camp.

Shadow was the first to say something, "A reasonable man would take your offer and be grateful, but I fear Sievert's pride or greed may lead him to treachery."

Eadgard nodded, "It is possible though unlikely at this time. We will have to keep him watched closely."

Wolf added, "But we will always be prepared for treachery. There is something not right here. I get the feeling Sievert is stalling. Let's play his game. Do you have scouts out in Sievert's lands Shadow?"

"Yes, Wolf. Some should have returned. Shall we go see what they report?"

The reports were all the same. Sievert had come with only a handful of men, leaving the rest at his castle in case it was attacked. They had brought two horses for each man of their party and one horse for each man was always saddled in the event they had to flee. Sentries had been set and those men were good. They probably knew they had been observed.

The next morning the men met again at the tent. This time Sievert seemed somewhat calmer.

"I have several issues I would like to clarify. First, if I am to have a king, am I to be the only one. What about Lord Eadgard?"

Wolf and Eadgard looked at each other. They both knew that Sievert was crafty and if he could not save face he would at least create dissension. Much to Wolf's surprise his future father-in-law replied before Wolf could answer.

"Lord Sievert, Aelle and my daughter Cenedred are to be married. On that day I suggest that we both pledge to Lord Aelle to be his subjects."

Shadow was not to be left out, "My good friend Lord Aelle had titled me lands and I would also pledge to him on that day." Both Shadow and Wolf knew Shadow had already committed to be Wolf's man.

Sievert nodded. On the surface, he now had a way to save face with his subjects and his men. "That point is agreeable if we can satisfy some other concerns I might have. What assurances would you give me that my family will still rule after me?"

Wolf thought for a moment. "Would it be agreeable if we draft a charter, signed copies of which are to be placed with the bishops and surrounding Lords, whereby we all make declaration that for all time our families shall hold their respective titles, lands, and rights subject to inheritance and will continue in their rules by right of family inheritance in each generation provided there is no treason."

The men all looked at each other. They said almost in unison, "Agreed."

Sievert was no longer frowning for he perceived these men might be here to make peace with him and not to bring him down. They were so naïve.

"In each of the lands, who will set the taxes and rents?" Sievert asked.

Eadgard looked at Wolf, "I suppose each Lord would."

First Eadgard, then Sievert and finally Shadow said "Agreed."

It had not been lost on Shadow that Eadgard and Aelle had in fact agreed to make him a lord. Knowing Wolf, he would probably follow through, even if this treaty turned out to be a sham. He supposed Shadow had his mother's interests at heart and had enlisted Eadgard's help. For whatever reason, Shadow was pleased at the outcome, for it might smooth the way for marriage with Ethelind. It would become formalized after Aelle's wedding.

Sievert sat back, "My last question is defense. You have limited my personal forces, what happens in the event of attack?"

Wolf took the lead, "An attack on one lord is an attack on all. A rebellion against one Lord is a rebellion against all. We all stand committed to mutual defense led by the War Chief who will command all our forces. I suggest, to avoid confusion, that each lord have a captain for his forces from his castle and such sergeants as needed. Is that agreeable?"

"Agreed" replied Eadgard, Sievert, and then Shadow.

Sievert had one more question, "Are my descendants to be burdened with the ten percent tax forever?"

Wolf responded, "Good question."

Eadgard leaned on the table, "To be fair we should all contribute to the overall defense on an ongoing basis. I propose, since we all will benefit from the arrangement, that we all pay a tax of ten percent of our rents and taxes to our King Aelle."

Sievert realized then that he had been drawn into completing the negotiations which he wanted to string out. If he raised other objections or made unreasonable demands now his enemies might become suspicious. Sievert responded, "I can live with that."

Shadow and Eadgard said almost in unison, "So can I."

Wolf looked at everyone, "Then, we have a treaty to formalize."

The priests were ordered to make a record of their agreement for signing and to start work on the charter that would be executed at the wedding. Wolf invited Sievert and his family to the wedding as well as his Captain, Siegfried and his family as guests of Wolf's family. Sievert inquired if the army would now be returning to Wolf's castle.

"I wish it were so Sievert. But now we march south and east. We have the lands of two other Lords to deal with. We may yet have to slash and burn though I would rather it not be so."

Sievert added, "Would it be acceptable if I surrender Ulrich into your care when I come for the wedding? I have the coin at my castle and will go fetch it. "

"You may give Ulrich over to my man Skjold when you arrive. As for the tribute, I will send a company to fetch it."

Wolf knew that something was afoot. There was no reason to delay the handover or payment of tribute. There had to be a reason for delay. As soon as Sievert left, Wolf motioned to Eadgard and Shadow to come to him.

"Treachery is afoot. Sievert just asked me if he could turn Ulrich over at the wedding and delay payment of the tribute. I wonder why Sievert was not with his troops in my lands. Why would he want a delay? My guess, Ulrich is not here to turn over, and Sievert is stalling for time. I suspect if we head south something will be at our back. Something very unpleasant. Any thoughts?"

Eadgard asked the obvious, "If three allies, why not more. If a little treachery, why not a lot? It could be possible that Sievert is playing more than two sides."

Wolf smiled, "We do think alike Eadgard, indeed we do."

Shadow looked at his two friends, "So what do we do?"

Wolf smiled, "We let him think he has taken us in."

Chapter 10 - War and Peace

The army marched south. Sievert's scout watched them until they were out of sight. He watched as the last thirty men mounted up to go in the direction of the castle. The scout smiled. They would be the first of many. Lord Sievert would take this little group and then the whole army.

Grimbold reported to Shadow, "They took the bait and we have our best scouts out. We will try to determine where the ambush will take place and where the main force has come from. The scout who went out the farthest has yet to return but he will be here within the hour.

Shadow motioned for the sergeants, "Turn the column!" They were headed north again.

The column had only gone a short distance when the last scout came back. His horse was ridden almost to its limit and was breathing hard. The scout dismounted and a man took the horse to cool it down. The scout went directly to Shadow.

"They are out there about a day's ride. I estimate about fifty mounted men-at-arms plus another seventy five on foot. They have no archers to speak of. They are headed directly south toward the road we are on."

"Where would be the best place to ambush them?"

The scout smiled, "Up the road there is a place where there are large hills lining both sides of the road and about seventy yards on each side there are woods. There is a large sharp bend in the road just at this end of the woods and you cannot see around it. The enemy column is moving at a fair speed. Their scouts are staying on the road ahead of the column. We could probably reach the spot at least an hour or two before they get there if we move quickly."

Shadow told the scout, "Well done. Get something to eat and a fresh mount."

Shadow commanded two hundred men. Wolf and Eadgard had taken seventy to relieve the thirty heading into ambush. They intended to ambush the ambushers. Yet Shadow's instinct told him this was just too fortunate. He had spent a lot of time in prayer last night and his discomfort had grown. He followed that sense of foreboding.

He called for Grimbold. "Something is not right Grimbold. I want two scouts sent out to swing east and west and scout the sides of the column that has been reported. Tell them it is urgent that I have the information so ride fast and light and take an extra horse. Call the leaders to me."

Shadow had made up his mind. The column waited ready to move on a moment's notice as Shadow conferred with his senior men.

"If we want to set up a defense on our side of the border, where would be the most advantageous place?"

The place they settled on would give them a slight geographical advantage but there would not be any surprise. The men who knew the area best advised on the disposition of the force and after discussion each man knew where to position the troops he led. The column moved toward the position.

The scouts came back after the army reached the destination. The reports were the same. The main column was indeed coming down the road, but there were two smaller columns all on mounts riding parallel to the main column. The one on the east numbered about forty and the one on the west about fifty. Shadow faced a force equal in size to the one he led. The mounted parallel columns had probably held back while the initial scouts were out. They had since caught up to their main force.

Shadow gave thanks to God. If he had tried to set up the ambush his forces would have been split and the enemy would have surrounded his force. Shadow sent a rider to Wolf and Eadgard to advise them to hurry to him that there was to be a battle and they were needed. The message also contained the number and disposition of enemy forces. Shadow trusted Wolf and Eadgard to know what to do.

Sievert had set the ambush for the men coming to collect the payment. He had twenty five of his forty one men hidden in the woods uphill on the north side of the road. They were just inside the tree line about two thirds of the way down the hill. The road here was on a narrow level area about a hundred feet wide. To the south side of the road was a steep incline that horses could not manage.

Siegfried had the rest of the men hidden on the road just where it went around a sharp bend and his men could not be seen. He would charge up the road as Sievert's men charged down the hill. What men they did not kill, they would force off the road to die under their horses. Then they would ride to join their allies and take Aelle and his forces by surprise from behind.

Sievert felt confident. The allies coming were good fighters and not the weak soft warriors Aelle's men had faced. Sievert had hoped the others would have done more damage to Aelle's forces. Sievert's scout came along the road and into the woods. He reported the company was about a mile up the road and coming at a walk. Sievert was getting impatient; his men had been in place for quite some time.

Finally the men he was waiting on appeared riding in column of two to his right. Suddenly the lead riders stopped and the columns swung out into battle line. Sievert heard a commotion to his left.

Uno was waiting for the charge signal when he was set upon from behind. The attackers came fast and hard. Uno barely survived the initial charge as he swung his horse to face the attack. The spear meant to take him glanced off his shield and his horse screamed as the spear cut deep. The horse staggered. His men were packed in a fairly tight spot and their closeness caused them to impair each other as they tried to swing around to meet the attack. His men were falling and Uno called to his men to retreat. Less than half were still in the saddle and were able to follow him as he fled to the more open level area where he could maneuver. He would lead these men below Lord Sievert's men where they could be attacked. Too late he realized he had erred. He should have tried to charge through rather than retreat.

Sievert had his own hands full. At the first sound of commotion men came from behind and uphill. They attacked Sievert's men from the woods above. Sievert was alarmed and tried to turn to face the attack but there was not room to maneuver freely in the woods and his horse screamed from a spear thrust. Sievert rode forward and turned on the level to face the attack. Those of his men still on horse followed. They had enough room to turn to form line. Sievert realized he had only about half the men he had started with.

He looked left and saw the thirty he had meant to ambush and to his right Uno faced about twenty with less than half that number. He knew he was dead when about fifty men appeared at the edge of the woods. One charge and his men would be driven back and killed by weapons or by falling under horses on the slope. He recognized two of the men, Wolf and Eadgard!

Eadgard surprised Wolf by calling out, "Sievert, I challenge you to single combat! Your men may surrender and live if you accept my challenge."

Sievert answered, "And if I win?"

"You get to face Wolf."

Sievert ordered his men to dismount. If he won he would live. Standing here was a death sentence. He could defeat these men; he would just have to take Eadgard quickly. Reputation and reality are not always the same thing.

Sievert moved to the right and waited for Eadgard to come to the level. As soon as Eadgard got to the level, Sievert charged. Instead of trying to turn into the charge, Eadgard spurred his horse forward at almost a right angle to Sievert's charge. Sievert shot behind Eadgard's horse trying to turn the mount sharply left to follow him but his horse reacted slowly for it was losing blood. In the meantime, Eadgard also reined in his horse turning it left. Both horses had now lost momentum and the combatants were opposing each other at a near standstill. Sievert had lost the advantage.

They moved their horses toward each other and sword and shield started clashing alternately. Wolf watched intently, he saw that Eadgard had an advantage. His horse was better trained and responded to Eadgard's knee commands with ease. Horse and rider were used to each other. Sievert's horse was moving sluggishly. In one maneuver, Sievert's horse hesitated in responding to a command and Eadgard's sword struck mail and Sievert lost his balance and in his effort to regain it, his shield dropped dangerously low and that was all Eadgard needed. Sievert was dead before he hit the ground. The men burst into cheers.

Eadgard faced the enemy. "Do you yield?"

Facing certain death and with no Lord to die for, the men went to their knees in submission holding up their swords. Uno came forward and did the same for Eadgard who took the sword. At

Eadgard's order one squad came forward and took the surrender of the other weapons.

The prisoners were bound and tied together. Five men were assigned to guard them and bring them south.

Wolf and Eadgard set out to rejoin Shadow moving quickly. After they had been on the road for an hour, a rider came to them with the message from Shadow. They increased their pace for they were not far from the main column.

Meanwhile, Lord Volmer advanced on Shadow's men. Volmer had sent out scouts in sweeping arcs. They started to bring him information. The enemy had not taken the bait and moved to the best position for ambush. Volmer considered that there were three possibilities. The opposing leader was not good enough to see the potential of the ambush site, he had no stomach to fight a force of trained men, or he was so good he had out guessed Volmer. Volmer's scouts had not encountered any force so Volmer's first assumption was that they were heading south oblivious to his presence. He sent out another group of scouts in arcs in front of the column.

Volmer was so concentrated on what was in front of him that he did not scout for any attack from the west. As a result, his scouts were arcing out in front of the column and did not detect Wolf and Eadgard's force. On the other hand, Wolf's scouts knew exactly where Volmer's force was.

Volmer received a report of where Shadow's forces had established their position. The report of their numbers came to Volmer. He had no reluctance to meet an equal sized force from these lands. It was his past experience that they were usually poorly trained, poorly armed, poorly led, and undisciplined. Having no stomach for battle, they were likely to break and run at the first sign of possible defeat, whereas his men had persevered through certain defeat to victory. He did not expect much of a fight. His men were eager for the rape and plunder that awaited them to the south. It never occurred to him that this was the first time he had fought on so large a scale or with men from this region.

Volmer had his army form battle line when they entered the plain facing the opposing army. His strategy was simple. He was simply

157

going to charge right through them as he had always done in the past when they raided. The opposing force was near the crest of a gently rising hill, but their small advantage would not stop his force.

His men of foot were at both ends of the line. They moved forward first and they advanced quite some distance almost to the bottom of the hill before Volmer had the mounted men charge. He had timed it right and both men on foot and mounted men charged the hill together. Volmer wondered what the enemy was waiting for because they did not counter charge. Suddenly the men at arms turned sideways and archers stepped forward. The arrows started raining down and Volmer realized they were not aiming for his men. The horses! All around him horses were crashing to the ground and riders were being thrown or crushed under them. The arrows continued until Volmer's force was halfway up the hill then the archers went behind the men-at-arms. Those men formed a shield wall!

Volmer was enraged. The enemy had never formed shield walls against him before. Then he saw the long spears and realized the archers had taken them up and they were protruding out between the shields. The clash as the two forces met was tremendous. This was a real battle that was engaged.

The charging horses reared and screamed as they were impaled on the long spears that had been braced against the ground. There was pandemonium. Volmer looked to his flanks. His men afoot had fared better but were being held back. It was then he heard the hooves on his left flank. He ducked a spear thrust and backed his horse off slightly. What he saw was unexpected. A large force of horseman was headed toward his left flank. Volmer suddenly realized he was outnumbered and outmaneuvered, but as in the past he hoped to fight through it.

Shadow ran up and down the wall with a small group of mounted men reinforcing wherever there was threat of a break through, giving time for the ranks to close. He was losing men but the enemy was losing more.

The battle had only been engaged for a few minutes when the Wolf and Eadgard charged into the enemy's left flank. They rolled it up and forced it back. Shadows right flank started to swing around the enemies left and this allowed Wolf and Eadgard to swing out even further and now they were attacking almost from the rear. The entire enemy army was forced to their right and Shadows line started moving forward. It happened suddenly; Volmer's men broke and ran. It became a blood bath.

Volmer was almost surrounded and fighting fiercely when he realized his men were breaking. This had never happened before. He always won. That was his last thought before the long spear caught him under the arm and he fell from his horse. The enemy swarmed him and he died.

Wolf dismounted for his horse was staggering. It had lost a lot of blood and was exhausted. It no longer had the strength to carry him. There were a myriad of small cuts all over the mount. Wolf was covered in blood, none of it his. His muscles screamed and he knew his body would be a mass of bruises, but they had triumphed. He watched as the enemy was run down and slaughtered or fought in small groups which were being overwhelmed. As always, some of the enemy would escape to tell of this battle.

He looked for Eadgard and found him still mounted. He walked toward him. "Are you alright, Eadgard?"

Eadgard was aghast. Wolf was covered in blood and it dripped from his sword. He was almost unrecognizable.

Shadow rode up, "Wolf are you alright? You look like something out of hell."

Wolf responded, "I had hoped to scare the enemy to death."

The men laughed the nervous laughter that often came after a battle before the bone weariness set in.

Shadow repeated, "Seriously, are you all right?"

"Yes, but every muscle in my body is screaming and my body is probably one large bruise. What about you two?"

Eadgard responded first, "No wounds."

Shadow added, "Same."

Shadow and Eadgard noticed the men were keeping their distance. Curiosity had the best of Shadow. He rode to the nearest soldier. "Why is everyone keeping their distance from Lord Aelle?"

The soldier looked up at Shadow. "Did you not see? He was like an angel of death. I have seen battles before and men in battle fury but nothing like that. The men are afraid to come near to him until they are sure it has passed. Until he cleans up they are likely to stay away."

Amongst the army that day Wolf was given a new nick name, Angel of Death, though no one would ever say it in his presence.

A few of the enemy were brought to Wolf. They were terrified to be brought before him for many had seen him at his grim work.

"Who was the Lord who led you?"

The one who was obviously the most senior responded. "Great Lord, it was Lord Volmer."

"Why did he come?"

The man was trembling slightly, his head bowed in subservience, "Great Lord, he and Lord Sievert had entered into an alliance with Lords Asbjorn and Yingvar to plunder and occupy your lands. They are now attacking your lands from other directions."

Wolf spat, "Sievert is dead. Asbjorn and Yingvar captive and their armies destroyed. Yours was the last. Thanks be to God!"

The man started to shake at the news but Shadow and Wolf noted that the man willed himself to control it. He said nothing.

The man kneeling there in the blood drenched dirt thought about what he had been told. He had been told the Christian God had died on a cross. How could it be that such a God's people could defeat Thor's men? There must be more to this God than he knew.

Wolf spoke to the man, "You came as a soldier to face us in open battle so you will be treated as a captured soldier and not a bandit. You will live. Do you have someone who will ransom you?"

"No, great Lord."

"Why did you not flee?" Wolf asked.

"Great Lord, I gave my oath to Volmer and I had to stand as long as he did. My men here did the same."

Wolf motioned for the men to be taken away. "Treat them well, they served their master well and with honor." The men bowed as they backed away.

Shadow had water fetched for Wolf and had some servants clean him up as well as his armor. Once out of his armor Wolf began to stiffen up. Indeed as he took off his uniform which was soaked in blood, it became obvious that his body was a mass of bruises. A clean uniform was fetched for him.

Shadow and Eadgard stayed with Wolf. The reports came in. The losses had been substantial. Thirty seven men had been killed and thirty four were wounded seriously enough that they would be out of service for some time. Two of those might not live. About thirty percent of their force had fallen. There were numerous smaller injuries that would not preclude the men from functioning. The sergeants had started having the men collect the spoils.

Wolf's men searched for Ulrich, and found a body that was reportedly his, but Wolf assured them it was not Ulrich when he saw it. Ulrich had apparently escaped.

Eadgard suggested they set up camp on the other side of the hill that night. It was agreed. Wolf did not attempt to put his armor back on but he called for a horse and went to visit the wounded. As always, it was the sergeants who were directing the after battle work. The army rested for two days. The dead were buried and a funeral service was held.

Fear and astonishment spread throughout the adjoining lands as the news of the annihilation of Volmer's army spread. The news of the defeat of the other Lords and their combined armies added to the reputation of Lord Wolf. There were stories of his ally Eadgard and the War Chief Shadow, but Wolf, the Angel of Death, was the main hero of the tales.

The army marched to Sievert's castle which surrendered without demand. Wolf took possession of the castle and left a substantial force to hold it. It was unlikely any would challenge his authority now. Sievert's lands were now part of his lands.

Wolf moved his army as though he intended to invade Volmer's lands. When he reached the border, emissaries came offering treasure for peace. Additionally, the family offered to provide hostages to ensure the peace. Wolf waited until the price got high enough before accepting with a condition. Wolf required agreement that priests were to be guaranteed right of passage in, into, and through the lands without persecution and the right to build churches from funds raised by the church.

Wolf did not press for continuing tribute. He knew that Volmer's family lands were relatively poor and they had been relying on trading. Fixing an annual tribute would have meant forcing the family into raiding in addition to trading and Wolf did not want that on his conscience.

The treasure and hostages including Volmer's heir, were brought to Wolf's camp. The identities of the hostages were verified and the army marched south as conquering heroes with much spoil. The wounded and the spoil were diverted to the valley castle, but the army did not stop but marched southward.

When Wolf's army had passed the most southern castle, emissaries came from Yingvar and Asbjorn's families. They knew where the army was headed. They pleaded that Wolf not attack their lands in retribution and also for their Lords to be returned to them. They offered a substantial treasure ransom and a fixed annual tribute to effect the result.

The money part was the easiest issue to resolve. Wolf increased the amount to be paid up front and made two additional demands. One was the provision of hostages to ensure the peace and payment of the tribute. The firstborn sons of both Lords would be raised in Wolf's castle. They would be returned to their families when they reached eighteen years of age or ten years had passed, whichever was greater. Secondly, priests were to be guaranteed the right of passage in, into, and through the lands without persecution and the right to build churches from funds raised by the church.

The financial demands were burdensome but would not impoverish the families. The emissaries accepted the hostage demands as a normal practice. The matter of the priests and churches they saw as of no consequence, but Wolf thought that this would be what would have the longest term impact on the people of their lands. One quarter of the ransom was to be paid immediately.

Wolf and Eadgard had calculated that these ruling families would not be able to maintain a large standing military with the funds they would be left with. The offer was better than the emissaries expected, so they agreed to the terms. Eadgard cautioned the families that he knew the heirs by sight and that any attempt at treachery would be dealt with swiftly. It was not unknown for families to try to send someone resembling an heir as the hostage. The balance of the ransom treasure was to be brought to Wolf. The

Lord's would be released when the hostages and the balance of the treasure were received by Lord Aelle.

The southern castle was reinforced and the army headed back north.

Chapter 11 - Home Come the Heroes

The army came home to heroes' welcome. The roads and lanes were lined with cheering folk. The people felt a sense of security for the first time in their lives. They worked hard and were prospering without fear of someone stealing the fruits of their labor. The people thought the army looked grand although it truth the troops were dirty and dusty from the journey and the uniforms and mail of most men needed repair of some sort.

The army marched proudly onto the field before the town. The bishop was there and led the army and those in attendance in giving thanks to God for their victory and His many blessings upon this land, His church, and His people. The expeditionary force was given five days leave and was to return thereafter for distribution of a share of the spoils. A cheer went up and the men left to see their families.

The families of the dead warriors mourned. The wounded were all taken home to recover excluding the two for whom there had been the greatest concern for their survival. They stayed in town where they could receive the best care.

During the next five days, Modig and a number of helpers would be very busy. The fortune brought back to the castle was enormous and more would be coming for years.

Wolf, Eadgard, and Shadow rode into the castle yard with their personal guards. There they were affectionately greeted by the women. When Cenedred embraced Wolf, she noticed he winced.

"Are you injured?" she inquired.

"Just sore."

Cenedred stated sternly, "I am so glad you are returned safely, but oh how you smell."

The men took the implied suggestion to heart went to get out of their mail and clean up so they could all have dinner together. Before dinner Wolf met briefly with Modig. Then he brought separately the Lords Asbjorn and Yingvar to meet with him. He inquired if they had been treated well. They stated they had. They had been well clothed, fed, and housed and appreciated that they had been allowed to walk outside for a time each day.

Wolf told each of them that they were being ransomed and the esteem in which their people held them by the terms of their ransom. He told them he expected they would be released soon.

The dinner that evening was a pleasant and boisterous affair as the warriors recounted their adventures. Wolf said little. Eadgard and Shadow reveled in the telling of their adventures. There were questions, so many questions, and jokes, and laughter. The women suspected that in spite of the joviality now, the reality of what these men had experienced was something different.

After the meal the women of the family went to sit around the hearth. Wolf asked the women to excuse him, Eadgard, Cuthbert, and Shadow as they had urgent business to discuss. They would rejoin them soon.

The men went into the library, the door was closed, and the men sat at the table.

Wolf addressed the men. "We four are as close as any men get. God has given us a great victory and our little part of His world has become a Christian stronghold. If we are to be good stewards of what he has provided, we must move quickly to consolidate what we hold."

Wolf looked at Cuthbert, "Grandfather, I know you are very wise. What is your opinion on the marriage of Shadow and mother?"

"I think Shadow should marry your mother. They have been in love since the day they met, but they obeyed God and acted honorably. Like King David of the Bible, it is time for their obedience to God's commandments to be rewarded."

Wolf nodded, "I agree." He turned to Eadgard, "I know you hoped for a union with your daughter Ava, but that would not be a good match."

Eadgard raised his hands in surrender, "I have come to realize that. She is young and I suppose there will not be a shortage of suitable young men to pursue her."

Wolf turned to Shadow, "I ask you not to postpone formalizing your betrothal. Neither of you are getting any younger."

The men chuckled.

Shadow said in jest, "My Lord, only if you insist."

Wolf continued, "We have four shires to combine. There are: my mother and father's ancestral lands, Eadgard's which will go to mine and Cenedred's first son, and Sievert's lands. Sievert was the first to try to cause dissension between us. He will not be the last."

Wolf paused for a moment. The others were listening intently. "The lands are spread out and there are some natural barriers as well as distances to consider. The effective defense of these lands requires castles: one here in the valley, my paternal castle, Eadgard's castle, and Sievert's former castle. Three of these four castles are I suppose for all purposes mine to rule although Eadgard has a partial claim to Sievert's, but that becomes mute when Cenedred and I marry for it will be our heir who shall rule over all. Although the cathedral town should be fortified, it can be overseen from here for now.

I propose, which will require Eadgard's agreement, a King for our lands, ruling a system of vassal lords and sheriffs to manage individual holdings. Your thoughts?"

Eadgard paused before saying anything, "The concept makes sense, and since your lands are the greatest, I would accept you as King once you and Cenedred are married, but what about the rest?"

Shadow nodded, "There must be some way to strengthen the likelihood the lords are loyal."

Wolf agreed, "There is. Family ties. I would propose to make Osmund lord of the land my father formerly held once he marries my mother. Perhaps we can find Ava a capable husband to rule the northern lands. Eadgard, you would of course rule your own lands and eventually hopefully a second grandson would rule your shire. Cenedred and I would rule from the castle here. Thoughts?"

Eadgard leaned forward, "The northern lands formerly held by Sievert will be the most difficult to rule and will need a strong hand. I suggest Shadow rule there. He would be able to hold that land by force of will and arms. If his sons are anything like him and you, they would rule there for many generations."

Shadow entered the conversation, "I thank you for the consideration, and if I am to rule an area, I agree with Eadgard, it makes more sense for me to hold the north. I have learned from you about governing and that land if managed properly, could also become a rich land. A combination of strength and generosity combined with hard work and the land would become a productive one."

Eadgard spoke next, "There can be no weak links. If Ava does not marry well then we will have to consider an alternative. I suggest we not tell her our plans until a marriage is decided. Now, to the matter of taxation, we must agree on a system of taxation by the king to finance our defenses and infrastructure. We are basically committing our subsequent generations to keeping up a system of government that will benefit the greater good."

Shadow jumped in, "Wolf is giving his mother and I, and your daughter and a future husband, lands without recompense, so I think the share of rents and taxes that should go to him should be substantial. Over time, our families will prosper from this generosity."

Eadgard nodded, "Agreed. And we should establish a charter as we discussed so there is a record of how this all came to be. In future generations we do not want some vassal Lord bellyaching about the level of taxation. If he does, the legal heir can pull out the charter and show him where the land came from."

Shadow nodded.

Eadgard went on, "And I particularly like the idea that Wolf, and therefore by practicality, Cenedred have to approve of Ava's husband in order for him to rule.

She is thus unlikely to be married to some handsome ne'er-do-well who marries her for income. Again, I assume that if she marries without approval, her husband will not be appointed to rule?"

Wolf shrugged, "Seems practical."

The men looked at each other and in turn agreed.

Wolf smiled, "Now as lord of this land, I get to tell my mother I have arranged a marriage for her."

The men left the library and joined the women who greeted them.

Lady Ethelind spoke first, "Well, have you finished your business concerning the affairs of state?"

Wolf looked down, "Yes mother. We were discussing the need for a lord to rule in the north and how to tie his loyalty to us. We decided on a lord and we are arranging a marriage of you to him."

Wolf could see his mother's fury and that she fought to control it.

She asked coldly, "And who is this lord to whom you would marry your poor mother."

Wolf looked at her with a warm smile, "His name is Lord Osmund."

Much to Wolf's surprise his mother threw her cup at him, which he ducked, then started laughing.

His mother exclaimed, "How could you be so cruel!"

"You find Osmund that unsuitable?"

Lady Ethelind got up and came to her son, tears streaming down her face, "My dear sweet son, you have made your mother the happiest woman." Then she turned to Shadow, "How could you let him torment me so? You will pay for this."

Shadow put his hands up in surrender, "I will willingly pay whatever tribute you require."

The whole family was now laughing.

Wolf broke in, "Now would someone care to tell me the plans for my upcoming wedding as my bride has not seen fit to inform me."

For the second time that evening a cup came flying toward Wolf's head. He avoided it and simply quipped, "I have never seen so many flying cups in one place before. Mother, I am afraid I will have to ask you to refrain from teaching my future wife your bad habits."

His mother started to pick up another cup, but Shadow rose and gently grasped her wrist, "My dear betrothed, your son is making your future husband Lord of the north so at least wait until that is done before you kill him."

There was more laughter.

Shadow then spoke seriously, "My sweet, he may be your son, but remember he is also to be king of these lands." It was a gentle rebuke, and then he looked at Cenedred who acknowledged his remark with a nod.

The women started explaining their plans for a wedding. It would be a grand thing with many invited guests here and feasting at each of the castles on the day of the wedding. There would be a feast in the village field for the people of the valley. The guest lists would be worthy of a great king. The Bishop had agreed to officiate.

Finally, Wolf got desperate and interrupted, asking for the answer he needed, "When?"

Cenedred answered, "The twentieth of next month for that is my parent's anniversary, if My Lord is agreeable."

Wolf nodded in agreement, "Of course."

It was late when the family members started to drift away to go to bed. At last only Wolf and Shadow were left. A servant came and asked if they wanted anything and they asked for a cup of ale. They sat sipping it.

Wolf spoke first, "Did you think a few short years ago that God would bless us so?"

"It is hard to believe that God took us from where we started."

Wolf became serious, "What I am concerned about is that although my family gains an Earl in you, we lose a commander of the elite forces. I would like you think about how we can manage that. Modig tells me my family can afford a standing army of about four hundred without strain. That is a huge force to keep the peace and enforce the law. That does not count what each under-lord can afford as a regional force. It has to all make sense. Right now I am at a loss as to how to organize it."

Shadow nodded, "I shall consider it and perhaps discuss it with others."

Wolf agreed and they retired.

The next morning Modig met with Wolf. Cuthbert and Shadow were present. Modig told Wolf that he had calculated that each man in the army would receive an amount equal to the better part of a farmer's annual income. There was concern about the impact this would have on the people if that kind of money flowed too quickly. There was also the problem of splitting up much of the wealth. Although some treasure was in the form of coins, these were of inconsistent sizes and much of the precious metal was in other forms. It was quickly decided that Aldwyn would oversee the conversion of the silver into coins of consistent size bearing a cross on one side and King Aelle's family crest on the other.

It was decided the men would be given a third of their share when they returned and another third in two increments six months apart. It would take that long to create enough coins working at a normal pace and leave time for the normal routine. The coin for the troops stationed elsewhere would be dispatched in portions under heavy guard on a secret schedule to lessen the temptation for raiders to attack.

Aldwyn and his helpers were guarded as they worked day and night to create coins from the silver that was in the form of jewelry, plate, cups, idols, ingots and such. Trusted men were brought in to assist in the heavy labor.

Wolf met with Beorn who brought a report on the trading business which was doing well. When Wolf saw the share of the profit that came to him, he was pleased. It had continued to grow. Beorn thought that one more boat would optimize their profits and he had found an excellent one for sale at a fair price. Beorn's share of the original boats was almost paid because the venture had been so profitable. It was decided to purchase the additional boat.

A request came from Wolf's mother for a meeting with him. He sent a message for her to come. He was surprised when she showed up with Cenedred and Hilde. The three women swept into the library where he had adopted the habit of conducting private business. They curtsied, but did not wait to be invited to take seats.

"What would you have of me, dear ladies?"

Lady Ethelind seemed in a particularly jovial mood and said a little impishly as she turned to Cenedred and Hilde, "I have failed as a mother. See he fails to greet us. Strictly business. No manners and much to my shame, I am going to have to leave it to you dear Cenedred to teach him."

Wolf could not help himself, he laughed. It had been a hectic morning of business and this was a welcome break.

"I am remiss and properly chastised. Welcome dear ladies. How may I help my dear mother, my beloved betrothed, and my esteemed future mother-in-law?"

The ladies smiled and Cenedred looked at Wolf's mother, "See, he learns quickly,"

Lady Ethelind turned serious. "We have a proposal that we will ask you to consider. When you and Cenedred marry, everyone will be here. They will come from far and wide at considerable expense. We will also have considerable expense related to the wedding and feast which it is usually customary for Eadgard as father of the bride to bear, but it is also customary it be held at his castle. However, as this wedding is more an affair of state, it would seem only fair that our family share in the cost."

Wolf thought for a moment, "This is logical. I agree."

Ethelind continued, "As you have arranged a marriage for your mother, that wedding will fall to you for expense, as my father's estate is now yours to rule, my son."

Wolf replied, "Yes, go on." He knew there was more.

"We ladies got to discussing it and we thought it would make sense to have both weddings here on the same day, yours first, then Osmund's and mine. The good bishop says there is time to publish the required announcements. What do you think?"

Wolfe looked at Hilde, "Lady Hilde, I did not realize how well you look after your husband. I see your hand in this. Now I will pay three fourths of the cost of the wedding."

Hilde was a little taken aback until the three others in the room started chuckling and she realized Wolf had been teasing her. It would take some time to get use to her son-in-laws informal and easy ways with his family. She loved her husband dearly, but sometimes he could be so stiff. Maybe some of her future son-in-laws informal ways would rub off on him.

Wolf concluded, "If Shadow and Eadgard can be persuaded, I am all for it."

Ethelind smiled, "They have already agreed"

Wolf muttered, "Conspiracy, conspiracy, conspiracies everywhere."

The ladies rose to leave, his mother and Cenedred kissing him on the cheek. He looked at his future mother-in-law, "Do you dislike your future son-in-law so much that you show him no affection?"

Hilde blushed and came and kissed him on the cheek. She thought that he would really take some getting used to. Not even nineteen and he acted like a wise old patriarch. Cenedred would have her hands and heart full with this one.

That day, Asbjorn's emissaries came to the valley, escorted by men from the southern castle. Wolf, Eadgard, Shadow and Cuthbert received them in the great hall. Asbjorn's men had been disarmed before entering the castle. The two sides were technically still at war until the ransom was accepted.

The ransom and the hostage were presented to Wolf. Asbjorn

was brought to the great hall where Wolf invited Asbjorn to stay and visit with his son. Wolf also told Asbjorn he was welcome to visit his son often if he would just arrange the visit ahead of time. An escort from the southern castle would be arranged.

This was a generous gesture for which Asbjorn thanked his host, Wolf no longer being his captor. He would like to stay and visit with his son for a day before returning to his castle and he would indeed come to visit his son from time to time. Asbjorn had been treated well so had no reservation in staying to visit or telling his son he would come to visit again.

Asbjorn and his son were invited to dinner that evening with Wolf's family and future in-laws. Asbjorn accepted. The meal that evening was delightful.

The next morning a single rider came under flag of truce. The rider came from Yingvar's family. Wolf received the rider in the great hall along with Eadgard, Shadow, and Cuthbert. The rider approached Wolf and Cuthbert's thrones. He fell to one knee.

"I have been sent, Lord, with a message which it is my shame to deliver. I have served my Lord Yingvar loyally for all my adult life as a warrior. This disgrace now falls on me. Lord Yingvar's family have betrayed their oath to you great Lord and renounced the treaty."

Wolf regarded the man, "The shame is not yours, warrior. You have served your master. The shame is the family that betrayed me and him. Take a seat faithful servant while your Lord comes."

Wolf called for Yingvar to be brought to the great hall. Yingvar recognized the warrior who rose from his seat in the hall and came and knelt before Yingvar, "I bear bad news, My Lord." The soldier looked to Wolf who nodded, and the soldier told his master of his betrayal.

Yingvar looked at Wolf, "It seems my enemies are more honorable than my family. It seems my life is now yours, Lord Aelle."

"Lord Yingvar, I do not hold your life cheaply. You may retire to your rooms, and with your permission, we will find your man suitable lodging and take care of him until a course of action is decided."

Lord Yingvar dipped his head in respect and left.

Wolf shrugged, "It is a good thing we have the army reassembling.

Shadow would you have a message sent to Herewood telling him we are on a war footing. We shall be coming with the army directly. This time I suppose we have no choice but to crush them."

Eadgard sighed, "I suppose not. What are they thinking?"

Shadow shook his head, "Most armies once dispersed take weeks if not months to recall. They are assuming they have until next spring to hire mercenaries to defend their lands. They may also assume we are still dealing with the northern Lords. They may not have yet heard of their defeat."

A man came to the hall and Wolf motioned him forward. "Lord, the captive Yingvar would like to speak with you"

"You may bring him to me in the library."

Yingvar came into the room surprised at the informal setting for Wolf's inner circle was seated around the table. Wolf motioned him to a seat.

"Yingvar, this is where we meet informally, so we dispense with titles here. Agreed?"

"Of course, and I thank you for seeing me." Yingvar seemed genuinely grateful, though how much of that was artful, Wolf did not know.

Wolf asked, "What would you have of us?"

"If it pleases my Lord, I will make my case. It seems my family has decided to deal with me treacherously. I fear for my son and suspect my brother has usurped. I still have loyal men in the land that will come to me to fight on my behalf. I have little to offer, but I do not want to see my people massacred and their land scorched. Based upon my experience, I know this is inevitable with the army you will raise. Even in captivity, I have heard of your conquest over the Lords of the north. My family must not know of that yet. It is a dangerous and treacherous game they play. I ask to go with you on your spring campaign and to be allowed to bring men to fight alongside you, and will agree to be your vassal lord and pay taxes and tribute if you will place me as ruler over my ancestral lands."

Wolf thought a minute. "That will not do."

Yingvar was obviously disappointed and made a gesture of surrender.

Wolf continued, "It will not do, because our army will leave in a few days. I will discuss your offer with my advisors and let you know of my decision."

Yingvar was stunned, "In a few days?" He paused, "Pardon my outburst Lord Wolf, I had not expected that."

Wolf smiled, "I understand. I require your assistance so we may decide. I will bring your man here. I want you to tell him to answer the questions we will put to him openly and honestly. After we question him, he will be allowed to report to you what we asked of him. Do you agree?"

Yingvar agreed and the man was brought and instructed under oath by Yingvar who then returned to his quarters. The man was asked what had transpired that Yingvar had been betrayed. He revealed that Yingvar's brother had fled home from the battle with some of his men, seized Yingvar's family and the family castle. Yingvar's men who were few were seized, so the word spread and those who did not go to the battle, but had been guarding the land, escaped and went into hiding. With less than thirty men-at-arms Yingvar's brother Sven had usurped his brother's domain. The man estimated that Yingvar's loyal men in hiding now only numbered about twenty given the defeat they had suffered at Lord Aelle's hands.

It was learned that the people of the realm had lived relatively well under Lord Yingvar for even though he was a hard man he was honorable. The people detested his brother Sven who was a cruel man. The man was obviously troubled and uncomfortable that his lord had ordered him on his oath to be truthful. He expressed his discomfort. Finally, when all the questions had been answered Wolf told the man to report to Yingvar and then he would be taken to his quarters.

When he left, Wolf looked at the group, "Well this is certainly an unexpected turn of events."

Eadgard leaned forward, "Indeed. The proposal of Yingvar carries some merit. We had not expected to rule the land just receive tribute. God has given us an opportunity."

Shadow smiled, "After the distribution, we will have willing warriors lined up for our service. Sometimes war is a numbers game and if we enter the land with a large enough force the family is just likely to run for the hills and Yingvar could handle the rest himself."

Wolf looked at his grandfather, "You haven't said much lately grandfather. What do you think?"

"I think it is good to keep your friends close and your enemies under even closer watch."

Everyone agreed with that sentiment. It was agreed that their guests would be invited to dinner and Cuthbert volunteered to brief the ladies on the situation.

That evening there was a formal dinner and Lord Asbjorn and his son and Lord Yingvar attended. The food was excellent and the wine and ale of good quality. It was a pleasant evening, but the guests seemed a little uneasy with the courtesy and friendliness offered them.

As everyone was leaving, Yingvar stayed back, and he was blunt in his question, "How did you accomplish so much in so short a time. I have been struggling for years and have nowhere near the success you have?"

Wolf answered simply, "My God is the one true God and He has blessed me and my family."

Yingvar shrugged, for he did not understand. As he was escorted back to his quarters he thought about the regular morning prayers of his captors. He thought about the things he had heard taught in the courtyard by the priest. The God of these people had died on the cross for the bad things people did, but the grave could not hold him. There was a promise that he would come back as the absolute warrior king to slay the wicked and to judge those still living and the dead spirits. He would slay a great army like the world had never known. What he had overheard the priest saying was not what others had told him about this God. He had thought about it for some time. He was still thinking about it.

It was a busy time as the castle prepared for war. Asbjorn was amazed for he had heard about Yingvar's family treachery and that the great army would march again in just days. He was amazed at how these people could do that. He might not have believed it if he had not been on the losing end of the great battle. He had seen the might of this king. He was sure Yingvar's people would regret their treachery.

The army was finally assembled in the field beyond the village. The role was taken. Those who had not been enrolled at the time of conflict were removed to the rear. There were very few missing from the ranks that should have been there.

The wounded were to the left of the tent where the lords and their families waited, while the families of the fallen were on the right and the army in front. When the Lords of the lands appeared there was a great cheer. Lord Aelle climbed up on an empty wagon in front of the army with Lord Eadgard, Lord Cuthbert and Osmund, but it was Wolf who spoke.

"The Lord our God gave us a great victory." A cheer went up. "He has allowed us to conquer land and gain great treasure." There was more cheering. Wolf held up his hand for silence. "Some of our comrades in arms gave their lives to defend our land and their fellow soldiers. Their families are here with us today to receive our token of appreciation for their sacrifice as you receive your reward." There was silence.

Wolf motioned with his hand and dozens of guarded hand carts were rolled to the edge of the ranks. They were filled with small cloth bags. Wolf announced, "Each man, as the cart passes is to take one bag. One only. Captains and Sergeants will receive their distribution afterwards. Remain in ranks. We will have quiet in the ranks during the distribution."

The hand carts started down the ranks and among the wounded and the families of the fallen soldiers. It took some time for everyone to receive a bag and there were only a few left of those men who did not come back. They would regret that decision. There was still a murmuring in the ranks as each man realized what he had received. This was more money than any of them, with the exception of Wolf's original elite personal guard, had held before.

When the distribution was complete, Wolf spoke again, "The dead and wounded made a sacrifice for victory. You made a sacrifice. You receive a share in our victory. You will receive more. Those who serve will receive a share in their victory. Those who stood guard over our homes and families also share in our victory!"

A cheer went up.

"But the memory of our fallen, our honor, and the peace has been threatened by treachery. The people of the eastern land have defaulted on their pledge and dealt treacherously with us and with their own lord." There was much booing and jeering.

"Are we going to let them get away with this insult?"

The sergeants initiated the chant and everyone was caught up in it, "NO! NO! NO!" and went on for several minutes. When it died down Wolf called out, "Are we going to make them pay?"

Another chant started, "Pay, Pay, Pay."

Wolf held up his hand for silence. "The people around us fear us now as they have never before. Their fear and respect is our greatest protection. If we do not march now, they will say we are weak and our enemies will mock us. Eventually they will bring the fight to us. I say we bring the war to them first. Strike first!"

A chant went up, "Strike first! Strike first! Strike first!" and it lasted for several minutes.

Wolf stepped down from the cart and Shadow stepped up. "The army leaves in two days, prepare to march for we will obtain victory and justice with God's help." A great cheer went up.

It was not until she watched Wolf address his army that Cenedred understood the full measure of the man she was to marry. She had been told how the men loved and respected him, but also feared his fierceness in battle. They called him "The Angel of Death" behind his back because of the dreadful killer he was on the battlefield. She had just now caught a glimpse into that man. Goose bumps rose on her arms even in the warm mid-day sun.

There was much celebration in the land that night though Cenedred was disappointed for her wedding would probably be postponed. Such sacrifices would be the cost of her love for Wolf because he ruled.

The next day the serious work of preparation for war got into full swing. To the last man, those who had fought, and some new men, worked together to prepare to gain victory. There were more new recruits than additional weapons. Beorn had to make a quick trip down river to buy shields, helmets, and weapons. He brought Modig who with the advice of Beorn hired many boats to transport troops for Beorn did not have enough of his own to transport the army. Going downriver by boat was the quickest, least expensive, and the easiest way to get to the army to Yingvar's lands.

Siegfried, the man who had been Sievert's War Chief and who was now a captive, was brought before Wolf. Wolf's inner circle was present as well as Yingvar and Asbjorn with his son Lucan. Wolf offered Siegfried employment on the condition he would swear oath to be his man. Wolf knew that the chances were among these folk, that once they gave oath they would keep it. Also there were many lord's present to witness the act.

Honor was important to the warriors. Now that Sievert was dead, his previous oath men were without a lord for Sievert had left no heir. His wife had only borne daughters. Siegfried knew that the lord he would serve was a strong ruler and a fierce warrior. This was the kind of lord warriors longed to serve. He would again have employment and a future. He accepted and gave oath there in front of the other lords and warriors.

This was also a lesson for Yingvar and Asbjorn, that Wolf would accept any who would put themselves under his rule. Wolf conferred with Siegfried in front of the others about the men who had been captured during Sievert's defeat. He told which ones would keep oath. Siegfried was prepared to vouch for all but three who had been mercenaries. The ones Siegfried vouched for were brought before Wolf and were made the same kind of offer as Siegfried. They accepted. The other three were to be exiled and given three days to leave Wolf's lands. They would be given a mark on their cheeks to identify them as exiles.

Wolf called Yingvar forward and asked him if he was still willing to make the agreement he had proposed. Yingvar stated he was. There in front of those present, he made oath. The implication was not lost of Asbjorn. He had seen the army that Wolf commanded, he had experienced the fierceness of it, and he had learned of Wolf's growing power. He had also learned the man did not seek raw power but took it as it presented itself only to ensure peace and prosperity. He did not seek to usurp the rule of others.

Asbjorn approached Wolf and asked if an alliance could be made between their lands for mutual defense. Wolf indicated he would be happy to consider and enter into negotiations for such a treaty. Arrangements were made for emissaries to meet for negotiations.

Asbjorn returned home leaving a great treasure behind which had been his ransom.

Wolf met with Yingvar and asked him how and what route his brother would use to flee if he fled. Yingvar provided his best guess and the routes he would likely use. Yingvar also told of the best way to reach those positions.

Siegfried was summoned to the library. Much to his surprise, the guards did not ask him for his newly issued sword. Siegfried was surprised at this for only the most trusted men were allowed into their lord's presence armed. He marched into the chamber and went to one knee.

"My Lord, you summoned."

Wolf smiled, "Rise Siegfried. In here we do not observe formalities, a head bow is sufficient."

"Yes, Lord," Siegfried said as he smiled.

Wolf continued, "I believe you know of everyone here but have not been formally introduced. This is my future father-in-law Lord Eadgard, my grandfather Lord Cuthbert, my war chief Osmund, whose warrior name is Shadow."

Siegfried acknowledged each one with a head bow.

"You are being appointed captain because Eadgard and Shadow know of your leadership ability. You will lead fifty men on a vital mission. You will go ahead of the army and block the escape route in the event Sven, Yingvar's brother tries to flee as we invade. Our reports are that his total force consists of about thirty household troops and forty mercenaries. Lord Yingvar will be travelling with the main army, but he will provide you with a man who will guide you. You will go mounted and all the men under your command will be good riders. Do you have any questions?"

"No Lord, I will ensure Sven does not cart Yingvar's treasure away. How else are we to be paid?" Siegfried said with an inflection that made the group laugh.

Wolf simply said, "Very good Siegfried. You understand your mission. We wish you well and will pray for your success."

Siegfried bowed, "Thank you Lord for your trust and I will not disappoint you."

It was this act of trust that bound Siegfried by the heart as well as by oath.

After he left, Eadgard stated the obvious, "We shall learn very quickly the value he will be as a warrior."

Shadow added, "I do not think we have to worry about that. He will honor his oath and I know from past experience he is very capable. Although he served a scheming master, Siegfried is a man of his word. I think he will be happier serving Wolf than he was serving Sievert."

Siegfried and his contingent left ahead of the main army.

Word started circulating down river about the great army that was going to be coming. Yingvar's family discounted the reports as wild rumors started to frighten them into submission. They had sent the call out for mercenaries but were not dismayed that the response was slight even though they offered good pay. The spring would bring more troops. They did not believe the reports of an imminent attack.

Yingvar's castle was less than a day's march from the river. Sven ignored the reports of an approaching army until the boats had disgorged over three hundred troops and they were marching toward the castle. Still Sven did not believe the report until he rode out and saw the enormous column in the distance coming toward him.

Yingvar had been right. Once it was known he was returning, and he was recalling his men, over thirty of the men who had been left at home or who had escaped the battle came to him. Yingvar greeted them as they marched and they were integrated into his company. When the army amassed on the plain in front of the castle they found the gates were open. Sven had fled and they entered unopposed.

*****

Siegfried saw the group coming. His troops were behind the hill and he and his sergeant were lying on the crest watching. The column had just come down a gentle slope and was crossing a wide open plain. There were about seventy troops in all and a large number of wagons as well as women and children. One of the wagons lost a wheel and was just left. As the column reached the midpoint of the plain, part of the group turned on the rest and a battle broke out. Apparently the mercenaries had decided to take the treasure. Siegfried watched the fight and waited until over half the armed men had fallen in the fight.

Siegfried slowly walked down the hill with his sergeant mounted up and went over and down the hill into the valley. His men formed line. They looked what they were, formidable. By the time those in the valley realized that Siegfried's force was coming there were only about twenty men on the field who had not fallen. Most dispersed and fled leaving the women and children behind.

Three men were brave enough to stay to protect the families. They were told by Lord Yingvar's man that the company was here to protect Yingvar's family. They were assured no harm would come to the women and children. The three men surrendered.

Siegfried and his men returned to the castle to find that the army had already camped and was preparing the evening meal. The captain went directly to Wolf who he found sitting in the kitchen eating. He bowed his head.

"My Lord, I have returned with the baggage train. The women and children have not been harmed; Lord Yingvar's family is safe. The column was in our sight when the mercenaries turned on Sven. I assume they were after the treasure. Sven died in the fight and I estimate about twenty men were still standing as we approached. The wounded had been killed by their opponents. The able bodied fled except for three brave men who stood to defend the women and children. When we offered quarter and assurance we would not harm the families, they surrendered."

Wolf motioned for Siegfried to sit, "Have something to eat with us, Siegfried." Wolf motioned to one of the men standing guard in the kitchen, "Find Lord Yingvar and tell him Captain Siegfried has brought his wife and family back safely. Bring the three men who were captured with the wagons."

Siegfried was already wolfing down some stew that had been set before him. He stopped long enough to say, "I have put the treasure wagons in the walled yard and placed a heavy guard on it. The men have been instructed not to leave it." He started eating again.

Wolf leaned back, "I wish all campaigns were this easy and bloodless."

Siegfried said something that took Wolf by surprise, "It seems your God puts the other gods to shame for he certainly gives you rule over their followers."

The three men were brought to Wolf and they knelt in respect.

"I understand you three men stayed with the women and children when the others fled. Why?"

One of the men answered for them, "Honor, Lord. We were not released with Lord Yingvar's death because we had made oath to our dead lord to make sure no harm came to his family while he went to war. "

The men were startled when they heard the voice from behind, "No one told me I was dead."

Yingvar strode forward and helped the men up. "I was in the care of my ally and my king, Aelle here. You honor me by your loyalty." Yingvar did something none of these men had experienced before, he embraced them.

Wolf interrupted, "Siegfried here,", Wolf said motioning to the man, "has returned with your wife and family. I thought you would want to know that they are in the courtyard."

Yingvar gave a head bow, which was not lost on the men who wondered at the strange events, and left.

They were in the presence of the great warrior lord and did not know what to do. Wolf motioned to the table, "Sit, eat, you must be hungry."

The men were used to obeying orders, but this they did with relish for the stew smelled good and as it turned out was delicious. They had not eaten in a day.

Wolf asked the senior man, "What is your name"

"Egon, great Lord. I am Lord Yingvar's castle sergeant."

"Yingvar is a lucky man to have men who would die for him after his death to protect his family. You did well."

The man lowered his head, "Thank you, Lord."

Wolf had finished eating and started to rise. There was no one left in the kitchen. The sergeant asked, "What are we to do, Lord?"

"You are a sergeant and this is your lord's castle. I am sure you can find something useful to do."

Egon looked at the great Lord, "We are not prisoners?"

"In case you hadn't noticed, Yingvar is now my vassal earl. Since you are his men you are my allies and subjects through him. Why would you be prisoners? Since you are still in your lord's employ, I suggest you be about his business."

Egon was stunned, "Yes, Lord."

Wolf strode from the building and went to find Shadow. Two men came from the shadows, but Wolf sensed them before they were visible and drew his sword in a flash and moved to the right so only that man could engage him. The man's sword thrust forward as his shield swept thin air and Wolf's blade which was of finest steel pierced the poor quality partial mail in his left side. In a lightening swift move, Wolf twisted and withdrew the blade and spun behind the other kicking the back of his knee brutally so he fell forward. Wolf put one foot on the man's blade and his blade at the back of his neck where he had no mail.

"Who sent you", Wolf demanded.

The answer came almost involuntarily, "Ulrich and Ragnar."

Men came rushing to the scene. Wolf ordered them to bind the captured man and take him to the stables. He ordered a man to go for Shadow and Siegfried. In the stables the man was seated on a hay bale. He hung his head. Wolf glared at him and the man got more uncomfortable as the minutes, which seemed like an eternity, passed. It was cool in the barn, but the man was sweating.

Shadow and Siegfried arrived together.

Wolf spoke first, "Assassins. The other is dead. They were inept though they did time their attack well. My half-brothers Ulrich and Ragnar sent them. I think it is time to deal with them."

Wolf put the tip of his sword under the man's chin and lifted his head, "You are going to tell us exactly where my brothers are and how you are to contact them if you succeeded. If you do not, well, I do not want to think about that. If you tell us all, you will live."

The man could not tell them quickly enough. He and his friend had been hired by Ulrich and Ragnar at a tavern frequented by soldiers seeking employment. A man named Gimm had actually paid them the first installment. The rest was to be paid after they had fulfilled the agreement.

Shadow and Siegfried had questions for him. Yingvar came part way through the interrogation. Wolf nodded to him in acknowledgement. After they knew what they wanted the man was taken to Yingvar's dungeon.

The men went to the kitchen to discuss the matter. They were brought beverages.

Wolf spoke first, "Any ideas how to deal with my treacherous half-brothers and Gimm?"

Yingvar answered, "Egon comes from the area where they are now. He knows the land and the town. His services would be useful."

Wolf answered, "That is a good start."

Siegfried volunteered, "Let me go with a chosen few, perhaps five. I see no choice but to kill them for otherwise they will continue their treachery. It will be done so that no one will know for sure though some may suspect. We will strike and leave."

Wolf looked at Shadow who nodded agreement.

Wolf was obviously uneasy, "I do not like to operate in the dark but to face my enemy in the light of day and face to face. However, they have forced the situation. Thank you, Siegfried, and may God be with you."

The meeting was over. Shadow walked with Wolf.

Shadow was concerned, "I think the time is past for you moving about by yourself. I think you should always have some of your elite company with you. Your family should be similarly protected. You are a ruler now, not just a soldier, and too many lives depend on your safety."

"Oh my friend Shadow, life has gotten so complicated. Former enemies like Siegfried have become trusted subjects while family has become bitter and treacherous enemies. I need the comfort of my God tonight so I must go pray. Please find the priest and have him come to pray with me."

Two days later the army was heading back north in the boats they came in. Yingvar's castle was manned with his loyal retainers who had come to him and it was now well known that any attack against him was an attack against King Aelle and his lords and army. To attack would be to let the Wolf Pack loose. It was enough to ensure stability of the hold.

Chapter 12 - On a Mission

Siegfried picked the best five fighters from the volunteers who came forward. Egon was there when the men were picked. Siegfried knew some of the men and the rest were well known to Egon.

He was allowed to choose from the best horses, and his men were well equipped though they made sure they appeared to be regular mercenaries. Some of the deception was as easy as sheathing quality blades in battered scabbards. Newly made spears that were strong were dipped in salt water so they would appear old and rusted and the shafts oiled and stained to look old and worn. Lord Wolf entrusted Siegfried with a goodly sum of money in the event bribes were needed and for their expenses. Siegfried distributed small purses to each of the men so they could operate independently if the need arose. With Captain Siegfried and Sergeant Egon leading, the men set out on the mission they knew was dangerous. They had been promised a generous reward for their success, but the honor of the success would be the greatest reward.

It took the unit several days to reach the town and they arrived during the day. The men who had been chosen were not only good fighters but intelligent. They knew how to blend in by partly being themselves while playing a role. The men entered the town in two groups of two and one group of three.

They did not draw attention to themselves but all ended up arriving at varying times on the same day at the same inn that was known by Egon as a haunt of warriors. Egon and his partner Sasko went to scout out the brothers. They learned by simply walking by and secret observation that the brothers were still staying in the rented house as the assassin had reported.

There was a tavern nearby. The men had only to buy a few drinks for some old warriors and inquire about who might be hiring mercenaries to discover a lot. They found out two brothers named Ulrich and Ragnar were staying with a man named Gimm, just as it had been reported. Rumor had it, that this Gimm was a disgraced bishop who had been exiled by some lord. The brothers were dangerous men and had earned a reputation of not being trustworthy, so most of the wiser soldiers gave them a wide birth.

Egon and Sasko were told that it was reported that a family in the east was hiring mercenaries. The pair feigned interest but the men did not know who was doing the recruiting. They already knew Sven would not be hiring more soldiers.

To learn the routine of the men the unit set up a revolving watch to track their movements. They found the men had hired about a dozen mercenaries who were housed on the edge of town. Each evening the two brothers brought them food and drink. Ragnar made the journey with his brother for he was now getting around quite well on a wooden leg.

Gimm seldom left the house and spent most of his time drunk with some cheap whore. At first they thought he was of no concern, after all it was the brothers the unit was after. Then they discovered by listening to gossip that Gimm was indeed providing the money for the brothers.

The seven men had never been seen together as a group as they were careful to avoid it. They did however interact in seemingly random meetings while drinking. The order was passed that they were to prepare and leave that day and meet at the rendezvous point.

The attack was to be made that evening. At the rendezvous Siegfried told them the plan. It was simple, but hopefully it would be effective. The trick was to do it quickly. The men were experienced warriors so there was bound to be noise, but they must be away without alerting the mercenaries or the townsfolk. They would attack the brothers on the path closer to the town than the barn where the mercenaries were barracked. Gimm would be taken at the house.

They hid until late afternoon then took their positions.

The brothers were making the evening trip to bring food and drink. Their hands were occupied with the sacks. They had also shared copious amounts of ale with Gimm. They were careless and five of the unit merely jumped and overwhelmed them. Gimm was easier, he was found by two of the men in a drunken stupor on his bed. Completely incapacitated it would have been murder not a warrior killing another in an attack. It would be a dishonorable murder so they dressed, bound, gagged, and blindfolded him. They searched for an hour before they found his treasure hide.

Back at the rendezvous point they had to figure out how to get their prisoner Gimm back. They could tie him on a horse but that would attract attention and they would have to avoid the main road. They would also either have to keep him drunk or he would start to suffer the shakes. They needed a horse drawn cart.

Egon came up with an ingenious plan. They took Ragnar's leg off, tied up his pant and smeared blood on bandages they wound on the stump. He was tied over a horse and Egon and another of the group brought him to a small village.

He was their wounded comrade who they were taking home. He had lost a leg in battle and was unconscious. The corpse was fresh so only close examination would have revealed the truth. They needed a cart and draft horse and they found one for sale.

As not to arouse suspicion they spent an inordinate amount of time dickering on price. Egon bemoaned the asking price denouncing it as banditry. As they got closer to a realistic price, Egon played the money card, saying that this was their highest price; otherwise they would not have any money to purchase food on the return journey. The price was now fair, and the seller did not want to antagonize two desperate soldiers so the deal was made.

Ragnar's body was dumped back near the mercenary barn.

This was how it came about that for four days Gimm rode across country jostled in the back of a farm cart. His bindings and gag were checked regularly and he was always closely guarded. At the river, Egon was able to sell the horse and cart to a local farmer while they waited for one of Beorn's trading boats to dock. Egon and the two men from Yingvar's castle who had accompanied them, stayed ashore to return to their Lord's service. The journey back to the valley castle was an easy one for Siegfried, his men, and the prisoner who welcomed the smooth ride after the torture of bumping around in a farm cart for days.

When they arrived back at the valley castle, Gimm was unceremoniously dumped in the castle prison until King Aelle gave orders for his disposition. The money that had been taken from Gimm was also turned over.

Bishop Aert had been on a mission. He was determined to reestablish the abbey and rebuild the Cathedral. The amount of treasure that Wolf had captured from former Bishop Gimm and returned to the church was more than enough to repair the abbey and re-staff it. The amount of money being tithed to the local churches and by the Lord Aelle directly to Aert provided more than adequate funds to not only rebuild the Cathedral but to build more local churches. His problem was finding skilled tradesmen and labor.

Much to Aert's pleasure, Lord Yingvar had sent a message requesting a priest be sent to explain the Christian God to him. Aert considered carefully who the right man to send was. In the end he sent Kenric who was plain spoken, likeable, and had a way of explaining the good news of Christ that even the unschooled could understand. He asked Kenric to inquire if there were tradesmen and workers needing employment for there were churches to build. Kenric chose his own temporary replacement at the monastery and went east accompanied by four warrior priests dressed as men-at-arms.

Soon tradesmen and laborers were coming from Yingvar's lands to help build churches. In the process they not only earned money for the support of their families back home, but came to know the people with whom they were now allied. Some accepted the new religion. Kenric sent a message that Yingvar had accepted Christ as his personal savior and asked for priests to be sent. Aert was pleased that many priests volunteered to be missionaries, but his abbey staff was getting smaller by the day.

Aert had also been determined that the abbey, monastery, and new cathedral should not be defenseless. He had continuously been training warrior priests.

Meanwhile, the women at the castle were on a mission to make sure that Cenedred and Ethelind were married before there was another crisis. They were busy preparing for the weddings which they had rescheduled when they received the word the army was on its way home. Two days later they heard the boats carrying the army had been sighted. This time they went to the docks with guards from the castle.

Wolf arrived home with the army to fanfare and cheering. They were again conquering heroes. They had brought home more treasure and there had been no casualties.

Wolf was pleased when he saw Cenedred, his mother, and Hilde at the docks. When he disembarked he greeted them with embraces and good words. He introduced Yingvar's eldest son Karsten who had returned with him as originally agreed.

The family enjoyed a lunch together. Shadow was not in attendance because of the press of his duties, but Lucan and Karsten were. Wolf told the boys they would be included in the family dinners and events for they were now valued family friends. Karsten was a little shy at first but soon opened up. Karsten was nine years old and Lucan was eight. They found they had both been sent by their fathers to the King. While Karsten was a guest and Lucan a hostage, they were both being treated as close family friends. Karsten had been afraid he would spend his time in a dungeon. They had not had strong family interaction in the castles from which they came and enjoyed being included.

Later in the day, Shadow presided over the army as it was finally all disembarked and assembled in the field. Aewel brought Karsten and Lucan to observe. The boys were awed by the size of the army. They asked questions and were surprised when Aewel told them this was only part of the army. There were three other castles and a fortification where troops were stationed.

The boys watched as the regular pay was given to each man according to his rank. They had never seen such a thing. Shadow announced the date and time to assemble for the next distribution and the part-time soldiers were dismissed to return to their farms and businesses. The regulars went to their respective assignments where the duty and leave rotations were announced.

The War Chief came to where Aewel stood with the boys and asked, "Are these the new recruits, Captain?"

Aewel tried to be serious, "Yes, my Lord."

Shadow looked at the boys who were looking a little intimidated. "Stand straight," he commanded in a stern voice. They obeyed.

"You come from a line of warriors and lords so we expect you will do well. Your training schedule will be as follows: First thing each morning you will attend the morning prayer meeting and breakfast with the troops and then you will have two hours of battle training with and without weapons. Because you are the sons of lords you will have a special instructor who will be training another half dozen boys of about your age who show promise. After lunch you will spend two hours schooling with the priests who will teach you reading and writing and you will study manuscripts.

You will have the evenings free to be with the family. There is no training on Sunday, but you will observe how we worship our God for about an hour in the morning and attend an hour of instruction in the afternoon to learn about our God so you will understand us. You will not go outside the castle without permission nor without guards for you the sons of Lords. Any questions?"

The boys stood silent. Aewel nudged them, "The proper response is yes lord or no lord."

The boys answered, "No, Lord."

Shadow looked at Aewel, "You may dismiss the troops and return with them to the castle."

Aewel was having a hard time keeping a straight face, "Yes, Lord."

So it was the boys' routine was established and they started integrating into the life of the castle. The boys were all puffed up and excited for although they had some training, they had never been treated like real warriors. They liked the idea.

That afternoon the boys were introduced to their tutor Father Feran. He assessed where the boys stood in their reading abilities and was disappointed in their level of progress. They would be a challenge, but Bishop Aert had stressed the importance of teaching the boys. This was of special importance given that Lord Yingvar had become a Christian. Aert hoped to impress the Lords with the value of a Christian education.

That evening's family dinner was especially entertaining. Lucan and Karsten were asked about their day and their telling of their experiences was enjoyed by all. After dinner, Wolf summoned a priest to chaperone as he and Cenedred walked arm-in-arm in the garden. Wolf honored the agreement he had made with Shadow and two guards accompanied the priest, following a discreet distance behind them and stationing themselves at strategic positions when the couple stopped and sat on a bench.

Cenedred leaned her head on Wolf's shoulder. He observed that the effect she had on his body was similar to what he experienced as battle approached, only this was pleasurable.

She sighed, "Is it always going to be like this, stolen moments?"

"No, for one thing we will be together every night except if I am at war or travelling. I expect we will have times when we will have more time for leisure together and other times when governing will take me away from you as I travel. Oh, I don't really know, this is new to me also."

She took a deep breath, "I guess we will have to work through it together. At least we won't be alone in the work of marriage, for we have God to help us."

"Yes indeed. He is my certain rock and shield. I could not have made it this far without Him."

They sat quietly together for several minutes and then Cenedred said, "As much as I don't want to, may we go back in? I am getting chilled." They rose and went inside.

Chapter 13 - Expected and Unexpected

Tents surrounded the valley town. What had started out as a castle village had grown quickly into a town in a matter of months as economic prosperity came to the valley. Soldiers applied for land lot grants. Modig had taken great delight in drawing up a town layout map for Lord Aelle's approval. As lots were granted or purchased, soldiers, tradesmen and merchants built homes and businesses with their new wealth.

Many new families were started and Bishop Aert had talked to the Lord about building a new church as the castle chapel was no longer large enough to hold the worshippers who attended mass on Sunday. The church was presently under construction. The river trade resulted in the opening of many new businesses, in some of which Beorn and his secret partner had an interest.

It was in this atmosphere of optimism that Lords and commoners, clergy and lay people, warriors and farmers, came to witness the long anticipated weddings. A large tent had been erected on the low rise hill just beyond the town. The castle chapel was too small for the weddings and the cathedral town could not host the weddings for the new cathedral was not yet fully built. At least this way people could gather around the hill and watch the ceremonies.

The appointed day turned out sunny, so the ceremony would take place. If the weather had been rainy, the event would be postponed. Usually the weather was good at this time of year and God had blessed the folk.

Something new would follow the weddings; the feasting would take place in the field. Already meat was cooking on spits over open hard wood fires and pots of slow cooking delicacies hung over others. In town, every available oven had been baking bread all night. Delicious aromas were everywhere. Workers were scurrying about unloading tables and benches from wagons. It seemed everyone was bringing what was needed. It was truly a community event and effort. It was a testament to the love the people had for those getting married that so many had volunteered to cook and perform other duties under the watchful eye of Wilfred.

Shadow, always the soldier, had tasked Captains Aewel and

Ragnvald with security. Ody, Eadgard's sergeant knew most of the invited guests by appearance and so he was in command at the Neck. Captain Siegfried commanded the river defenses and had experienced sergeants screening incoming vessels. Skjold was given temporary command of the southern castle, so Herewood could attend the wedding.

At eleven o'clock with the sun high in the sky, the first to arrive at the ceremony tent were the honor guards who marched from the castle and took positions at each of the tent poles. People waved small strips of cloth as they marched. The Bishop's procession was next and Aert walked with two priests leading and two following. The people waved small pieces of colored cloth and shouted greetings and Aert waved and smiled. He was enjoying the festivities. The clergymen entered the tent and stood in front of the makeshift altar facing the crowds. Next were Lord Aelle and Osmund on horse followed by the members of the Wolf Pack who were not on duty elsewhere. There was cheering and vigorous waving. Aelle and Osmund waved to the crowds. When they arrived at the tent, they dismounted and two men took their horses.

The guard marched in twos to the upside of the tent and turned facing the crowd. Lord Eadgard and Cenedred rode out of the castle with two of Eadgard's men marching in front and two behind. Eadgard was on the right and Cenedred was riding side saddle on the left, her horse led by the man in front. Her horse was decorated with flowers. Next were Lord Cuthbert and Lady Ethelind in the same manner. Next came the bride's family. As the retinue travelled to the wedding tent, the crowd cheered and vigorously waved small pieces of colored cloth.

The brides entered the tent accompanied by their fathers. The ceremony took about an hour and the crowd gathered around the tent stood in solemn silence. First Aelle and Cenedred exchanged vows and then Osmund and Ethelind. As each groom kissed his bride there was enthusiastic cheering which caused both brides in turn to blush even though they were smiling broadly. As arranged, directly after completion of the weddings, an installation ceremony was held and Osmund was appointed Earl of the northern castle under the rule of King Aelle. Again there was much cheering after which the lords, ladies, bishop, clergy, and soldiers marched down the hill to participate in the festivities.

As the reception line was being organized by Wilfred so all the dignitaries could greet and congratulate the newlyweds and their families, Captain Ragnvald discreetly whispered something to each of the lords. He knew they would notice any increased presence or proximity of the guards.

Lucan and Karsten, who were included in the line, did not notice the two guards that moved up close behind them. They were enjoying their part and were proud of the uniforms Wolf had given to them. They resembled the uniforms Wolf's guard wore, except they bore their father's crests. Each wore a small knife in an ornate scabbard, a gift from Lord Aelle.

After the dignitaries had passed through the line, Cenedred and Ethelind had pleaded to keep it open for the people of the valley. Wolf allowed it for he knew to give in to fear was to surrender. The people loved coming through the line. There were lots of curtsies and bows by men and woman who had not had the opportunity to practice such niceties and they enjoyed it. After about an hour the ladies stood barefoot and after two hours, chairs were called for so they could sit. It made the greeting no less appreciated by the people. Bishop Aert who still practiced at arms daily stood the entire time as did all the lords, except at hour three Lord Cuthbert called for a chair.

The people were very well behaved and only two men who had a few too many ales were removed from the line by Wolf's guard. At least they were wise enough to go quietly. Wolf noticed that during the distraction one man approached without as much scrutiny as others had been given by the guards. The hairs on the back of Wolf's neck stood on end. There was something about him. He was not looking anyone in the eyes. Wolf who was third in line stepped forward and took a quick two steps and was in front of the man standing just a little to his left before the man realized it. He grasped the man's right wrist with his right hand as his left hand held the knife blade against the man's side with enough pressure the man's breathing quickened.

Wolf leaned over and whispered in the man's ear, "Come quietly and live, resist and die here and now." The man was wincing in pain from the twisting grip Wolf had on his arm that Wolf was not about to release. "Let go of the knife." The man did. Two of Wolf's guards had quietly come up and taken a hold on the man. Wolf smiled and said loudly, "Certainly friend, these good lads will show you the way." It happened so quickly hardly anyone other than Shadow, Eadgard and the closest guards noticed the encounter.

It had become very hot and a small awning was erected to keep the Lords and Ladies out of the sun. Food was now being served so the waiting line dwindled and the guards at Shadow's direction stopped any additional people from lining up.

This day would be the topic of discussion for weeks. People who had never seen their lords and ladies up close would recount their personal exchanges. They would recount this day to their children and grandchildren as the soldiers recounted the battles fought.

The brides were still smiling. Wolf smiled as the last of the line passed at four o'clock and leaned over and whispered to his wife, "Let this be a lesson to you that no good deed goes unpunished."

His new wife just smiled and whispered back in a playful tone, "As you say, Majesty."

The wedding party went to their tent and started eating for they were all hungry. Everywhere there was much laughter and joviality. As dusk approached, Wolf noticed Captain Ragnvald came and spoke in Shadow's ear; he nodded and said something softly to the Captain who left.

The newly wedded couples adjourned to the castle at dark accompanied by soldiers carrying torches and followed by dozens of impromptu singers who serenaded the couples on the way home.

While the Lords Aelle and Osmund and their brides enjoyed their wedding night, Aewel and Ragnvald pieced together information about threat that had been averted.

It was one of the newer sergeants Leof, who had prevented the greatest threat. He had been tasked during the previous period of war with the roving patrols of the northern valley. There it was possible for a small group of infiltrators to climb into the valley along the creek bed coming from the mountains. When his captain gave the order to make sure the valley was secure for the weddings, he started roving patrols on his own initiative.

It happened he was leading one of the four man patrols when he found a band of infiltrators. His men took up an ambush position and when the infiltrators came to that position he walked out and asked them what they were doing here. They moved to attack him.

For most of them it was the last mistake of their lives. As the seven infiltrators moved to attack what they thought was a lone soldier, Leof's men attacked from the sides. Leof took the first man as he hesitated and looked toward the side attack. Leof then moved on the second man and engaged him. Five infiltrators were killed; one was seriously wounded and captured. Two of Leof's men were wounded. The alarm horn was sounded and reinforcements came. A hunt began for the one infiltrator who had escaped. He eluded capture and was the one King Aelle had stopped.

Shadow had been informed by Aewel of the encounter, but not wanting to ruin the wedding day, told the captains to carry on and notify the guards.

It turned out that the drunken men had actually been paid. They were told it was a practical joke and had been drunk enough already to believe it because they wanted more money for ale. At the time they probably did not know they had been a distraction for an assassination attempt. Now they were terrified once they learned what had happened. They had been unwitting pawns, but they realized that their actions might result in a death sentence. The captains determined they were of no further use and they were thrown in the dungeon. A few days there might just serve to cause an attitude adjustment.

The captains interrogated the two captured men who had infiltrated the valley. They started with the wounded one because they thought he would be the most susceptible to persuasion. He was in great pain and pleaded for help. He was told he would get it, but first he needed to answer some questions which he did. The man wanted a promise of help and life and the captains agreed.

The man told the captains who they had been sent to kill and the bounty that had been offered. It was a fortune so the captains surmised that the overall contract would have been a lord's ransom. The leader of the group was the one who had eluded Leof's troops.

His name was Dag and the group with him had not worked for him before. They had been hired through an arranger named Elvard. The man did not know where the arranger could be found but only of the tavern where they had met him. The information he provided would be enough to eventually find Elvard, though it might take some time. A healer was called and the man received treatment and some relief.

The two captains did not go to see Dag, instead they sent someone else to see him. He was the least impressive looking man they could find but very quick witted. The man went into the cell where Dag was chained. Dag sized him up as a person of no importance and spat at the insult of being sent such an interrogator.

"What do you want? I will tell your masters nothing."

The man shrugged, "I was told if you were cooperative I was to take your measurements for your coffin. The Christians here will give your body a proper burial. They told me if you were uncooperative not to bother, they would just put your body in a hole for you are just a pagan anyway."

"You think I will be tricked by you?"

"Can I take your measurement or not?"

Dag almost growled it, "I will say nothing."

"I do not think my captains care, Dag, because your friend has told them all they need to send men after the arranger Elvard. Measurements, yes or no?"

Dag was taken aback. If they knew his name and that of the arranger they probably would just execute him. They must have captured another from his group and he had talked. It occurred to him he might have some small thing to offer.

"Tell your captain I know where Elvard can be found. Perhaps I can save them great expense in return for my life?"

So it was that the captains came to know not only who the target was, but the person who arranged the attempt and where he could be found. Elvard could be made to reveal who had hired him.

It had been agreed the captured men's lives would be spared. They would leave, however, with an exile mark and without a thumb on their dominant hand so they could not grip a weapon. They would be guests in the dungeon until Elvard was dealt with.

The newlyweds mainly stayed to themselves for two days eating in their rooms. On the third day they came out of hiding to eat a mid-day meal together for Eadgard and Hilde were preparing to leave. Eadgard had been away for some time and needed to return. Shadow was also thinking that he should go to start work in the northern lands. There was discussion about whether Ava might stay with her sister and Aelle for a while.

Eadgard cornered Wolf after lunch, "Son-in-law, I think it is time you inform me about how your spies communicate so quickly with you."

Wolf took Eadgard to the library where he explained about the homing pigeons. He took Eadgard to the pens on top of the chapel tower so he could see some of the pigeons. Eadgard was impressed. They arranged for Eadgard to be included in the system though it would take some time to raise pigeons that would home to his castle. The spy perch would be used in the meantime.

After lunch, Wolf was advised of Siegfried's return. Wolf and Shadow met with him regarding his mission. The report was succinct and yet full. Wolf asked that Bishop Aert be told of Gimm's capture and imprisonment and that Lord Aelle would like to discuss the matter with him at his convenience.

Aewel and Ragnvald came to report on the assassination attempt. Wolf greeted them heartily.

"These attacks are getting tiresome. Have you got any idea who is after me this time?" Wolf inquired.

Ragnvald was the one who answered, "You were not the one they were trying to kill."

Wolf was a little surprised, "Who then?"

Aewel pointed at Shadow and proceeded to tell them what had happened. Wolf agreed to honor the arrangement the captains made to spare the men's lives and to the punishment the men would be subject to. It was agreed the men would not be punished and released until Elvard was found and the two captives would be informed they would be held until Elvard was located.

Wolf, Shadow, Ragnvald, Siegfried and Aewel sat to discuss a plan of action. Someone had to find Elvard and find out who wanted Shadow dead. It must be someone important for the amount of the bounty must be enormous considering what Dag and his men had and were to be paid. It was enough for them to risk an almost suicidal mission. Yet, Shadow could think of no enemy he had made that was powerful enough to pay to put this plot into effect.

In order to find out who was behind the plot, someone would have to travel west to find Elvard and discover what he knew. The group discussed how many should be sent and who it might be. To send a group would be to draw attention. There was concern about authorities in the area being suspicious of outsiders who had no legitimate reason to be there. Wolf's captains and sergeants were always stopping and questioning visitors who had no apparent reason to be here.

One man could work more freely, but if he needed help to carry out a plan, he would not have it. They discussed having one capable man going and having some others stay nearby in case they were needed. The major concern voiced was that Elvard was reported to be located in a heavily populated area. It might be possible for individuals or two men to travel to the area if they had a legitimate reason to be there. A few individuals or partnered groups could have intersecting meetings to pass along any plan or need to the group. The problem was to come up with reasons for the men to be in the area.

Wolf directed the captains to seek the trader Beorn for suggestions and told them they could trust him completely in this matter. He gave them a sealed letter to give to Beorn.

Shadow left to prepare to travel to his new castle with his new wife.

Wolf met next with Bishop Aert regarding what should be done with Gimm. Aert always the practical one identified some possible scenarios: one, they could try Gimm as a normal citizen and that could open them up to conflict with the church because it could be claimed he should be tried in an ecclesiastical court; two, they could send him to the ecclesiastical court, but that would cause all sorts of inconveniences for Aert and Wolf and it could end up being expensive as the church might claim the local officials should pay for the prosecution; three, they could leave him in prison, but eventually the fact he was here would come out and they could be accused of denying Gimm a fair trial. The way Aert saw it, Gimm was just a problem and a thorn in their side.

Wolf suggested another possibility. They could just take him back where they found him and drop him. Without money, Gimm would have to find work. A paper could be drawn up granting Gimm release pending an ecclesiastical hearing based upon his having returned the remaining money to the church, which had already been done. It would then be up to church authorities to recapture him, which under the circumstances they would probably not care to do.

Aert thought this was a wonderful idea and said he would make the arrangements which he did. So it was that Gimm ended up back where he had been taken.

The men who brought Gimm back left him at the outskirts of town with a small purse with enough coin for a week's sustenance.

Gimm had not eaten the morning before he arrived, so he walked to the local tavern where he ordered food and ale. He was eating and thinking about what he could do when a strong hand clasped his shoulder and he found a knife at his throat.

"Thought you would avoid paying us did you? We want the money you owe us, Gimm."

Gimm was terrified and dropped the wooden spoon he had been using to eat the stew he had been served. The man holding the knife was not alone, another man was with him and came around the table and sat. Gimm knew then who it was that held him hostage; it was two of the mercenaries the brothers Ragnar and Ulrich had hired.

"You can either pay us or we will take it out of your hide."

Just then the tavern door burst open and several men in uniform entered. The man holding the knife quickly sheathed it and sat down. One of the men in uniform pointed in Gimm's direction.

"Arrest those three," was the order.

The two mercenaries tried to flee, drawing weapons as they ran for the kitchen and the back door. They ran out the door and into five uniformed men who saw the drawn weapons and did not hesitate but fell on the two men. There was a brief skirmish in which the two mercenaries were killed.

Gimm was indignant and demanded to know why he was being arrested. He was stunned to find he was being arrested for the murder of Ulrich and Ragnar.

Justice in the town was swift. The resistance of the two mercenaries found with Gimm and their fight to the death was considered by the magistrate to be ample evidence of Gimm's guilt. The magistrate's previous investigation had revealed Gimm's reputation as a man of poor morals who had recruited mercenaries for obvious illicit activity. Gimm was no lord who needed soldiers for a legitimate purpose. He was convicted and executed the same day.

*****

The captains met with Beorn. They gave him the letter from Lord Aelle which he read. They then explained the problem to him. Beorn knew the town where Elvard was located. He also had a way to get a small group there legitimately. One of Beorn's boats periodically took cargo there to trade. The trip necessitated going far down river and going up another. Along the route cargo was sold and others bought and loaded, then sold and unloaded at least twice. Five or six men could thus easily be infiltrated into the town and stay for two or three days without arousing suspicion. The crew usually stayed on the boat at night to guard the boat from thieves, but half the crew was off the boat during daylight hours between on and off loading.

Beorn did not have a full cargo for the first leg, but under the circumstances the first leg would not be a problem. Beorn was sure the boat would have a full cargo when they arrived at their destination. All the captains agreed this was an ideal solution. A tentative departure was set.

Siegfried suggested to the other captains that men who had long experience as scouts, sometimes spying out enemy towns, would be good choices for the expedition. They were used to going unseen and were good fighters. It was agreed Siegfried would recruit the team.

Siegfried had known Magnus for many years. He was a man of just a little above regular height and when he wore his normal clothes looked very ordinary. If one saw him without his shirt, one would be struck by the thick knots of muscle that covered his body. The man was stronger than any other Siegfried had ever met. He was also quick of mind and a deadly fighter.

One thing about Magnus that was hard to understand, given his talents, was that he was not ambitious. He had great initiative when given an assignment, but had no desire to be responsible for the long term leadership of men. It was not that he could not lead; he just had no ambition to. If he needed to assume leadership in battle he could and would, and had with great success. Magnus was a very useful soldier. Siegfried thought it was a shame that so much leadership potential was being wasted. This was the man Siegfried approached about the assignment.

Siegfried knew Magnus could keep his mouth shut so he gave him an outline of the assignment. Magnus said he was intrigued by the challenge and asked if he were successful if it might result in a promotion. Siegfried was totally taken aback by this turn of events, but agreed to give him the next promotion if he succeeded. Others had tried to bring Magnus into a leadership role without success. Siegfried did not care why the young man had changed his attitude; he just knew this would benefit the army.

Unbeknown to Siegfried, Magnus at twenty three had met the first girl who had really gotten his attention. She was a pretty daughter of a local merchant. She was totally taken with Magnus, but told him he would have to provide a better income than that of an ordinary soldier before she would agree to marry him. When she found out he had twice turned down promotion to sergeant, she chastised him. She told him if he could better himself, she might consider marrying him.

Siegfried told Magnus for his assignment he would lead a unit of five men. Magnus asked who the five would be. Siegfried told Magnus that would be up to him. Surprisingly, Magnus agreed readily to recruit the unit. Siegfried told Magnus he was immediately being released from his present unit and duties and would report directly to him. Siegfried impressed the need for secrecy. A detailed briefing would be given the team before they left. Siegfried wanted the unit to leave within forty eight hours.

Magnus knew there was a lot riding on the success of the mission, so that day he gave a lot of thought to whom he wanted on the team.

He would seek them all out the next day. That evening he told his woman friend that he was going on a patrol and when he returned he might again be offered promotion. She asked him if he could obtain land for a house, for she knew Magnus had the money from his share of the spoil with which to build one. He told her when he returned he would apply for a land grant. The young woman was very happy and Magnus was very motivated.

Magnus spent the next day talking to the men he had chosen. In order to talk to two of the men it was necessary to tell their sergeants that he had been sent by Captain Siegfried and if there were any questions they could verify this with him or Captains Aewel or Ragnvald. Magnus had chosen another scout, Aldin, to be his second, and four others who were excellent fighters.

Magnus considered Aldin the next best scout in the entire army. He was intelligent, could blend in anywhere, and was a deadly fighter. The four other scouts were seasoned killers who knew how to take orders but still exercise initiative, could keep their mouths shut, and were not prone to drink too much. Each of the men on the sketchiest information agreed to join a special scouting group. Magnus gave Siegfried the names and the men met with Siegfried and Magnus that evening. The men got to know each other.

Siegfried liked what he saw. No one could have picked a better team for this mission. He told the men they would be briefed in the morning and to be prepared to be gone for several weeks. They were told they didn't need to bring their own mounts.

That night the captains went to see their lord. Siegfried explained the plan and the team that would be going. Wolf thanked the men for their work and said he prayed for their success.

The men left their uniforms behind but went armed. They were to assume the role of ship guards. Beorn had put together a new crew for this trip, so the men did not know each other.

Men liked to work Beorn's boats for they always went protected by capable guards who it was rumored were often hired soldiers of Lord Aelle. Beorn's crews were seldom challenged or bullied in ports. It had very quickly gotten around that to fool with Beorn's cargo or crews could be bad for one's health.

The "guards" of the new group led by Magnus, in addition to

standing watch, helped on the oars when needed. This gained them appreciation from the crew.

Nodens had captained boats for Beorn for many years. All he knew was he was to deliver the six cargo guards to a certain town stay for as long as reasonable without raising suspicion, and leave with them and possibly one other passenger. The captain had undertaken unusual trips for Beorn in the past and as always did not ask questions.

Beorn was not just an employer to Nodens, but a trusted friend. Beorn had taken care of his loyal employee for many years. Since rebounding from his ill fortune, Beorn had ensured Nodens had shared in the new prosperity. Beorn's crews worked regularly and under good conditions. Working for Beorn was considered a prize berth for he paid well, though he expected hard work, and all his crews were treated fairly.

The journey down river was uneventful. The first cargo was unloaded without a problem late in the day. Nodens expected a further cargo and it was already waiting. It was loaded the next morning and they headed down river. At the next stop they unloaded the cargo, but the new cargo had not yet arrived. Some of the crew went into town.

One member came back to sound the alarm that the crew had encountered trouble. Two guards stayed with the boat along with the remaining crew while Magnus and three of his team grabbed helmets and shields then ran into the town following the crew member who had come for them.

When they entered the tavern, there were seven men holding down the three crewmen and beating on them. Magnus knew immediately these were not town's men.

Magnus shouted, "Arms, ambush, surge, back way!"

His men understood. This was no tavern brawl and swords were drawn as the group charged forward and four of the enemy fell before they could draw weapons. The other three fell quickly and in less than half a minute the three crewmen were hustled out the back door. The enemy had meant to draw the men into a restrained conflict until others could enter to overwhelm the guards. Without the element of surprise, the enemy had no chance.

Magnus urged the group toward the boat and they arrived just ahead of their pursuers. Much to the surprise of the men chasing the small party they encountered a wall of two armored men with shields and weapons blocking the narrow dock. It was a bottleneck into which the attackers were forced and their rush stalled. Three men died against the two defenders. Then there were four armored men. The enemy were hacked, stabbed and slashed to pieces against the four man wall. It was only a few moments until the wall surged slightly forward and six armed horrors were decimating the attackers.

The attack broke after just a few minutes. The guards did not chase them. Eleven attackers lie dead or dying and others were fleeing aiding limping and wounded comrades. Had the thieves just tried to steal the wrong boat or was their more to it. The scouts found two men who could not escape because of their wounds but who could still talk.

"Tell me who sent you and live." Magnus demanded.

The man spat on him and Magnus executed him. He moved to the next man who was now shaking, whether with fear or shock Magnus did not know or care.

"Tell me who sent you and you will live."

The man moaned, "I will bleed to death anyway."

Magnus shook his head, "Tell and I will have you bandaged and I will not kill you."

The man nodded agreement and said, "Lenarth," and then he died before he could be bandaged.

Nodens had heard the exchange and said, "Lenarth is Beorn's competition. Because Beorn deals honestly and fairly he has been taking much of Lenarth's business. Lenarth had depended on the attack on Lord Aelle's lands being successful and Beorn being put out of business. A pox on Lenarth," and Nodens spat.

Magnus asked, "Is this the first such attack."

"Crews have been bullied and attempts made to intimidate them, but they were unsuccessful because of the guards. The townspeople quickly learned it was better not to take Lenarth's money than to suffer the wrath of the boat guards. It seems this time he was after the guards and did not use townspeople."

Magnus looked around before saying, "Nodens prepare the boat for departure just in case. Aldin you stay here with two, you two come with me." The three guards staying moved to stand at the narrowest point of the dock. Nodens returned to the boat. Magnus marched back into town.

Magnus could find no townspeople. He became very concerned. The last place he searched was the church. There he found them. Men, women and children were lying dead everywhere. The parish priest was nailed to the large alter crucifix.

Magnus and his two men changed tactics. They were scouts again and followed the blood trail of the retreating enemy. They found eight able bodied and half that number of wounded camped around a fire in a small clearing in the woods. No command was necessary. They merely stepped from the woods and began killing the enemy. No one escaped and only the wounded remained.

Magnus looked at the wounded man who looked to be the most likely to survive. The man thought he was going to die. He started to shake.

""Tell me the truth and I will let you live. Was it Lenarth who sent you?"

The man unable to speak because of fear nodded vigorously wincing in pain while he did so. A thought came to Magnus.

"Was he allied with Elvard?"

The man again nodded in the affirmative. Magnus ordered a stretcher made for the man. By the time it was finished the other wounded had died. Magnus left with his men who carried the stretcher. The men returned to the boat and sailed back to the valley castle. Magnus saw this as something far more sinister than an attack on Beorn. When he returned unexpectedly, he was brought to Siegfried directly and then to Lord Aelle.

Magnus knelt to his king, "Majesty, I am your servant."

Wolf motioned him to rise and sit at the table, "Magnus, here in the library we are informal. This is the place of soldiers, a head bow is sufficient."

"Yes, Sire."

"Tell me what happened."

Magnus recounted the events without the results of the interrogation. He also gave his observation that there was more here than met the eye.

Wolf asked him, "Why are you so concerned and suspicious that you postponed your mission?"

"My Lord, two of the men interrogated admitted that Lenarth had sent them. On a hunch, as both men are based in the same town, I asked the one if Lenarth was allied with Elvard. He confirmed it. I believe him for he knew that I already knew about Lenarth so he probably assumed I had pre-knowledge of Elvard. I brought him as prisoner."

Wolf inquired, "Why not go directly after the two?"

"I surmise that the western Lord Feliks, who rules the land in which the town lies, is not a part of the conspiracy. If the attack succeeds there is stress between you for it is of such a scale that you would think he was behind it or allowed it. On the other hand, if it fails and there is retribution, it is an attack by you on his lands. Alternately, if those who are known to be close to you cause problems in his area of rule, he might be persuaded that you have ambitions there. Any of these might entice Feliks into an alliance against you. So far these have all been avoided. I could not grasp all the possibilities, but it seemed under the circumstances ill-conceived to proceed without further orders."

Wolf smiled at Siegfried, "You made a good choice, Siegfried. And you Magnus have shown you have intelligence, initiative, and courage, and I am glad we have sergeants like you serving us."

Magnus bowed his head, "Thank you Sire, you are most generous."

Wolf smiled, "Tell your men they will not be needed until tomorrow morning and then we may have a further assignment for you."

Magnus bowed and left.

Wolf said, "He is insightful and intelligent. He will be very useful, Siegfried. Please have everyone come for council."

Magnus went directly to see Leola at her father's shop. She greeted him with a hug and a kiss on the cheek as her father looked on. Her father made a strange "harrumph" sound and looked at Magnus.

"I have told her she can do better than you. There is no future in being married to a soldier."

The remark struck Magnus the wrong way, for he had always been proud of his service. He walked up and got in Irwyn's face, "I am proud to be a sergeant in my king's service and you would be well to mind your place."

That was the first time that Irwyn had seen the warrior's side of Magnus and it was frightening. At that moment he realized that this man could probably tear him limb from limb and not work up a sweat.

"Calm down, Magnus. I was just jesting. I meant no harm or disrespect."

Magnus nodded, "I accept your apology, friend."

It was then that Leola realized what Magnus had just said, "Is it true you are a sergeant? Is it? Tell me?"

Magnus shrugged, "Yes, it is."

She spun and giggled; "Now we can be married."

It then occurred to Magnus. "I have not proposed marriage nor has your father agreed. He has in fact, said over and over he is against your marrying a soldier."

Leola looked at him with a shocked look on her face. It was true, but surely he wanted her, "Yes but …" she trailed off realizing he was right.

Magnus' mind was racing a mile a minute. What a fool he had been in so many ways.

"What makes you think I would marry a girl whose approval is conditional upon my station in life? Where would you be if I were maimed in battle? You would flee home to daddy. A soldier needs a real woman not some girl parading as one. You are a sweet child, of whom I am fond, but you are not a soldier's woman and your father is right that you are not suited to be a soldier's wife."

Magnus marched off. Leola watched him leave, her mouth open. Well, she thought, there were more deer in the woods and she could do better anyway. At the time she did not realize how wrong she was.

After stopping to buy two apples, Magnus returned to the castle to obtain the new uniforms he would need that indicated his new rank. He might as well use his time wisely. He went to place his order but the man in charge of the stores was away and he would not be back for half an hour. Magnus went to find a place to wait. He found a cool spot on a stone bench under a tree. He sat down and started eating an apple. Magnus was lost in his thoughts about how the day had gone.

A feminine voice came seemingly from nowhere, "Nice looking apple."

Magnus did not even look up but pulled out the other apple and said, "Be my guest."

"Thank you."

Magnus turned and there sitting beside him was the prettiest young woman he had ever seen. She was chomping, not nibbling, on the apple. Between mouthfuls she managed to speak while Magnus sat there speechless.

"I am famished. It's not that I could not get something, I have just been preoccupied. My sister's recent experience had really made me consider."

"Consider what?" Magnus inquired.

"How I see life. I have been so self-absorbed. Now that I have been brought to reality, I have to decide how to live the rest of my life."

Magnus nodded, the beauty of the girl being lost to the conversation. "Me too. So much has happened to me recently that I have realized how selfish and unrealistically I have been living. I also have changes to face."

The young woman said, "Tell me."

Magnus did. He did not tell about the details of his mission but other than that he was bluntly honest about his personal life. He confessed to wanting to avoid responsibility and had wasted his potential. When he finished, he just waited in silence for a few moments.

His guest finally said, "It seems we have a lot in common. Our stories have many similarities. What is your name?"

"Magnus."

"I am pleased to have met you, I am Ava. I hope we have an opportunity to talk again."

Magnus smiled, "That would be nice. Do you work here?"

Ava smiled, "No, I am visiting relatives. Perhaps we can meet here tomorrow and talk some more."

Magnus shook his head, "I will probably be sent on patrol tomorrow but when I return, if it is acceptable, I will ask for you and perhaps we can talk again."

Ava smiled, "It is acceptable."

Magnus watched her leave. It again struck him that she was a beauty, but there was more. He did not know that a few weeks ago the "more" had not been there.

Chapter 14 - Emissaries and Scouts

Present at the meeting with Wolf were his grandfather and his captains; Eadgard and Shadow had gone to their own castles. After much discussion, it was decided that an emissary would be sent to Lord Feliks to inform him of their suspicions and to assure him that they had no ambitions for his realm. The emissary would be authorized to agree to an alliance if Feliks seemed so inclined and brought the matter up.

It was also agreed to reinstitute the mission to find out who was behind Lenarth and Elvard's treachery. It was unlikely that any enemy lived after Magnus' encounter and if they did, they were unlikely to identify him as he had worn his helmet during the encounter. Magnus and his team would be sent again on the original mission, but this time there would be more guards on the boat including some archers. With the help of a good captain and three able sailors the guards would be the crew.

Nodens captained the vessel downriver. This time it was a larger vessel with more men. They proceeded gently as the soldiers learned their duties. They were strong and quick learners. They would do. There were several dockings along the journey so they could practice that most delicate part . It was necessary that they would appear accomplished at their final destination.

While Nodens was going down river in one vessel, Siegfried was going in another. He was on a diplomatic mission, a role that was new to him. He would disembark just down river adjacent to Asbjorn's lands and travel west to Feliks's castle. He had an entourage with him as one would expect an emissary to have.

Siegfried came alongside the dock of the first village in Feliks's lands. There he found a greeting party. His boat displayed the appropriate flag indicating he was an emissary come in truce. The man in charge of the docks told Siegfried's captain that his passengers could not disembark until he received orders. The captain was leery and told the man they would then anchor off shore and wait for permission to disembark. The man in charge tried to persuade the captain to stay docked, but the captain pushed off.

They were about a hundred feet from shore when a group of

armed men arrived. They were not Feliks's troops. By this time the boat was prepared to repel borders if necessary. The man who was in charge at the docks argued with the armed men who marched away. The man then left hurriedly and returned shortly with some baggage and a chest, boarded a small sail craft and went quickly downriver.

Siegfried's vessel remained anchored and vigilant the rest of the day and through the night. It was late morning when twenty troops showed up at the dock. They set out pickets and two men were sent on an errand and came back shortly with a villager who talked to the man in charge of the troops and then went down stream. He came back a few minutes later rowing toward the boat in a one man punt.

The man hailed Siegfried's vessel, "Lord Feliks has sent his captain to meet you. The Captain is named Mann. He invites you to come ashore and begs forgiveness for the way you were greeted at first. He will accompany you and your people to Lord Feliks's castle."

Siegfried ordered the vessel to dock. Siegfried was the first off the ship and strode up to the Captain.

"Captain Mann, I am Siegfried, emissary of King Aelle, who has sent me to Lord Feliks. We come in peace bearing gifts and with good intentions."

Captain Mann smiled, "Since when are renowned warriors emissaries?"

"Since their King so appointed them and gave them orders to carry out," Siegfried replied in a jesting voice.

"Welcome, Siegfried. How many men do you have with you?"

"Twenty five men-at-arms and two priests and four bearers."

Mann whistled, "Quite an entourage. A full company?"

Siegfried shook his head, "By no means. The company I normally command has over fifty men-at-arms not including archers."

Mann asked, "How many captains?"

Siegfried knew it was probably common knowledge so answered, "Four, not counting those supplied to or employed by his under Lords."

Mann whistled, "Then it is true that your King has a large standing army."

Siegfried nodded, "The largest I have seen, and the reserves are numerous and train regularly. Ah, I am like an old woman, I say too much."

Mann smiled, "The reports and rumors indicated as much as you have told me. If I may suggest, let us get organized and ready to move out for if we march hard we might reach the castle by nightfall. I must admit I am glad you brought such a guard. As you have seen, our land has been tormented by raiders."

As they marched, Siegfried and Mann compared notes about the battles they had seen and warriors they might know in common. Mann made note of the fact that the soldiers with Siegfried were in excellent physical shape and well disciplined. There was no griping and the hard march seemed like a stroll in the woods to the men. Mann had been concerned the emissary's entourage might slow them so they would have to camp along the way. To the contrary, the pace they kept up was almost too much for Mann's men and when they approached the castle in the early evening his men were exhausted but Siegfried's men were jovial and joking.

Siegfried's sergeant Leof had the banners unfurled and held up as they neared the castle and the men fell into a formal march. Mann had noticed that this was all done without any orders being given by Siegfried. Mann looked at the Wolf banner and became inquisitive.

"Is this the Wolf pack?"

Siegfried laughed, "Oh no, this is less than a tenth of the houschold guard."

"I have heard of both the wolf pack and the wolf horde, what is the difference?"

Siegfried had been conscious of the information he had given. It mostly confirmed common rumor and knowledge, but now Siegfried meant his answers to impress with the truth. It was obvious Feliks was in trouble and needed an ally and was trying to determine the strength of Lord Aelle and if that was where an alliance should be sought.

"The Wolf Pack is the group of my Lord's personal guard. The horde refers to the entire trained army including those at his other castles and of his under Lords, relatives and loyal men to whom he has granted holds."

Mann turned this information over in his mind. If the men with Siegfried were less than a tenth of the personal guard then it followed that total was over two hundred and fifty. It was known that Lord Aelle held other castles and fortifications and had under lords, Earls, who must command fairly large numbers. The under lords were all thought to individually be stronger than Lord Felix. This meant that at any time the Wolf could field an army of several hundred not counting reserves. It was a mind numbing number.

Mann considered the implications. It was probably true that if King Aelle had ambitions for his Lord's lands he could just march in with a small part of his forces and take it. It was therefore probably a safe assumption that it was true what was said about Aelle. He was a true Christian Lord, fierce when provoked, but not covetous of his neighbor's lands or possessions.

Siegfried was met in the courtyard by Lord Feliks in an informal but friendly greeting. It was a warrior's greeting not a diplomat's. Leof's stood his men at ease but in truth they were being vigilant for betrayal. They only appeared to be relaxed in ranks.

Feliks's castle was small and so with apologies, Siegfried was told his men would have to be quartered in the chapel. Siegfried laughed saying that would be heaven compared to many of the places they had slept and it probably would not be the first time they slept in chapel, though usually through a boring sermon. Feliks decided he liked Siegfried. Siegfried told Leof to quarter his men in the chapel and the castle sergeant volunteered to show him the way.

Leof observed that the small chapel would be easy to defend but hard to escape from. There were only two doors and the windows in the stone walls were tall and narrow, easy to defend but difficult to escape through. Leof had his men move all the benches so they could sleep against the walls and the benches were pushed against each other and positioned so as to impede any possible charge into the room.

Leof set up a sentry schedule and instructed that only two men could be gone from the chapel at any one time. Leof had just settled the men in when the sergeant came to the door and asked to see Leof who agreed. The older sergeant entered without being asked and noted the position of the men and the benches.

"You know your business. I would have a time rooting you out of here with three times the men you have and I do not have that many. You have no worry about being attacked here, but I do not fault you for your caution. It is good soldiering. I came to invite you to my home for supper once your men have been fed. About seven? Food will be brought for your men."

Leof nodded, "Thank you, I would be pleased to take you up on your invitation. Do you live in the castle?"

"Yes, just ask anyone how to get to Sergeant Karl's."

The man held out his hand. The two sergeants clasped arms and Karl left.

Leof turned to his second, "Be sure the men follow the caution for eating unknown rations."

Siegfried was meeting with Lord Feliks. Feliks was a rural Lord who had no time nor desire for formality. Feliks shared a cup of ale with Siegfried and Mann sitting at a small table. He stated that his was a small shire castle in what had been until recently a rural holding that hardly any outsiders bothered with except for a few river traders. His people had been happy and content with their simple lives and it had been easy to keep the peace. Recently, much to his surprise, large numbers of armed men had been causing havoc along the river. He did not understand the reason for this change.

Siegfried shared the story of Captain Nodens' merchant ship and the attack. He related the story of the guards thwarting the attack and what they had found and done. Siegfried also explained what their suspicions were. With respect, it seemed that Feliks was being used as a pawn to manipulate perception of the lord's further west. Feliks thanked Siegfried for the information and ordered he be shown his quarters. Feliks told Siegfried that perhaps they could talk again after dinner.

When Siegfried left, Feliks consulted with Mann. Feliks might be content to be a rural Lord, but he was no fool. What Siegfried had told him fit the circumstances, but could it be that King Aelle did have ambitions? Mann gave Siegfried his insights and conclusions. If Aelle wanted the land he just needed to send twice the number of men accompanying Siegfried, which he could easily do, and take the land. Mann was convinced that Aelle was sincere.

That evening, Leof had no trouble finding Sergeant Karl's home. His wife was a jovial woman and the sergeant had three children, the oldest of whom was a fourteen year old daughter. Leof was made to feel at home and thoroughly enjoyed the evening even though it was apparent that Karl was up to some subtle matchmaking. Leof excused himself after a visit of about two hours thanking Karl and his family for their hospitality.

After Leof left, Karl said to his wife, "He is young but very capable. I get the feeling he and his men would be fierce to face in battle, a mixture of young and hard as well as experienced and hard. Some in his command are old enough to be his father and I could tell by watching them that they respect him. He will advance. He would be a good prospect for a son-in-law. I must go now to report to Lord Feliks." He kissed his wife and left.

Feliks found he enjoyed Siegfried's company. He asked Siegfried how he had come to be in Aelle's service. Siegfried saw no reason not to, so told him, giving the general story. Without going into details, Siegfried told how after making oath, Lord Aelle had given him an important mission and trusted him to carry it out. Siegfried said matter-of-factly that his ascension in the ranks of his Lord's trusted followers was in accordance with his ability, experience, and loyalty.

Feliks was impressed by the story. It was obvious that Siegfried was now totally Aelle's man. Feliks thought this Aelle must be a special leader to create such loyalty in former enemies.

The men agreed to meet again the next morning to discuss business. After Siegfried left, Feliks received a report from Karl. It seemed the perception of Feliks men was that the emissary was truly here on a mission of peace and were as concerned about possible treachery as was Feliks.

Siegfried met with Feliks for an early morning meal after which the men got down to serious discussion. Feliks needed help in taming the raiders in his land and wanted an ally against whoever was behind the moves. Feliks was forthright with Siegfried that his incomes had fallen in half. His farmers were continually in fear, his officials along the river had been bribed or murdered so his taxes from trade had fallen off, and his forces were too small to overcome the marauders.

Siegfried told Feliks of Eadgard's, Osmund's, and Yingvar's arrangement with Aelle. He also told of the alliance with Asbjorn and the cost that was paid for the alliance. Feliks found the arrangements a little troubling from a pride standpoint, but had to admit to himself that economically and militarily it made sense to be an under-lord of Aelle.

He asked Siegfried to give him time to consider the matter and asked if he were to agree to come under King Aelle how long it would take to receive military help. Siegfried said the troops here could start immediately if they could obtain mounts until their own arrived and reinforcements could arrive in a matter of days. Siegfried asked what King Aelle would do if Feliks decided not to enter into an agreement.

Siegfried simply replied, "Nothing, unless an attack comes from here and therefore my Lord is forced to respond. We will continue to be good neighbors with a hands-off policy."

Feliks thought about the matter for two days. His mind was made up for him when he received reports of thirty armed men raiding the river trading docks and fishing villages. He called for Siegfried who came to him straight away.

"Siegfried, I have received reports that a group of armed men are attacking my river settlements. Because I accept your assurances that these raiders are not yours, if your men would take some of mine and rid me of this threat, I will agree to become King Aelle's vassal lord."

"How many do the reports indicate are in the band?" Siegfried asked.

Feliks replied, "About thirty."

Siegfried thought a moment, "How many mounts can you provide?"

Feliks looked to Mann, "How many?"

"Twenty six or seven sound ones."

Siegfried nodded, "If you permit, Lord Feliks, I will take my men immediately and I suggest Sergeant Karl and one other come."

It was left unspoken that Feliks could thus be assured that the raiders were not some treachery to pressure Feliks to accept Aelle as King.

Feliks looked at Mann, "Assist these new allies of ours to prepare."

Leof and Karl were put to work to prepare the troops to move out. Provisions were gathered, water bags filled, and mounts were saddled.

While preparations were being made, Mann got a map and showed Siegfried where the reported attacks occurred. The enemy was making tracking them too easy moving from north to south along the river. It was a predictable route. It was as if they were trying to lure Mann out to engage them. Siegfried told Mann as much and warned him to be prepared for an attack on the castle. The enemy might not know that Siegfried and his men were here in addition to the castle soldiers. Siegfried wrote and sealed a letter to King Aelle and suggested to Mann that it be sent up river as quickly as possible as it would bring reinforcements.

Siegfried's men were told to remove their distinctive uniforms and carry them in their saddle bags. From a distance they were to look like the soldiers from the castle.

Within the hour the column rode out of the castle. As they headed south, one of Siegfried's men saw a scout in the woods and the word was passed discreetly forward. Another scout was spotted and by then Leof had two of his best scouts out. One enemy scout would never report back and the column's whereabouts would not again be established.

The raiders sent scouts north and west but could not establish contact with Siegfried's column. The raider's leader assumed they were moving too slow to catch up with his raiders. The next day the raiders came to a fishing village that was deserted; they fired it and rode quickly on.

The next town the raiders approached was the main river trading port in Feliks's lands and there would be plundering there. The scouts from the north and west came in and reported no contact. The leader thought they could be in and out of the town and set an ambush before the trailing column could reach them.

Unknown to the raiders, Siegfried's men had ridden past dark, rested for only four hours without making camp, and rode again. They made very good time and had cut straight across country, through farm fields, along cow paths and foot paths in single file, and through woods where rough country pathways had been worn down. They did not follow the twisting roads that made for easy riding that the raiders were using.

The raiders' leader trusted his scouts' reports. They spied out the town which seemed busy at work. There were two boats docked and they were just now being unloaded. If they could get close to the boats without being noticed they could keep them from leaving. Then the town was ripe for picking. The scouts told they could only approach the docks along the riverside without being seen.

The leader ordered his men to dismount and they slipped along the woods and started down a narrow street next to the river which led directly to the docks. The raiders went quietly so as to postpone drawing attention as long as possible. They had entered the town without the alarm being sounded as they had in so many others. Everything in this town was theirs for the taking including the boats.

The men at the rear turned to see a cart being drawn from a courtyard entrance into and across the street. Before they realized the significance men came into the street ahead of the raiders and formed a shield wall across the street. The shield wall was advancing five abreast across the entire street and it was at least two deep. The raiders had few shields being poorly outfitted for combat against experienced and well-armed troops.

The leader yelled, "Trap. Back."

The street was very narrow and retreating was a problem for the wagon behind them was wedged between two stone walls and suddenly was ablaze. The hay in it was burning furiously; there would be no escape there. The leader tried to make his way back to see why his men were not retreating when he saw the smoke. On the river side was a low retaining wall and a fairly steep bank to the river and on the other side houses.

"Into the houses!" the leader ordered. His men started to break in doors and then wished they had not as they succeeded for they were met by some of the wolf pack. The men saw the distinctive uniforms and shields. Some panicked and fled to the river while others died. The shield wall rolled down the street and warriors poured out of the houses. The slaughter was great as the raiders were outnumbered two to one.

A half a dozen raiders who could swim had jumped the wall, abandoned their heavy weapons, and started swimming across the river. The wolf pack drove the raiders against the retaining wall and down the river embankment. Only a handful lived to surrender.

Siegfried was amazed. These men had been poorly armed and trained. They were just thieves with weapons and had fallen like wheat to a farmers scythe. Siegfried went to the dock area where the only open space in the small town existed. It was the trading and loading area. He sat on a box and had the five men who had been captured brought to him. Karl stood beside Siegfried. Leof was busy collecting weapons and doing the things sergeants did following a battle and another sergeant was standing on the other side of Siegfried.

Four of the five captives hung their heads. One was insolently staring at Siegfried his hands behind him twisting as though he would somehow loose his bindings.

"Bring him," Siegfried ordered pointing at the man. The man was brought to Siegfried and forced to his knees. "Who sent you" he demanded.

The man did not answer.

Siegfried rose and struck the man. "Take him and hang this murdering thief." Siegfried ordered pointing to a pulley arm used to load and unload cargo.

The man shouted as he was dragged to his feet, "I am no thief; I am a soldier!"

Siegfried looked at him, "Then who is the Lord you serve if you are a man-at-arms and claim you are a prisoner of war?"

The man blurted, "Lord Sebbe."

"And who is this Lord Sebbe you speak of?"

"He is a lord from the west. His lands border the river to the west that runs parallel to this one."

Siegfried looked at Karl. Karl nodded.

"How do I know you speak the truth?"

The man was no longer insolent, "My horse is over the hill and in it is my letter from my Lord authorizing me to raise a company to raid here."

Siegfried sent men to fetch the horses and the letter. Siegfried sat and waited. The letter brought to him was no doubt authentic and it did show that the man had acted under authority of Lord Sebbe. What was unclear was where he was authorized to raid. The letter did not contain that essential piece of information.

Siegfried looked at the man, "Can you read."

"No, but a priest told me what was in it."

"Was yours the only party told to raid here?"

The man shook his head, "There was another, but I do not know where they are now."

Siegfried frowned, "In hell."

Siegfried looked at Karl. He ordered his men to take the prisoners away for they would be going to Lord Feliks's castle. The town's people had already started coming out of hiding. The men, who had been brave enough to continue working the docks, knowing the danger, were from one of the two boats docked there. It turned out both of the boats were Beorn's. One was headed upriver and the other was headed downriver. It was a blessing that it was the one captained by Nodens and Magnus and his troops had been put to work in the ambush. The raiders had been like lambs to the slaughter.

The after action report was positive. Only two of the men had been injured seriously and were not fit for duty. They would be sent up river on the vessel headed for the valley. Karl went with Leof to search the captured horses for useful information and to see what the raiders were carrying.

Siegfried, Nodens, and Magnus went aboard the vessel. They discussed the possibility that Sebbe had sent the assassins against Shadow. That made no sense. There was no gain for Sebbe so there must be a piece of the puzzle still missing. The plan would proceed.

Chapter 15 - Treaties and Treachery

The next morning Nodens' vessel sailed away and Siegfried returned to Feliks's castle with Karl. The other boat would sail upriver. Feliks's horses were returned and the captured horses were now the mounts for Siegfried's men. Feliks listened intently to Karl's recounting of events. He went to the dungeon to question the captives himself.

Feliks was a man of his word and was prepared to be allied with and be a vassal lord of King Aelle. Now that things were stabilized, Feliks suggested that he go north to meet Aelle. He further requested Leof stay here with his men so that he and Karl would have enough men to go about the countryside assuring the people that things were now under control and to defend the castle and Feliks's family. Siegfried agreed and he and Feliks went upriver the next morning.

It had been some time since Feliks had been on the river and never as far north as he was going. He thoroughly enjoyed the trip and Siegfried's company. He was impressed by the river defenses and that the boat was stopped and checked as a matter of routine. Siegfried knew the sergeant on duty and they exchanged friendly pleasantries and Siegfried introduced Grimbold to Lord Feliks.

Feliks was impressed by the lush fields and friendly people they passed. People were always waving to them and calling greetings. As they approached the castle, Feliks noted the town close to the castle was a large and bustling place full of activity. When they arrived, four boats were already docked. Increased trade had led to building of three more docks and now there were a total of six.

A young man was waiting on the docks with two men-at-arms when the boat docked. He embraced Siegfried and welcomed him home. Feliks came down the gang plank to where the men were.

Siegfried turned to Feliks, "Lord Feliks let me introduce King Aelle."

Feliks was stunned for a moment; this is not what he expected. After a moment Feliks regained his senses bowed his head and said, "Majesty."

Aelle stepped forward and embraced Feliks much to his surprise,

"Welcome, Lord Feliks. I am pleased to have you visit. Let me take you to meet my family."

Feliks enjoyed the walk to the castle. People were bowing their heads and smiling as they passed, acknowledging them but keeping a respectful distance. It was a bustling place. It was not lost on Feliks that this king was loved by his subjects, so much so that he could walk among them without a lot of men-at-arms ringing him.

As they entered the castle, several people came out to meet them. Wolf introduced Feliks to his wife Cenedred who surprised Feliks by embracing him. He was then introduced to Lord Cuthbert and Bishop Aert who also gave him a hearty greeting. They went to the garden where they were seated at a table and drinks were brought to them. Feliks was somewhat surprised that Siegfried was still with them. He was even more surprised when two more captains came to the table to join them. Ragnvald and Aewel were introduced to Lord Feliks and chairs and drinks were brought for them.

Cuthbert had met Feliks many years before, when Feliks was but a lad, and was especially pleased to trade mutual memories of past experiences and people they had known. It was a pleasant social gathering. Feliks asked if he could have a tour of the castle and the town. Cuthbert volunteered to show him around and Feliks agreed. When they left, Siegfried told the others of his adventures in the west and of the developments.

Feliks was fortunate for this was market day and he got to see the vendors and all the goods that were sold or traded. He purchased a belt with a beautifully worked small silver buckle for his wife and a bolt of cloth for his daughter. He enjoyed the extended negotiations for he had not been able to do that for a long time. The word had gotten around as to who Lord Feliks was and the two lords were greeted cheerfully by many and received warm greetings. The vendors made a special effort to attract the men.

The town was quite large and there were a lot of new homes and a few permanent small shops. The lords visited the shops and Feliks bought his wife a spun wool blanket. They even stopped at the local tavern for a drink of ale. The men there were friendly but respectful. Feliks could not remember having such a good time. He told Cuthbert he would have to come here with his family. Cuthbert told him he could catch a ride on one of Beorn's river boats anytime and they were best because they had guards who would bolster any guard Feliks brought.

As the men were returning to the castle they ran into Karsten and Lucan who Cuthbert introduced to Lord Feliks. The boys were respectful but at the first opportunity drifted away to enjoy the rest of the day as they had finished their work. Feliks inquired as to how the sons of the lords came to be here and Cuthbert told him. Feliks said that they did not look like hostages nor act like it.

Cuthbert laughed, "Those boys are like a part of the family and they act it. They are industrious and have fit in here quite well. Their studies and warrior training are progressing nicely."

Feliks was intrigued, "You teach them to fight?"

Cuthbert replied, "Of course, we want our family and our allies to be able to defend our lands."

Feliks asked, "May I see their training tomorrow?"

"I am sure that can be arranged. It will necessitate rising early as their day starts at sunrise."

Feliks smiled, "I think I can manage that, even at my advanced age."

The men laughed, because unlike Cuthbert, Feliks was just approaching forty and still in good health and a vigorous man.

The dinner that night was a very pleasant family affair. Feliks told how he would like to revisit in the near future with his family. Feliks had four children, a daughter who was the oldest, and three sons who were younger. The family expressed that it would be a delight to have them come.

The next morning Feliks rose before the sun and Cuthbert took him to observe the general morning routine and training. They attended the morning prayer, the breakfast, and observed the weapons and physical training of the household guard. Feliks was impressed and was told they practiced daily for the wolf pack members were the full time soldiers.

Feliks was then taken to where the boys trained and watched Lucan and Karsten train with the other boys. Feliks was impressed with the discipline of the boys and how able they were for their age and size. Cuthbert told him they were given uniforms that identified them as members in training and they would lose the right to wear them if they dishonored the unit. The boys knew the uniform was a privilege and with it came a monthly payment though of course it was not what the men received.

On the return walk, Feliks heard the clash of practice swords and shields and asked if he could watch.

Cuthbert hesitated, "Usually spectators are prohibited, but in this case an exception is in order, but I ask that you not repeat what you see here."

Feliks replied, "Of course."

They went up some stairs and quietly through a small door. They were standing on a small viewing gallery over a fairly large room. Three warriors were attacking a single warrior. They were all dressed in mail and helmets but were using only practice weapons and shields. The three men kept trying to hem in the single combatant, but he was lightning fast and seemed to foresee their next moves. The sound of clashing sword and shield were like the fast drumming of rain. One of the three left the attack bent over and limping moved away. The single combatant made a signal and the other two ceased.

The man went to the injured soldier and talked to him. He seemed genuinely concerned for the man's wellbeing. The other two had taken off their helmets put up their weapon and shields and went to their comrade.

The injured man finally spoke, "That last blow knocked the wind out of me and the one before would have broken my leg if your sword had not been a practice one. I am alright now, except my pride is injured."

The single combatant laughed, "You who has given me more bruises than anyone else and you have the nerve to complain because you get a little payback?"

The other men laughed.

The man who was the brunt of the comment rose and limped over to put his weapon and shield away, "One thing about these exercises, the last time I was in a real battle the opponent seemed to be moving in thick mud. This may be a little hard on the pride, until we face an enemy, then we know how fortunate we are to have these opportunities."

The single combatant spoke again, "That's it for today; I have other work."

The three men bowed and left while the remaining man put up his weapon and shield. Feliks waited for the man to remove his helmet. He was not surprised to see it was King Aelle and now knew that his warrior name Wolf was appropriate. Feliks had no idea that at one time it had been used as an insult.

Cuthbert and Feliks slipped out the door.

"Does he practice like that every day?" Feliks asked.

Cuthbert answered with a shrug, "Usually he practices longer, unless he is travelling. The men compete each week to be his sparring partners. On a couple of occasions, he has been slightly injured as have some of his practice partners. The troops consider it the best training opportunity available. You heard the one man; in battle our soldiers are quicker and better than their opponents."

A short time later Cuthbert and Feliks went to the library where Wolf and Cenedred were waiting.

"Welcome. Please Feliks, take a seat," Wolf said, motioning to a vacant place.

Feliks dipped his head in respect and then took a seat.

Wolf sighed and started the discussion, "Are you willing to go forward? Do you have any hesitation?"

"I am willing to go forward on the terms Siegfried set out but have a few minor conditions."

Wolf tilted his head, "What are they?"

"I would like my two youngest sons to come here to be trained with the other boys. I would also like my eldest daughter to come here for an extended stay. I understand that here women are not prevented from learning to read and I would like her to be taught. I would also ask that a worthy warrior and a few men be stationed at my castle to train my eldest son and supplement my castle guard until my lands attain their full prosperity."

Wolf nodded, "That is most agreeable, but you must know that training with my men will mean no special privileges. Everyone trains the same and on the same routine. As for your daughter, my wife would have to agree to safeguard her."

Cenedred paused for a moment, "I will want to meet her first before I commit to mentoring her."

Feliks laughed, "I agree to your most reasonable conditions and would have it no other way."

Wolf nodded, "We will arrange a formal ceremony to sign the necessary documents and make the public declarations."

Feliks smiled, "Perhaps my family could be brought here for the ceremony. I will provide a letter for my wife and a boat could bring her and my children here."

Wolf declared, "It will be done."

*****

Magnus and most of his men enjoyed the river trip from the start. There were a few men who could not swim and being on the water made them very uncomfortable. In the evenings when they were anchored or docked, some of their comrades began to teach them to swim. Many river boat men could not swim, so the teaching did not draw any suspicion. The peer pressure motivated the soldiers to learn quickly. It was not long until they could stay afloat and a few days more and they could swim a small distance. After a week they could probably swim to shore at the widest part of the river. Swimming became a regular part of the crew's routine.

By the time the boat was reaching the river fork where it would turn north up the other river, the men had fallen into a routine. By the time they approached their destination they were practiced in handling the boat and making it look as though the boat crew was not on alert when it was. They had found ways to hide their weapons and armor and were practiced at quickly preparing for battle. The group had drilled and drilled. At first it had been awkward for half the crew to keep rowing while half donned battle armor and then to change places without hardly missing an oar stroke, but they had worked it out.

It had been decided that if they engaged boat to boat they would not wear mail, for more men drowned in their mail than died from weapons in boat to boat encounters according to the captain. Many of the men had been at the river defense and now that they all could swim concurred with the decision. Going ashore to do battle would be a different matter.

The boat they were in was one of the two repairable seagoing raiding vessels that had taken part in the river attack. It had been put back into service by Beorn as a river trader. Yet, it was still essentially what it had been constructed to be. The size of the crew meant that Magnus commanded almost a full company. Part of their cargo was new uniforms packed in a crate. The men did not have other uniforms, but new ones were on board as trade goods manifested to be delivered upriver and were there if needed.

The boat arrived at its destination and docked without assistance of a pilot or smaller craft, usually a sign of an experienced crew. The goods bound for here were quickly and efficiently unloaded and the fees and taxes paid. As the receivers came to pick up their cargo, the payments were received by weight of coin and silver and the money taken on board. During the transactions Nodens did not try to hide the fact that at least some of his crew were there to guard him, the cargo, and the money. This was in keeping with past trips he had made and had come to be expected. Anyone trying to steal from Nodens would not have easy pickings.

Once all the cargo had been picked up, Nodens took two men and went looking for new cargo to purchase that could be sold on the return journey. Nodens found a smith that specialized in making farm implements of very high quality. No purchase was made on first viewing. Nodens made some inquiries and with a few well-placed small gifts discovered the smith had found it difficult to sell his goods as the farmers in the region were having a difficult time. When Nodens returned, he was able to purchase the smith's entire inventory at a price that would yield a very good profit up river.

In the meantime, under the guise of seeking cargo, Magnus and another man roamed the town striking up conversations and by buying a pint here and there learned about the politics and business dealings here. At the same time, Aldin was scouting with a companion in another part of the town.

Magnus found a man who apparently made very good arrows. The hunters in the area frequented him, but he had a hard time selling enough to more than scratch out a living.

Pehr was with the crew so Magnus took him to examine the arrows. In talking with the man who made the arrows, Pehr discovered the man also made bows. Several were brought out and Pehr purchased one for himself and a bundle of arrows at what Pehr later told Magnus was an extremely good price. The man had a wife but no children. One of the problems that Wolf's archers encountered was a shortage of high quality arrows.

The next day Magnus went with Pehr and purchased, at a very cheap price, almost all of the bows and bundles of arrows the man had made. Later in the morning, Magnus went back and made the man whose name was Rheged a personal offer of employment. A wage was negotiated and a good faith payment made to the man that was the equivalent to what he made in three months. The man was enthusiastic as his tools, his wife Alta, and their few meager possessions were taken on board.

The rest of the day was spent scouting for other cargo and accumulating information. A few of the crew went into town in twos but never more than a half dozen were away from their vessel at any one time. They learned much about Sebbe, Elvard, and Lenarth.

Magnus went around the places where Elvard and Lenarth did business. He did not know what he expected, but Elvard seemed to be marginally on the edge of criminality here, but not a man of great influence. He had just two body guards who were more show than fight from what Magnus observed. Much to his surprise, inquiries revealed that Lenarth was not really a merchant. His shipping business was but a sideline that it was rumored allowed him to carry out all sorts of criminal and mercenary activities. It was those activities that allowed him to force smaller river shippers out of business. It was rumored that Lenarth worked as a client for Lord Sebbe. Rumor also had it that Lenarth now received a percentage of the income from the docks for protection and thus river trade had stabilized.

That evening Magnus, Aldin, and Nodens discussed what they had learned. It seemed that taking Lenarth was out of the question now that they had established he was under orders and the protections of Lord Sebbe. Elvard was apparently the weak link, but how much he knew was questionable. It was probable that Elvard was used by Lenarth to contract the assassins. He was probably directed to do so by Lord Sebbe. That Lord had no reason for wanting Shadow dead so must be allied with another lord. Anyone approaching Elvard from the boat would probably be reported immediately up the chain of command and the boat would be attacked by bandits of unknown origin.

Magnus decided to find out if emissaries from other lords had been visiting Lord Sebbe in the last few months. That was the kind of information that would be part of the local gossip and easy to obtain. It took only an evening to find out the answer. Two different sources told of Lord Sebbe entertaining delegations from Lord Asbjorn and from Shadow's family. Rumor was that Lord Sebbe was paid a large sum of money to dispose of a potential challenger for lordship of a western hold.

Aldin had obtained similar information that evening at other pubs. He had learned that it was rumored that Sebbe had failed in the mission to kill some heir and the payment had not been forth coming. It was rumored that Sebbe was in debt and could not meet all his commitments.

That evening, the scouts compared their information. There was no rumor as to why Asbjorn had sent a delegation to Sebbe, but the fact that he had was troubling. The return cargo hold was just about full with goods that would be taken directly to the valley for therein was the most gain. Tomorrow would be their last day here. To stay beyond that would raise suspicion for it was obvious the cargo hold was almost full. They would concentrate on finding information from the west.

That night the scouts concentrated on finding visitors from the far west and trading rumors with them over pints. Shadow's family estates had been racked by war and lost many of the sons of the lord there in battle. Of the seven sons, amazingly only two were left alive and with the death of the father by a suspicious illness, the youngest son had assumed control. It was rumored his father had been poisoned. The other brother was rumored to be in eastern lands and he was a threat to the youngest son as long as he lived. It was reckoned that his death had been arranged.

It seemed the puzzle was solved. The next day the boat left to go downriver so it could later go upriver to the valley. The return trip went quickly as the downriver current was strong as rains upriver had swollen it. The crew had to be wary of floating tree trunks, but having oars in the water would be counterproductive. The current and the sail were used.

Going back upriver was a little more difficult, for the current here was strong against the boat and even though the wind filled the sail it was necessary for the crew to row. They travelled without docking, anchoring in quiet backwaters at nightfall. On the upriver trip, they had some full moons when they made way, though slowly under just sail, all night.

They arrived at the docks in midafternoon and a messenger was waiting with instructions that Magnus should come directly to the castle. Magnus delegated to Aldin the command of the guard. Nodens ship was already having Beorn's employees unload the cargo. Magnus, much to the surprise of his new employee, gave him money for food and shelter for him and his wife along with directions to the inn. He told him he would meet him there as soon as possible.

At the castle Wolf, Cuthbert, Cenedred, Siegfried and Ragnvald were waiting for Magnus' report. After a prayer for God's guidance, they listened intently to the information and how it had been obtained. Magnus explained that it had not been necessary to confront any of the parties, and because of the relationships he had deemed the dangers involved in doing so made action unwise. Magnus told them his unit had acquired the necessary information without exposing their true mission. As it was, no one knew they had been there or that they had gathered the intelligence. The one thing they did not know was why Asbjorn had sent a delegation to Sebbe.

Magnus was asked to stay for the discussion of what to do next. It was recommended that Shadow should be immediately informed of the findings and the great council called so all the lords could consider the matter. Aelle agreed. In the meantime Lucan's freedoms were to be curtailed and a close eye kept on him.

Magnus suggested a scouting party be sent along the river to see if there were any rumors or information regarding Asbjorn's intentions. Magnus suggested Aldin and a small group of special guards accompany the next boat departing to trade on Asbjorn's side of the river. The group was in agreement with his proposal. No further action regarding Sebbe or Shadow's family lands would be taken until

Shadow arrived.

After the meeting, Magnus asked his Lord for an audience. He told Wolf of his plan and asked if his Lord would allow it or assume the employment of the bow and arrow maker. Wolf smiled, for the young man had become quite enterprising and this pleased Wolf. Magnus was told that as long as it did not interfere with his military duties, he could own the business. Wolf summoned Modig and told him to immediately arrange a grant for Magnus who had to start arrangements as he might be needed for other duties on short notice. Modig was always good at reading between the lines, and assigned Magnus a prime location. He told Magnus the grant of title would be prepared forthwith but as of now that land he could consider his.

Magnus went to the chapel to offer thanksgiving for the success of his journey and the business opportunity. When he finished praying, he noticed Ava sitting nearby. He nodded to her and got up to leave and she did also. Outside she spoke first.

"Just back from your patrol?"

Magnus smiled, "Just returned this afternoon."

Ava asked, "Routine patrol was it?"

Magnus shrugged, "More or less."

Ava laughed, "I expect it was less routine and more something else. I hear things and I somehow think that you were more on a mission than a patrol."

Magnus frowned, "Someone has loose lips. That could be dangerous."

"I guess that depends on who is speaking to whom."

Magnus asked without thinking, "May I take you to dinner?"

Ava smiled coyly, "I am having dinner with my family. Would you care to escort me?

Magnus dipped his head, "It would be my honor. Does your family live nearby?"

Ava strained to keep a straight face. It was true she was not widely known like her sister, but that he did not know her was amusing.

"Yes, my family lives nearby. Meet me here at evening prayer then you may escort me to dinner."

Ava picked up her skirt slightly and scooted off.

Magnus went to the inn to see Rheged. He took him to see the site of the new shop. Modig had recommended a tradesman who would build for him. Magnus asked Rheged to design a shop that would be an ideal one for him and three apprentices. He was also told that he was to discuss with his wife living quarters to be constructed for them. It would be two rooms initially, a hearth room and a bedroom. They were to decide where on the property they would like it built, keeping in mind the possible expansion of the shop in the future.

Rheged was stunned and kept thanking Magnus for the opportunity. Magnus then really got Rheged's attention. He asked Rheged if he would like to be paid the agreed wage or share in the money made by the business, say one fifth. This brought Rheged to his knees in gratitude. He had worked so long and hard just to feed his wife and himself. Rheged was no fool; he knew the volume of goods he could produce with a good shop and three able apprentices. He would be well-to-do and so to would the man for whom he would work.

Magnus explained that Rheged would have to run the business as he would be occupied by his military duties much of the time. He asked Rheged if he thought he could hire the men needed as apprentices and Rheged said he had no doubt and he knew what to look for. In the event a man did not work out that man would just have to find other employment. Rheged would have the building sketch ready the next evening for the builder to examine. Based upon what Modig had told Magnus, he had more than enough money to start and maintain the business for some time.

That evening Magnus went to prayer service in his best uniform. He entered and took a seat next to Ava who sat alone in the second row of pews in the half filled chapel. After the short service, they left and Ava took Magnus' arm and led him down the stone path from the chapel to the castle's main building.

Magnus started to say something, but Ava put a finger to her lips, and Magnus remained silent. She led him into the building through a back entrance. Magnus almost bumped into his king and queen as they entered the hallway.

Magnus dipped his head, "My apologies, Majesties."

Cenedred was the one to speak, "I see your taste in men has matured little sister. Please follow us."

Magnus turned to Ava stunned, and she did the most unwomanly thing. She stuck her tongue out at him. He could not help it but laughed out loud. His king and queen glanced over their shoulders and said something to each other that Magnus could not overhear. It was their turn to laugh at a private joke.

Magnus had expected great formality at his king's table, but instead it was a delightful time of conversation and friendly banter. Magnus sat to the left of Ava with Siegfried his captain to his left and Lord Feliks and his wife sat across the table. He would have thought that he would be uncomfortable, but he was not. It was delightful.

After dinner, the king and queen announced they would take a short walk in the garden and invited any who wanted to join them. Usually no one accepted. This evening Ava motioned to Magnus who stood and pulled out her seat and she took his arm and they followed Wolf and Cenedred into the garden.

Magnus sighed, "You could have warned me."

"And have you run off in fear of what my brother-in-law or big sister might say. Never! You may be brave and experienced on the battlefield, but in spite of being much older than I, it is my observation that you are not experienced in matters of the heart."

Magnus shrugged, "Alas, you have taken the measure of your adversary well."

"Oh, I hope you are not my adversary. That would not at all suit me."

Magnus smiled and sighed, "I am corrected and humbly accept the correction with pleasure."

Ava shook her head, "Oh no, perhaps you are silver tongued like my sister's husband. He won her heart with his kind manner and words."

"There is much I can learn from my king."

They quietly followed the king and queen on a short walk around the garden.

Cenedred smiled at her husband, "I think my sister is quite taken with your man Magnus. It seems different from the frivolous pursuits of her past. Is he a worthy man?"

"Not of noble birth, but a loyal Christian man of ethical character. He is intelligent and finally developing ambition. Not the wrong kind either. I would have no objection to a match if it should happen."

"Ah, but what will father think. He is not as egalitarian as you."

"True, but we have discussed what would have to happen if she was properly matched and Magnus' loyalty and service is beyond question."

Aelle and Cenedred started a second circuit. It was not lost on the couple that Ava put her head against Magnus' shoulder as they walked. The others were still in the dining room when they returned. The men decided to adjourn to the library. There they sat all about and cups of ale were brought for them.

King Aelle spoke first, "I did not know you were interested in my sister-in-law Magnus nor her in you."

Magnus shrugged, then remembered who he was addressing, "Neither did I, sire. I mean I did not know she was your sister-in-law. She neglected to tell me when we talked. It seems she enjoyed my momentary discomfort when we came here tonight."

Aelle laughed, "That is Ava. She has become much like her sister these last few months. By the way, for everyone's information, Shadow and my mother will be here tomorrow. We will discuss the matter of what to do about the attempted attack on him when he arrives. Magnus, I want you here."

"Yes, Sire."

The men spent time discussing the growing trade and prosperity throughout all the holdings. It was a decent hour when the socializing ended. Magnus returned to his barracks room where he was tormented by thoughts of a certain young woman.

The next day Magnus went to the inn after morning weapons practice to see Rheged. He found Rheged and Alta sitting on a bag on a grassy area near the inn.

"Why are you not at breakfast Rheged?" Magnus asked.

"We have been put out of the inn and my tools have disappeared from the shed. Apparently the lock on the door is gone. The innkeeper told us he needed our rooms but refused to give me my money back. I paid him for a week using the money you gave me."

"Wait here," Magnus ordered and went marching toward the inn.

He wanted to be furious but controlled his anger. He entered and saw the innkeeper and motioned him over.

"What can I do for you, Sergeant," the innkeeper asked solicitously.

"You know the man Rheged and his wife Alta who were staying here?"

"Yes, sergeant, troublemakers, and I had to put them out," the innkeeper claimed.

"Who is staying in their rooms now?"

"A respectable river merchant who can afford the nice accommodations I provide," the innkeeper replied.

Magnus drew his short blade and felt the sharp edge, "You do know what the penalty for thievery here is?" Magnus asked looking at the man's right hand. "Rheged is my man and the money he paid you was my money. The tools stolen from the safekeeping in your shed were my man's therefore mine. Now I am going to tell you what is going to happen. I will come back in two hours and all my belongings will be locked in the shed as they should be. A purse will be here with the refund for Rheged, and as my man has been good enough to yield his rooms to the river merchant, the purse shall contain the amount that man paid. If not, well then things will become very ugly and official. Do you understand?"

The innkeeper was now sweating even though the day was not that hot.

"Yes, sergeant. I understand."

"You know the king does not tolerate unfair dealing here. You are new and may not know how seriously he takes honesty; you obviously not being a Christian man. You may want to consider changing your ways or selling your inn and moving on." Magnus sheathed his short blade turned and left.

The innkeeper left his help to prepare for the noon meal, and went to talk to a man who was said to know everything and everybody in the region. He paid the usual copper and asked about Magnus.

"Have you crossed Magnus?" the man asked.

The innkeeper answered directly, "Yes."

"You have made a very dangerous enemy. He is a warrior of great renown and influential. He keeps company with the king's sister-in-law and betting has already started when there will be a wedding. If they are wed, Magnus will be promoted further, perhaps even titled. How have you crossed him?

The innkeeper told him.

"The economy is good now. My advice, based on what he said to you, is to sell your inn and move far away."

It was not what the innkeeper wanted to hear, but it was advice he knew he would follow. At heart, he knew he was a coward and facing a man like Magnus did not appeal to him. It took less than an hour for the tools and goods to be put back in the shed and locked. The purse was readied.

Beorn paid well for information so he was the first approached. When he found out the inn would be for sale and the circumstances, he made a bid and a quick sale was finalized at somewhat below market value and more than it had cost the innkeeper to establish the business. Beorn's business interests, and thus Lord Aelle's, were expanding. He had learned from Aelle and knew a man who would make a good honest innkeeper and be happy to run it for a share of the profits.

Magnus went with two hired men pushing a cart and Rheged to fetch the tools and the money. The builder had just finished a small house that was not yet occupied by the new owners who would be moving from down river. Magnus had been able to rent it for a month while a new house was constructed and the shop was started.

True to his word, Rheged had a sketch for the builder to look at. The shop was somewhat large but Magnus noted the living quarters were very small. He asked the builder to double the size of the hearth room, much to Rheged's surprise and Alta's joy. The price quoted was very reasonable based on the advice Modig had given. Magnus could easily afford it. He had almost every penny he had been paid or been given as share. Rheged would hire his three men now and they would help in the construction.

The builder was a man of integrity and he was also a smart business man. He knew that the future might hold greater works commissioned by Magnus. Besides, the sergeant certainly travelled in exalted circles.

Magnus returned to the castle to find another invitation to dinner. He was pleased. He suspected that if he had not been interested in Ava, and told his king so, the invitations would have ceased. The fact was that he was more than interested.

Magnus went to a certain weaver and ordered two new uniforms. At the rate things were going, the two he had would be worn out from washing in no time. Not that the washer woman complained about having a uniform of his to launder each day. She just smiled one of those knowing women's smiles and took his money.

It was another pleasant evening meal. Yingvar had arrived and Magnus was introduced. There was another pleasant walk in the garden with Ava.

Ava asked Magnus what he was doing in town. He explained his business activities. Ava was interested. She suggested an associated product for him to consider and he was impressed with her idea and said he would discuss it with Rheged.

After dinner, King Aelle called Magnus aside. "I suppose you noticed that Ava has taken a very keen interest in you. She has talked to Cenedred about you in the most serious manner. What are your feelings for her?"

"Sire, may I speak freely?"

"Yes, what you say in this regard need not affect your position in our army."

"Then Sire, I will tell you that if she were not the daughter of a lord, I would have sought to arrange a marriage. She is intelligent and beautiful and life with her would be full of surprises. As I have no family to act for me, I would have hired an intermediary. The fact is that she is the daughter of a Lord and the sister-in-law of my great king. She is way above my station and I am at a loss as to what to do. My heart wants to go forward and my common sense tells me I tread on very dangerous ground."

Aelle nodded, "You put the matter straight. It is certainly a complicated matter."

Magnus shrugged, "I would understand and not hold it against you Sire, if you send me away, though my heart would break."

Aelle smiled, "A broken heart, or in this case two, may not be necessary. There is a solution. It seems, according to Bishop Aert, that one of the prerogatives of a king is to grant titles. The matter of status can be easily remedied. I could make you Lord of Docks. How would that suit?"

"Sire, if it meant I could marry Ava, I would be pleased to be Lord of Privies."

Aelle laughed, "Well said good Magnus, well said. I do think I can do somewhat better than that. We will discuss this matter further when Lord Shadow arrives. Until then, be assured Cenedred has persuaded me that you and Ava would be a good match."

Magnus bowed his head, "Thank you, Lord. I will always be your humble and loyal servant."

"I am counting on it, Magnus. You may go."

The castle morning routine started out as usual on the morning of the arrivals. The routine was disrupted when Eadgard and Hilde arrived at mid-morning. Shadow and Ethelind in the company of ten men-at-arms arrived at mid-day. Shadow was anxious to get a full report so the advisors were summoned for an immediate meeting. Ethelind insisted on changing out of her dusty clothes, so they did that while the others were on their way. Magnus and Siegfried were the first to arrive and in a short time everyone was assembled.

Magnus repeated his report for Shadow. Shadow asked a few questions and he and Ethelind sat quietly.

Wolf asked, "How large and rich are your family holdings?"

Shadow answered directly, "The lands of my family hold are about as large as all the lands under your control and were very rich and should be for the land is fertile and the people are hard workers."

Wolf asked, "What do you want to do?"

Shadow looked at Ethelind, "I am your man Wolf and that will not change. My younger brother Abreean was the worst of our family. I have three younger sisters and I am concerned for their welfare now. The people of my family lands will suffer under Abreean. He needs to be removed and I have the best claim. I think I should give up the northern shire to someone else, claim my right to my family lands, and it will become part of our joint family holding and your kingdom. Only Sebbe will be keeping us apart geographically. I think Ethelind should stay with you for the time being, a trusted Captain should go to the northern castle, and I should go with part of the army to claim the land. The taxes from those lands will fund a much larger military to protect all our lands. Our trade base will be expanded."

Cuthbert asked, "How are you likely to be accepted."

"I believe some men who I have fought with will come to me, but I have been gone too long to know how many. If Abreean is in control, the family forces must be decimated. I do not see how there can be more than seventy to seventy five men-at-arms in the land if all my brothers are dead. To win a war at that cost is a tragedy."

Wolf asked everyone their opinion. It was unanimous advice. Shadow would go to claim his ancestral holdings. Yingvar was of the opinion that it was unlikely there would be a problem related to an attack on his lands. With the southern castle reinforced, Asbjorn would be unlikely to make a move. Pending the outcome of Shadows expedition, Asbjorn would be reluctant to make a pact with Sebbe for to do so might result in being caught between two large military powers which he turned into enemies. Feliks also pointed out that now there was a strong and loyal force between Sebbe and Asbjorn. There were many problems with Asbjorn and Sebbe moving to join forces at this time.

It was also decided to place scouts on the west of Sebbe's lands to watch for any movement by Sebbe to attack Osmund's rear. Feliks agreed if Sebbe moved to do that he would send for reinforcements from Aelle and immediately move to attack Sebbe's rear as he attempted to engage Osmund. They would then take all the lands of Sebbe and they would be annexed to Feliks's hold.

After much discussion, it was decided that Herewood would go to the north castle as commander. He had proved to be a capable administrator. Aewel, as commander, would take over the southern castle which would be reinforced because of the concern about Asbjorn. Modig would go with him temporarily to assist him in administration and further development of the economy there.

The matter of raising the expeditionary army was discussed. Shadow suggested that volunteers be asked for. The riches of his family lands would be distributed as shares to entice the volunteers. Wolf said the lands would have to be revitalized as the valley had been. He would waive his share so the holding could be revived.

Wolf was also concerned about leaders because he wanted to keep both Ragnvald and Siegfried to command the defenses for the land in the event a force had to be sent out.

The captains and Magnus were asked to leave and wait outside.

After some time the captains and Magnus were recalled. They were told of Wolf's decision. Shadow would go by ship with a hundred men-at-arms and thirty archers. The group would include Magnus' group and the rest would be volunteers. Magnus would be promoted to Captain effective immediately. He would choose two to be his sergeants. Siegfried was now promoted to War Chief and Ragnvald to Valley Commander.

There would be seven Earls - Osmund was to be Earl of the West, Eadgard Central Earl, Yingvar Eastern Earl, Feliks Central Western Earl, a Southern Lord, and a Middle Lord for the land between the valley range and the eastern river, and a Northern Earl. The last three would be titled later. As planned and agreed, Eadgard's lands would eventually go to one of Aelle's male offspring out of Eadgard's lineage.

While they were together, the progress of prosperity was discussed. The lands were thriving and incomes were up. The people were content and the army had no trouble recruiting men when openings occurred.

After the meeting adjourned, Wolf and Cenedred asked Eadgard and Hilde to stay.

Eadgard simply said, "I have heard reports. Is it true?"

Cenedred replied, "Yes father. They have been chaperoned. Nothing inappropriate has happened."

Eadgard protested, "He has no title, no lands!"

Wolf shrugged, "I can remedy that, probably the same way our families were long ago. I intend to make him an Earl."

"You would do that for my daughter?"

Wolf shook his head, "Not unless it was also a wise idea. He is an accomplished leader and he has a lot of potential. He could be a good asset to our family. He is frugal, loyal, and intelligent."

"What holding would you give them?"

"I am inclined to title the Cathedral Town and lands between the mountains and the eastern river. It is rich and close. It is difficult for me to govern from here and a defensive fortification there needs to be completed and manned. In addition, there is a great potential for trade up and down the eastern river which is untapped. He has knowledge of river trade and I believe he could develop it."

"What about the northern and southern?"

Wolf opened his hands, "For the time being they are being administered and I have some options, but I want to see how they develop. It will be interesting to see what the situation is with Osmund's sisters."

"Why the middle land for my daughter's proposed husband?"

Wolf smiled, "I really believe that with time it might become the richest of all the lands if properly administered.'

Eadgard asked the apparent question, "What if I object."

Wolf shrugged, "Cenedred and I have discussed it. I will not allow the marriage if you do not agree."

Eadgard asked, "If I object would that preclude titling some other future candidate to be her husband?"

Wolf was not evasive, "As I previously stated, it will be dependent upon the character and ability of the man."

For the first time Wolf could remember Hilde interjected, "Eadgard, do not be such an ass. He is a nice and capable young man who will make Ava a good Christian husband. Please do not let pride deprive our youngest daughter of happiness. You know how close a thing it was getting my father to accept you."

Wolf did not know the story there, but he saw the look on Eadgard's face and said nothing.

Eadgard took a deep breath, "Very well, I agree. Perhaps we can announce the betrothal at dinner and then arrange the public official betrothal. "

As dinner was ending that night Wolf stood, "I have an announcement. I am naming Magnus, earl of the land between the eastern river and the valley mountains, between Eadgard's lands to the north and my southern lands. However, he will not be released from his duties as a captain in Lord Osmund's forces until after the upcoming campaign."

Most of the party sat in stunned silence including Magnus.

Eadgard stood, "I have arranged a marriage for my youngest

daughter Ava."

Ava froze and her heart seemed to sink. Her stomach was in a knot.

Eadgard continued, "She shall marry Lord Magnus."

Ava started crying, rose from the table, and went around to her father and hugged him. "Thank you, father. Thank you. You have made me so happy!" She was sobbing.

Applause broke out and congratulations started. Magnus was speechless. Was this really happening?

Ava came back around the table and embraced Magnus saying, "I will be a good wife."

Magnus simply said, "I trust so, my love."

There were toasts and the women went away to talk about marriage arrangements and dates. The men went off to discuss matters related to the upcoming campaign.

Chapter 16 - The Expedition

Feliks went home with twenty five additional men-at-arms and twenty archers to reinforce his castle in the event a force had to go forth to engage Sebbe's rear. Ten of Eadgard's men came to join the expeditionary force. Of the two hundred and fifty standing men-at-arms of Aelle's forces, ninety went with Osmund, forty were at Feliks's castle, sixty were at the southern castle and sixty stayed in the valley. Forty reserves were called up for the valley defense and thirty recruits nearing completion of training were put into service on the valley duty roster.

It was quite an impressive flotilla of seventeen boats that went down one river and up the other. Magnus' boat was significantly ahead of the others because of its design and crew. It got to the landing site first. All of Magnus' crew disembarked in mail with Shadow. Shadow had his helmet off. The crew formed line as they went ashore. They were at the bottom of a long sloping hill.

Two men approached signifying truce. Shadow and Magnus went forward to meet them.

One of the men smiled and embraced Shadow, "I thought that was you coming, Osmund."

"Beadwof you old dog, how have you survived this long? It is good to see you. Let me introduce Lord Captain Magnus, my second."

The two men clasped hands.

Beadwof shook his head in disbelief, "I could hardly believe it when I received a report a boat was nearing. I knew if it was you the landing would be here. I see you have some men with you. Good. I brought about twenty so that makes us over sixty. Your brother has about the same number. It will be a good fight."

Shadow made sure he heard correctly, "He only fields sixty?"

Beadwof shrugged, "We won the war and lost everything. Strange world."

Just about then other boats started to come into view.

Beadwof strained to count the ships. "How many?"

"A hundred men-at-arms and forty archers. A dozen mounts. Seventeen ships."

Beadwof whistled, "Your little brother will soil himself when he sees us coming. The treacherous little coward will probably try to run. You staying?"

Shadow smiled, "Yes!"

Beadwof smiled, "Good. The lads will be very happy to hear that."

The army disembarked and camped at the top of the hill that night. There was significant catching up to do. Shadow knew some of the older soldiers. Shadow's exploits had been heard of even here as had Wolf's. They broke camp at first light and started the march inland. Shadow took forty men ahead in order to draw Abreean into the open. It was a mixed force of twenty he had brought and the twenty Beadwof had brought to Shadow.

Magnus followed not far behind with the main force. Experienced scouts ranged out on the mounts ahead and to the sides as well as behind. The reports started to come in. Abreean had apparently taken the bait and wanted to finish his brother once and for all.

Unbeknown to Magnus, his force had been spotted and reported to Abreean who assumed it was Lord Sebbe come to reinforce him and attack Shadow's rear. Abreean, based on the report thought he and his ally outnumbered Shadow at least two to one and an attack on the enemy from Sebbe was imminent.

Shadow baited his inexperienced brother by apparently putting himself at a disadvantage where Abreean's sixty were atop a steep hill while Shadow's forty were in the hollow. Shadow's men formed a shield wall that had obvious openings because of the rocky terrain. Abreean's force charged downhill and Shadow's band backed up as preplanned to a more level spot and formed a solid shield wall upon which the charging force faltered.

Then Abreean's nightmare began as the woods on both sides seemed to vomit more men into the fight and Abreean's force was rolled up on both flanks and quickly surrounded. Abreean too soon realized these men were better fighters than he had ever seen and then he saw him. His older brother cutting his way through the mass of men cramped together in an ever collapsing circle. Then Magnus was in front of him and Abreean was no match for Magnus. There was no surrender. All but three of the enemy died, including Abreean. The three survivors were found wounded covered by the dead bodies of their comrades. The hollow was a bloody mess.

The three were tended to and bound and would be taken to Lord Shadow's castle until it was decided what to do with them.

Shadow came to Magnus, "Thank you."

Magnus looked up, "No one should have to kill their brother."

Magnus called for one of his sergeants and ordered him to bring the after action report. Beadwof came limping to where Shadow and Magnus were standing. He knelt before Shadow, "My Lord."

Shadow smiled and pulled him up. The other local warriors came and did the same. It was now official.

Beadwof looked at Magnus, "Your men are well armed, armored, and trained. This lot didn't stand a chance. What I wouldn't give for mail like yours."

Shadow smiled, "All our men will have it soon. Your men and the new recruits will also have armor. Beadwof, you and I will have our work cut out forming a new army. My friend Lord Captain Magnus will be returning home, but we will be rebuilding this land."

Beadwof had lost four men and three of Shadow's men had perished. Four of Shadow's men had been wounded seriously, mainly broken bones, and one of Beadwof's men had a serious cut. The lighter casualties Shadow's forces had incurred spoke to the value of better weapons, armor, and training.

Abreean's men had been poorly armed and had almost no mail or armor and the helmets and shields were of poor quality. Shadow thought his brother a fool to fight with men who were so desperately in need of rearming. So many brave men had died for nothing.

*****

The spy's report had come to Feliks's castle that Lord Sebbe was going to march West with fifty men-at-arms. Reports had circulated about men going upriver in a long boat and a rider had come from Abreean to call for Sebbe's men. Men left Feliks's castle before Sebbe's men had left theirs.

Sergeant Leof led assisted by Sergeant Karl. There were forty men-at-arms and twenty archers all mounted. Sebbe's men were on foot so it was inevitable that they would be overtaken. It happened at the western river ferry early in the morning the same day the encounter between Shadow and Abreean took place.

Leof's scouts reported that a large area had been cleared around the ferry crossing. The ground sloped gently down to the river and all around the clearing the area was heavily forested except for the road that had been cleared to the ferry. Half way down the cleared portion of the slope was the ferryman's house which it appeared Lord Sebbe was presently occupying based on the comings and goings. Sebbe's forces were still asleep around fires in groups of six. The ferry was small and only five or six men could cross at a time. There were only two sentries and they were asleep.

Leof had his men dismount and they prayed quietly for victory and God's protection. Leof explained the plan and ordered the sentries killed. They then slipped into the forest to take positions at the edge of the wood.

Sebbe's men started crossing at sunrise. The first group of a half dozen men was being pulled on the raft across the river. They had loaded but were not wearing armor for the river crossing. Sebbe's troops on shore were at a disadvantage as none of them were in armor either. The ferry swayed in the current and Sebbe had decided the chances of men going in the water were greater than being attacked here.

There was no doubt what Sebbe intended as his men were camped in groups of six and the group that would cross next was waiting at the ferry. Most of Sebbe's men were just rousing when Leof signaled the start of the attack.

The first flights of arrows had killed a dozen men and wounded at least than many more before Sebbe's men instinctively grouped behind the ferryman's hut where there was some shelter from the arrows. It was then that Leof's men-at-arms charged in from the sides. They ran across the open ground and engaged the remainder of Sebbe's force that had been caught flat footed.

It was Leof who encountered Sebbe as his second opponent and Sebbe was good but he was not wearing mail. Where Leof was bruised, Sebbe was cut. Soon Sebbe started to tire as his bleeding increased. It seemed to be a rhythmic clash of sword and shield.

Michael O'Gara

The two were evenly matched and if it had not been for the armor
the outcome would have been in doubt. Finally, Sebbe slipped and
was mortally wounded.

It was a bloodbath, in spite of the fact that some of Sebbe's men
were experienced fighters. The chainmail made the difference and
Sebbe's forces had suffered early catastrophic losses. The battle was
over within a half an hour. The outcome was immediately evident to
the six of Sebbe's men who had crossed the river, so they did not
attempt to return but rather cut the ferry's ropes. Of Sebbe's men six
escaped and five surrendered. The rest perished.

Leof had three wounded soldiers who would need to be
evacuated. Karl oversaw the collection of the spoil. Lord Sebbe's
corpse had a significant amount of coin in a purse hidden under his
tunic. The mail and weapons were collected. A wagon was hired
from a nearby farm to which the bound prisoners, tied in column by
a rope around their neck, were attached to the back. By mid-day the
column was headed along the river road.

It took only two hours to reach a point across from where the
boats carrying Shadow's force had landed. Leof signaled and one of
the small boats came across. Leof advised that he had come to
reinforce Lord Shadow. He was advised that word had come in the
last hour that Abreean had been defeated.

Leof had his men establish camp, post sentries, and prepare a plan
of defense. He left Karl in charge then took the prisoners and
wounded across the river. Lord Magnus returned with his troop and
established his camp on the hill overlooking the boats. Thus there
was a troop on both sides of the river.

Osmund had moved to take possession of his family castle and
Magnus' force was still considerable. Magnus decided to move his
force across the river and join it with Leof's. They would move in a
show of force through what was formerly Sebbe's shire and occupy
the shire castle. The idea was to consolidate control over the lands.
The boats would be sent to Feliks's docks with the boat crews and a
skeleton crew on the largest vessel. The wounded would be sent
back to the valley on the smallest boat. The next morning the boats
ferried Magnus' force across the river then sailed away after mid-day.

Magnus' column was an impressive sight. It marched across the land. People expected this army would take what it needed. They were surprised when the army purchased what they needed, though they haggled for a fair price and people were reluctant to press their luck. They were told their new Lord Feliks was a fair man and served the just and fair King Aelle. Aelle's army and those of his earls would protect the lands.

The army sowed the seeds of good will as it travelled. As word went ahead that people need not fear the approaching army, people came to see it pass. The local priests, though few and far between, were impressed when they were asked to come and minister to the army. They were overjoyed with the gifts of coin they were given.

When the army reached the castle, the gates were open and eleven men-at-arms presented themselves outside the gate to surrender. Magnus and his men searched the castle and found Sebbe's widow and her two daughters hiding. They started to cry when they were found.

The widow and daughters were brought to Lord Magnus in the great room. The woman immediately went to her knees and her two young daughters followed. The daughters could not have been more than three to five years in age.

The woman pleaded, "Great Lord, please do with me what you will but have mercy on my daughters."

Magnus replied in a quiet and gentle voice, "What kind of men do you think we are that we would make war on a defenseless woman and her daughters. Please stand. What is your name?"

"Goda, Great Lord."

"Lady Goda, I am Magnus, an Earl of King Aelle. Feliks by decree of King Aelle will be Earl here because Lord Sebbe made war on one of Aelle's Lords and lost. You have my condolences on the death of your husband."

Lady Goda did not respond as Magnus expected, "I will not mourn he who was my torment and the scourge of my daughters. I forgive him, but I know the kind of man he was, a wicked and perverse man. My father told me he regretted arranging my marriage to Sebbe, although at the time he had little choice. My father may pay some small ransom for my return."

"Who is your father?"

"My father is Lord Aldred, his lands border to the south."

"There is no need for ransom. Is there someone you can send to your father to arrange for your return?"

"Yes, my Lord."

"Then let it be done. Would you and your daughters do me and my officers the honor of dining with us this evening? The fare may be simple, but we will endeavor not to bore you with soldier talk."

Goda smiled, "It would be our pleasure, Lord."

"You will need help packing for the return to your father. I will assign two trustworthy men to help you. You may take your personal jewelry and possessions, but the goods of Lord Sebbe are forfeit. Is there any treasure in your rooms?"

Goda nodded, "No, Lord. You are generous, Lord. Thank you."

Magnus turned to Leof, "Please arrange helpers for her."

"Yes, Lord."

Leof was no fool; he was being charged with ensuring only personal possessions and not castle treasure left. He knew just which two men to assign. They would be courteous yet firm. He left and got them.

The search of the castle was continuing and in the absence of Lady Goda her rooms had already been searched. A large hide had been found, behind a false wall, and it contained chests of treasure. This was immediately reported to Leof who reported it to Magnus. He countermanded the order to let a rider go to Goda's father. Lady Goda had not yet returned to her rooms and was on her way when she was intercepted and returned to Magnus.

She came into the room and curtsied to Magnus. She was no fool and recognized his demeanor had changed.

"Lady Goda, I am rescinding my previous offer. You are to now consider yourself my prisoner. We offer you kindness and you return deceit."

Magnus motioned and one of the smaller chests was brought and laid before him. Goda was horrified, not at her actions but that she had been caught. How had they found her hide?

"Your personal goods are forfeit. Your father will be contacted regarding your disposition. It seems your wicked husband had a viper for a wife. Take her away and lock her up."

Goda was taken to a humble room with a small table and a bench and a bed and a few candles. Two changes of her most modest clothes hung on pegs in the room. Goda did not repent but rather cursed her bad luck. She had almost won out.

Her daughters fared much better. Being small children they were placed in comfortable rooms with a servant who had been their nanny. The girls did not miss their mother who spent little time with them anyway, and they just enjoyed their day in the absence of their mother's temper, which was vented on them each time they saw her.

The search of the castle uncovered considerable other riches. A considerable share would go to Aelle and Magnus, and the rest would be distributed to the army. Feliks would acquire the rule of the lands. Magnus stayed in the castle two days. During that time the goods and treasure to be returned to the valley were prepared to be moved on wagons.

A courier was given a message to take to Goda's father. Magnus told Aldred his daughter and granddaughters would be returned to him if he would arrange a time when they could be brought to the border. No ransom would be asked.

Karl was left in charge of the castle with command of twenty five men-at-arms and ten archers. Magnus and his men made their way back to Feliks's lands. Feliks came out to greet him. There was a celebration.

The next day a letter was delivered from Aldred who said that he would be grateful for the return of his granddaughters and appreciated the generosity of the king's earl in not requiring a ransom. He set a time and place for the return of his granddaughters. He also stated that if it were to please his fellow lord, he would appreciate it if his daughter was not returned. Aldred also stated that he would be pleased if the gift he sent in appreciation would be accepted.

Aldred's message was obvious. Please return my innocent granddaughters, but here is treasure that I hope will convince you not to return my daughter. Magnus decided the world was indeed a strange place and there were some daughters even a father could not love.

When Goda was told what was to happen, her concern was not

for being separated from her daughters, but what would happen to her. Magnus told her she would be taken to the far northern lands and given into a convent. If she ever entered any of Aelle's lands her life would be forfeit. Goda knew this meant she would never be able to go to her father to plead for sanctuary. She threw a fit and had to be physically removed, kicking and screaming curses.

Magnus personally escorted the granddaughters to meet their grandfather. He went with twenty five men-at-arms to the border. He saw this as much a diplomatic meeting as an act of compassion. During the trip, it occurred to Magnus why Aelle had made him a lord before he returned. It put him on a necessary footing for some of the work he might have to do. It occurred to him that he had much to learn from Aelle.

As Magnus journeyed, he had two scouts out as was his habit. The report came back that almost fifty men were camped at the meeting point. Magnus assumed this meant that the girl's grandfather had indeed come in person. When Magnus troop was within sight of Aldred's camp, the troop was halted and ordered to dismount and wait. Magnus went ahead with the one warrior and the two girls. It was as much as to protect his men as to show no hostile intent toward Aldred.

Aldred walked down the road with two men to meet Magnus who dismounted and led his horse toward Aldred. Aldred was a man in his late thirties bearded and heavy set but who moved like a warrior and was probably very muscular in spite of his girth.

Magnus spoke first, "I presume you are Lord Aldred?"

Aldred had obviously expected some gesture of subservience. "And who might you be?"

"I am Magnus, earl of the central hold and under the orders of Aelle my King and future brother-in-law."

"Forgive me Magnus; I had thought you to be a soldier ordered to bring my granddaughters."

"Aldred, I am indeed a soldier and I do have your granddaughters. Let me bring them to you. Magnus turned motioning for the girls to be brought forward.

Magnus went a few steps, knelt on one knee, motioned the girls to come and spoke to them, "This is your grandfather, Lord Aldred. He will take care of you from now on."

During their stay and the trip, Magnus' kindness to the girls, of which they had little experience and enjoyed, as well as them seeing him as a protector had developed an affection between them. The girls hugged him and he took their hands. All of this was not lost on Aldred.

"Girls, this is your grandfather Aldred. If you ask him nicely, he might just hug you."

The older one asked, "Are you my grandfather?"

Aldred laughed, "Yes sweet child, I am and you may hug your grandfather," and the man went down on one knee and opened his arms.

Magnus put a gentle pressure on her back and she went into Aldred's arms and then the youngest went too. Their grandfather embraced them both.

"I am so happy you are here children. I and your grandmother will take good care of you."

Aldred took the girls by the hand and a woman came forward. She was a woman in her mid-thirties, a reasonably attractive woman, wearing a smile that would light a dark night.

"Girls, this is your grandmother." Aldred just had time to say it before the girls were swept up by the woman who laughed and swung the girls, one in both arms. The girls laughed and Aldred shrugged his shoulders.

"Magnus, would you and your men like to join us for a meal before we all depart?"

"Of course, Aldred."

During the meal Aldred asked about Aelle, if all he heard was true. Magnus clarified the factual parts of what Aldred had heard and dismissed those things that were embellishments. Magnus told that Aelle was the most accomplished warrior he had ever seen. Aldred asked Magnus how he would fare against Aelle.

"I would be fortunate to last a minute."

Aldred continued, "So the reports of the victories are true and Aelle now is king of these other lords?"

"Yes, but Aelle is a different King. He does not covet what others have. He would be content to just rule what he holds. It seems however that others are intent on provoking him to war with them and to conquer their holdings. Others judge him to be a fair and just man and bind with him as a way to ensure the protection of their people and so voluntarily become his subjects. It is strange. Of course God works in mysterious ways his wonders to perform."

"Where did you hear such a thing?" Aldred inquired.

"From my Lord Aelle."

Aldred took this all in, "My conscience has been keeping me awake. I did not want Goda back but neither should I have wanted her harmed. What has happened to her?"

Magnus told him.

"Was this your idea?"

Magnus did not avoid accepting responsibility, "Mine alone."

"A wise resolution for you have caused her no harm, no offense to anyone, her future is in her own hands, and you keep your promise to me."

Aldred resolved to never mention her name again. He knew she was a wicked and treacherous woman who would turn on her own daughters or parents for the sake of her ambition. Aldred had little hope of her changing; however if it was to happen it just might do so in a convent. Aldred had an impression that convent life was much like being in the army and the discipline might effect change in Goda.

Aldred asked seriously, "I understand you and your Lord Aelle are followers of the Christ?"

"We are." Magnus answered.

Aldred asked Magnus to explain Christ to him and Magnus did. Aldred was full of questions. As the night got late, Aldred asked if Magnus would stay another day so they could talk more. Magnus agreed and they did. Aldred was much impressed by Magnus and Magnus invited him to visit. Aldred said he would send word and indeed would come to visit and meet the king and the other lords. He also would like to meet Bishop Aert.

The two groups departed with the exchange of gifts and many pleasantries.

Chapter 17 – Consolidation

Magnus was preparing to return to the valley when word came that he was to return, but his men were to go to reinforce Osmund. Leof would be in charge during the trip to join with Osmund. So it was that some sailed north and most of the troops sailed south. The western river being high this time of year and the only ferry being out of service, the boats would have to travel around to ferry the troops so it was just as easy to transport them around. The men arrived rested and marched unopposed to Osmund's castle.

Leof arrived at Osmund's castle to a flurry of activity. Osmund came out to meet him.

Leof dismounted and took a knee, "My Lord Shadow, we are here at your service as ordered."

Shadow pulled him to his feet, "We are soldiers and a head bow is sufficient in these circumstances Leof. I am glad to see you."

They started walking into the castle, "I am blessed for I found my sisters and they are well. They fled to a convent. I do however have a problem that needs to be resolved before I bring them here. It seems my brother had an ally whom he allowed to settle part of my family lands. I have asked him to leave and he has refused. He claims the lands are now his by right of possession and the fact my brother gave them to him. I pointed out to him that they were not my brother's to give."

Leof smiled, "Let me guess, he did not agree with your assessment, and now we must dispossess him of your land."

Shadow laughed, "You are a remarkably fast study, Sergeant. We plan to march tomorrow. Are your men ready?"

"Yes, my Lord."

And so it was that Shadow led his force from the castle. The scouts ranged ahead. Two enemy scouts were detected and were dispatched to an untimely grave by Shadow's scouts who were more skilled and experienced. Shadow knew their failure to return would tell the enemy he was near but hopefully not how many nor the disposition of Shadow's forces.

The scouts reported the enemy held high ground and were waiting to be attacked. Their position had been prepared. Shadow asked about approaches from the other sides. The enemy had its back to marshy area on three sides and the only approach was to take them head on. Shadow asked about the nearest water supply and learned the enemy would have to travel a quarter mile to avoid drinking the brackish marsh water once their fresh water supplies ran out.

Shadow's forces would have no trouble foraging but the enemy would have to come past Shadow to get to food in any quantity though eels, snakes and such could probably be found in the marshes. Shadow could not believe the enemy had been so foolish. He sent scouts out a great distance for he thought surely there must be some trick here.

The reports came back. The enemy had pillaged, raped and burned in the area. The folk who had originally lived here hated the invaders who had forced the local residents from their homes by a program of terror. Observations and reports from the displaced confirmed there were no other enemy forces within days of this place.

Under the circumstances, Osmund put his forces to work. Each day they prayed then, under guard, they started surrounding the enemy with barriers of thorn bushes and bramble. They worked from both sides moving toward the middle as the enemy watched. At the same time the scouts reported to Shadow that the imported settlers were leaving or being killed, as without the protection of the men-at-arms on the hill they were being driven off by Osmund's farmers.

On the hill the enemy commander Nord watched Shadow's men; he had not expected this. There would be no quick battle. There would be no advantage of geography against a foe that seemingly had a slight numeric advantage but was inexperienced. Abreean had said his brother was a rash fool and incompetent. The enemy commander had only found out when his last scout had arrived that Abreean's brother Osmund was also called Shadow Killer the renowned warrior and commander. It was then he realized who had been the fool and his own limitations. He had been a decent sergeant but as a captain he had led his men into great danger.

As fresh water supplies and food dwindled, Nord knew he was going to be forced into a straight face to face fight or see his force start to dwindle in effectiveness from hunger or disease from drinking bad water.

Nord started marshalling his force for battle. Shadow did the same. The two forces would meet in the flat of the valley where it would be that the best fighters would win. Only Nord did not intend all his force to go straight into the enemy, some would veer off and open a hole in the bramble barrier and attack the enemy's flank. He did not know that Shadow's archers were prepared for just such an attack.

Shadow's men-at-arms stood in the opening. A truce messenger was sent to Nord telling him he could still leave if his men left without their weapons and swore not to return. Pride and desperation would not let the man accept Shadow's terms.

Shadow's men were steady as the charge came. The shield wall was solid and at the last minute the long spears appeared through and over the shields and the slaughter started. Twenty of the enemy veered off and several with axes started chopping at the brambles. Suddenly flaming arrows struck on the other side of the brambles and the hay that had been placed there in the dark of night caught fire and burned furiously engulfing the brambles and two of the axe men. The others were driven back by the heat and flame.

Almost simultaneously both sides of the opening were afire and the only way out was through the opening in the bramble wall in which Shadow's men stood. Men on both sides were falling in the battle but Shadow's wall was moving forward making the opening smaller and smaller. The enemy troops were experienced fighters but the addition of the eighteen new men rushing to reinforce the wall created some confusion and a break in the enemy's line occurred and in that moment Shadow's well trained men wedged into it automatically as they had been trained. The enemy started to back away.

Shadow was in the wedge but at the side. Nonetheless the damage he inflicted on the enemy was significant. The wedge broke through and men poured into the gap and forced a wider intrusion into the enemies shield wall. Threatened with being surrounded the enemy started to retreat. Nord was defending himself against an able warrior when his men started backing up the hill and he followed backing away quickly. It extricated him from the man in front of him only to be faced with Shadow Killer who stepped in front of him. The man, recognizing his adversary, knelt and offered his sword. It was like a domino effect. The other survivors seeing their leader surrender did likewise. So it was that seventeen men of the enemy force were taken captive.

Shadow took his weapon and demanded, "Who are you and where do you come from?"

"I am Nord, a mercenary who was promised land in payment for past services. Lord Abreean could not pay in coin so gave me this land."

"What services did you render?"

Nord hung his head, "When the last battle against invaders was won, I was not paid as promised. The land had been ravaged by war. Abreean promised to make me Sherriff here if I would overcome his older brother which I did. He then approached me to fight another brother, but his promises of payment had proven unreliable so I refused. Abreean said he had found another ally and would come for me after he killed his last remaining brother. I heard of his defeat and supposed that was the older brother he had referred to. He had only referred to you as Osmond and I did not know you were the great war chief Shadow Killer until I had already defied you."

Shadow looked at Nord and asked a question to which he did not expect an answer, "What am I to do with you?" After a pause he added," I could have forgiven you defiance Nord, but the pillage and rape of the innocent and defenseless is unpardonable."

Nord answered, "Such acts are unpardonable, but if you investigate, you may find that such acts were the work of your brother's men and not mine. The atrocities did not occur at the hands of my men. After my refusal to fight with Abreean against you, he sent his men as raiders."

Shadow thought for a few moments then committed, "I will investigate the matter and in the meantime you and your men shall remain prisoners." Shadow sent patrols to make sure there was peace in the area. The scouts were also sent out to make inquiries. The army made camp.

The reports came back. Nord's men had forced the people by

threat of violence from their lands. It was not until after the farmers and merchants left their lands with their possessions that the robbery, murder and rape occurred. This seemed to support Nord's claims.

There were witnesses to some of the attacks who had escaped. They were to be brought to the camp as were the three prisoners who had been captured in the battle with Abreean. When the witnesses arrived, three of Shadow's men, three of Nord's, and the three prisoners were put in a line and the witnesses brought to identify them. Of the group the witnesses could only identify two of Abreean's men. The two men confessed to their guilt, but it seemed the third man had stayed at the castle the whole time. They were taken away and Nord was summoned.

Nord came into Shadow's presence and knelt, "My Lord."

"It seems Nord that you told the truth, so you and your men shall be spared. The question still remains, what am I to do with you?"

Nord was quick to respond, "Take my oath and give me a place in your service. I have no lord, no money, no prospects, and no home. A place was the one thing I wanted more than all else."

"What about your men?" Shadow inquired.

"They are sworn to me, but I will release them into your service so they may also have a place."

"Discuss this with your men. In the morning they may choose independently. If they do not wish to join my service they will be exiled but freed to go. At that time I will accept your commitment if you are still willing. If not, you also will be freed to go into exile. Each man will be taken by a guard through the camp and will be allowed to talk to any man of his choosing about being in my service."

The next morning the men were polled. With no other prospects and having learned that the life of a soldier in this army was better than any they had experienced, that soldiers were allowed wives and many of the men had wives at their base stations, they all willingly became soldiers in Shadow's service. They were however broken up and went into various units. They would not be stationed together.

One of the scouts discovered a small abandoned ancient outpost on the outskirts of one of the larger villages in the area. Shadow took a patrol and went to see it. It was a circular stone structure with two floors and the stone works were in good repair but the roof and floors would need replacement. It was surrounded by a stone wall which formed one side of covered horse stalls which were collapsing. The gate was gone as was the door to the building. The area around needed clearing as it was overgrown.

Shadow decided on the spot to man the position. With repairs and some furniture, it could serve as a small unit base from which to keep the peace. Eight men were assigned to man the station and get it into shape. For the time being the unit would be relieved every sixty days by three revolving units of eight from the castle.

An acting sergeant was named and put in charge. Shadow delegated the responsibility for repairs to the man. He was given a purse, for which he was responsible, to pay for repairs, provisions and furnishing of the station. He was told a regular rider would come for reports and to relay orders.

Shadow returned to the main body and sent out riders to advise the population that the trial of the two perpetrators would be held at mid-morning. Their Lord would also be hearing delegations. Shadow conducted the court with dozens of spectators in attendance. The accused men were found guilty on the testimony of the witnesses and were hung. The people then knew that law had come to the land.

Based upon the delegations' reports, Shadow realized that the people needed help getting reestablished in their share farms. Their sheriff had been murdered. A clerk made a record of the requests of the people and some who had immediate survival needs were given small amounts of money to tide them over. Shadow promised to appoint a new sheriff.

The next day Shadow and his troops left for the castle. Leof and a patrol went to fetch Shadow's sisters. He carried a letter of introduction from Shadow to his sisters. One of Shadow's sisters, the youngest, refused to leave the convent saying she was at peace there and was going to stay. The other two returned with Leof.

Shadow found that men and women who had served his father and who had fled when his brother Abreean had arranged their lord's murder, started to come to him. Some of his concerns about staffing were thus resolved. Soon there was a household staff. There was even a trusted man; his father's only surviving sheriff, to send to tend to the tenant farmers who had been evicted by Nord. Their need was greatest.

So the rebuilding started.

A month later Ethelind arrived by boat bringing some of their wealth with her.

Chapter 18 - The New Lord

Magnus returned to the castle a hero and a proven leader. The family met him when his boat docked in early evening. Wolf congratulated him; Ava embraced him as did Cenedred, and Cuthbert clasped forearms with him in a warrior's greeting as did Ragnvald. Ragnvald stayed to supervise the treasure Magnus had brought.

As the group walked together to the castle, Ava was arm in arm with Magnus telling him about the wedding plans that had been completed. They had only to set the date. The hour being late, the family took Magnus directly to dinner over his protests that he should first clean up and change into a clean uniform. The family wanted a firsthand account of the western campaign. Magnus told them of it and answered their many questions. Dinner was followed by a walk in the garden.

The next morning after breakfast, Magnus went to see Rheged with Ava who insisted on coming. They were accompanied by a guard and a priest chaperone. In his absence, Magnus' business enterprise had prospered under Rheged's enterprising oversight. The buildings were completed and production was in full swing with the apprentices hard at work. Rheged stopped the work and introduced the Lord and his betrothed to the new employees. Rheged also introduced Ava to his wife Alta.

Rheged then took Magnus aside to give an account of the business profits while Ava listened and observed. The suggestions Ava had made had been added – spear shafts and metal tipped walking staffs. There were back orders for bows, arrows, and spear shafts. Rheged was very enthused because he was becoming quite well off and Magnus was becoming wealthier by the day. Magnus was impressed by the income the business was bringing in. Magnus and Ava returned to the castle.

Magnus attended his king and provided him with a military report on the campaign. They also discussed the potential visit of Lord Aldred. Wolf gave Magnus an accounting prepared by Modig of the disposition of the treasure Magnus had brought back. It was then that Magnus realized that he was truly a wealthy man. They discussed the need for Magnus to travel to his new lands and approve work to be done on his fortifications.

After their meeting, the lords had lunch with the royal family. Ava was distressed that Magnus would be leaving on business so soon. Her spirits were revived when a date for the wedding was set. She thought she should go to see where they would be living and inquired if she shouldn't have some input into the changes at their future home. Cenedred agreed with Ava, besides they would be married at the cathedral so they should visit Aert to finalize the arrangements. Ethelind hinted that Magnus would do well to let the women come to keep peace in the family. The men relented and agreed to the ladies going. Wolf had business to attend to so would stay in the valley.

The next day they departed for Magnus' lands with thirty men-at-arms and ten archers. Magnus enjoyed the company of the ladies as they travelled, even though they went at a more leisurely pace than Magnus would have liked. The ladies saw this as something of an outing rather than a business trip. Magnus realized they had the knack for making the routine interesting. He wondered if he would ever be able to adopt that attitude, then realized his responsibilities required that he always be on guard. His role was different and he would enjoy some of their enthusiasm when he could.

They arrived at dusk and camped on the hill next to their future home. The tents were erected and the military routine for protecting the camp being second nature, everything required was quickly done. The new Lord and the ladies first planned act was to visit their friend Bishop Aert, but he was nearly to them as they were leaving to go see him. They were greeted warmly and they went to Magnus' tent and shared a drink. Aert told them they must come have breakfast with him. He would then give them a tour of the new cathedral and his new adjacent quarters in the morning. After a short visit, they all retired for the night.

The morning breakfast was enjoyable and the friends exchanged news of their latest adventures and work. The bishop's took them on a tour of his new quarters which were very functional. There was a meeting room, dining hall, library, a kitchen and humble sleeping rooms for the bishop and his staff. The meeting and dining hall were humble but attractive while the rest of the building was very plain. It spoke of a bishop and staff more concerned with work than comfort.

The cathedral was a very large church constructed of wood. The carpentry work was excellent and the carving intricate and beautiful. The pew benches were well crafted and when the party sat down was surprised at how comfortable the seats were. Ava expressed to Aert how she looked forward to worshipping here. Aert was pleased that Magnus did not plan to add a chapel at his new home but come to worship here.

The party had lunch in the dining hall and afterwards walked back up the hill to the building that would be the new lord's fortifications. Magnus called for a man to make a list as they toured. First he inspected the walls which were about ten feet high. He had a note made that a four foot wide and six foot high deck would need to be made around the inside of the wall so the wall could be defended. Because of the slots in the wall Magnus suspected such a construction had been a part of the original design. The gate to the courtyard was really more ornamental than defensive. He made a note that a second defensive gate should be constructed inside the other if possible or the ornamental gate replaced if necessary.

The stone building which had previously been the bishop's residence was in very good condition inside. Four long hallways ran the entire length of the exterior walls of the building. There were five narrow tall windows on each side. The four doors to the interior rooms, one opening on each hall were offset so no door was opposite a window. The building was obviously designed to be defended.

Magnus had a note made to have metal shutters made for each window. Upon close inspection it was obvious from the stone work that this would also have been part of the original building for hinge anchors were in the stone. The interior doors would need to be made to be strong defensive barriers not the ornamental doors that were now mounted on the strong hinges. The doors now mounted were not bracketed to be barred. Magnus walked around the hallway back to the main entrance.

There was a great hall at one end of the building facing the main gate and door to the building. The hall had been the bishop's throne room. Magnus had a note made to have two lockable iron gates made to place on either side of the entrance to the main hall to prevent unwanted guests from entering the outer hallways. There was a large hearth on each of the outer side walls and a number of small rooms on either side of the hearths. The walls were all made of stone. Upon inspecting the rooms it was apparent that these rooms would make excellent barrack rooms. They would be cool in summer and the hearths would keep them warm in winter.

To either side of the central interior wall to the sides of the throne dais were two doors which led into a dining hall. On the wall opposite the doors was a hearth and on either side of that were two doors leading into the kitchen. On the wall behind the dining room hearth was another hearth that was used for cooking. This kitchen was large and again there were rooms against the hallway walls. Ava stated these would be for the household staff.

Proceeding on there were two more doors which led into a room and on either side against the hallway walls were broad stone stairways leading to an upper level above the kitchen. On the far wall in the center was a hearth and to the side the door to the hallway. Wherever possible the walls of the room were lined with wooden shelves which former bishop's had installed. This would be the library.

The party went toward the far end of the room and climbed the stairs. The second level of the building was simply a large open space above the kitchen. It had a double hearth in the middle of the room. There were two tall narrow window openings on each wall. This was obviously directly over the kitchen and dining room hearths. This would be the lord's quarters.

Magnus instructed a note be made to have metal shutters made for these that could be barred and defensive doors installed at the top of the stairways.

The building contained no furniture and Ava and Cenedred saw it as their mission to see that this was remedied. They were enthusiastic and full of ideas. They would need draperies and rugs, pots and pans, utensils, and furniture. Ava asked to be allowed to make these arrangements. Magnus agreed on condition he would give the women a budget to work with and that the soldiers' quarters would be furnished by the castle captain. The ladies both found the terms agreeable. Cenedred had not been able to do the same at Cuthbert's castle out of respect, so she had taken active participation in her sister's opportunity to "nest".

Magnus ordered a ladder be brought and a carpenter summoned. It was as he had suspected, the roof needed some minor repair.

Magnus asked Aert, who had just finished the cathedral rebuilding project, if he had a person who could help them hire the appropriate tradesman and develop costs for the projects. Aert invited the group for lunch and said he would have his staff arrange appointments with the needed tradesmen for midafternoon.

After lunch, the group returned to the castle. When they arrived, there were two priests and several tradesmen waiting. They were introduced to Lord Magnus and the rest of the party by Aert. There were two furniture makers in the group and they went off with the ladies and a priest who would make a list of what was needed and a tally of the prices quoted.

Aert went with Magnus and the other priest. The notes from the morning were used for reference. The carpenters examined the walls and two of them wanted to build the wall decks and the gate. A sort of bidding war started. Magnus intervened when it became obvious the men were getting carried away in the competition and Aert had to whisper to him the price was now too low for anyone to make money. He told the men he did not want to take advantage of their desire to work and was willing to pay a fair but not exorbitant price. The men could split the job. Each man would do two sides and they would build the gate together. They came to an agreement, with Aert advising Magnus, on price and a guarantee of workmanship. Only seasoned hardwoods would be used. Magnus told the men that there would be more work once the castle was completed and he expected their work would be of a high standard.

They then went into the building and to the top of the stairs where the placing of doors was discussed. Magnus wanted the door to open outward to make it more difficult to force them open from the small landing in front of the door. The men discussed how this could be done and they agreed on a common plan and each would do one of the doors.

The carpenters could see no way that the ornamental gates could remain in place if a solid defensive gate was to be installed. They would have to be removed.

The three workers in metal were asked if they could use the gate material to build the hallway gates. They were all of the opinion it was be less costly to build new ones. The window shutters were discussed and that would be a reasonably easy project to do.

The metal workers were all asked to go to the priest and privately give him a price for the work. The three men had never done such a thing before and wanted to compete openly. They were allowed to do so and finally the bidding stopped. Two of the men said they could not match that price. The low bidder was taken aside and asked why he could so much lower than the others. He said he had purchased a stock of metal some time ago at a good price from a river trader. He had been storing it and it was already on hand. He had also been purchasing scrap metal and refining it when he wasn't busy doing jobs for others. As a result, he had enough metal on hand to do all the fabrication and still make a profit. The metal worker was given the job.

He offered Magnus a reduction in price if he could take the ornamental gates to melt down. Magnus declined for knew the metal was of sufficient quality to make spear heads and arrow heads and he had plans for that metal.

The tradesmen were all given an initial payment witnessed by the priests and the rest would be paid when the jobs were completed. The tradesmen left to start work. Magnus was pleased for the prices negotiated were less than he had planned.

The women came to him with lists and prices. They decided, it being late that the furniture makers would be sent away and told to come back the next day. The group adjourned to have a meal and review the lists. It seemed the furniture makers were each better at some particular thing according to Aert and so they should choose according to the makers specialty to get the best quality rather than decide based only on cost. The group concentrated that evening on furniture.

The most expensive piece would be the large dining hall table which would be made of one slab of hardwood. It was to be so large that it would barely fit into the dining room on its side because of its width and length. The maker would have to find just the right tree, tall and straight. The benches would be made from the wood of the same tree. Cenedred announced that the dining table would be her and Wolf's wedding present to them.

When the cost of the furniture was tallied it was just a little more than Magnus had allowed for but he had saved enough elsewhere to more than make up the difference. The ladies decided they would go look at what the local merchants were offering in the morning. Aert offered to have his cook go with them to select the best quality pots and utensils and advise the ladies regarding local prices. The ladies recognized that Aert was diplomatically suggesting the cook could negotiate the best price. They accepted his offer.

In the morning, Magnus was pleased to find the carpenters already bringing wagons loaded with wood to the courtyard shortly after sunrise. The ladies set out with four guards and two servants with a small cart to bring back the purchases. Just before midday there was a rain shower and work stalled for a while as the workers took cover and the opportunity to eat a cold meal.

Magnus was surveying the river front and talking to river men who fished up and down the river. There was only one dock and it was really not sufficient for significant river trade. It was Magnus intent to build three commercial docks and two warehouses. The river men were very helpful and asked if a better dock could be built for use by them. Magnus discussed this with them and agreed to consider this if the dock were built some way from the proposed commercial dock and trading area.

The banks in front of the town were soft and the river men said the shallows were soft mud in which a man would sink to his waist. The shoreline was very shallow for about thirty feet from the shoreline. The area around the dock was a flood plain for quite some distance back from the river before the ground sloped up to the present town site. Each spring the floodplain filled and the single dock was submerged. The fishermen grounded their boats during flood stage. Unfortunately, the river men reported the banks were like this on both sides for a day's journey in both directions.

Magnus knew that docks could be built to float up and down on piers sunk into the silt for he had seen it done. Here in dry season there would be a lot of dock sitting on dry land. The docks would have to be at least one hundred and twenty feet long. In order to get wagons from the docks to the hilltop across the soft soil would require building of some kind of road several hundred feet long. It would be expensive. Magnus now knew why the river trade here had not developed even though the location was ideal to serve a large area.

As he walked uphill the old Roman roads that still existed here and there came to mind. If the ground was excavated for a road and large rocks were used for a bed then river bed stone was used to cover the large rocks, such a road might hold small wagons even when the ground was wet. Magnus immediately went to visit Aert and explained what he wanted to do. Aert had one of the priests arrange for laborers to dig some test pits for the Lord. Magnus had markers placed and the men went to work.

Magnus went back to camp to eat but saw on the way that goods were being brought into the residence. He went to investigate. Ava came rushing to meet him and gave him a big hug. Cenedred followed a short way behind.

Ava was very pleased, "God has blessed us, and we were ever so successful and now have enough kitchen ware to cook meals here. Everyone can be fed from the kitchen. This is going to be a wonderful home for us."

Magnus was buoyed by her joy and enthusiasm.

Cenedred arrived, "I did not know I would enjoy the outing as much as I did. I also learned a lot about bargaining this morning. Aert's cook is a marvel at it. I will have to do some buying for our castle when I return home."

In truth, Cenedred was happier about the changes she saw in her sister than the experience of the morning. She had silently given thanks to God for the positive changes she saw in her sister's character. She was maturing quickly now and was no longer the self-centered child she had been a short few months ago.

They ate a cold meal together at the camp. Magnus explained his plans. The women talked about how this would make it so much easier to travel between castles to visit.

After lunch, Magnus went to see how work was progressing on

the fortifications. He was amazed at the progress. Framing for the decks was already being erected. There were many men working on the decks and both the carpenters came to greet him. They had heard he wanted to build docks and they said they would like to discuss this with him. He told them generally about his plan and they said that working together they could do the work. They had both seen it done before and the metal workers here could make all the appropriate rings, anchors, and chains necessary. They suggested that if it pleased the Lord, they would prepare plans and costs.

Magnus told them he would make no commitment but would consider their plans. Magnus knew that the men wanted to keep the work here and the earnings in their pocket. He appreciated their enterprise. They asked him some questions about details of the project their men were working on and made some suggestions. The discussion ended when a priest came to tell Magnus that his presence was needed at the shore. Magnus went with the priest.

The work at two dig sites had been stopped because the laborers had run into bed rock. The bedrock of the pit nearest the water was struck just a little over three feet down and the next about forty feet up the bank about four feet under the surface. The men were amazed that Magnus was happy about this. He told the first group to dig another pit about eight feet from the water line and the other he had dig a pit between the two which had already been dug. As he walked uphill the third group hit bedrock about five feet down. This was better than Magnus had ever hoped. He put out some additional stakes.

By early evening the pits that had been dug made Magnus certain that the bedrock sloped uphill fairly close to the surface. He just needed to know if the bedrock was wide. He marked spots for the next day's pit digs to determine if the rock was underneath the whole hill.

In late afternoon a messenger came to him asking if the party would again share a meal with his Excellency the bishop. Magnus accepted and instructed the messenger to advise the ladies.

Magnus then went about inquiring where large quantities of large stones could be found. He was told that there was not much naturally occurring loose rock in the area. One of the locals said that the old ones probably had collected them all to build the stone fences that were abandoned down river. When asked, he told his lord where the fences were. Magnus called for mounts and four guards and went down the road that followed the river. About a mile from town near the river he found the system of stone fences that were overgrown and falling down. The fences had originally probably been three feet high. He dismounted and pushed some over and picked some up. They were large but a man could lift them and there was more than enough stone for the road he wanted to build and probably dozens more like it. Wagons could bring the stone to the dock site making several trips a day and with a crew loading stones at one end and another unloading at the other a great number could be moved in a day.

Magnus thought he knew what the ancient builders had made the fences for and now he had another possible enterprise in mind. He would implement that plan later.

The evening meal was pleasant and Magnus shared his discoveries with his new friend the bishop and his family. Aert realized the impact Magnus's plans would have on the prosperity of the people, the population of the town, and the church. Aert was pleased that the relationship with Magnus was similar to the one with Wolf. They had just naturally fallen into the same pattern as both men genuinely liked each other.

The next day revealed that the bedrock was indeed at least a hundred feet wide and probably a lot wider. Magnus went about hiring a large number of laborers to dig and wagons to hall rock and dirt. Magnus consulted men who hauled heavy loads in wagons and they advised that it would be best if the road angled slightly to decrease the incline even more. They even agreed on how to achieve the best angle. Magnus had the road bed staked out and the digging and hauling started.

Late in the day a messenger came to Magnus with word that Lord Wolf was coming to visit Magnus. He returned to the residence and found the ladies had hired a cook and servant girl. The cook was preparing a hot meal of stew and fresh bread in quantity sufficient to feed the soldiers and a meal of lamb for the Lord's family.

The next day at mid-morning Wolf arrived and warm greetings

were in order all round. The ladies insisted on taking him to see the work in progress at the residence. The tradesmen in charge were introduced to King Aelle who was pleased with the joy his wife and sister-in-law were taking in making this place a home within a fortress.

After the tour of the residence, Magnus took Wolf to see the work at the shore. He shared his plans and his discovery. The roadway was being excavated and another part filled with stone when they arrived. Wolf was impressed with Magnus's plans. He inquired how much this was all costing. Magnus told him that after the docks and warehouses were built, almost all his share of the treasure from the campaign with Osmund and Sebbe would be invested. Magnus calculated that with the taxes and rents from the lands that were being presently generated, he could maintain it all, without taking into account the potential of river trade or his other business enterprise.

It was then that Wolf knew he had made a good decision in Magnus. Wolf stayed two more days and then returned to the valley with the ladies. The date for the wedding was set keeping in mind when the residence would be furnished and the defensive construction completed. Magnus was pleased that the repairs to the roof required much less work than he had anticipated.

Magnus made time to tour the land meeting the people and interacting with local head men. He became known as a fair lord, paying a fair wage for a hard day's work but tolerating no slackers as a few ne'er-do-wells had discovered after being fired from his crews their first day. He meted out justice impartially. When travelling, he always visited the parish priests or attended worship with the locals. Everyone thought they were fortunate he was their earl. He loved and protected his people and worked for the prosperity of all those who lived peacefully in the land as did King Aelle. The lords did not tax oppressively and the people could see that much more than the taxes and rents they paid were being spent to improve life in the land.

The work at the home was completed two weeks before the wedding and the road had been completed as well as construction of the first dock. Two others had been started. One warehouse was substantially complete and the frame had been started for the other.

The wedding was attended by all the lords but Asbjorn, who sent polite regrets and no explanation.

Prior to the wedding Aelle called the great council together to discuss Asbjorn's absence. Aelle's spies reported that Asbjorn had not been in good health and his grip on power was slipping. Asbjorn's disease seemed strikingly similar to what Cuthbert had experienced. No one was sure whether Asbjorn's brother or his uncle was seeking to replace him but a power struggle was obviously occurring.

Aldred, Feliks and Yingvar also expressed concerns about the reports they were receiving. There was some military build-up and the people of the land were being subject to oppressive taxes. It was agreed that the southern castle would receive further reinforcements. The Lords all agreed to use some of their increased prosperity to pay for the recruitment, equipping and training of an additional ten men-at arms each. This would increase the King's standing force by eighty men-at-arms.

Wolf took Magnus aside and presented him with a small chest. It was filled with treasure. Wolf told him it was a wedding present from him and Cenedred. Magnus was most grateful. The couple received many wedding gifts from wooden spoons to silver goblets to fine tapestries. They were overwhelmed by the generosity being lavished on them.

The area around the town was filled with fancy tents and humble shelters as many came to celebrate the union. There was a grand parade to the cathedral and a simple wedding ceremony with Eadgard giving his youngest daughter in marriage in the new cathedral with his Excellency Bishop Aert officiating. It was Aldred's first wedding since becoming a Christian.

As with Wolf and Cenedred's wedding, there was an outdoor feast and again a reception line but this time an awning had been erected and there were seats. The wedding party stood to receive the lords, ladies, officials, captains and their wives. Guards channeled the visitors into and through the covered reception area.

Osmund and Ethelind enjoyed seeing the family again. They had travelled by boat and theirs was one to the first to use the new dock. Osmund's two sisters had never been away from their family lands and saw the trip and visit as a great adventure.

Aldred attended the feast and talked with Yingvar who told him he had prospered with the peace and increased trade that King Aelle had brought to the region. Eadgard attested to the fact that his lands were also prospering in the absence of continual war. Aldred had seen what Magnus had done at the river front and was thinking about how he could emulate that. He inquired of Magnus who told him he could have a copy of the plans for building the floating docks. The other Lords also expressed interest.

Herewood and Aewel approached King Aelle about marriage. They both had been administering the lands they had been given stewardship over very well and those areas were prospering. They were both unmarried and wanted to be wed and raise families but had no suitable candidates for marriage. Aelle said he understood and would talk to Cenedred about the matter.

He mentioned it to Cenedred and in minutes she, Ethelind and Hilde were conspiring. Both of Osmund's sisters were of marriageable age, as was Feliks's daughter and the youngest sister of Aldred. The women conspired to introduce the young women to the eligible men. Aewel was the older of the two and the women thought he might be the most difficult to pair up but it turned out Aewel, in spite being older, was more attractive to the young women for he was a rugged and handsome man.

Introductions were made. Herewood was younger and perhaps better natured but not as attractive as Aewel. Only Osmund's oldest sister Gytha seemed to have an interest and she attached herself to Herewood. They walked through the feasting visitors socializing and introducing themselves. Gytha's interest in Herewood was not lost on Osmund.

When the festivities were over, all the officials and lords except Herewood and Osmund departed for their own castles. Herewood stayed for several days and he and Gytha spent considerable time together chaperoned by Ethelind. As the days passed, Herewood and Gytha found they were pleased with each other's company. The time came for Herewood to return to his duties but he had one last thing to do before he left.

Herewood was no stranger to danger and had faced and overcome his fear before, and when he came to Osmund he had to practice that same discipline. There were so many reasons that Osmund might refuse his request. He was eleven years Gytha's senior, and though she was beyond the normal marrying age, he was not a lord. Much to Herewood's surprise Osmund was not angry when he asked Osmund for permission to marry Gytha. Osmund burst into laughter and slapped his knee.

"Ethelind and I were wagering when you would come to me. We had already decided we were in favor of the match. Come let us see if we can talk Wolf into it."

Aelle and Cenedred were sitting on the terrace having a morning meal when the two men came to request an audience. Wolf had them come and invited them to join him and his wife. Wolf asked why they had come to see him.

Osmund spoke, "I come as the patriarch of my family, to request your approval for a marriage I have arranged."

Wolf looked serious, although he was not, for he and Cenedred had been in on the wager with Osmund and Ethelind, "And who are the parties to this arranged marriage?"

"I have arranged, subject to your approval, for the marriage of Herewood and Gytha."

As Wolf shook his head, and Cenedred looked away to keep from laughter, Herewood felt as though his heart went into his throat.

"Herewood is valuable to me where he is. I cannot see releasing him from service to go back to your castle, Osmund my friend."

Herewood was now the warrior, "Sire, if I may?"

"Yes, Herewood."

"It was not my intention to leave my post or my position in your service. Lady Gytha is agreeable to living at my post, wherever you make that. I beg you Sire, to approve this marriage."

Cenedred could bear it no more and burst into laughter, "Good Herewood my husband is having you on. We have all discussed this possibility. Tell him husband."

"Forgive me Herewood, but we are having our fun at your expense. Of course you may marry Gytha, but I must admit that I am disappointed in you Herewood."

"Why so, Lord?"

"Well, you neglected to hold Osmund up for a dowry."

Herewood smiled, "Yes, Sire. I was neglectful in that."

"Well seeing as Lord Osmund has arranged this marriage for his sister, and you are in my service, I will have to negotiate for you."

Herewood was now enjoying the game, "I would be ever so grateful, my Lord."

Now it was Osmund's turn to play a part, "Oh my friend Herewood so quickly you turn my disadvantage to your own advantage.   It is my own fault; I should have known to negotiate with you for you are so love stricken you would have accepted a set of candles for dowry."

An informal announcement was made at dinner that night. Gytha feigned surprise though everyone knew she must already know. His Excellency Bishop Aert would preside at the wedding. There would not be a long betrothal because Osmund and Ethelind had to return to their lands.

The couple was married and everyone returned to their own duties. Wolf and Cenedred promised to come and visit Osmund and Ethelind.

The harvest was good again that year. The farmers had gotten used to planting as much as possible because they could now turn that which was excess to their family's needs into cash by selling it for shipment by boat either north or south wherever the price was best.

Rheged was continuing to make Magnus wealthier. The receipt of arrowheads, spear tips and casing for spear ends made from the old bar gates increased profitability. Magnus had arranged to have the gate metal melted and recast at cathedral town and shipped to Rheged by boat.

The river trade prospered and the cathedral town grew and people started calling it Cathedral Town. Magnus built more docks and merchants built warehouses on land rented from Magnus at miniscule prices. Magnus was no fool for the docking fees and taxes were where the income came to him and he was not greedy.

For the next two years all the lands prospered and the standing army of Wolf increased in size and trained hard and regularly. Most of the soldiers married and built small homes with the wealth from the previous campaigns. They were not disappointed by the lack of a war for they were paid regularly and lived well. They were occasionally away from their families on patrols and missions to intercept the odd raiding party, but generally they enjoyed garrison life and kept the local peace. The people always welcomed the soldiers for the Wolf Pack was well behaved and disciplined. Tarnishing the image of one's comrades brought several levels of discipline. Each of the lords also had their own forces and they had grown substantially.

Word came that Lady Ethelind was with child. Wolf's half-brother was born in late spring before Wolf's child. He was named Penrith. His father Osmund now ruled a very prosperous land as had his father. The people were happy and Osmund commanded a formidable force of warriors and archers who secured the peace in the land.

King Aelle and his queen came to visit the lords and their garrisons regularly and he and his queen went among the people. They often showed up at country churches to worship with the locals even when Lady Cenedred was with child. They were much loved for their love of the people and the prosperity they had brought.

Aewel remained unmarried for a time then requested permission from Wolf to take a leave to visit Aldred. His interest was Rowena, Aldred's sister who was the eldest of the available Christian women of acceptable rank. Aewel had been writing to her and wanted to spend some time determining if a match was possible. Lord Aldred was happy to entertain Aewel. Wolf approved the leave. The visit resulted in another wedding.

All of the matches resulted in contented marriages. Some of the married parties were happily in love and some contentedly in love. Some loved with passion and some with tenderness, but all the couples relied on God in their marriage and they all grew together.

Babies were born and Asbjorn died. There was civil war in the southern lands as Asbjorn's family killed one another for power. In the meantime, Asbjorn's son and rightful heir Lucan was safe with Aelle. Because of the civil war the tribute did not come from the southern lands and because of the treaty the lands were legally forfeited to King Aelle.

The great council was called by the king and met to discuss the matter of the southern lands. It was decided to let the family of

Asbjorn become weaker by fighting among themselves for power. When they had exhausted themselves in their sin, the land would be claimed and Lucan would become Earl. Lucan had become a devout Christian and though not an outstanding soldier, he was good. Where he excelled was in his understanding of things administrative and political.

He had come to Aelle to discuss the problems in his family lands. He acknowledged that Aelle had the legal right to claim the lands, but requested that Aelle consider accepting him there as earl even though he was only twelve though he would soon have his thirteenth birthday. His familial claim would blunt much of the opposition and his people were sick of war. If he came with a sizeable army after his family had drained themselves of their resources, it would be rather easy to seize control. It would then become a matter of rebuilding.

He made the argument that he had learned from Aelle how to govern and would be good at restoring his people's prosperity with some financial assistance from the other lords. Of course, he hoped King Aelle would provide him with an advisor until he was well established. In addition, his people were more likely to accept Bishop Aert's missionaries once Lucan was in place.

So it came to be that for the first time in years an expeditionary force was preparing to go into the field.

Chapter 19 - A Righteous Cause

Aelle's spies brought regular reports on the situation in the southern lands. Over the years Aelle had developed an elaborate intelligence network. He knew in detail what was happening in his own lands and the lands surrounding his. He also had a strategic knowledge of what was happening farther away. The conclusion was that an expeditionary force into the southern shire in support of the rightful treaty claim and Earl Lucan would not bring any other lords into the fray. In any event, it would take a complex alliance to raise a force to challenge Aelle's. The further lords were happy not to awaken the sleeping giant that was Aelle's standing army.

Aelle sent messages to all the surrounding lords that Aelle's forces were going to assist Lucan to assert his right as a loyal earl of King Aelle in regaining his family lands. Lucan would enforce the King's claim to the lands under the treaty. He assured the lords that he and his earl's policy of non-aggression unless attacked was still their guiding principle. He also let them know that any attack on Lucan's lands would be considered an aggression against King Aelle.

The reports were that there were less than thirty capable men-at-arms left in the entire southern lands. Lucan's uncle was ruling, but his hold was tenuous. The spies reported that two lords of adjoining lands had started to raise troops to invade Lucan's lands until they received the message from Aelle. They had thought to double their lands as their force outnumbered what Lucan's uncle Blad could field and his forces were worn from continuous fighting. They were in no way prepared to face King Aelle so abandoned their ambitions.

Ragnvald led a hundred men-at-arms and twenty five archers into Lucan's lands. The column also had a long train of wagons following for the land they were entering had been decimated by civil war. Many of the wagons contained grain, salted meat, and seed.

The reputation of the Wolf Pack went before them. It was said they did not abuse the civilian population and they purchased what they needed instead of seizing it. A few people came out to meet the column and found this to be true and word spread. The soldiers bought fresh fruit and vegetables or traded grain for it.

When the people learned Lucan was with the column some of the sheriffs came with their people to greet the earl. Lucan had learned from Aelle, and met with the heads of hundreds as they came out of hiding assuring them of his and King Aelle's love for the people. Increasingly the company was welcomed as liberators for the reputation of the peace and prosperity of the lands Aelle ruled was well told and the reports of the kindness with which they treated the people went ahead of them.

The force moved forward with the scouts continuously out collecting intelligence. Lucan's uncle Blad thought he would be in a strong position in the castle for a small force could defend it. However, war had drained the stores and the castle could not hold out against a long siege. When he saw the size of the force that came and camped around the castle and the many wagons with the column he started to despair. This force was prepared for a long siege.

The next morning Blad came out under a truce to talk with Siegfried. Lucan was by Ragnvald's side. Blad did not recognize Lucan.

Blad spoke first, "Who are you that invade our lands?"

Ragnvald replied, "Who are you that would deny the king and his rightful earl of their right to rule here. Who murders their brother with poison and his family by the sword? Who ferments rebellion against the legitimate rule?"

Blad struggled to restrain his anger. The insults were bad enough, but how did this man know about the poison. Blad always believed the best defense was offense.

"Who are you to question me?"

Ragnvald smiled, "I am Ragnvald, War Chief of King Aelle, who demands you surrender this land to be governed by its rightful king and Earl Lucan."

Blad tried another tactic, "If you are indeed friends of my nephew Lucan, you are welcome. Bring him to me and we will rejoice and he will be our leader."

Ragnvald was now angry, "You make me to be a fool and insult me gravely. This is a personal insult and not covered by truce. I challenge you to single combat."

Blad's anger started to rise and he realized this was his opportunity; defeat this man and his troops would go away, "I accept here and now!"

Blad had only to claim protection by truce and return to the castle, but his own poor reasoning and his anger got the best of him. Blad was wearing mail and his opponent wore a uniform and cape. This Ragnvald would be at a disadvantage and defeating him would be easier. Blad was not very observant in his anger.

Ragnvald dismounted while taking his helmet from his saddle horn and placing it on his head. He threw off his cape and Blad saw that his arms were covered in mail and that meant the tunic he wore was over mail. Blad then realized his opponent wore mail leggings as well. Siegfried's shield came up and he drew his sword.

Blad now knew that he faced a formidable opponent and before Ragnvald could react, Blad mounted his horse and fled for the castle. Blad's companion did not have time to follow for Ragnvald was upon him and he surrendered.

Ragnvald's mounted warriors needed no order from their War Chief. Sergeant Skjold saw the opportunity and gave the order and a full pursuit started from the lines. Blad had a head start and started from a point closer to the castle, but the mounts of his pursuers were stronger and faster. He entered the gate with several mounted warriors less than a horse length behind and the defenders could not close the gate fast enough to keep out the attackers.

The men at the gate were engaged and more of Ragnvald's men were forcing their way in through the gate as Blad's men tried to close it. The rest of Blad's men rushed to the gate, but they could not stop the incoming tide of warriors and in fact they only slowed it as long as it took Ragnvald's men to cut them down. The castle fell without a siege.

Only twenty three men had defended the castle and all fell in its defense. No prisoners were taken inside the castle. Only the man who had surrendered to Ragnvald lived. Ragnvald's men searched the castle and found little of value.

He sent Skjold to question the prisoner and find out where Blad's home was. Skjold was then sent to search it for wealth. Skjold took twenty men, drew three days provisions and immediately set out. They arrived at Blad's estate to find it abandoned. They questioned the local people who were happy to tell them that Blad's wife and her family had left with three wagons several hours ago. After determining the direction of their travel the patrol set out in pursuit.

The family had camped in a small clearing just off the road well after dark. They were just rousing from their sleep when the patrol stepped from the woods and four rode up the road to block any escape. The grandfather and an aged uncle and two servants were the only males with the wagons. The rest of the family group consisted of women and children.

Skjold spoke in his parade ground voice, "We have no desire to harm women and children. We come only for the wealth that belongs to Earl Lucan. Assemble and sit on the ground here leaving any weapons while my men search the wagons, then you will be allowed to leave. Resist and we will use force."

The men and women did as they were told and herded the children to the indicated spot where they all sat in the grass that was wet with dew. The search yielded a large amount of silver and gold which was confiscated. The men were searched and it was found that each man, including the servants carried substantial wealth in purses upon their person.

So it was that Skjold announced the women would have to be searched. He told them he would do it as gently as possible if they did not resist. The servant women were subservient and they were patted down as respectfully as possible and each was found to be carrying purses. They were allowed to remove them from under their garments themselves. The purses were confiscated.

The family woman decided to struggle to protect their wealth. Blad's wife pulled a knife and lunged forward at Skjold who drew his short blade and struck her with the hilt knocking her unconscious. Her uncle jumped up and rushed Skjold and met the business end of Skjold's sword. Skjold searched the unconscious woman and removed several purses. He had her bound. Some of the other family women had to be held down to be searched and the purses had to be forcibly taken. As a result, their experience was much less tolerable than those of the servant women. Those who fought were bound up.

Under the circumstances the families other goods were all unloaded and searched. The clothes and other goods were strewn all over the ground. A chest of coins was found as well as several more purses. There were silver plates, candle holders, cups and vessels and utensils. One sack that was found contained precious stones. One searcher by accident found a dress had precious stones sewn into the hem so all the clothes had to be examined. This resulted in many garments being cut open.

After the search had been completed, Skjold made up a humble purse and approached the grandfather, "This purse contains enough to leave this land and support your group until you can find work. You may pack up your personal goods and leave this land with one of the wagons. We are taking the other wagons. If any of you ever return to any of the lands of King Aelle your life will be forfeit. Do you understand?"

The grandfather nodded and simply said, "Yes."

The amount of treasure that the family had tried to escape with was astounding. Without the wagons, the patrol could not have brought it back to the castle. Even so, the wagons were heavily laden and they travelled slowly.

With Lucan's agreement Ragnvald made Skjold Captain of the far southern shire and temporary advisor to Lucan. Skjold was left with twenty five men-at-arms and ten archers to keep the peace. He would have to recruit and train an equal number of men-at-arms for Lucan before he came home. The weapons and armor captured in the campaign would be used to arm Lucan's force.

Skjold was left with most of the provisions in the wagons and enough coin to pay for and provide for his troops for several months. Lucan was given enough money to recruit young men to train at arms and pay them and to maintain his castle and give aid to the farmers who might need it.

Ragnvald suggested to Lord Lucan that he might want to consider building docks and becoming involved in the river trade as the other lord's had. Aelle had given Ragnvald authority to assure Lucan that if he wished to do so, next spring the king would be willing to help him with such an enterprise.

Two days later, the troops being rested, Ragnvald and the majority of his force marched north toward home.

Word had gotten down river that Ragnvald had gone south with an army of more than one hundred. There were some who did not believe the reports of the size of the armies of King Aelle and his lords. They saw the expedition of Ragnvald with what they thought must be the majority of King Aelle's army as an opportunity to raid. Two Danish raiders came upriver to raid Cathedral Town. Each boat was large and had a crew of a little over forty men.

Magnus had always positioned scouts up and down river so he knew of the approach of the raiders. The raiders' first view of the town led them to believe they had come unobserved as they saw men running away from the docks. There was a half loaded wagon and bales near the dock but no boats. The raiders did not pay any mind to this for they thought they had caught the town unawares. They knew the residence was above the town and well-fortified, but they did not need to take it to loot the town and the cathedral.

The two boats docked and the warriors disembarked and started running up the hill. They were half way up the hill when the hundred men-at-arms who had been hiding on the other side of the hill appeared at the crest. Magnus's troops had been reinforced by Bishop Aert's priest warriors. At the same time, mounted warriors came from the right side behind the line charging up the hill.

The raider captains both realized at the same time that the mounted warriors behind them were going for the boats. This was a trap. With a precision that came with months of practice the warriors dismounted and four men rode off leading the horses. The dismounted warriors ran down the dock in column of two. Some in the rear at just the right spot stopped and turned making a shield wall across the dock that was two deep. The rest of the group headed for the boats. The men on the boats were experienced warriors and climbed up on the dock to form a shield wall but they were close to the middle of the boats where they organized so some of their attackers came straight at them and some jumped onto the end of the boats running along the boat to flank the shield wall.

Realizing they were outnumbered and likely to be flanked the group gave up on the shield wall and charged. It was an ugly fight. The raiders engaged in the fight did not realize that a number of men were swimming downriver with the current and climbing onto the boats behind them. These men were not meant to be combatants and waited for the fighting to end. The boat guards were outnumbered two to one and though they fought bravely they were overcome fairly quickly. All but three of Magnus's warriors went back to reinforce the dock shield wall while the men who had swum to the boats brought the wounded warriors aboard and cast off and guided the boats downriver.

While the fight for the boats was underway, the raiders on the hill fell back to establish a shield wall facing out from the dock while others attacked the dock. Magnus's warriors attacked the shield wall and the fighting was fierce. The raiders attacking the dock wall were caught in a bottle neck and could make no progress and became desperate when they saw the boat guards being slayed. Some tried to wade along the dock to engage Magnus's men on the dock from the side. They quickly became trapped in the sucking mud and could neither go forward nor back and continued to struggle and sink until they were waist deep in the mud. The raiders were trapped between the dock shield wall and the shield wall of the large force. Once the boats were taken the raiders all knew they would die.

The ground was slick with blood as Magnus and his men inched forward.

The men from the castle locked it down with Ava and two guards locked upstairs and came to the battle. The raiders were all trapped and fighting as only desperate men could. They had fought out of many hard places, but the foe they fought now was well trained, armed and disciplined. Minute by minute they grew increasingly aware the chances were they were going to die, but they all would rather go the warriors' hall than surrender in disgrace. The surviving raider captain gave an order and his men formed a wedge and tried to force their way through the wall. The raiders did not see the dozen fresh warriors from the castle coming downhill to the fight. They reinforced the point where the raiders wedge was attacking.

The wedge was surrounded and the intensity and desperation of the fighting grew. Men were slipping in the blood. One of Magnus's men fell backward and as another took his place Magnus pulled the fallen man back and up, then both went to the fight again.

Only three raiders survived, they were ones pulled out of the mud. Two others refused help in being extricated from the mud and were left there cursing out of reach of spears and waving their weapons threateningly. The archers came and had target practice at point blank range. It seemed cruel but not as cruel as letting the men die of thirst or starvation.

The cost of the battle had been high. Thirty one of Magnus's and Aert's men had perished. Eleven more were wounded. Eighty one raiders were dead and three captured. The captured were in shock. They had never before experienced such defeat.

The raiders' boats were brought to the dock and tied up. They contained a substantial amount of loot from other raids, but no amount of money could make up for the men who had lost their lives.

In small groups the men were giving God thanks for the victory and praying for the families of the comrades they had lost. The company mourned greatly for three of their companions who had not yet been saved from their sins through faith in Christ. They knew that though the men had been honorable and loyal by worldly standards, they fell short of God's standard and were bound for hell, for they were not cleansed of their sins by faith in Jesus.

The wounded were taken by wagon up the stone road to be tended to. The wounded would all probably survive and only one was unlikely to go back to active service. He would probably be a permanent garrison sentry.

The three men who were captured were tried and were hung. The word spread quickly of the large battles almost simultaneously fought in the south lands and the central lands. At first many believed it could not be true, but there were too many witnesses for it not to be. In fact, the size of the battles was large enough in reality so there was little embellishment needed to make the stories entertaining.

The ferocity of the battle of Cathedral Town was retold all over the lands and up and down the rivers. The proof became evident when Magnus put the captured boats to work as river traders. It took thirty six hired men to man all the oars of the boats, though they seldom had that large a crew because they were just used on rivers. They were guarded by men who had fought and some of whom had been wounded in the battle of Cathedral Town. They were large vessels that could hold a lot of cargo.

The taking of the southern castle was recounted in all the lands inside and outside of Aelle's lands. Magnus's and Ragnvald's reputations as warriors grew.

*****

Aelle was reviewing the reports of taxes collected and incomes when they came for him. His wife was in labor and the child was coming. He went to his wife. She was covered in sweat and in obvious pain.

"It is time husband." She grimaced in pain, "This is all your fault!" She laughed through the pain.

The women hurried him from the room and sent him away to wait. One of the midwives told him his wife was having a hard labor. He went to the castle chapel to pray. Bishop Aert arrived and was brought to Aelle. They prayed together. Word came for Wolf to come. Bishop Aert followed him as he rushed to Cenedred. He knew when he entered the room. He went to her she was pale and there was a lot of blood.

She spoke almost in a whisper, "My dear husband, I love you as I know you love me. God is calling me home, but He has allowed me to leave you with a healthy son. I will be in that better place waiting for you." Tears ran down her cheek, she smiled, and then she was gone.

Wolf started sobbing and Bishop Aert came and led him away. Aert took his friend to the library, locked the door, and did what he could to comfort him. They cried together, they prayed together, they reminisced about the good times with Cenedred.

After Aelle was composed, he went to see his son. He shed a tear as he held the baby and asked forgiveness for not coming sooner. He decided the child's name would be Aethelred. He was assured that a wet nurse would be found quickly.

Magnus was the closest so he was the first to arrive with Ava who was not coping well. Eadgard and Hilde arrived next. Hilde took Ava into her arms both literally and figuratively and the women comforted each other. Osmund and Ethelind travelled the farthest and were the last to arrive. Everyone was praying together for strength and acceptance. They did not allow the death to destroy their faith but were strengthened by each other and by turning to

God.

It was a state funeral with Bishop Aert officiating. Hundreds came and left wildflowers at and around the town church. The church looked as though were besieged by flowers climbing several feet up on all the exterior walls. During the funeral the fields around were filled with people who had come to pay their respects.

The funeral procession to the burial plot was almost a mile long. At the site Aelle saw the marker for the first time. It read, "Queen Cenedred, Beloved Wife of King Aelle, Loved by All, Blessed by God." Tears flowed down Aelle's face. He looked at his son who was beside him in the wet nurse's arms.

In the evening, the family and lords met for dinner. It was as pleasant end to a trying day as could be expected in the circumstances. All those present traded their good memories of Cenedred. There was laughing and a few tears. It was all part of the mourning process. Though they knew Cenedred was in a much better place, they would all still miss her and it was the missing her that caused them to mourn.

A meeting was set for the lords for the next morning. As the dinner guests were leaving Feliks approached Aelle and asked for a private audience. He said it was an important matter they should discuss before the next morning. Aelle granted his request and they went to the library.

When they were seated Aelle asked, "What is it that I can do for you, my dear Feliks."

Feliks sighed and took a deep breath, "Sire, you have been most kind and generous to me and I do not wish to seem ungrateful."

As Feliks paused, Aelle could tell he was almost in tears. Whatever was on his mind was troubling him greatly and he bore a great burden.

Aelle used as comforting a voice as he could, "Feliks we have known each other long enough that you should know that you may request of me anything without fear of giving offense, for I trust your goodwill."

Feliks hung his head, "I have always been but a country lord. When my lands were small I was capable of ruling them and did so well. Since my king so generously increased my holdings, I have become painfully aware of my limitations. I cannot govern well all the lands you have given me. I can see there is so much more prosperity that can be obtained for the people in the annexed lands. Lord, I mean no offense, nor am I ungratefully, but I ask that you let me just rule the lands I originally held."

Aelle sat back in his chair for this is not what he expected. He asked, "Will this make you content my friend?"

"Yes, if it pleases my king."

Aelle thought for a moment, "You have prayed about this and you request this of your own free will?"

"Yes, Sire," was the reply.

"Then I will make it so."

Feliks looked up and fell to his knees in front of Aelle, "Thank you my King and my friend." Felix said it with tears running down his face.

Aelle lifted him up. "Let us pray together and then you get a good night's sleep." Aelle did not though, and spent the night praying about what to do.

The next day the great council met to discuss business. All of the lands were prospering, but Lucan needed to become more involved in the river trade. The lords all agreed to contribute a portion of an interest free loan to allow him to do the necessary work. Lucan expressed his appreciation.

Magnus and Eadgard had started a lumbering enterprise. Logs were cut, dragged to the streams, and floated whole downstream to the rivers and cut into lumber at saw sites. The tree cutting was selective so the forests would regenerate. The finished planking was shipped on the river to places where the hardwoods were not as abundant and prices were higher. It was proving to be very profitable.

The men discussed trade and agricultural matters. Herewood had imported some grain seeds which seemed have a higher yield and he offered to share the seed with the other lords. The meeting was very productive. This group of men was related by the blood of the battlefield, family lines, or marriage and it was a mutual loyalty that they all hoped was last for at least a few generations.

The last item discussed was the request of Feliks, which surprised all the other Lords. Aelle announced that Feliks' request should be granted and he would rule his original lands. The others asked Feliks questions and it was obvious to everyone that Feliks was pleased and relieved. Feliks stated he could leave with the other lords, content in the knowledge that he would rule only that which he could manage well. The issue of who would rule where was discussed and the council's advice was in accord with the king's thinking.

That evening at dinner, Aelle announced that Herewood and Aewel would be made earls of their shires and Ragnvald would become earl of the shire that Feliks was giving up. Siegfried would be known as Lord Commander of the Army and would be given a large estate as a thane of the King. Everyone was pleased with the announcements, especially the men involved and their wives. The official ceremony would be held before the lords returned to their homes.

After all the others had dispersed, Wolf, Cuthbert and Aert retired to the library. There they shared a cup of ale.

Aelle was introspective, "I never wanted all this. I just wanted a little piece of land to call my own, a place to raise a family. They call me King Aelle because I have gathered so many earls. Cenedred was indeed a queen, of my heart and of the people. I did not have ambition to be king."

Aert sighed, "Sometimes what we want is not what God wants. He has given you a genius for governing and leading, and you bring His church and His people prosperity."

"Aye, but it is all by His grace and not of my doing."

Aert considered, "That is true, but He gave you the gifts and talents and you have used them for His glory and for others, and in that He has blessed you. Accept your place."

Cuthbert added, "I saw this specialness in you my grandson. It is why I stepped aside. God laid it upon my heart to do so. As a result, I have been blessed."

Aelle shrugged, "Our lands have become known as a place of fierce warriors, strong Christians, and a hard working prosperous people who give glory to God. Sometimes men live by their reputations and sometimes reputations draw conflict. I fear my reputation will be a mixed blessing, but until I die I will defend the faith and my people."

Chapter 20 - New Beginnings

Aelle felt as though he was starting over again. The castle seemed empty without Cenedred and though he had many who were loyal to him, all his friends were now far away from him. He turned to God first for comfort and strength, then his grandfather for companionship, and his son for joy.

He threw himself into his work and made government work for the good of the people. He travelled his realm keeping in touch with his earls and going among his people, talking to them, and worshipping with them in community churches. He was blessed and successful in all his undertakings.

In the two years after Cenedred's death, the lands still prospered and Aelle's heart healed. The farms were productive and the rents and taxes kept increasing, and the river trade was growing as were the taxes and fees from it. The profits from his business enterprises with Beorn continued to generate wealth. Of all this though, the thing that gave him the most pleasure was the growth of the church, much of its missionary work funded by the money from Wolf's wealth.

Wolf had completed his latest visits to the castles on the southern and western loops, stopping to see Feliks, Ragnvald, Osmund and his mother Ethelind, Aldred, Aewel, Lucan, and Yingvar. One of the captured raider boats became Wolf's main means of transport and it was crewed by his warriors. It was the most efficient means of travel and allowed Wolf to purchase cargo as he saw opportunity.

Heading north he stopped at Cathedral Town to visit Bishop Aert, Magnus and Ava. They were all at the dock when he arrived. They were all so happy to see each other and after embraces and niceties they exchanged news. Magnus and Ava announced that Ava was with child. Magnus was eager to tell Wolf about all the things that had been accomplished and the status of the lands under his rule. It seemed things were going well in all the areas he visited.

Wolf reported that his son Aethelred was growing like a weed and healthy.

Aert welcomed Wolf warmly and they spent a lot of time discussing the missionary work under way. Aert told Wolf about the welfare of the various parishes. There were now an adequate number of churches in all the shires under Aelle's rule. The vast majority of the population was now Christian.

Wolf stayed in a visitor's room in Bishop Aert's residence and the guards with him took turns on sentry duty. After visiting the town for several days, the troop returned to the valley as the trip to the northern castles would require a journey by horse.

Wolf was happy for the chance to visit with his grandfather and son. Aethelred was a toddler of immense curiosity who spent much time in the presence of men, either his father or grandfather. Cuthbert had given the child a small wooden sword and miniature shield and sometimes the grandfather and father would take turns on their knees fending off the attacks of the small warrior. It was play, bonding, and training. This was the play Aethelred liked best. He also loved to listen as father or grandfather read him stories. His favorite story was that of David and Goliath.

After a week at home, Wolf left accompanied by Captain Leof and thirty men-at-arms to visit Eadgard and Hilde. They travelled the inland road that was a more direct path to Eadgard's castle. Wolf was always dressed in the same uniform as his troops with the exception of his helmet which was fit for a king. As was the habit Leof commanded the troop and Wolf allowed himself to be accompanied.

The officers appreciated the fact that Wolf not only respected but trusted their command of the guard. Wolf was riding in the midst of the column talking to one of the soldiers as they approached a small town on the border of Magnus's and Eadgard's lands. It was a clean and industrious town, the center for trade by farmers in both Eadgard's and Magnus's lands. This would be the place where they spent the evening.

Wolf took off his helmet and placed it on his saddle pommel as he dismounted as the other troops did. The soldier he had been talking with took the reins of his horse and Wolf went to find a place to sit and wait. He spied a nice size rock just by the road and went and sat on it.

He watched as a young woman came along with a pail of water and a gourd vessel for dipping. She offered the soldiers fresh water and they accepted, each drinking a gourd full. The young woman saw him and came and offered Wolf a drink.

"Would you like some fresh spring water?" she inquired.

Wolf nodded, "Yes, thank you," he said and drank it all. It was fresh and good.

The young woman smiled, "You seem weary compared to your friends?" It seemed more of a question the way she said it than a statement.

"Yes, that is true. It is perhaps that I have more on my mind than they."

The woman laughed, "And what weighty matter would a young soldier like you have that would weigh you down so mightily and take away your joy?"

Wolf had to laugh.

She tilted her head so slightly, "What is so funny in that?"

"Nothing and everything."

She looked a little stern, "I may be a simple country maid, but I am not one to be made fun of if you know what is good for you." She was shaking the gourd at him.

He laughed harder. She hit him gently on the top of his head with the gourd. He could have prevented it but was enjoying the game. Two soldiers came running, but he motioned them away. The young woman was quick and noticed the soldier's reaction.

"It is true what they say that the Wolf Pack looks out for one another, but I hardly think you needed two reinforcements to deal with me. Another one would have been enough."

She smiled at her own jest as did Wolf.

"He patted the rock beside his, "Sit and visit with me, please. Have pity on a weary soldier who is need of jovial company. What is your name?"

"My name is Aethel, and yours?"

"My name is Aelle."

She smiled, "A noble name and the same as the King's."

Wolf smiled, "Yes. Does not your name mean noble?"

She laughed, "You are not as dimwitted as it would first appear. My mother was married to a cousin of Lord Eadgard the father of our saintly queen, may God bless her departed soul. But alas, my father and brothers are simple farmers. How did you get your regal name?"

"My mother."

This response drew a light blow on his shoulder with the gourd. The company was making ready to disperse so Wolf knew he had to act, "May I come to visit you?"

"If your captain will allow, why don't you come for supper? The fare is good in our house. Our home is on the top of the hill," and she pointed to the west about a quarter mile. "Come at seven."

"I will look forward to it," Wolf replied.

Later, when Wolf left for dinner at the farm, outriders and scouts were riding unseen behind and to either side of Wolf. It was a very prosperous farm and the house was well above average in construction. It was not quite a small manner house but close. He tied his mount to the post in front of the house and went and knocked on the door. Aethel answered the door.

"You are early. Are you sure you have permission?"

Wolf gave a mock bow, "I apologize, my lady. In my impatience to see you again, I am indeed a little early. If I have given offense please accept my humble," and his speech ended when the young woman smacked him gently with her open hand on the top of the head.

"Just like a man, always having to have the last word. Well, you are here now so come in and meet my mother. My father and brothers will be back directly."

Aethel introduced Aelle to her mother Indonea. They made pleasant conversation for about a half hour and Indonea made Wolf feel very welcome. Aethel had obviously gotten some of her mother's traits for Indonea was a straight forward, jovial, and friendly woman, apt to say what was on her mind.

"You are the first young man Aethel has brought home. I am surprised for she has had many suitors and none have made it to the front door, let alone past it. You do seem nice enough, but I never expected her to bring home a soldier."

Aethel protested, "Mother, please!"

Her mother continued anyway, "She must see something special in you. She has had well to do farmers and merchants coming to seek her out and she chased them all away. I must admit that somehow you are different, not that to be so is necessarily bad, just different. I actually find you quite likeable."

Wolf nodded, "Thank you. From such a direct and noble woman, I truly appreciate that you like me."

Indonea laughed, "Has she told you about her noble name. She had never done that before."

Aethel interrupted, "Mother, he already knew the meaning of my name."

Indonea nodded, "Good, I'd hate to think you are getting uppity as an old maid."

Aethel gasped, "Mother, I am not an old maid."

Indonea tilted her head toward her daughter, "Already twenty and not married, I don't know what else you would call it."

Aethel stomped her foot, "Enough, mother!"

They both started laughing. It was contagious and Wolf could not help himself. This was a joyous happening. It was while they were laughing that Aethel's father and brothers came into the room.

Her father spoke first, "I see we have a guest," and offered his arm in a warriors greeting which Wolf took.

"I am Paul, and these are my sons Mark and Luke. I know they are not common Saxon names but they ..."

Wolf interjected, "The apostles."

Paul nodded, "Well that is one point in your favor. Are you a follower of Jesus the Christ?"

Wolf nodded, "Yes."

Paul smiled, "Good, otherwise we would have fed you and sent you packing."

Aethel interjected, "Father!"

Paul just shrugged his shoulders, "Still, it is true; we will have no unequally yoked in our family."

Mark and Luke were big lads, and it was Mark the older that started it, "He looks rather small for a soldier."

Wolf laughed without thinking.

"You find that funny?" Mark asked.

Wolf tried to contain himself but was still stifling a laugh, "I meant no offense, brother."

Mark's reply was curt, "I have no sword, but if we were on equal footing, I would box your ears."

Wolf's reply surprised Mark, "Oh some good sport before dinner. Let us go outside"

Wolf turned to Paul, "With your permission of course."

Paul smiled, "This I have to see."

Aethel exclaimed, "NO, NO, NO!"

Wolf took off his mail, uniforms and weapons, but not his under tunic. He stepped away from the house and Mark smiled.

"Now I will teach you a thing or two," and he charged Wolf who suddenly was gone and Mark felt a boot push his rump vigorously and he lost his balance and went face first into the ground.

Mark rose to his feet but did not make the same mistake a second time. He started to circle his opponent who just stood there. When Mark was behind Wolf, he swung. Wolf had positioned himself so that he saw the shadow of Mark's blow coming. He ducked and the force of Mark's swing went high and Mark lost his balance momentarily and then darkness and stars were all he saw as he felt himself falling. He lay there trying to catch his breath. His brother Luke helped him up. Wolf was already putting his uniform back on.

Mark looked at his brother through glazed eyes, "What happened?"

Luke chuckled and said, "The little fella beat you," as he helped Mark into the house.

Mark was a good sport and congratulated Wolf, "You fight well. Who taught you?"

Wolf told him, "A seasoned warrior of great ability whom I was honored to have teach me. What would have happened if you won?"

Mark replied, "If you were a good sport about it, I would have respected you none the less. If you had been a poor loser then I would have known your true character."

Paul just nodded and the sons remained silent.

Wolf smiled, "Very wise Mark, very wise. You ever think about joining the army?"

"Father needs us here. The farm is large and we have only two hired men to help."

Wolf knew the other part of the answer was implied. The sons had considered it, but their family loyalty came first and he respected that.

The meal was good and the conversation was friendly and Wolf enjoyed the company of these good people.

Paul came right out with it, "What are your intentions toward my daughter?"

Wolf answered directly, "I am a Christian man and my intentions would be honorable."

"Have you been with a woman?"

Wolf answered honestly, "Yes."

Paul asked, "How then can you say your intentions are honorable?"

Wolf sighed, "I have been with one woman, my wife who died."

"I am sorry for your loss, but as a father I trust you understand my wanting to protect my daughter's innocence."

Wolf replied, "I understand and respect it. May I call on your daughter again? I will bring the parish priest to chaperone if that is acceptable."

Paul was hesitant, "I think our good father will be too busy for such a task."

His response was interrupted by a knock on the door. Indonea got up and answered it. The guard captain was at the door. Aethel felt sure then that Aelle had come without permission and she would not see him again. Indonea invited him in.

Leof went to Aelle and bowed, "Majesty, riders came with urgent news, your orders are needed."

Wolf stood, "Thank you, Paul, for your hospitality. I have not enjoyed myself so much in years. Please excuse me."

Wolf left and the family was sitting at the table speechless looking at each other.

Aethel was the first to speak, "Well, he did tell us his name was Aelle."

They all started laughing.

Paul was the next to speak, "Girl, if you send this one away, I will send you to a convent."

They all laughed the more.

When Wolf got back to the town, he was surprised that the whole troop was assembled and ready to ride.

Leof's report was succinct, "Raiders came ashore between here and Eadgard's castle. Their boat landed them upriver and is now beached near the Abbey. The raiders seem to be headed in an arc and the Abbey will be the last place in their attack. It appears they are headed directly here."

'How many?"

Leof shrugged, "One report says three dozen the other about thirty."

Wolf nodded, "We will be evenly matched."

Leof smiled, "The reserve will be here within the hour and we will have thirty more men."

"How long before the raiders arrive?" Wolf asked.

"They are camped about four hours away. If they leave at sunrise they will be here at mid-morning, but if they start in the dark they would be here at sunrise."

"I would be here at sunrise if it were me. We need to send a rider to have Magnus send men to the Abbey to seize the boat and block any who escape. What is your plan?"

Leof paused, "I have patrolled this road before when I was a sergeant. The road goes through open fields with little cover. There is one place very close to here where there is a deep but gently sloped gulley in which mounted men would not be seen from the road. It runs parallel to the road for about a hundred yards and arcs away on the ends. It would be dry at this time of year. The raiders will have to pass a steep hill on which there are some woods on the east side before they come to the area. It would seem to someone who does not know the area that the woods are the place from which an ambush would come. They will no doubt scout the woods. At this time of year, men could hide in the fields on this side of the woods for the crops will be high. They could come in from this end and thus not give any telltale signs. Men can be hidden on both sides of the road. "

Wolf nodded, "Disposition of men?"

"Half ours on both sides to bolster half the reserves."

Wolf nodded agreement, "Which side do you want?"

Leof thought for a moment, "I know the area better so it would make sense for me to lead the men into the crop field."

Wolf nodded, "Let's do it. You assign the men."

Leof said, "Yes, Sire," and hurried to organize things.

Leof split the men and gave Wolf a local who took Wolf's group to the gulley. One of Wolf's men had a hunting horn he would blow to signal the attack. The need for quiet until the moment of attack was stressed. They were all in place within two hours. The raiders came an hour before dawn. The road was visible, but it was still dark in the areas where the quarter moon was not lighting the ground. As Leof had thought, the raiders let down their attention a little after passing the wooded area.

There was momentary surprise when the attack came. The horn sounded and Wolf and his men hit their flank first and the raiders turned to defend against them. A moment later, Leof's men burst from the field and caught the raiders with their backs turned. A few fell immediately to Leof's men. These raiders were however experienced warriors and did not panic. They formed two outward facing walls quickly and started moving sideways down the road. The fight moved several hundred yards laterally. There were men falling and the raiders were losing the most men. When the raiders were closest to the trees they changed their tactics and fought into the woods and then many of them were gone in the thick brush in the dark.

Wolf had the recall signal blown and the men returned to the road. The Wolf Pack and the reserves returned to the Town. The reserves were left under the command of one of Leof's men and ordered to form a defensive perimeter to protect the town just in case the raiders circled back. The regulars gathered their mounts. Only two of the Wolf Pack members were unable to ride off with the others due to injury in the battle.

Two wounded raiders were bound and held. Eleven raiders were dead back on the road along with four of the reserves. Five reserve soldiers were wounded. Wolf and Leof knew where the raiders were going and could get there faster and they did. When they got there, Magnus was waiting. Three of his men were already standing in as the boat guards and all the rest of the men were hidden. The raiders did not come until almost twenty six hours from the first encounter.

The raiders arrived jogging down the hill leading five horses loaded down with loot. They were exhausted and surprised when Magnus's forces attacked from the sides. The second battle was one sided. Some tried to make a run back to the woods. They ran right into Wolf's men attacking downhill. Wolf killed the first man he encountered within seconds, but the second man was the leader and an experienced warrior in good mail. He fended Wolf off for almost a minute before Wolf killed him. There were no survivors.

The raiders were being stripped of everything valuable and the loot was being put in the boat. Soon sentries were posted and the men rested. The after battle report was brought. There were twenty one dead raiders and three of Magnus's men and one of Wolf's had been killed. There were five wounded; none of the men were suffering life threatening injuries.

Wolf and Magnus came together and embraced.

Wolf smiled, "We have to stop meeting like this."

The men went and sat leaning against a large tree drinking water. One of the men brought them some cheese and bread. They took the food, gave thanks to God, and began eating.

Magnus shook his head, "Why do they keep coming? We have successfully met every raid or attack? When will it stop?"

"My friend, I do not think it will. Men are driven by their sinful nature and will seek to destroy what is good and fulfill their own lusts. It will never end, so we must always be on guard."

Magnus shrugged, "I know you are right, but I wish we could stop all this."

Wolf stated, "It won't end until the second coming."

The men sat quietly and ate.

Wolf's men sailed the raider's boat back to Cathedral Town with the wounded and Magnus accompanied him. Leof led Magnus's men back leading the mounts of Wolf's patrol and detouring through the border town to recover the wounded.

There was much relief when the king and the lord returned unharmed. They were greeted and ate together at Magnus's home. After the meal the men excused themselves to conduct an investigation.

The men were concerned as to how the boat containing the raiders had gotten past the town without being reported. Within an hour they had the answer. The boat had been inspected going north with a small crew and a cargo. The boat had regularly made the trip as a trader. The question then was how the boat came to be in the possession of the raiding party.

The two wounded raiders from the first encounter arrived at the Town and were questioned. They told that the boat had picked them up on the west shore well past the town. The boat was beached further up river by the captain and the raiders went ashore on the west bank. The captain had been paid a large sum and left after beaching the boat near the abbey and the three raiders who accompanied the boat murdered the unarmed crew. The raiders had marched from the east and planned to move in an arc and return to the boat's new position. The men had been paid in advance and were ordered to take what loot they could and create as much disturbance as they could quickly and leave. They had planned to leave for several days and then do another raid.

Wolf said nothing, but there was something strange about this. If the raid had been successful, which it would have been if Leof's men had not been in the area, it would have created disruption. Wolf immediately sent new scouts and spies to look for small groups of armed men on the east side of the river who might be preparing to raid on the west side. He sent messages to Yingvar and Eadgard warning them and asking them to advise him of any suspicious activity and to watch for raiders.

The company rested up and the wounded were tended. Bishop Aert had a memorial service for the dead soldiers in the cathedral. Magnus met with the families of his men who had died in his service and Wolf was present for those. Leof travelled to the valley to meet with the family of his dead comrades. Depending on the family circumstances a financial provision was made.

Wolf stayed in the Cathedral Town until Leof returned with fresh troops. Those presently with their King were released to go back to the valley to rest. Leof wanted to go with Wolf but was ordered to go home and get some rest. Eadgard had sent his captain, Aldin to accompany Wolf.

Wolf planned to make a stop on the way to Eadgard's castle. He wanted to visit the families of the reserve soldiers who had died and those who were wounded. He would also go to see Aethel and of course being king he could do so.

When he arrived, his first act was to see the families of those who died and those who were wounded. The families of the dead were still grieving but seemed to be faring well. They were getting a lot of support from their community and the wounded were doing well. The financial help they received from the king would help them bridge the difficulties. One of the wounded was using a crutch and struggled to get around. A man had been hired to help him with his farm for the season.

Wolf heard more than one person say they thanked God the patrol was here when the raiders came or the death toll and misery would have been wide spread. People came to express their gratitude to the troops with Wolf even though those were not the ones who fought in that battle. The reserve men were heroes in their own community. Many in the community remembered a time when raiders ravaged the land at will and life was much more dangerous.

After attending to business, Wolf went to Paul's farm early in the evening. He found Paul working in a field. Paul saw him coming, said something to his sons, and came out of the field to meet him.

Paul knelt saying, "Majesty."

Wolf smiled, "Paul, rise. Please walk with me."

Paul rose and went with Wolf.

"Paul, I must tell you I have made inquiries about you and your family as my duty requires. Does that offend you?"

Paul shook his head, "No, I would expect nothing less. We are who we are and have nothing to hide. Our imperfections are apparent. I have friends in the valley and also inquired about you. Sometimes a public reputation is not the same as a private reputation."

Wolf laughed, "Well done Paul, well done. I would like to visit with your daughter and ask your permission."

Paul replied, "Does the king require my permission?"

'No, I suppose not, but the Christian man does."

Paul simply said, "I give it. I have no doubt that you would be the sort of man who could tame my daughter if he so chose." Paul chuckled, "You should be aware though, that the dowry will be a farmers and not one fit for a king."

They walked to the house and around to the back door. Paul washed his hands in a bucket that was there for that purpose. They entered and saw Indonea who was busy baking bread.

Indonea was at a loss as how to act, so asked, "What is the proper way to greet my King?"

Wolf smiled, "I would rather you greeted a guest in your house with a hug."

Indonea smiled, wiped her hands on her apron and gave him a motherly hug.

Wolf sighed, "I would like to do away with formality and be as we were the last time we were together."

Paul shook his head, "Easy for you to say. Last time we did not know you were the king."

"How about this, in here I am just Wolf, in Town you may treat me like the king. Paul that would mean a head bow as we have spent time together, and Indonea a half curtsey."

Indonea mocked him with an exaggerated curtsey and broke into laughter. The ice had been broken. Paul sat with Wolf in the kitchen and as they shared a cool drink of well water. Paul asked about the encounter with the raiders. He had heard so many rumors he did not know which was fact and which was fiction. Wolf told him the essential facts of the encounters including the casualties on both sides.

Mark and Luke came to the house. They were at a loss as how to act until their father told them to sit and have a cup of water.

Luke looked at Wolf, "My brother has been bragging about how he was bested by the king. It is the only time I've heard him brag about losing."

Mark cuffed Luke playfully on the back of the head, "It was the only time I lost. There is no dishonor in losing to a better fighter."

When asked by the brothers about the encounters with the raiders, Wolf patiently told the story again.

Aethel came into the house, "Oh dear, I did not expect company" she said brushing back her hair with her hand.

Wolf could not help himself, "And who said I came to visit you."

Aethel walked over and started shaking her finger at Wolf, "Just because you are king don't think you have the right to mock me. To me you are just another soldier boy." She threw back her head in mock indignation.

The family all froze.

Wolf laughed and then said, "Well played Aethel, well played."

She went and drew herself a cup of water and came and sat at the table, "Well after the last go round, I did not think you came to practice fighting with my daft brothers. You took your time in coming round."

Wolf smiled, "Well you know us soldier boys, we have our duty and our lives are not always our own."

Aethel rolled her eyes, "Alright, I surrender."

Wolf simply said, "Good."

Indonea spoke, "Seeing as how my husband has forgotten his manners, will you stay for dinner?"

"I'd love to."

Indonea was an excellent cook and the meal was delicious. The family was curious about news from around the land and Wolf shared the general news. Wolf enjoyed the conversation and the family interaction. After dinner, he and Paul went outside and sat on a bench.

Paul spoke first, "You seem comfortable in these surroundings. It is not what I had expected."

"I feel very comfortable. This would be what I would choose for myself, but it seems God has chosen me for another role for which He has given me unique talents and gifts. I cannot desert my people."

Paul nodded, "I guess it is like farming. Once the crop is in the field, it cannot be left alone; it needs tending. And once the field has given you life, you are loath to leave it."

"Yes, exactly. We just each have different fields God has given us stewardship over."

The men sat quietly for a few minutes just looking at the stars on this clear night. Wolf heard a noise behind him. He glanced back and Aethel was there.

"Father, may I have some time with Wolf?"

Paul got up and left and Aethel sat down, "I am glad you returned.

I worried when I heard about the raiders and that you had gone off to fight them. I knew you had a reputation as a great warrior, but until then it really did not strike me what that really meant. I did not think you would return."

"Sometimes the protection of the people requires those warriors who serve put their lives in jeopardy."

Aethel put her head on Wolf's shoulder, "What was the queen like?"

"She was intelligent, witty, and pretty. She had been brought up in a lord's castle so she was fragile and well-mannered, but with a sense of humor that made her seem somehow down to earth."

Aethel sighed, "You loved her?"

Wolf nodded, "Yes. Next to God, I loved her most and well. I grieved her loss."

"Am I anything like her?"

Wolf thought, "Not really. She was a fragile pretty woman, but you are a strong handsome woman. She seemed down to earth and you are down to earth. She liked the life of a lord and you could be content anywhere. She never did hard physical labor, but you labor daily. She was delightful, but you are playful. She was intellectually independent, but you are fully independent. Not really alike but both attractive and loveable in your own right."

Aethel thought about what he had said, "I am glad of the differences. I never have to worry about being measured against her."

"No, that you do not. Would you like to come visit my home, with your parents of course?"

Aethel's reply was practical, "I would like that, but it will have to wait until the crops are in, perhaps in the fall."

Wolf rose, "Let's go inside."

The family was sitting at the table when the couple came in and joined them. They had been talking but stopped when the door opened.

Wolf spoke first, "Paul I would like for you, your wife and Aethel to come visit my home and meet some of my friends and family. Before you object, I can have two good soldiers who were brought up on farms help Mark and Luke while you are gone. I can also provide a good cook and housekeeper. When you come back, I will leave the soldiers so Mark and Luke may come and visit as I think they would enjoy that. If you would like, I could probably have the farm tended while you all visit at the same time. You do not have to answer now, think it over."

Paul shrugged, "I must confess I have never stayed in a castle and it has its appeal. I am not sure we would know how to act."

"Just be yourselves. In my home my guests do not observe niceties unless there is a formal occasion and I try to limit those as much as possible."

Paul and his family thanked Wolf for the invitation. They would talk it over and let him know in the morning, which meant Paul would have to decide how to best manage the trip. Wolf returned to where the company was camped on the edge of town. The sentries and scouts had seen nothing out of the ordinary.

Early in the morning a messenger came who had ridden all night. He brought a report that four of those scouts and spies that had been sent had found parties of armed men gathered at four towns on or close to the east bank. They were being ignored by the local authorities who seemed to have a hands-off policy in place. Rowdy drunkenness that normally would not have been tolerated was. This seemed to indicate that the lord of those lands was conspiring against Wolf's people.

Three of the groups were making inquiries about obtaining boats and the fourth seemed to be concentrating on gathering maps of the southern roads. Wolf sent riders with orders to Ragnvald, Eadgard, Magnus, and Yingvar. These bands could not be allowed to raid successfully.

Wolf went to Paul's home to discuss the visit. Paul liked Wolf's suggestion and the family would visit as had been suggested. Paul asserted that he did not want to be gone for more than two weeks, although others of the family might visit longer, meaning Indonea and Aethel. Wolf told Paul he was being called away on urgent business and the visit would be arranged for when he returned.

Paul asked outright, "Is the urgent business the raider kind?"

Wolf nodded, "Do not tell anyone."

"I will not, but what about Aethel?"

Wolf thought, "She will need to be told, but tell her it is secret and many lives hang on it remaining a secret."

Wolf and his troops left that afternoon and headed north. They met Eadgard's troops led by Captain Aldin. They did not make camp but slept dismounted for just a few hours and rode most of the night. A new rider came in the morning with updated reports and was surprised to find the group on the road and so close to the river. The report indicated that one of the armed groups had rented a boat to take them across the river. It was a small group of about twenty five and Wolf knew that the crew of the boat would not be sailing the boat away based on past experience. They would be murdered for the boat which would be beached at the escape point.

Wolf now had a confirmed crossing point and the troops rode there. The scouts reported that the group was in the process of loading the first group into the boat on the far river bank. The boat was small and it would take two crossings to bring all the men across. Wolf wanted them all on this side of the river.

Wolf's command was nearly twice the size of the raider company. He liked the idea of a quick surprise attack with overwhelming force whenever possible. The scouts reported no other enemy in the area and the soldiers dismounted quietly and slipped into the woods. Deep in the shadows they waited for the enemy to all be on this side.

The first group across formed a defensive perimeter that was mostly show for the men were so widely spaced that they could not hold against a determined foe of equal numbers let alone a larger force. When the others got to shore, they quickly murdered the three man crew of the boat and disembarked. They pulled the boat onto the shore and formed into a column of twos and started marching up hill. One man was left to guard the boat.

The raiders were three quarters of the way up the hill when the attack started. Wolf led the charge and running full speed put up his shield and knocked the first man he came to over and as the man went down slashed his throat. The second man tried to take Wolf while he was killing his friend, but did not realize the quickness of the warrior he faced. His swing of the broad axe was deflected by Wolf's shield and Wolf swept his sword low almost severing the man's unarmored leg. As the man toppled Wolf killed him. Wolf was now in the killing zone and it seemed as though suddenly he was alone. He had cut his way through five of the attackers before some of the troops had run to the battle line.

Wolf's men were all staring at him. He wiped his sword on the nearest victim.

"Casualty report," Wolf ordered.

The two sergeants quickly took the roll and one reported, "No dead, two wounded, minor, and twenty three enemy dead with one captured, the boat guard."

Wolf nodded, "Thank you, Sergeant. Carry on."

The sergeant snapped to attention and bowed, "Yes, Lord."

The enemy had been taken completely by surprise and been slaughtered. Several of the raiders had tried to run back to the boat, but several of Aldin's men on horseback had galloped to the boat and had intercepted them.

Wolf covered in blood, looking like the angel of death again, went to the boat guard, "Who sent you?"

The man stammered an answer, "My cap, captain," and pointed to one of the dead men.

Wolf's voice became threatening, "Do not try my patience if you want to live. Who sent your company?"

The man was so afraid he was having difficulty speaking, so he pointed across the river and said, "That lord."

"Bind him, he is coming with us."

The man started crying, realizing he was going to live.

Wolf called, "Aldin!"

Aldin was now mounted and came down the hill.

Wolf looked at him, "Take all the bodies into the woods and bury them. Clean up as much as possible, I do not want evidence that this group was intercepted. Tell your men they did well."

Wolf then called, "Wolf Pack to me," and his men came running.

"You all did well, I am proud of you. Any of ours wounded?"

The men looked around and all shook their heads no.

'Good, help Aldin's men get these bodies into the woods. We do not want to give warning to the others that we know they are coming."

His men all looked at each other with knowing smiles.

*****

The southern raiding party of thirty three men was just fifteen minutes across the border into Yingvar's lands. They were marching down the rough seldom travelled road through the woods. They were really mercenaries but poorly equipped for battle against a trained enemy. They did not yet have scouts out. They should have.

The attack came from the woods on both sides. As the battle engaged, some raiders tried to run back only to find the way blocked. Some tried to go forward but found the same. Yingvar's men outnumbered the raiders almost three to one and most of the raiders died in the first fifteen minutes and the last three alive surrendered.

Yingvar questioned them. One of the three knew who had sent the party. Yingvar knew his answer would mean war. He sent a rider to Wolf and moved his men to make camp near the border.

*****

There were two groups crossing the river almost simultaneously. Wolf and Aldin waited at the most northern crossing while Magnus and Ragnvald waited at the one to the south. The crossing points were less than six miles apart. It was assumed one group would swing north and the other south to raid. Neither group was expecting what waited for them.

The group opposite to Wolf's command was again going to have to cross in two trips. The boat used would only hold about fifteen men at a time and then it was overloaded. The first wave came ashore. These men were better trained though and sent two men to scout the woods. The second wave was only half way across. Both scouts had to be taken out and were killed quietly in the woods. The man in charge on the shore was obviously concerned that his scouts had not returned.

Wolf could hear him shouting at the boat crossing the river. "Turn back and come back for us. The scouts have not come back."

Wolf gave Aldin a quiet order and he took twenty men back to where the horses were tethered.

The boat kept coming, "They probably have gone too far and not yet returned."

"I don't like it. Let's withdraw."

The man in the boat was having none of it and was obviously the one in charge, "We don't get paid to stay on the wrong side of the river."

His boat beached and the men came ashore. The two men had a quiet conversation. A patrol of six men was sent up the hill. The rest of the men stayed near the boat. The patrol was almost on top of Wolf's men so he had no choice but to charge. The patrol was overwhelmed as the wave of men swept down the hill.

The mounted men came across the hill with their horses running full out to stop the boat from leaving with many of the raiders. The raiders were fighting for their lives and some were being killed because they were so focused on getting on the boat. The boat did leave but only with five men on it rowing as hard as they could for the opposite shore and safety. The rest were left to fight and die. Half the men on shore were slain when the rest, all wounded or badly injured, knelt in surrender and were taken prisoner. Wolf had only killed two of the enemy before the surrender.

Wolf's first act was to get the after action report and to his amazement he had lost no men and the wounds and injuries were slight.

Wolf looked at Aldin, "Not bad for a day's work. Could have been better but not bad. Let's clear the dead and question this lot."

The prisoners were bound and questioned by Aldin. The result was repeated. Most of the men had no idea who hired them but in this group two did. The confessions were all leading to the same conclusion.

*****

Magnus and Ragnvald looked at the reported landing site. The line of sight from the shore was good. The raiders would have to be allowed to come quite a way inland. The troops were deployed so the enemy could be engaged in whichever direction they set out. The enemy would be on foot and Magnus and Ragnvald commanded mounted troops that could deploy and maneuver more quickly.

They awaited the crossing all day, but it never came. A scouting report came from across the river that the enemy had retreated to the east and apparently were not going to cross the river. A rider was sent to Wolf and returned shortly to tell that Wolf's troops were almost here.

The forces merged and made camp. There was now an army camping in the open fields. Wolf, Magnus, Ragnvald and Aldin met to discuss the situation. Spies and scouts reported that apparently it had become known that the other raiding parties had been destroyed. The last party had retreated when the received word that a large force had left Cathedral Town and another was north. The leaders discussed how they would conduct the campaign.

The reports had come that Aewel's troops had joined Yingvar's so there was an army on the northern border of Yingvar's lands ready to invade from the south. Herewood had men ready to invade from the north. The enemy would be outnumbered by at least four or five to one. The boats would be arriving tomorrow to ferry the army across the river.

In the early morning, a truce party was on the eastern shore asking permission to cross. An emissary came and Wolf sent Aldin to deal with him.

The emissary announced officially, "I have come to meet with Aelle."

Aldin replied arrogantly, "King Aelle does not meet with mere emissaries. Sometimes he will meet with lords, but never with minor officials."

The man sputtered, "I am no minor official!"

Aldin smiled, "You are a minor official of a minor lord. The armies of King Aelle, the Wolf Pack and the Wolf Horde and the men of his lords are marshalling on your western, northern and southern borders as you are no doubt aware. Your lord after invading our lands does not even come himself to beg for peace. It is insulting. My king deigned to send a senior officer to meet with you and, as distasteful as it is, because he ordered it I came. What do you want? "

"My message is for Aelle, er, His Majesty King Aelle."

Aldin dismissed the man with a wave and started walking away, "Leave the truce is over."

The emissary was left with his mouth open as Aldin walked up the hill.

A sergeant looked at the emissary, "If I were you I'd get back in that boat and go back across the river. And if you have family over there I'd gather all I could and make for another realm for I think there will be nothing left of your lord's lands when the Wolf is done with him. The army will soon be assembled."

Aldin and the sergeant reported to Wolf and his comrades who all had a good laugh. It was serious business, but Aldin and the sergeant made the emissary seem so comical.

The emissary returned to his Lord, Daegel, and told him of the encounter. His Lord threw a fit of temper. He would not humble himself. He asked the emissary about the force reports. There were about a hundred and fifty men-at-arms marshaled on the southern border, three to four hundred on the western bank of the river, and another hundred plus coming from the north. This did not include the numerous archers.

His Lord sat dismayed, "What about our allies."

The emissary shook his head, "We suddenly have no allies since the armies appeared in such strength on our border and so quickly. These are reportedly just the regulars. If they called up reserves? Those who encouraged this want no part of it now."

His lord hung his head, "So I have no choice?"

"Two. Either you run or surrender. These are the only practical alternatives. Perhaps if you negotiate you would be allowed to leave with some wealth. The lords on your borders will not allow you to cross there for fear Aelle would use it as an excuse to enter their lands. If you escape in that direction you will not be able to take much."

The next morning Wolf's boats arrived about the same time as the Lord Daegel came across the river under truce. He was met by the Commander of the Army and brought to the Wolf's open sided tent.

Wolf was seated talking to his officers and lords. It was of course all show.

Ragnvald asked Daegel for his sword and then said, "It will be returned when your audience is over."

Ragnvald led Daegel to the king's tent and announced, "Your Majesty, Lord Daegel has come under truce to talk with you."

Wolf rose and went to the raised dais and sat in the throne chair and became King Aelle. Lord Magnus came to stand beside the throne chair. The rest of those gathered took up standing positions on either side.

"He may come."

Lord Daegel entered and bowed slightly before Aelle, "Your Lord, I make no excuses. You have come to seize my lands which you have the force to do. To prevent unnecessary loss of life I am prepared to surrender my lands under some small conditions and will provide you with further important information and documents as part of our negotiations."

Aelle tilted his head, "What do you ask and what do you offer?"

"I ask that I be allowed to leave my lands and go downriver safely with my family and fifteen percent of the wealth I presently hold. I will provide documentary proof that my neighboring lords to the east and north took part in the conspiracy to destabilize your realm."

"Five percent, and it is agreed"

Daegel knew he was being treated generously and simply said, "Agreed."

Wolf turned to Ragnvald, "Lord Ragnvald take possession of the shire. Once the documentary proof is in your possession, have the documents of surrender signed, make sure this man gets his share and safe passage warrant to go downriver with his family."

Ragnvald bowed, "Yes, Sire.'

Ragnvald motioned Lord Daegel to leave the tent.

Wolf turned to the others, "I think while we have the army assembled we should put a little fear into our enemies. Notify Yingvar to go north to the castle and Herewood as well. We will all converge there."

The army arrived at the castle which was in the center of the shire. The wealth of Lord Daegel alone made bringing the army here worthwhile. The documents provided by Daegel were proof positive of the conspiracy. It was an interesting situation. It would require a delicate touch. One of Wolf's sergeants was ordered to do it and so was seemingly drunk in the wrong place at the wrong time.

He just happened to tell a drinking companion, who was buying him drink, how his captain was preparing for an invasion because the king was furious having found documents proving certain lord's conspired to destabilize his realm. He was calling up all the reserves and this was going to be the war to end all wars. He would soon be rich.

It took less than ten hours for word to get to the lords who were part of the conspiracy. They came in truce to meet with Aelle. When they came they became afraid. The army at the castle was massive. A little show was put on for their benefit.

A company in transit was slowed and given orders when to appear. Their scout was watching and as the rebellious lord's came into sight, the company rode over the hill and came to the fork at the same time as the lords. The Captain said within their hearing, "I thought more would have been here by now. I will take the men over there to camp sergeant. Go and report to the lord commander of the army that our company is here."

The sergeant turned his horse as he acknowledged the order and rode toward the castle. There were so many here that the lords could not count them all. They knew there were hundreds and just with the army that was already here their troops would be washed away like sand by a tidal wave. With more coming their position was pitiful.

They went into the great hall and knelt before King Aelle.

"Your Majesty we come to beg audience," the lords said in unison.

Aelle replied, "You who conspired to kill my subjects and destroy the peace? Why are you here? "

The lords looked at each other, "We beg you do not destroy us and our lands."

Wolf laughed, "And why should I not?"

Their answer was not at all what Wolf expected.

"We want the same sort of conditions for surrender as Lord Daegel, to leave with our families and ten percent of our wealth."

Wolf sat back and looked at his lords and commanders, "I did not come for conquest but for justice. I will take your offer into consideration. You will be our guest until I decide. In the meantime, as a show of good faith, I will halt my military build-up and take no action against your lands."

The lords were taken to their quarters and kept under guard.

Wolf and his advisors started their meeting with prayer and then spent several hours discussing the situation. On a strategic level they considered what accepting the offer would mean. They discussed what other lords would perceive about Aelle's ambition from the inclusion of the lands into the realm. On the other hand, they continued to be attacked even though they were not aggressors. They came to the conclusion it was better to be strong because it seemed no matter what they did, the attacks on them would continue.

Discussion moved to how to integrate the lands into the realm. Recent intelligence put the number of men-at-arms of the two lords at less than seventy to eighty in total. Even if they all accepted an offer of employment they could be absorbed into other units and an occupation force put into place. The lands were rich and would yield much wealth and even more if integrated into the realm. The life of the people would be improved.

Where missionaries had been martyred in the lands, they would now be able to go about their business without being persecuted. The gospel could be spread even wider.

The next morning the two lords were summoned back to an audience with King Aelle.

"We have considered your offer. Lord Daegel was given five percent of his wealth to take and we offer the same to you."

One lord answered immediately, "I accept, Lord."

The other had hesitated, "I accept also, Lord."

Wolf nodded, "Then let it be so. Lord Ragnvald, please make the arrangements for these men including signing the documents of surrender."

"Yes, Sire."

Aelle rose and everyone bowed for this was a formal occasion. Aelle left the room. So it was that Aelle's kingdom grew.

Afterwards, the leaders met to give thanks to God for their success. They went back to their respective companies and prayers of gratitude were again offered.

Almost all of the full time men-at-arms who were offered employment under the new king or one of his earls accepted knowing they would be sent elsewhere. Their prospects would be dismal if they did not have a wealthy family to go back to.

The men of the Wolf Pack knew there would be significant opportunities and land grants now that the king had such a large realm for there was much un-worked land. They also knew it would take some time for it all to be ironed out. All of the original Wolf Pack were told that there status would be as thanes and they would be granted land though their continued service was expected.

The lords and commanders in the field were left to secure the annexed lands until permanent arrangements could be made. The majority of the forces returned to their garrisons. All those who served were richer than when they came and of course none more so than King Aelle.

Chapter 21 – Betrayal

The troops returning to their various bases were treated again as conquering heroes. Each shire celebrated the triumphant return of their earl and his troops. Aelle sailed home stopping at Cathedral Town to send a message to Aethel and her family inviting them to come to the valley to visit. Magnus offered to send a half a dozen men to accompany them.

When Aelle arrived home, the first thing he did was spend time with his grandfather and son. It was good to be home. At home he fought battles with a little warrior and read stories. He spent time conversing with his grandfather and being brought up to date on what was happening in the valley; who had died and who had been married and such.

Aelle had a lot to consider and do. Aelle knew it would be a major undertaking to organize the three new shires so they would work as well as the existing ones. Only Daegel's shire had any semblance of a sound working administration and Siegfried, as earl there, would have his hands full.

The ten shires that were previously a part of Aelle's realm were already well organized having lords already in place. These earls, Magnus, Eadgard, Herewood, Aewel, Lucan, Yingvar, Feliks, Osmund, Ragnvald and Aldred, already had administrations in place and a stable system of sheriffs, elders and thanes. The new shires needed the same level of organization. Aelle put off appointing earls for the two other annexed shires. They were relatively small and the northern one could be integrated under Herewood and the eastern one could be easily combined with Siegfried's new shire, but Aelle was reluctant to do that. The garrisons needed at the castles for these shires would be small and manageable. The income would greatly outweigh the costs even with a reduction in taxes and rents. He was still considering new earls for them.

Modig for his continued service to his king was granted the status of thane and the valley manor house that had once been occupied by Staffan. He also received the incomes that were associated with it. The Wolf Pack now numbered over three hundred. Captains Grimbold and Leof were promoted to commander and each given command of approximately half the troops, about three companies each. They were given authority to appoint two captains and four sergeants each.

All of the original Wolf Pack members were now thanes with land grants and with their wives and families had their own homes in the valley. From all reports, Skjold had done a superb job as Lucan's advisor and his promotion to captain was made permanent and as one of the King's Thanes he was granted lands and the associated incomes in the newly annexed northeastern shire.

Aelle met with Beorn. Their business enterprises were doing very well. Aelle granted Beorn a land grant along the river in the northeastern shire and status as a thane. It had become common knowledge by observation that Beorn was Aelle's man so there was no longer any advantage in keeping the relationship secret. Beorn was also granted land near the town so he could build a larger estate home. He was also appointed commander of boats, so he would carry authority during time of war and draw a salary during peace time. He would also thus become a member of the great council.

Aethel's family arrived a week after Aelle at midafternoon on Friday. He, little Aethelred and Cuthbert met them in the courtyard and greeted them warmly. Aelle hugged the ladies and introductions were made as servants took the family's baggage to their quarters. Paul seemed a little uncomfortable with this for a moment but then decided to enjoy the pampering. Aethel easily made friends with Aethelred who took up with her immediately. The boy was also amused by the similarity in their names. He pointed at himself and said his name then pointed at Aethel and said hers and laughed, which caused everyone to laugh.

Aethelred's nanny tried to take him, but he was having none of it. He wanted to stay with the group. Indonea picked the boy up, though he was quite heavy and carried him as they went inside. Surprisingly, he just smiled and enjoyed it. The group went to the great room where they sat down. Aethelred went and sat in his father's lap. Aelle asked them if they would like to rest after the journey. They were all too excited by this adventure. After a little conversation, Aethel suggested a tour and off they went.

Aethelred kept going back and forth between Aethel and Indonea holding their hands as they walked. As they went, Aelle or Cuthbert would introduce them to the staff. From what Paul could see the staff was very comfortable in the presence of their lords and apparently found nothing unusual in being introduced. He was just a little uncomfortable with the polite head bows and small curtsies that accompanied the introductions.

Aelle promised the group a tour of the town and the valley when they had time, perhaps after breakfast in the morning. He suggested as the hour was getting late, perhaps they would like to retire to their rooms to refresh before dining.

At the appropriate time, a servant went to the rooms to advise the meal was to be served shortly. The family was taken to the family dining room which was warm and intimate. Aelle and Cuthbert were already there as was another man. Aelle introduced his Excellency Bishop Aert, a dear friend who would be joining them for dinner. Aelle did not sit at the head of the table, instead Cuthbert did. The seating had been arranged so Aelle sat next to Aethel, Paul and Indonea sat across from Aelle, and the bishop sat at the end of the table. Aert was in a position to see all the interactions.

Aelle asked Aert to offer the blessing which he did and then the food was served.

Paul fell into his down to earth pattern and spoke first, "How long have you known Aelle and how did you two become friends?"

Aert laughed, and Paul looked a little embarrassed.

"Paul you are delightful. Usually people keep me at arm's length, so it is refreshing to be personally engaged."

Aert told the story of how he and Aelle had met and become friends. Even though he summarized, the telling took a little time. The family was intrigued by the story and Aert had a sense of humor that most people never saw and he interjected it. There was laughter and questions. In getting to know Aert, they were also getting to know Aelle better. At the end of the telling, Aert turned the tables.

"So now it's your turn. How did you come to meet my friend?"

Paul turned to his daughter, "I suppose you must tell this story."

Aethel did, with self-deprecating humor, not leaving out her quirky behaviors. Aert and the others laughed at the telling of the story for her mother and father had not heard the first part. It was an altogether delightful dinner.

After dinner, Aelle suggested they retire to the hearth room which they did. The room had chairs with cushioned seats and backs.

Aethel sat, "These cushioned chairs are very comfortable. What is in the cushions?"

Cuthbert answered, "Goose feathers. Once in a while a small one will escape. They help keep one warm in winter when the fire is going in the hearth."

"I have never seen anything like them."

Aelle interjected, "They were a gift from my friend Beorn, a river trader who imported them. He should be arriving back from business soon and I will introduce you."

Aelle turned to Paul, "How would you and your wife like to accompany me and Aethel on a walk in the garden?"

Paul did not have an opportunity to respond for Indonea answered, "Wonderful, romantic, let's do it!"

The couples left for the garden.

Cuthbert turned to Aert, "What do you think?"

"They are most refreshing, truly humble and honest. Their parish priest says they are genuinely Christian people of faith. They are hardworking, generous, and loved in the community. He is a respected sheriff. He is known as an impartial, fair, and wise judge. His monthly community court is run efficiently and his oversight beyond reproach. His family farm is also very prosperous. His sons are well thought of even if the older Mark is a little prone to hand fighting. Aethel is a young woman of good reputation, known for her kindness, virtue, common sense and quick wit. There has been no lack of suitors, but it seems so far she has been very discriminating. She has rejected wealthy men of weak character, in fact all men of weak character, men of slow wit, men of harsh nature, and handsome men from good families with little ambition, but most of all men of little or no faith."

Cuthbert merely stated the obvious, "A very discerning young woman."

"Yes, it seems she would rather live life alone than with the wrong man."

In the garden, the couples were enjoying their walking tour of the garden. Indonea and Paul were as though on a second honeymoon. They were walking arm and arm quietly and Indonea had her head against her husband's arm as she would not reach his shoulder.

Aethel asked, "Do you always wear a sword."

"Yes. You should know that twice there have been assassination attempts. Once it happened while I was with Cenedred. If I had not been armed we would both be in heaven now. That is why there are always guards around when I am outside. If we were to marry there would be guards at your parents' also."

Aethel nodded, "With great privilege comes great responsibility, and with great responsibility comes danger."

"Yes. It is something to consider."

"So then marriage is a possibility, even given my family's lowly status?"

Aelle laughed, "Half my lords are such because I made them such, and only because God has put me in a position to do so. Status is a fleeting thing that can be given or taken away, but character is ours to develop and keep in accordance with God's precepts."

She looked at him, "Well and wisely said, but you evaded my question."

"Sorry, I did not mean to. It seems more a probability than a possibility, don't you think?"

"Yes," and she rested her head on his shoulder while they walked in silence.

Aelle was about his military business early the next morning though the three he was fighting got the better of him that morning. Though he was distracted, Wolf made no excuses but rather praised the men for their accomplishments. They went away feeling a sense of accomplishment for they knew they had improved though their king had not been at his best that morning.

After his training, Aelle went to see his son. It had become part of the morning routine that Aethelred expected daddy to fight with him in the morning and so the little swords and shields came out and they did battle. Aelle played with his son for a half hour, dying several times with too much squealing and laughter before they went for the morning meal.

When they came into the dining room everyone else was already there. Aethelred made straight for Indonea and climbed up into her lap.

"Good morning, everyone," Aelle said.

Bishop Aert announced the food had already been blessed.

Cuthbert asked the standard question, "How many times did you die this morning?"

"Seven," Wolf replied.

The visitors looked at each other, puzzled by the conversation.

Cuthbert looked at his great grandson, "He is improving then?"

"Yes, he is looking to get under my shield or by it. He now has the idea and is not just hacking away."

Aelle noticed the puzzled expressions of their guests. Aelle explained, "Aethelred and I fight with play swords and shields most mornings, and it is really as much training as play. He loves it."

The faces around him showed understanding and Aethel said, "Our children must be trained early if they are to reach their potential, but not be driven at too early an age."

"Yes, and at his age he will enjoy it for about a half hour, so that's all we do," Aelle added.

Indonea asked, "It is a pleasant day, are we still going to tour?"

"Of course. Have you been to the valley before?" Aelle asked looking around the table.

Aethel and Indonea shook their heads no but Paul said, "Before I met Indonea, I was here when I served in your uncle's company."

"You perhaps knew Osmund?"

Paul's eyes lit up, "Yes, he was my captain and I his sergeant. He is a good friend and an able warrior. I have not seen him in years."

"You don't know?" Aelle asked.

"Know what?" Paul responded.

"Osmund trained me and was the captain of my Wolf Pack, then commander of the army. He is now married to my mother and earl of his ancestral lands, a part of my realm. How did you not know this?"

Indonea interjected, "We heard of your marriage and that your mother was marrying some lord but not the details."

Paul added, "I heard she was marrying some fellow with a strange name, Shadow I believe."

"Shadow Killer is Osmund's warrior name," Aelle announced.

"He was not called that when we served together. I had heard of the renown of the Shadow Killer, but I did not know it was Osmund."

Wolf shook his head, "Strange. You will have to come and spend time with him when he comes to visit next time, which I hope will be soon," and Aelle looked at Aethel who knew what he meant. Paul missed the look but Indonea did not.

After breakfast, Aelle excused himself as he had business to attend to. He said it would take about an hour and then they would leave for their tour of the valley.

In the library Aert and Cuthbert sat with Aelle.

Aelle started, "Please inform me for I am anxious to know what you can report to me."

Aert repeated in more detail what he had told Cuthbert the evening before. He added details from the records about Paul's military service. He had been a highly competent warrior and had been promoted. He was injured in battle and appointed sheriff and granted lands for his loyal service. In short he was a man of good character, although in his youth he had been inclined to drink too much and when he did he was inclined to get into fights.

When he met Indonea, she straightened him out. Before she would marry him he had to swear off alcohol and get right with God. For him the first part had been the easiest. Finally he had truly surrendered to the will of God and his life of course changed. He became sergeant, a responsible married man, had children, and then became a gentleman farmer.

Wolf then asked his grandfather about the man. Cuthbert told how Paul had rendered great service to his brother and his brother had interceded on his behalf to have him granted the office and lands he now held. He knew of Paul and could verify what Aert had learned.

The tour of the valley was a pleasant outing that started with a tour of the town. They rode to town and tethered the horses then went on a walking tour. Only two of the guards walked behind them. The others stayed with the horses.

The shops and homes were well laid out and everything was so clean. A wagon went by loaded with upright barrels from which a horrible odor was coming.

Aelle shrugged, "Sorry about that, but every morning the honey wagon collects the contents of the night pots and brings it to a cesspool about three miles away where it is disposed of and the barrels then are brought to the river and washed. It helps prevent disease and filth."

Paul smiled, thinking he was being humorous, "I suppose like our outhouses when the pit is filled you add lime and cover it over?"

"Exactly," Cuthbert responded.

Aethel being curious asked the question, "Where does your drinking water come from?"

Cuthbert answered, "We are over a shallow underground river and our four community wells, the first of which is in the castle, provide crystal clear cool drinking water. We also have cisterns that collect rainwater which we use for washing clothes and bathing. During a siege it could be used for drinking. Poisoning the three wells outside the castle would not pollute the upstream well in the castle."

The town was alive with activity. They visited the shops and walked the streets and Paul noted that it must not be unusual for the king to be amongst the people for they all took it in stride just bowing slightly or gently curtsying when they crossed his path. After their walking tour they mounted the horses and went riding.

Aelle should have suspected Aethel and her mother would be good riders given their lifestyle. They were very comfortable on horseback and had worn long loose dresses to allow for it. They stopped for a cold lunch of cheese, apples, and bread beside the river. Blankets were laid out and they sat and ate as the river flowed by. While they were eating, Beorn came by on one of his boats and shouted greetings. The party waved to him.

They saw a small part of the valley that day and returned to the castle for the evening meal, where they enjoyed friendly banter and the women talked about what they had seen in the shops.

The next morning, it being Sunday, they all went to church in town. Before the service people went about outside greeting one another. The parish priest was a friendly man not the least bit intimidated by the fact his bishop was with them. He greeted the guests warmly. The parishioners greeted Aelle, Cuthbert and their guests. Aethel and Indonea were dressed in their finest and presented an attractive picture.

After service, the party went back to the castle for a noon meal. Beorn and his family came by invitation of the King and were introduced to the visitors. It being such a beautiful day, the party was served in the garden. After the meal, the ladies gathered together to talk and so did the men.

Paul was curious about river trade and how it added to the prosperity of the lands. Beorn explained it in summary and Paul appeared very thoughtful.

After a moment's hesitation he spoke, "I often do not plant all my fields for I do not want to see crops go to waste. If I were to bring excess crops to the river, could arrange to sell them downriver?"

Beorn smiled, "That is what the valley farmers have been doing for some time now."

Paul looked at Beorn, "May I come to see you to discuss this more?"

"Of course. Come when you can get away. I will be in town all week."

Paul thanked Beorn and said he would indeed come to see him. Paul said that perhaps they could do business together.

The gatherings broke up when the heat of the day came.

During the next two weeks the families spent a lot of time together. There were pleasant outings, long walks and rides, and conversations. There was play time with Aethelred and it seemed he had adopted Indonea and Aethel.

The family had been given permission to go about the castle as they wished. Paul being a farmer was used to being up early and one morning during his morning exploration he went by the door to the gallery overlooking the practice hall and heard the practice. He quietly went in.

Paul watched the sparring intently. He realized why Aelle was a legendary warrior. The three warriors facing him were obviously very skilled. Paul realized they were better skilled at war than he had ever been and he was good. Still, they had their hands full with this one man which he assumed must be Aelle. He had been watching for a half hour when the practice ended and the men, covered in sweat, took off their helmets and put the practice weapons away.

"You are getting very good. The time I can hold you off is continually decreasing. It started at two hours and now it is down to less than one. Each team is improving. I am proud of you."

The men were smiling broadly for they knew it was true.

Paul slipped out of the gallery and went to the garden to think. His potential son-in-law was truly a formidable man. There was no doubt his daughter would not do better. He contemplated living in the shadow of such a son-in-law and realized he had already been as the man was his king. He was now just closer and the shadow was cast completely over him. This was a little bit like when he first came to know Jesus, overwhelmed but realizing he was lucky to be His subject. He prayed and was relieved of his prideful concern.

On the Friday morning two weeks after their arrival, Paul came to see Aelle and Cuthbert was in the library with him. A servant asked if Paul could have an audience and was told to bring Paul in. Aelle motioned Paul to a seat.

Aelle greeted him, "Good morning, Paul."

"Good morning, Majesty."

"Tell me Paul, what brings you here before the morning meal?"

"With your permission, I need to return home to tend to my business. Next week is also the monthly court. I can think of no other way but to ask you directly, should I take my ladies back with me?"

Wolf smiled, "May I have until this afternoon to answer that question?"

It was Paul's turn to smile, "How can I deny my king?"

"Good then let's go eat with the others."

The cook had prepared boiled eggs, ham, and spiced apples. It was very good. After breakfast, Aelle asked Aethel to walk in the garden with him. As they left the room everyone saw that a priest and two guards followed along behind them.

Aethel spoke first, "You seem preoccupied this morning."

Aelle smiled, "I am. I have something to ask you."

It was her turn to smile, "If you are going to ask me to marry you the answer will be yes, if it is anything else I will be mortified."

Aelle smiled, "Good, I will ask your father, but it is a little more complicated than just that."

He explained his plan to her and the ramifications it would have for them and for her family. He asked for her insight. Some of it she saw no problem with and the rest were of uncertain outcome though she thought it might work out.

They went to the hearth room where the families were seated with bishop Aert.

Aelle started, "Paul I want your blessing to marry Aethel. I would have her as my queen."

Paul smiled and interjected, "Indonea and I have discussed it and you have our blessing."

Aethel and Indonea came and hugged Aelle and everyone was giving congratulations.

Aelle looked serious, "There is more. When my mother and Cenedred were here, they were a part of family decisions. Would you care to continue that or should the men retire to the library? Bishop Aert is one of my closest advisors and has knowledge of my governance, so he would be included."

Paul looked at Aelle, "I have no secrets from Indonea and if Aethel is to be your wife, I see no reason she should not hear what you have to say."

Aelle nodded, "I would have you give up your present position and lands and move to another shire."

Paul seemed ready to obey, "Yes, Lord." He showed no anger or disappointment, "May I ask to what purpose you will use me, Sire?"

"I would have you be earl of my newly annexed northeast shire."

This took Paul by surprise, "Truly?"

"Yes, I need you and I have three reasons. First, I have considered your experience, skills, and character. Secondly, I would have family and loyal men in positions of authority so my offspring do not have to worry about treachery. Thirdly, Bishop Aert, I, and Cuthbert and a lot of parishes have been praying for God's guidance in the appointments. We three, as well as others, feel comfortable with this first appointment.

I will appoint one of my other loyal men to take over your present holding. I will also offer your sons positions as recruits in my personal guard so they can learn skill at arms. It is the best training available, but they need to understand they will be treated the same as all other recruits. They may decline the offer if they so wish.

There will be challenges in this new shire and it is on the frontier. Your military and administrative background will be invaluable in keeping the peace, guarding the border, and governing. I have many agents in the area and you will be privy to their reports."

Paul asked, "When would you have me go, sir?"

"I would need you to go and take control as soon as possible. There are already a capable captain, sergeant, and troops in place who will remain there until you recruit and train your own men. I have examined the incomes that would go to the earl there and it is many, many times, your present income after expenses. Those expenses were calculated with the establishment of a permanent company of twenty five men-at-arms and as many archers. With proper management of river trade, our incomes from the shire could be a lot more.

Arrangements will be made for the shipment of your personal items to the new castle. It is similar to this one but somewhat smaller."

Paul knelt on one knee, "Thank you for your generosity, Sire. I never dreamed of rising to such high station and I will do everything in my power to repay the trust you have put in me."

Aelle pulled Paul up, "I believe and trust you will. Now let us celebrate. It will be some time before the official proclamation of the betrothal is published and becomes official, but in the meantime we can celebrate your new station. We have a special treat the cook has baked with apples."

The others who had been silent got up and started congratulating Paul. Aethel came over and slipped her arm around Aelle's.

"You know this was supposed to be my moment future husband. You are truly either a brave man or totally naïve."

Aelle smiled, "Let's assume I am naive. Do not worry Aethel for I intend to make it up to you."

Aethel smiled and said mischievously, "Oh, you certainly will."

At the table Aelle had Aethel on one side and Paul on the other. He wanted to talk further with Paul, "I think you will need to return to your hundred soon to prepare for your departure and to introduce your replacement. Your new station may be announced for Bishop Aert has arranged that the new appointment will be announced in the churches on Sunday. The formal induction will be held later, the day after the wedding so all the earls will be here."

Paul smiled and replied, "I assume my wife and daughter will stay to plan the wedding."

Aelle turned to Aethel, "Don't you think that would be appropriate? The initial behind the scenes work can be started before the official betrothal is announced in church."

Aethel smiled, "Oh yes. A state wedding is a huge and expensive, I mean expansive affair that requires much planning."

Aelle laughed. Paul looked puzzled.

Aelle let him in on the joke, "She promised to get even with me for taking away attention from her on her day. I now suppose she will have the grandest wedding, therefore the most expensive, in the history of the shire."

Aethel laughed, "Do not worry future husband for your future wife is very practical and knows how expensive it will be to raise our many future children."

Paul left for home. He was accompanied by six of the elite Wolf Pack, his replacement, Sheriff Ware, and his three sons. When he arrived with the soldiers the people of the area already knew of his new status. His sons came out to meet him and he took them aside to talk.

He told them of their sister's coming betrothal and of the offer the king, their future brother-in-law, had made. He explained to them implications of this offer with him being earl of a rich shire. Only those who could both fight and govern would have such a rich inheritance. The brothers were eager to take on the challenge and said they would both go into service.

The first two days back, Paul did not get any work done for his friends and neighbors kept coming to congratulate him. Mark and Luke spent their days showing Ware's sons the farm and the crops and the special things a farmer needs to know about a certain piece of ground. Ware's sons were experienced and the work went quickly. Soon Mark and Luke were spending their time collecting the belongings that were going with their father to the new shire.

During the trip Paul had come to know Ware who was reported to be an honest Christian man. Paul found him to be a straight forward no nonsense man. He was an experienced farmer and a quick learner. Within a week of arriving, he held his first monthly community court. He showed himself to be a wise man with a common sense approach to justice. Paul knew that much thought had gone into his appointment.

Ware assured Paul his goods stored in wagons in the large storage barn would be kept dry in the barn until they were taken to go north. Paul left his two hired men. He had offered them employment in his new home and they had agreed to come. Their goods would be added to the empty wagon in the barn for transportation. They and their families would come with the wagons.

Ware purchased the farm equipment and tools from Paul at a fair price. Paul kept the wagons and horses to carry his goods to his new home. Within two weeks, Paul was headed back to the valley with three of the Wolf Pack and his two sons. Three of the pack had stayed to protect his goods. For the first time in years Paul wore his sword and helmet and carried his shield tied to his saddle. A spare horse was led by Luke and carried coin and other family treasure.

When Paul arrived, his wife, daughter, and Cuthbert came into the courtyard to meet him. Aelle was not at the castle. Mark and Luke embraced their mother and sister whom they had not seen in weeks. They were introduced to Cuthbert. After the introductions, Paul took Cuthbert aside and asked him how they could safeguard his family treasure. Cuthbert made the arrangements.

Aelle came back about an hour before the evening meal. He came into the hearth room to see the Indonea and Aethel telling the brothers about their visit and the plans for the wedding. Aelle felt sorry for the brothers who were displaying the fidgety signs of boredom. He marched into the room.

'Paul, Mark, Luke, it is so good to see you," Aelle announced. He added," Hello, everyone."

The men rose as Aelle came and clasped their forearms and then embraced them. "It is good you are back, Paul. Mark, Luke, I want to steal you away for a talk, we will be back in time for supper."

Paul had his back turned to the women and had a pleading look on his face so Aelle took mercy on him, "Paul, why don't you come with us?"

He took the men into the library, "You looked so miserable in there, I just decided to take pity on you."

The men smiled.

"Mark and Luke have you made a decision about the army?"

First Luke then Mark replied in the affirmative. Aelle told them they train at Aewel's castle there they would be away from the distractions of family and besides Aewel had been the Wolf Pack's original trainer.

The family dinner that evening was very pleasant and Paul and the sons told of their preparations for the move. As the dinner ended and the family was leaving, Wilfred asked his king if he could have a private meeting. Aelle excused himself and took Wilfred to the library.

Aelle sat down, "Take a seat, Wilfred."

Aelle could tell Wilfred was almost in tears. Wilfred told him about the secret he had discovered and all Wolf could say was, "You are certain?"

'Yes, the servants witnessed the sign each morning, vomit in the night pot."

Wilfred could see the pain on Wolf's face. Wilfred could hardly restrain his sadness and had tears rolling down his face. He had come to love his king. Aelle called for Cuthbert and had Wilfred repeat the report. The second telling was too much for Wilfred who broke into sobs. Wolf told him he could leave, embraced him and thanked him earnestly, and ordered him to secrecy. Wilfred left the room.

Cuthbert asked, "What are you going to do?"

Wolf stood and started pacing, "I am going away on the king's business and will be gone for some time. Please take care of Aethelred."

Cuthbert nodded knowingly, and uncharacteristically came and embraced his grandson who was obviously deeply troubled and hurt. When they left the room Paul's family was in the hearth room. In a display of authority, Aelle called for the duty sergeant who quickly came into the room.

"Sergeant, prepare thirty mounted men for departure within the hour. They may tell their families that they will be gone for some time."

"Yes, Lord."

Aelle turned to Paul, "Paul I will need you to go to your new post. I will be gone for an extended time and so it would be proper for your wife and daughter to go with you. I will be in touch with you when I return. Mark and Luke you will start your training here and then go with the next boat going to the southern castle. I am sorry, but I must leave tonight."

Aethel asked, "What about the wedding?"

Wolf was now in military mode, "No public announcement has been made and the king's business requires I be gone for an extended period. No announcement will be made."

Wolf turned and left the room and went to make ready for leaving. He said goodbye to his son and Cuthbert who seemed as distressed as he was. He called for Modig and Captain Grimbold and asked them to arrange for Paul to get to his new post.

Meanwhile, Aethel and Indonea went to their quarters. Aethel was stunned. What would she do? She turned to her mother.

"He seemed so cold."

Indonea turned to her, "I have seen it before, warriors in crisis become stone men and all emotion gets locked away. One of two things has happened, either there is a military crisis or he suspects. If it is the latter, you have put our family in great danger."

Aethel pleaded, "It was just one mistake, so surely I can be forgiven?"

Indonea's response was harsh, "The man can forgive you, but the king has responsibilities. The implications for him are profound. It is over."

Aethel started crying, "When will you tell father?"

Indonea's response was direct, "Tonight."

A half an hour after Wolf left, Indonea told her husband. For a moment he was furious and then he did something his wife had never seen him do before, he started sobbing, and then Indonea knew it was for his daughter.

Wolf and his escort rode most of the night, not making camp and grabbing just a few hours of sleep, then setting out again. When they arrived at Cathedral Town, even though it was early morning, Wolf went directly to see Bishop Aert. His friend could tell Wolf was greatly troubled. Aert was a good friend for he listened; he grieved with, and prayed with Wolf, then advised him on how to proceed.

The next day Paul came alone his horse near exhaustion. He asked for an audience with Wolf. It was granted and Aert was present. Paul came and took a knee before Wolf, "I beg forgiveness Majesty, for my wife has confessed to me. My family has caused you great shame."

Wolf shook his head, "Rise, Paul. The sin is not yours. You need no forgiveness."

Paul had tears in his eyes when he rose, and Aelle said to him, "Sit, Paul."

Paul kept on, "I did not know and my wife kept it from me when she found out. What was she thinking? After all these years, I cannot believe my own wife would keep such a thing from me."

Wolf said, "Who can understand women? I have been praying with my good friend for God to give me a heart of forgiveness and He has. As king though, you understand I have a duty."

Paul could see that Aelle was fighting his emotions, "Yes."

The men sat quietly for a few minutes lost in their own thoughts before Paul said, "Lord, I will take my family far away. I have acquired wealth and can start over somewhere outside your realm."

Wolf replied, "No, there is no need. The sin is not yours, Paul, that you should be punished. You will go and take the position I have appointed you to and you will be a loyal man. Your sons will be trained as I promised."

"Yes, Sire. Thank you."

Aelle continued, "Bishop Aert has generously offered to arrange for Aethel to stay at a convent until the baby is born. Do you know who the father is?"

"Yes, Lord. My daughter confessed."

"Do you wish your daughter to be married to him?"

Paul started sobbing lightly, "There can be no marriage for he is a married man."

Wolf had not considered this possibility, "I do not wish to know the man unless he is one of my trusted men."

"No Lord, he has no connection to you."

Wolf considered, "Tell him it is a royal command that he must make a private documented confession to the local sheriff and agree to pay support for the child to the church. If he does not agree, and do it immediately, then you will threaten to tell the king his name and the king has promised to see he is prosecuted and probably thrown into prison for his crime of adultery and offense against the virtue of an earl's daughter." Wolf looked at Paul before continuing.

"Aert advises I cannot prosecute the man for treason because of the adultery; there was no public announcement of the betrothal, so it did not officially occur. It is just as well. I do not wish to see someone die over this sin. Tell the sheriff it is a royal command that this matter be kept private to protect you. My dear friend, the bishop, will give you the royal order document which is being prepared. It seems the only option is the convent and then Aethel can come to you after the baby is born if you so wish."

Paul answered, "It will be done as you order."

"I am going to visit my friend Eadgard and will return in a week. Please have this matter resolved by then and Aethel gone to the convent. I cannot bear the misery of seeing her now."

Aelle could tell Paul was as dejected by the events as he was, "You may go now, Paul, and leave me with my friend here to comfort me."

Paul rose, bowed and left. The bishop's men gave Paul a meal and place to sleep. When he awoke, he prepared and started back to the valley.

Chapter 22 - Again Into the Fray

Aelle was not a coward and never had been. He faced many enemies and had overcome his fear and turned it against them as battle fury. Now was not the time to become a coward. So it was that he went by boat to see his mother some months after Aethel had been sent away. Bishop Aert had decided to come along to visit the newly established churches. Aelle knew and Aert knew that the real reason he was coming was to be a part of the matchmaking.

They left from Cathedral Town and sailed south and along the way briefly visited with Yingvar, Aewel, Lucan, Aldred, and Ragnvald. The shires he travelled through were prosperous. The shires were like flowers in the sun; the extended peace was the sun that nourished them. The peace had come thanks to God.

Every time they docked, people came to greet them. These people were genuinely happy to see their king and their bishop. It was an altogether enjoyable trip.

Osmund's lands were prospering under his care. The people had responded with enthusiasm and hard work to their new earl for it quickly became apparent that he had their best interest at heart. He had spent a fortune helping the farms become productive and establishing the river trade. There was peace, justice, and a sense of security. Their lord had made it known that their king had contributed substantially to the fortune spent rebuilding the land. The people had been further encouraged when they found they were paying less taxes and rent and the increased productivity actually resulted in more income for the earl and the king than there had been at any time in the history of the shire.

A new river town had sprung up around the port that Osmund had built. It was situated in a river bay and there were six docks. Osmund had learned from Magnus and had seen that the town was built on a hill overlooking the docks. He had built two roads from the docks to the town.

When Aelle's vessel came to the port there were four trading boats at the docks. His company disembarked and guards were left with the boat. The tax collector had started down the dock and when he realized who had come knelt and gave his regards. Aelle told him to rise and asked him where there was a good place for his company to camp. The tax collector offered to give up his home, but Aelle told him that he always stayed with his troops when travelling. The king purchased the only two good horses that were for sale. The group set up camp and many came to greet the king; both the prominent and the humble. Aelle treated them all equally. Finally as dark approached the troops politely but firmly shut the camp off from visitors.

The next day, after stowing the tents back on the boat, the party started marching for Osmund's castle. They were all fit and would march until they arrived. They marched all day and into the night. The fact that they were marching at night probably saved them. The horses had not been for the king or the bishop but for the scouts. The scouts reported the sighting of the force camped in their way. Wolf had thirty of the Wolf Pack with him and as the opposing force was larger he decided to avoid rather than engage them.

Two of the men had been with Magnus on the campaign with Osmund. They had some knowledge of the area though it was sketchy. The group made its plan. Wolf sent one of the scouts to report to Osmund on their situation. The scout took both horses so he could ride hard and alternate them.

Wolf ordered the men off the main road. They marched to the northwest through the woods. They found the rough road they were looking for in the early morning and followed it to the place the men had told about. It was just off the road and looked like it would be easy to defend. The rock ledges were steep. The pathway between the ledges they followed was narrow and two men could hold it against dozens. At the top the area was small.

It became apparent there were three paths to the top and they were all narrow and winding between the cliffs. They could see the brook from the top. The place was very defensible and they would be able to see the enemy coming from a distance. Wolf sent three men to the brook to fill the canteens and told everyone they were to go on half rations. The three days rations they had could thus be stretched to six.

Wolf, Aert and Sergeant Ord examined the accesses. They

decided the best way to defend the top was near it. If the enemy came they would let them channel in the narrow accesses and fight them head on where a flanking could not be achieved. The two archers would stay at the top to deal with any climbers. The walls were steep and twenty feet high but rough. Half the men would defend the paths and the other half the top. Anyone who climbed there would be easy to engage with spears as they neared the top.

There was a round depression in one of the larger rocks and Wolf poured some water into it. The stone was not porous and the water stayed. He ordered two men to fill it from the canteens and then refill them at the brook. They would cover the water with a shield to keep it from going into the air.

The men were tired so Wolf set sentries while the rest slept. The enemy did not come until late afternoon. Each guard shift had gotten six hours rest before the enemy came into sight. It had taken the enemy some time to realize the troop had left the road and then to track them. When they finally arrived, they were not happy with what they saw.

Wolf observed two of the enemy, obviously the senior men, arguing. Half the force left leaving about forty men to attack Wolf's group. The leader sent scouts out. No attack came and Wolf figured the enemy would not attack until night. By evening Wolf had come to the conclusion that the enemy was content to keep his force penned up here. Wolf was used to following his instincts. He and his men prayed.

It was early morning when the enemy guard started to doze and as soon as he did, he died quietly. Wolf's men slipped by without making a sound. A quarter of the men they attacked died in their sleeping rolls before the alarm was given then another quarter died trying to get their weapons and the other half died in direct engagement. Of the two other sentries guarding the pathways one had escaped west and the other had died, taken from behind, starting toward the camp.

Wolf called for an after battle report. Two of his men had been injured too badly to travel. His men collected food and canteens and took some of them back to the top. They helped their injured comrades up and brought extra spears from the enemy. The enemy shields were used to block the pathways. Aert would stay to minister to the wounded until someone could come for them. The three men had enough food and water to last a long time. A canvas shelter was erected to keep off sun and rain.

Wolf and his men set out for Osmund's castle and they had not gone far when they met the scout coming from the other direction leading the exhausted horses. Osmund's castle was under siege. The scout had immediately set out to warn Wolf. Wolf told the scout to go back to the river and get word to Ragnvald to send all the reinforcements he could muster quickly. He was to take one horse. Wolf asked Ord which of his men was the best horseman. That man was given a horse and was told to ride to Aldred with the same message. Aert produced paper and wax from his pack and Wolf wrote and sealed messages for both men.

He and his twenty six remaining men set out for Osmund's castle. They arrived near the castle at night and found a hidden place in deep woods to rest. Sentries were put out and before sunrise Wolf went with a trooper and did some scouting. He returned.

He gathered his men and spoke quietly, "The castle is surrounded and there are too many for us to attack. Their baggage train is between us and the attacking force. If we move stealthily and act quickly we could kill the guards and have the wagons on fire before the main body can reinforce the guards. It will be a quick attack and then retreat at the run. I repeat, kill, fire, and run. I want each of you to repeat that to me."

Each man whispered it.

Wolf continued, "We meet back here and then move deeper into the forest. They will have to start scavenging and we will attack the bands of scavengers they send. The more men we pull away from the castle and kill the longer the siege lasts. That means delaying the enemy until reinforcements arrive. Understand?"

The men were nodding.

"This is not about honor but keeping our people alive. Kill, fire and run, remember it."

The baggage train was lightly guarded. The thirteen guards did not have a chance. There were two sentries who were only half awake and leaning against the wagons. Most the wagon guards died in their sleeping rolls. There were over two dozen wagons and they were all set ablaze using branches from the campfire. The Wolf Pack was in and out in less than two minutes and carried away provisions to last several days.

The enemy commander Ramm was woken when the smoke was spotted. He dispatched twenty mounted troops under the command of Sergeant Holt. The fires had been raging for five minutes when the patrol arrived. The wagons could not be saved. The sergeant leading the troops was enraged when he saw the baggage guards had been killed in their sleeping rolls. He made an enormous mistake and led his patrol into the woods.

His mounted troopers went further and further into the woods in search of the attackers. Holt's patrol did not find them, but Wolf's troops found the patrol. The men were riding single file through dense woods when they were attacked. Riders were speared out of the saddle, horses screamed when speared and riders fell. Holt's men dismounted and formed a shield circle, but the enemy was no longer attacking. Holt realized he had only nine of his patrol around him. He waited a few minutes then checked his fallen men. All eleven were dead

Wolf's men found a place to stop and rest. None had been lost in the attack. Wolf smiled, "You all did well. That is now our method of attack. Once they figure out what we are doing they will try to lure us into a trap. We must be ever vigilant. Ten minute rest then we move."

Osmund had been called to the wall. The smoke was thick.

Beadwof turned to Osmund, "What do you think happened?"

Osmund smiled, "I think Wolf happened."

Beadwof chuckled, "So they did not find him."

"I think not. That also tells us reinforcements will be on the way. Wolf will have sent riders just as we sent pigeons."

Aldred's company entered Osmund's shire first, but Ragnvald was not far behind. The pigeons had arrived at Ragnvald's castle but not at Aldred's. The riders had both gotten through and Aldred being closer and having no river to cross got there about the same time as Ragnvald who had to cross the river. The rider Wolf sent had met Ragnvald at the river.

The alarm had gone throughout the lands. Leof and Grimbold knew their business. The reserves were called out and every earl was alerted. Two thirds of the standing army went with Leof by boat and one third of the reserves. One third of the regulars and two thirds of the reserves stayed to protect the shires. Boats were commandeered and the river traffic was all going one way within a day.

Both earls had scouts out. As a result the two companies were able to find each other and consolidate. They were a half day from the castle when they saw the little battle. Wolf's men had attacked a scavenging party. The scavenging party was just about overrun when the companies appeared flying their banners.

Some of the scavengers fled and left Wolf and his men. Normally Wolf would have retreated into the woods, but he recognized the banners and started marching toward them.

It was Ragnvald who said in a loud voice, "I should have known he'd beat us to the fight." The men who heard the remark started laughing and the comment was passed down the column.

The two earls dismounted and came to Wolf who before they could observe the formal welcome embraced one then the other,

Wolf said, "You do not know how glad I am to see you. Have you recovered the two wounded?"

Aldred replied, "A patrol was sent and should be returning anytime."

Wolf nodded, "Good. We have been having a grand time harassing the enemy."

Ragnvald asked, "Are you and your men hungry?"

"No, the enemy has been feeding us very well, thank you."

The remark drew laughter from those within hearing.

Wolf added, "I and my men are tired of walking all over the country though; do you have some mounts you can spare?"

Ragnvald laughed, "It just happens that my friend Aldred thought to bring some."

Wolf asked, 'How many warriors do we have?"

Aldred replied, "Between us we brought one hundred and forty."

Wolf sighed, "I have twenty four. Some of my men have been killed in the attacks."

Ragnvald calculated, "That makes us about one hundred and sixty plus. How many enemy?"

Wolf calculated, "I estimated they started with a little over two hundred and fifty, we have killed perhaps," and he looked at Ord.

"Thirty nine, Sire."

Wolf continued, "Which means they have a little over two hundred left. Shadow had about a hundred at the castle and I doubt he has lost many in the siege, so we probably outnumber them slightly, so let's get to it."

Wolf's men mounted and the column set out.

Ramm was summoned by one of his captains, "What is it."

"Lord, we have a scout report. A column of about two hundred is less than a half day's march away. Another report says there are boats on the river carrying several hundred more men and about a hundred will probably land today."

Ramm shook his head, "It is not possible that they could mobilize so quickly! It is impossible! It should be weeks before reinforcements could get here. "

"Nonetheless, Lord, they are here. What are your orders?'

"Are you certain?" Ramm asked still not able to comprehend the reality.

"We have multiple reports and confirmations, Lord."

Ramm looked at the castle and shook his head, "We must withdraw. Organize it."

'Yes, Lord."

Osmund watched the preparations. He turned to Beadwof, "Prepare the men to join the pursuit column."

Beadwof smiled broadly, "Yes sir, with great pleasure."

Ethelind came to the wall and watched the activity, "What does it mean?"

"It means your son is coming with a relief column of a sizeable enough force to challenge our friends out there."

"What is Beadwof doing?"

Shadow smiled, "Preparing the men to join the pursuit column."

Ethelind looked at her husband seriously, "Good, they need to pay for the evil they have done here."

Shadow put his arm around her and she laid her head on his shoulder and sighed.

As soon as the last of Ramm's men left the field a rider came from the woods at full speed carrying Wolf's banner. He came into the castle out of breath and Shadow went to meet him.

"His Lord sends his regards and cordially invites you to pursue the enemy. He has veered off with his command to cut the enemy's escape route." The messenger smiled broadly.

Shadow laughed, "Well done. Would you care to accompany us to the dance? We can supply a fresh mount."

"There is nothing that would please me more, my Lord"

As a new horse was brought and the messenger changed over his saddle, he noticed that Shadow's men were already mounting up. Beadwof had arranged that a skeleton guard would be left to defend the castle. The company rode out with Cenedred waving from the wall as the gates closed.

Shadow sent scouts ahead with extra mounts. Ramm's scouts knew that they were being followed but did not know the size of the force and it was closer than he anticipated. Ramm hurried toward the border. He pushed his column and kept going after dark for there was enough moonlight by which to travel.

Shadow's column kept coming also. It was about one in the morning and Ramm's column was strung out and tired. They were straggling along the road. The attack started silently, the men just came from the woods on both sides and started cutting down Ramm's men in the center of the column. It did not take long for a large number of Ramm's men to be cut down. Then the enemy was gone.

The column was in disarray and did not move. Standing back to back Ramm's warriors stood silently waiting for an onslaught, but after a quarter hour Ramm decided one was not forthcoming and the column started forward.

An hour later, the adrenalin rush was gone and the warriors in Ramm's column were starting to become distracted when it happened again at the end of the column. It was a quick attack and only part of the column was engaged. Some men turned to reinforce the rear and as they ran back the front of the column was attacked and the attack at the rear ended as quickly as it started. Wolf's men who attacked the rear disengaged and as they returned to the woods started howling. It was a spontaneous thing but the superstitious men of Ramm's column became truly frightened.

The attack on the front of the column ended quickly. It became a joke and Wolf's men started howling as they returned to the woods. The column stayed frozen for half an hour. Ramm had difficulty getting the column moving and the men moved slowly watching the woods. Multiple false alarms stalled the column. Ramm's men marched in fear all night. The attacks by the men led by Wolf and Aert had not only slowed the column substantially but reduced the number of warriors.

The column moved into open land just as the sun was rising. Ramm took count of his men. To his surprise he found he had lost thirty seven men in the woods. His men were exhausted but the border was within a half day's hard march so after a ten minute rest he moved the men out. As they topped a rise he saw them. The hill ahead was a mass of warriors. He ordered his men to move to the woods but the men did not want to go into the dark shadows of the woods. A few obeyed. There was a terrifying howling and one man came from the woods his guts spilling out.

Spontaneously, Ramm's men charged forward spreading out as they ran. It was a long way to the warriors waiting at the top of the hill. Ramm's men were tired to start with. The last of their adrenalin rush wore off as they reached the hill on which Ragnvald and Aldred waited.

Wolf's army had received reports of the murder of men, women, and children, of rape, and pillage as they had travelled here. It was a time to mete out justice. Wolf's men attacked the front and Osmund the rear of Ramm's men. It was a massacre. Some were able to escape into the woods.

Wolf's army rested and camped.

Wolf was sitting against a tree drinking water next to Aert, 'Why do they keep coming? Why when they know what is likely to happen? So many souls have gone to hell."

Aert sighed, "It is the nature of evil."

While they were camped, the rest of the reinforcements arrived. Wolf went to greet them. The army rested a full day. Investigation revealed Ramm had escaped. That meant the war was not over.

Wolf and his men were exhausted. They and Osmund would return to the castle. Leof would pursue Ram into his shire. He would take the wealth of the land and bring it back to make reparations.

Wolf's men were exhausted when they reached the castle. Wolf hardly had the energy to embrace his mother before going to sleep. He slept for nineteen hours straight. He rose, relieved his bladder and then went to the kitchen to get something to eat. Shadow was there nursing a drink of water.

Wolf sat down, "You know Shadow, I marry, my wife dies, I fall in love with another woman and she has a baby by another, I come to have my mother match-make and get in the middle of a war. It is enough to make a man give up women."

Shadow started laughing and could not stop. Wolf did not think it was that funny until he recognized that the cook was bent over in pain, she was laughing so hard.

Wolf shrugged, "What does a king have to do to get something to eat?"

The laughter grew.

Wolf finally got fed when the laughter ran out. He ate then fell asleep at the table with his head resting on his arms. He awoke to the gentle shakings of his mother.

"You smell son, go get cleaned up."

He did. There was a clean uniform as well. He went to see his mother. She was in the small dining room. He went to where she was sitting and kissed her on the forehead.

"Shadow told me what you said."

"I was really tired," Aelle replied.

"Yes son, but because your defenses were down and there was truth in it, it probably is an accurate view into what you are feeling."

"Perhaps."

Ethelind looked sad, "I know there is a temptation to give in because of the hurt, but there is someone else out there for you. God knows who it is. Let us pray together and Aert and I will work on it."

They prayed together.

Wolf took some time off. For several days he relaxed, rested, and read scripture. He took long walks, and spent time talking about mundane things with his mother and theological concepts with Aert. He also received the reports from Leof.

Leof led the Wolf Pack into Ramm's lands. They did not go burning, pillaging, and killing. They did demand food in an amount equal to the annual tax Ramm levied. It was quickly recognized that this was no army like any had ever known. If it was sold food, it would just move on and there would be no suffering.

Leof sent a fast company ahead with extra horses to Ramm's castle. They rode almost without stopping. Their mission was to prevent treasure from being removed. When the few castle guards who were there heard of their coming, they left quickly with what they could carry. The patrol took possession of the castle and those who fled did not get far before they were run to ground.

The treasure room had an iron door and several locks which apparently the guards had not been able to get past. It was left locked pending Leof's arrival. When Leof arrived, the treasure room was opened and it became obvious how Ramm could afford to field such a large army. The amount of treasure it the castle was massive. It would take several wagons to transport it.

Leof sent large patrols out to search for Ramm. He was not found. Leof took some comfort in the fact he was now impoverished and without an army. Leof placed a bounty on Ramm and had it announced throughout the land. Because of the bounty, Ramm was given into their hands.

Leof started purchasing the provisions the army needed and the quality and quantity brought for sale in the market near the castle increased dramatically. Leof had learned that Ramm would often take what he needed and not pay for it, so the market had not been vibrant during his reign.

After Ramm was captured, earls came from three surrounding shires. They were amazed to find that Leof was a commander of only a portion of the king's army and not a high lord of the king. They made a plea to him anyway. Their lands were in dire straits for Ramm had taken all their wealth. The farmers were barely surviving and there was no force to keep the peace. They were faced with disaster. Leof invited them to stay and sent a message to the king for direction. Instead Wolf came escorted by a company.

Wolf met with Leof and the senior officers first when he arrived. He viewed the treasure room and discussed the situation with Leof. He also shared an overview of some of his intelligence from his spies with Leof. The king received the earls accompanied by Leof standing at his side. The earls were announced and two of them came into Wolf's presence and knelt before him and paid their respects. The third approached him arrogantly. Wolf examined him for a minute. This was Rinc, cousin to Ramm, and he was as the reports had described him.

Wolf turned to that man, 'Do you come seeking my help and give no respect? Are you so arrogant that you would potentially sacrifice the good of your people for your pride? Leave, you have truce for just as long as it takes you to leave this shire."

The man sneered at the King and left the room.

Wolf turned to the other two, "Rise, come let us share a meal and discuss your situation."

They adjourned to a small dining room where they sat informally. Food and beverage was brought and Wolf asked them already knowing the answer, "Why was your neighbor so hostile?"

One of the men, Tedman, spoke, "He is a cousin of Ramm, and was not as hard pressed as we. Ramm left him with somewhat more than he took from us. We had only fifteen men-at-arms each and Ramm oppressed us more than his cousin. His cousin would often enter our land and steal from us. We did not have the men to stop him. We were doubly oppressed and our lands are near collapse."

Wolf said, "You have truly been put in a difficult position. Why did you ask for my help and what do you ask and offer?"

The other Earl, Magan spoke, "We came to you because you have a reputation far and wide as a just and generous king. It is known that your people prosper in peace and we would have the same. We have been told your taxes are fair and as evidenced by your presence here, that you defend your subjects and guard the peace. We would have you as our king and protector, and will be your loyal subjects if you will help us in our time of despair."

Wolf finished chewing the bite he had taken and then spoke, "I know of your shires. They were and can be prosperous. Make a list of what you need and what your incomes are now and what they could be. We will review them and pray about this. Then I will give you my decision. When can you have the lists?"

Magan spoke for them, "We have prepared a list of needs and we have advisors with us who will help us prepare the information on taxes and rents. We could probably have everything ready for tomorrow."

Wolf nodded as he ate, "You know that your young men will be subject to the military call as is custom and that they will be required to train and serve one month in twelve?"

Tedman nodded assent, "We know. We also know you encourage your lord's to have enough men to keep the peace and your taxes are such that they can afford to do so."

Wolf nodded while saying, "Good. We will meet tomorrow afternoon to discuss this further."

Within the week, the realm had again expanded by voluntary treaty with two earls and the conquest of Ramm's shire. The earls had a king and a large loan to help their people and put their shires back into production. They each had a sergeant with twenty men-at-arms assigned to assist in establishing and keeping the peace. All the troops sent were single with a reason for there were lots of eligible women in the shires and a shortage of husbands.

Leof would not be returning to the valley for he was now earl of the shire formerly held by Ramm subject to a list of land grants his king would make. Troops were left with him until he could heal the land and raise his own force. After arrangements were completed, Wolf returned to Osmund's shire with a majority of the army and the acquired treasure.

Osmund and Ethelind were happy to see Aelle return. They greeted him in the courtyard. After the greeting, he went to clean up and the troops were dismissed. He would see his mother and Osmund at the evening meal. After cleaning up, Aelle had some time so he asked a servant to bring him a cup of water and went to the garden where sat on a bench and relaxed. He had been there for some minutes when a young woman came and sat on the other end of the bench.

She sat there doing needlework.

Aelle asked her, "Do you do a lot of that kind of work?"

The young woman nodded concentrating on the piece.

"Do you come here often?"

There was another nod in reply.

Aelle smiled, "You don't say much do you?"

She sighed and put down her work in her lap and looked at him with piercing blue eyes, "You will please forgive me. I came from a place where I wasn't expected to speak much and I am finding it hard to fit in."

Aelle nodded not saying anything. The young woman went back to her work and Aelle sat there enjoying the smells and quiet of the garden. His last thought was how amazingly quiet it was and how the garden walls kept outside sounds from being heard. He dozed off. He awoke to a gentle shaking.

"Wake up."

He looked up at the young woman with the piercing blue eyes, "You were snoring like an old fat sister. I came here to enjoy the quiet. Won't you go somewhere else to make that noise?"

Wolf smiled, "No, I like it here with you."

She made a harrumph sound and went back to her place. He quickly dozed off again. This time he was woken by a soldier who told him that the evening meal was ready and his mother had called for him. He arose and went to the family dining room.

When he entered he saw the young woman with the piercing blue eyes. His mother got up and hugged him. She pointed to the young woman, "Edlin, this is my son, His Majesty King Aelle."

The young woman did not seem at all flustered but stood and curtsied, "We have met."

Ethelind was a little surprised, "You have?"

Edlin smiled, "Your son sat down, fell asleep, and was rude enough to snore while I was trying to enjoy the quiet of the garden."

Osmund interjected sternly, "Edlin, you do realize that you are speaking of your sovereign who could order you returned to the convent."

Aelle could tell Edlin was on the verge of tears and said, "Edlin, you will have to become immune to your brother's teasing if you are going to survive here."

Edlin sighed deeply, and Aelle could tell she was relieved.

Ethelind piped in, "My dear husband, you must remember where Edlin came from and everything there is said in ernest."

Osmund appeared truly sorry, "Forgive me little sister, I am sometimes just a crass soldier."

Edlin spoke, "I am sorry Majesty and you are forgiven my brother. I have led such a sheltered life these many years."

Aelle sat down and everyone else followed, "Edlin, what happened that you left the convent?"

She looked up, "Sire, it..."

Aelle interrupted, "Here I am just Aelle. The family only uses honorariums in public."

She continued, "Aelle, I finally came to the conclusion after years of prayer that it was not God's plan for my life, though I confess I do not know what is."

Aelle nodded, "I was content just to live and be an earl, but it turned out God had other plans and now I am king of a sizeable realm."

Edlin was surprised, "You have not always been king?"

Aelle looked at Osmund who then retold in brief while they ate, the adventures they shared, the growth of the kingdom, and the tragedies they had endured. From time to time Edlin would ask a question.

At the end of the telling Edlin stated simply, "It is such a sad story."

They finished eating and went to the hearth room to sit and talk. Edlin followed them.

Ethelind started, "We have no progress yet on our little project. The candidates we identified all had a problem. So we are not giving up but starting over."

Edlin asked, "What's the little project?"

Osmund smiled, "It's a secret little project?"

"So what is the secret?"

Wolf laughed, "They are trying to find me a wife and cannot find a suitable women."

Edlin asked, "What are the requirements?"

Ethelind replied, "A young Christian woman of noble birth,

virtuous, innocent and who could make my son happy."

Edlin said innocently, "What about me? I have all those requirements?"

Aelle, Ethelind and Osmund looked at each other. They could think of nothing to say. They all looked at Edlin.

"Well, I am Christian and from a noble family. No one can say I'm not virtuous or innocent because I've been locked away in a convent. The reality is no one makes anyone else happy. Happy is based on circumstances. Our joy is in the Lord and a happy marriage can best be achieved following God's precepts."

Again, Aelle, Ethelind and Osmund looked at each other. They were speechless. The silence was overwhelming. Edlin just sat there innocently. Wolf started laughing lightly and then belly laughing. Edlin, Ethelind and Osmund were not laughing at first, but as Wolf's laughter escalated, it became contagious.

After the laughing ceased, the group just sat there for a time. No one knew what to say.

Aelle finally asked, "It would be strange for Edlin is my step aunt; is there such a thing?"

Ethelind smiled looking at her husband, "I wonder if it would be a problem even if they are not related by blood?"

Osmund pondered, "Bishop Aert can tell us when he gets back from his visits to the church. Perhaps even our own priest could answer the question."

Aelle threw his hands in the air, "You are all crazy!"

Edlin looked at Aelle and said a little quietly, "I am sad that you have such a low opinion of me."

Aelle started laughing, "Absolutely crazy and it has nothing to do with you Edlin."

She shook her head and said calmly, "How can you say it has nothing to do with me? It seems to have everything to do with me and you are laughing at me."

Aelle leaned back in his chair, "I surrender. Forgive me, Edlin."

"Of course I forgive you, Aelle," she replied with a smile, "I can't lose."

Aelle was taken aback, "What do you mean"

Edlin smiled, "I either have a nephew or get a husband who is king. I can't lose."

Aelle started laughing again and not alone. Edlin was so beautifully and innocently naïve. She said what she was thinking without putting it through some filter. She seemed to see things clearly.

Aelle finally said, "Edlin, I love you already."

"Of course you do, the question is how you will love me."

Osmund suggested they retire and pray and consider the matter. Some guidance from the clergy was also required. Osmund and Ethelind were so taken by the idea that they summoned their priest and asked him to review the matter. There was a lot of overnight research of the scriptures by the two priests of the castle.

In the morning, the family came to eat a morning meal together. Edlin, who seemed to have a joyful nature anyway, was in an especially good mood. The family prayed over the food giving thanks to God.

After Osmund had finished offering the prayer, Ethelind asked, "What makes you especially cheerful this morning, Edlin?"

Edlin's response caught Aelle and Osmund with a mouthful which they had trouble keeping in their mouth because of Edlin's answer.

"I find I am quite pleased with the prospect of being married to Aelle." She reached across the table and took some food to put on her plate.

Ethelind was taken aback, "Do you always say what is on your mind?"

"You asked and aren't we to always speak in truth?"

Aelle interjected, "She has you there, mother."

Ethelind gave her son one of those looks only mothers can give when they are displeased with their offspring.

Aelle couldn't help but start laughing, "Mother, you haven't looked at me like that since I was a child. You must really be confused by the situation."

Ethelind put her head in her hands and sincerely prayed, "God help me in the time of my trial."

Edlin added, "Amen."

Ethelind looked at Edlin who was innocently eating her meal.

Aelle chuckled. He could not remember enjoying himself so

much. It was a pleasant change from the life that had been forced upon him. His spirit was lightened. He had prayed last night about the situation before retiring and had slept peacefully. Edlin was a joy.

They were almost finished the meal when a servant came and whispered in Osmund's ear. Osmund nodded and said something to the servant.

The priest came into the room and knelt before the king saying, "Majesty."

Aelle smiled, "Rise good priest, in our own quarters a head bow is sufficient."

The priest rose and gave Osmund and Ethelind a head bow, "My Lord and Lady."

Osmund smiled at the priest, "Please sit. What news have you?"

The priest sat and began, "We searched the scriptures and especially the Book of Leviticus, and there is nothing that would prevent the marriage you described."

Osmund smiled, "Thank you. Have you eaten?"

The priest nodded, "Yes thank you, Lord."

Osmund said, "Thank you again. You may leave us."

The priest rose and left the room. Osmund looked around. Ethelind was looking perplexed but Edlin seemed oblivious or perhaps just taking it all in stride. Aelle was smiling looking at Edlin. Aelle changed his focus to Osmund.

Aelle could not help himself, "What can an earl offer a king as dowry, Osmund?"

Osmund started laughing, Edlin just looked up, and Ethelind turned red and spoke deliberately, "How can you take this so lightly?"

Aelle looked at his mother, "What makes you think I am taking this lightly, mother"

Ethelind then saw that he was perfectly serious.

Aelle smiled at Edlin, "I find her to be joyful and she is not at all hard to look at. She does meet all the qualifications you laid out. She has already indicated her willingness. It might complicate our family tree, but you must admit it is not all in all an idea to be discarded."

Edlin looked at Aelle, "I am pleased that you do not find me hard to look at."

Aelle smiled at her, "Actually Edlin, you are a very attractive young woman."

"Thank you," she said. She was obviously pleased by the comment. She added, "I had no way of knowing until you told me. I have no experience in what men find attractive or not."

Osmund appeared deep in thought, "I see what you mean about the dowry. What do you have in mind?"

Ethelind could stand it no more, "Are you all mad? Are you serious?"

Aelle smiled, "Now mother, last evening I was chastised for saying it was a crazy idea and you were the one considering it seriously. Now I have warmed to the idea and you are the one who is saying it is madness."

Ethelind sighed, "My emotions always get the best of me when I am with child."

Aelle jumped up and hugged his mother, "That is wonderful." He went and congratulated Osmund.

Aelle thought for a moment, "Perhaps we three are touched and Edlin is the only sane one. My mother has a grown son who is king, a toddler son, and is now with child. My former captain is now an earl and my stepfather. Edlin may be the only one looking at this without clouded perception. "

Edlin smiled, "Thank you, Aelle."

Ethelind had to stop and think. There was a few moments silence before she said, "Are we really going to do this?"

Aelle looked at Edlin, "Would you consent to marry me?"

Edlin smiled, "Of course."

Aelle looked at Osmund, "Do you as, patriarch of your family, approve and are you willing to give your blessing?"

Osmund replied, "Yes, if we can agree on the dowry."

Aelle looked at Edlin, "One small chest of silver coin would be the dowry."

Osmund said, "Agreed."

Aelle looked at Edlin, "I would have asked for more, but your brother is such a tightwad I was afraid he might refuse."

Edlin laughed delightfully and the others followed.

Aert returned late that day. He confirmed what the priests had determined and was very pleased with the betrothal and thought it was a grand solution that would solidify the family lineage, loyalties and inheritance.

It was the king's prayer, and the hope of all his family and friends, that their children and grandchildren would not be born into conflict.

www.ingramcontent.com/pod-product-compliance
Lightning Source LLC
Chambersburg PA
CBHW070407260626
47161CB00001B/312